I0551873

Thanks to Rue Frischmuth for designing the cover.

Nonymous

To Rue again, because my love for you could never be encompassed in just one book.

Also, yes that is the same Rue who did the cover, I have cooler friends than you :P

Author's Note

Disabled people & characters do not exist to educate others, and that's especially true for the ones in this book. Lots might *seem* like an expert at times, but that's only because she's a blunt autistic teenager with a penchant for research and access to the internet. Just because she says she's doing something based off of 'research' doesn't necessarily mean it's accurate/the right thing to do (especially since she very vocally admits that a lot of her 'research' is pop psychology articles). Please for the love of god don't think reading this silly little book about faeries and summer camp is somehow going to turn you into a scholar on anything.

Lots sends incredibly unedited emails home to her sister throughout the course of the book full of text speech, a lack of commas & apostrophes, and typos. I think the ways characters text are super interesting and advise trying to read them as is if you have the capability to, but if you're using a screen reader a lot of the abbreviations she uses won't come across properly. **https://tinyurl.com/lotsemails** has all the emails in order as plain text if you run into anything that confuses you.

Lots communicates via text/writing a few more times throughout the book, but she edits herself a lot more when talking to other characters, so the linked document only includes her emails to her sister.

Chapter 1

I could be a terrible person.

I'm not (a statement that I recognize might actually be even more indicative of terrible-personhood), but I could be. Maybe I am. People tend to be horrible at identifying traits within themselves, actually, and I have alexithymia, which puts me at an even bigger disadvantage there. But if I am terrible, at least I don't want to be. I've spent years researching how *not* to be. That, I think, has to indicate at least some level of goodness.

But while my incessant need to research every possible decision so that I can most effectively define my own version of morality has likely been amplified by my autism, the fact that that morality exists in the first place has nothing to do with it.

Autistic people are not innately good. Allistics wouldn't have spent decades coding so many of their iconic villains and anti-heroes as autistic if they truly believed that we were.

Still, allistics seem to hold this weird belief that all autistics will instantaneously get along because of the mystical, all-encompassing powers of an autism diagnosis. Because sometimes, beliefs and biases never make it past our subconciouses. With allistics, I've found this to be an even more prevalent issue. In fact, over the course of my sixteen years on this planet, I've learned that one should always assume that neurotypicals are at *most* half right about whatever they're telling you. Whatever intangible thing in their brain that keeps them from forgetting to eat for days on end for the sake of finishing a project or series or thought also appears to keep them from engaging too deeply with their own minds. And so, allistics are capable of reading our traits as off-putting and inherently villainous while simultaneously reading our diagnoses as the key to eternal childhood and innocence.

Autistic people can be rude. Sometimes, we even do it on purpose. Autistic people can drink. Some of us do drugs. Some of us swear, some of us fuck, and some of us are almost definitely serial killers.

And Faith Harris is a massive bitch. *And* incredibly autistic.

Autism and bitchiness have never been mutually exclusive.

July 3

My dearest Alice,
Hellllooooooooooooooooooooo.

Bet u didnt think ud b hearing from me this quickly huh?

Anyway Im here. Still alive and all that. I supose you wont be able to write back & conferm that you are too until you escape phone prgatory at the end of the summer (haha! Bet ur wishing u were the disabled one know huh?)

Anyway miss u already. Def not just bcuz Im still waiting for M to get here.

(I do miss u for real 2. Im just a lot better at remembering I miss ppl when Im bored).

Have a good summer & talk at u soon,
Charlotte

Chapter 2

I refuse to believe in the concept of soulmates as a matter of principle.

I also have two of them.

The first is my sister, Alice. Twins statistically tend to report feeling emotionally closer than siblings with age gaps. Since no genetic rationale has ever been found to explain this, many revert to calling it an "indescribable bond".

I do not like things that are indescribable. So, while I might not be able to rectify that issue for the rest of twin bonds, I can at least explain mine.

Alice and I are fraternal. I am roughly four minutes older, though I round up to five whenever we're talking about it to annoy her.

There is no definitive scientific explanation for why Alice and I have gotten along better with each other since infancy than either of us has ever gotten along with anyone else, but I don't need one.

Alice is the kind of person who chews on pencil erasers while she's working on homework and who hums while she's pretending to. She is the kind of sister who complains about you leaving drawers open and clothes on the floor and hair in the sink and then yells at your parents for reprimanding you for the exact same thing, because "oh my god, Charlotte's trying her best, alright?". She is the kind of teenager who's shy and unassuming until the moment someone says something remotely homophobic or ableist about her (technically older) sister.

Alice is not the kind of person that anyone could spend a lifetime alongside without deciding that they want to keep doing that forever.

Our parents probably would have fully given in to our codependency had they not been smart enough to also set Alice up with a part-time therapist once kindergarten started and my autism and ADHD referrals began pouring in. Both of our therapists reassured them that being close likely wouldn't negatively impact either of our developments, but they also recognized that summer camps and after-school programs' frequent tendency to count on Alice to navigate my support needs might. It can be hard to remember to be a child when none of the adults around you give you the space to be one. My parents first found Corrain as a way to try to mitigate that.

Then, I came here, met Morgan, and decided to keep coming back forever.

Morgan's name isn't actually Morgan. I called her "Megan" for years until Gator convinced the entire Caribou Crew that we all needed nicknames at thirteen to ensure we were getting a 'proper camp experience'. Now, calling her anything other than Morgan would just feel wrong.

Morgan's camp name is the most confusing one since it's technically also an incredibly common first name (and one that bears a striking resemblance to her legal one at that), but Morgan insists that we use it anyway since "Morganizer" is kind of a mouthful.

Officially, (when we were seven and she was still "Megan"), our counsellors paired us up constantly because we were the only new girls starting the same week in our age cohort. Our current theory is that they were actually secretly hoping we'd catch a bit of each other's autism and balance things out better.

I was the kind of seven-year-old who never knew how to shut up and Morgan was the kind who was so good at shutting up that she didn't speak at all for the first half of her life. So, whoever decided to start shoving us together at every given opportunity likely thought that we would somehow emerge as one semi-functional child capable of talking exactly as much as allistic seven-year-olds were supposed to.

That and we looked excellent in photo ops. Both women and people of colour are statistically under- or late-diagnosed with autism, so having a ghostly pale, eternally sunburnt little girl eager to drag her much more demure Black best friend in front of any and every camera possible definitely helped with publicity. I'm no longer naïve enough to think that the only reason Morgan and I were prominently featured all over the Corrain website when we were younger was because our bond was so strong that even the counsellors knew it demanded to be captured.

(I'm no longer naïve, but I am nostalgic. I went through the camp archives in eighth grade and hunted down each and every picture of us. They currently live in a folder in my bedside table).

What the counsellors who paired Morgan and I together might not have accounted for, was how completely content we both were with each other's communication styles. In me, Morgan had found an ally so completely unaware that talking to counsellors could possibly be daunting that I'd eagerly deliver any and all messages and complaints on her behalf. And in her, for the first time, I had found an uninterrupting audience seemingly completely unbothered by my inability to take turns in conversations. Morgan claims it actually took me days to realize that she didn't talk since I was already so used to never letting anyone else get a word in edgewise. I'm never completely sure if she's joking about that. Her memory's just good enough (and *I* was just self-involved enough) that she probably isn't.

"Lots!"

Morgan's the only member of the Caribou Crew that I keep in consistent contact with throughout the school year, so she should logically be the person I'm least excited to see again every July.

I have never once been logical about Morgan.

Since the day we met, neither of us has ever spent a moment at Corrain without the other. We plan out the activities we want to sign up for in December to ensure we're both mentally and physically prepared to do them together come July. We coordinate trips home, weekends away, and family vacations to make sure neither of us ever has to exist here alone. Now that we're old enough that parent drop-offs have ceased to be formal, meticulously scheduled events, we've made a tradition of waiting for each other in the parking lot so that we can cross the camp property line together. I've already exchanged goodbyes with my parents and made them park on the other side of the lot.

(It's not that Morgan has anything against them, she's just not a fan of adults in general and I'd rather not have our reunions be full of awkward parent-maneuvering.)

I push myself up off the curb and grin as Morgan jogs over to meet me. She's already wearing a purple camp t-shirt and a pair of black leggings. One of the many, many extraordinary things about Morgan is that you never have to wonder what she'll look like. She's a massive advocate for the benefits of wearing identical or near identical outfits daily, so the routine of camp wardrobe suits her perfectly. Even her hair is eternally familiar. Morgan's worn it in short cornrows ever since the first day I met her, and I can't imagine her ever changing that. There are few things she hates more than physical inconsistencies, so a hairstyle that hugs to her scalp is not the kind of thing that she'd ever willingly part with.

When Morgan finally reaches me, I have to slouch down to let her throw her arms around my neck. Morgan and Alice are the only two people who are allowed to touch me without announcing it first. I don't necessarily hate touch, I just normally need time to prepare myself for the unexpected smell or heat or texture of other people's skin. Morgan and Alice have both always felt like too much of myself for that to matter.

I kiss the top of Morgan's head. She kisses my cheek. Her mother (who always refuses to acknowledge the benefits of waiting at the other side of the parking lot) arrives behind her with her bag and waits expectantly. Our luggage is shipped to Corrain ahead of time to make move-in day run more smoothly, but we all carry smaller knapsacks around with our electronics, water bottles, accessibility tools, and other essentials.

"It's nice to see you, Charlotte." Morgan's mother pats my shoulder even though I know for a fact that Morgan's told her to never do that without warning me first multiple times already. I don't need people to ask permission (I actually hate it when they do. It makes physical contact a lot more burdensome to navigate), but I at least need them to announce it.

I love Morgan's mother for making Morgan and for raising Morgan and for doing her best to advocate for Morgan whenever she has to. I do not love Morgan's mother for consistently managing to forget that I am, in fact, also autistic and not just her daughter's non-disabled, personal support worker.

I flex the muscles in my cheeks because I want to ensure that Morgan's mother continues to like *me.* "You too."

I don't know what I'm supposed to say in the silence that follows because, despite what Mrs. Ross seems to think, talking a lot does not, in fact, mean that I'm good at it.

I link my arm through Morgan's. "We'd better go!" I announce. "Sign-ins to finish, unpacking to do... lots of stuff. See you in two months!"

I wave with my free arm then drag Morgan off before her mother can grab me again.

We whisper and stumble and giggle our way up the hill then pause at the point where the outside world ends and Corrain begins. I am not a superstitious person and neither is Morgan, but her fingers slip down my arm and intertwine themselves with mine. She squeezes my hand once and then, in sync, we step over the property line together.

And just like that, we're home.

Chapter 3

I don't like talking about Corrain with people who have never experienced it in person.

This isn't because I'm ashamed of Corrain, my friends, my autism, or myself. I've spent so much time talking over those possibilities in therapy after a middle school teacher decided to inform my parents that I was 'lying' about how I spent my summers that I'm fairly confident that my lack of transparency does not arise from any kind of repressed shame or self-hatred.

I just prioritize truth and accuracy. Assuming that all autistic people do is a stereotype, but that particular stereotype is one that fits me excellently. And I've learned that sometimes, (especially when dealing with allistics), lying is the easiest way to avoid mistruths.

Whenever I explain Corrain to someone for the first time, they seem to expect it to be some kind of miraculous, transformative experience. There's the obligatory "aww" that they never manage to catch in time. The "well, isn't that just wonderful!". The "Gosh, I bet you just *love* being around so many other kids like you, huh?"

There is a delicate balance to answering these kinds of questions without accidentally feeding into confirmation biases. I *do* like camp. Spending nine summers here would have been a nonsensical choice if I didn't. I also tend to feel closer to other autistics than I do to allistics, but the same could probably be said if I attended any other camp centered around some kind of shared life experience.

Theatre camp kids tend to prefer the social climate of theatre camp to mainstream education because it provides them with a peer group that shares their hopes, dreams, and pop culture reference points. Science camp kids are probably more likely to befriend strangers met at science camp than those met in their daily lives because they can relate to each other more. But when someone talks about going to theatre or science camp, they don't typically conjure images of kumbaya circles and conflict-less utopias.

Which is, perhaps, a bad example since the kinds of kids who go to those camps are also probably more likely to benefit from a camp centered around some kind of neurodivergence, (not because theatre or science are specifically linked to neurodivergency or anything. Any specific-interest based camp would just probably boast a higher neurodivergent population than its more generalized counterparts. Neurotypicals tend to abruptly become boring in their teenage years and don't start developing hobbies again until their thirties), but it's an example nonetheless.

I get along with more people at Camp Corrain because we share a lot of life experiences and outlooks, not because autism instantly leads to peace and harmony. I tend to get along with autistic people better than allistic ones because they tend to make more sense to me, not because they're innately more likable.

Truthfully, my penchant for autistic friendships has always felt more spurred by allistic reactions to me than any conscious decision-making on my part.

I can normally only get a few sentences in with allistics before I notice it hitting them. The skin around their eyes goes a little less crinkly. Their eyebrows inch millimeters closer together and their lips part ever so slightly. There's a look to the side (there's almost always a look to the side, whoever told allistics that they're subtle was a massive liar) as if they're waiting for someone to come and rescue them.

That's another thing that allistics are always getting wrong about me. They hear that autistics struggle to read facial expressions and assume that that must mean that we never pay attention to facial *changes*. I am paying attention all the time. I notice shifts in vocal tone and pitch and speed and monitor eye movement and skin crinkles and wrinkles. I'm just too busy tracking all of that to pull it together into anything meaningful.

Anyway, Camp Corrain is not a utopia, but I've found that whenever I tell people that I spend my summers at an autistic summer camp, they seem to expect it to be one. So, I lie. Slightly. Depending on who you ask. I still tell people I go to camp, I just never specify that it's an autistic one. But since neurotypicality is the expected default, some people (especially nosy middle school teachers) read neglecting to mention my autism at every given opportunity as an intentional deception. When pressed on the subject, though, I try to stick as close to facts as possible in order to avoid any further prescribing.

Corrain is technically on private property. The founder thought it would make it easier to safeguard campers if she didn't have to worry about them wandering off with strangers. Her original mission statement was incredibly independence-centric and it would have been a massive liability issue to give a bunch of disabled kids free-reign on a plot of land that anyone else could be using. Said founder also partially named the camp after herself. Lorrain Bishop founded Corrain out of frustration that her son, Joshua, was frequently left out of activities in the other camps that she enrolled him in. Why she named a camp that was meant to be for her son after herself still evades me. Supposedly, the slight consonant change came from Joshua's affinity for alliteration, so at least there's that.

For a while, Camp Corrain was exactly that: a camp for Joshua. This wasn't entirely Lorrain Bishop's fault, of course. Corrain was founded while Asperger's was still its own diagnosis, so as far as Lorrain was aware, creating a camp for children with her son's disability would mostly just consist of structuring things around his own much narrower needs.

Once Corrain broadened things to include more autistic kids, the mission plan needed to change. Corrain was founded to give one lower support needs autistic teen a place where he could partake in as many camp activities as he wanted to without feeling different or isolated or *autistic*. Corrain survived because it slowly started consulting enough professionals and support workers to realize that the majority of autistic kids—even those of us requiring the most marginal of supports—cannot, in fact, choose to stop feeling autistic. Over the years, it's adjusted to acknowledge that an autistic utopia is not a place where autism ceases to exist, but one where it's constantly kept in mind.

Independence is still a big part of its core goal, but what that looks like is assessed on a camper-by-camper basis. Campers can choose which activities to do and when, but only if they've been approved to do said activities and only with the additional supports or adaptations that they require. Older campers with lower support and supervision needs can relatively keep as much to themselves as they want, but only if they stay with a buddy and check in over text or walkie with their cabin leader every half hour. Camp Corrain's a lot less likely to lose or kill a kid now than it was a few decades ago.

That's not to say that it's perfect. I don't think any camp ever could be, and public and professional opinions on what autistic supports should look like are in a constant state of flux and debate. But I've been coming here since I was too young to know about any of that and by the time I was old enough to begin to recognize Corrain's various red flags, they'd already shifted to a permanent pinkish.

I'm so lost in thought breathing in the camp air and taking stock of each new child and lawn chair that I don't notice Morgan going through her bag for her cue cards until there's already one in her hands.

I gnaw at my cheek. I have a huge chewlery collection and always have at least something chompable on my fidget lanyard (always a pink charm, of course. I care more about colour than shape), but sometimes keeping my anxiety less visible is worth destroying the inside of my mouth.

Morgan mostly communicated via flashcards and AAC apps when we were kids, but she always got too frazzled to navigate any of that when she was overwhelmed. So, when she started talking around more and more people at nine and her diagnosis shifted from non-verbal to selectively mute, her support team started experimenting with other forms of non-verbal communication. Morgan's far more likely to enter verbal shutdown when she's already anxious, so relying on something that makes her even more discombobulated was unnecessarily burdensome.

They landed on written communication. Morgan has hypergraphia, so she already carried pens and papers everywhere for impromptu writing or doodling. It was such an obvious solution that I still don't know how no one came to it earlier. And an inconvenient one for me since reading wasn't and never has been my forte, but other people's accessibility tools have nothing to do with what I'd find most convenient.

When Morgan first started speaking verbally, most of what she said outside of her house was delivered via cue cards. Now that she's able to speak more often than she isn't, she still pre-writes the cards every now and then. For conversations that she's worried will make her anxious enough to push her into shutdown. Which is, admittedly, incredibly anxiety inducing for everyone else involved, but I like to think that I've trained myself into doing a pretty good job at pretending that it isn't.

Morgan's eyes flick up to mine for a moment and she sighs. "You're freaking out."

"I'm not freaking out." Morgan's not a fan of looking anywhere near other people's faces, which normally works incredibly well in my favour when I'm trying to deceive her. Except that she knows me so well that she's mastered catching me exactly when I'm least ready to be observed.

"You're sure the cards aren't—"

"Love them. They're like, 'scary conversation incoming' warning signs." I don't know if I'm lying. My alexithymia makes me struggle to decipher even my own emotions sometimes. Those are a lot more difficult to study through research papers and other external sources. I still get all the baseline symptoms, but after years of research, I've been forced to conclude that the physical sensations that accompany most emotional reactions are at best nonsensical, at worst identical. I do know that I love Morgan being able to tell me things though, so I shake my wrist at her. "Give."

She hands over the cards and recites as I read. She gets every single word right. Morgan always does, when she's using her cue cards. I've never been able to figure out if that's because she spends so much time poring over them that she's accidentally committed them all to memory, or if it's just a side effect of Morgan being Morgan.

"I'm starting the Leadership program this year."

I freeze. "Morgan."

We're supposed to do Leadership after we turn eighteen. That way, Morgan can still have volunteer material for her resume by the time we enter the adult world, and *I* can keep putting off facing my fears of children, role delegation, and responsibility for as long as possible. We'd agreed on that all the way back when we'd mapped out our entire futures at twelve. The plan's always been to never sign up for something that the other isn't absolutely certain she'll be able to do.

Morgan's perfect at rules. She's the only reason I have any semblance of a routine. And yet she's apparently about to break one of our biggest ones.

"You're pissed." Morgan tends to dictate other people's emotions for them. This is normally an excellent compliment to my inability to read my own, but sometimes, I'd rather remain oblivious.

"I'm not—"

"I know I should have warned you." Her wrists begin to smack against her sides. Her steps speed up and become uneven. "But I didn't want to... it won't be a huge deal, okay? I talked to Janine and..."

Cabin leaders are only contracted to work during the summers. I know this because my parents tried to reach out to get Janine to weigh in on an IEP re-evaluation when I started grade nine, only to be met with an 'out of office' email and redirected to some off-season admin person I'd never even met. Morgan is not impulsive enough to have organized all of this over the course of the last week or two.

I wonder how long my best friend's been planning on abandoning me.

"Lots?"

I blink and she's suddenly right in front of me. Her hands are on my arms. It's a lot easier for me to focus on someone when they're the only thing I can see. "It's a transition phase thing, okay? I'll only be with the Leadership kids or CITing every few days at first. And I told her I'd split activity time half-and-half tops by the end of the summer, and that's only if it ends up working out, okay? And she said I can still bunk with the Caribous every night. Obviously." She scratches at her leggings. Black and plain and skin-tight and constant. Like her. Or unlike her, maybe. I don't know. "I wouldn't be able to... I can't... I don't think I'd be able to switch over all at once. Neither does Janine. Waiting until eighteen wouldn't have—"

"We could've talked about it." I'm not supposed to interrupt Morgan as frequently as I do. I got a whole lecture on it once when we were ten and her speech therapist stopped by for an on-site visit. All that accomplished was making me feel even shittier every time I did it from that point on.

It's not like I'm making a conscious decision to cut other people off either, I just wasn't built with whatever innate sense tells everyone else when interjections are conversational instead of disruptive. Morgan interrupts me right back now, so I try to tell myself that it's fine. Mostly.

"You don't want to do Leadership yet," Morgan says.

"I would've. If we talked about it. I obviously would have—"

"That's why I didn't warn you. You don't want to do it. I don't want you to." She drums her fingers together then wraps them around mine, raises our fists between us, and keeps drumming. I mentally count each tap. "Janine says I should try. But if it ends up being too much for you, I've already let her know..."

"It won't be," I decide. It *can't* be. I survive public high school just fine without Morgan being there for every second of it. Doing the same a few hours a day at a camp specifically built for people like me should be easy. Even if I haven't had to spend a single second doing that since we were seven. I have no right to stop her from doing this. "It'll be fine. Yelling at five-year-olds will be good for you. Make you appreciate how much more independent than them I am."

"We're generally not encouraged to yell at the children."

"Right." I nod. My throat feels too warm. "Yes, of course."

"You'll tell me if you need me, right?"

I roll my eyes. "I'm sure I'll manage. The five-year-olds—"

"Fuck the five-year-olds." She squeezes my fists. "You'll tell me, right? Promise."

I smile. Sometimes it feels like Morgan is the only person who truly understands how I function. Teachers and classmates at school are consistently either underestimating my capabilities or abruptly deciding that I must not be disabled at all just because they've seen me do one thing that another autistic person they know can't. My support needs are low enough and my ability to mask is high enough that when I'm the only disabled person in a room, everyone else decides that I need constant coddling, and yet the moment I'm around other more visibly disabled people, they seem to expect my own needs to abruptly disappear. After a lifetime of growing up together, Alice tends to get me mostly right, but sometimes having different neurotypes interferes with any twin telepathy powers we might possess. If twin telepathy is real, that is. Almost all the scholarship on it would disagree.

Anyway, I am just as dependent on Morgan as she is on me, our codependency is just more visible in one direction. I might be good at navigating her anxiety and at speaking up for her when she can't, but if anything, she helps me more. Morgan knows how to gently guide me through remembering to eat and sleep and take my meds and brush my teeth and comb my hair without it feeling like she's patronizing me or like I'm inconveniencing her or even like she's actually telling me to do anything at all, most of the time. Somehow, she's even mastered just reminding me to breathe. Morgan is as vital to me as my own nervous system and she's far better at keeping me alive than that's ever been. She also knows me well enough to trust that I'll be able to tell her when I do and don't need micromanaging.

"I promise."

She gathers my fists together and kisses them. "This is going to be a good summer." She declares. "I can sense it. You'll be so busy having fun that you won't even notice that I'm not there for some of it, okay? Plus, the more time we spend apart, the more stories you'll have to tell me, right?"

I take a deep breath and make myself smile. She's going to be so good at convincing her campers that everything's going to be alright.

Chapter 4

For someone who insists on plaguing our cabin summer after summer, Faith Harris is ridiculously difficult to keep track of.

And to make matters worse, no one else ever seems to notice.

No one at Corrain is supposed to be allowed to go off on their own until we reach eighteen, even after support team consultations. Even once we hit fifteen and can get away with being considerably less supervised since we'd technically be old enough to camp counsel elsewhere, the most alone anyone's ever supposed to be able to get is partnering up with someone, then leaving each other alone once you get to wherever you've told your point-person you're going to be.

Still, I've lost count of the number of times I've been struck by the unusual realization that no one's made me want to scream for the past hour, looked around to find Faith nowhere in sight, and then realized that everyone she could have possibly been paired up with was present.

We're at the Welcome Back Bonfire when I notice it for the first time this summer, sitting beneath our tree a good several feet away from the actual festivities. The moment we were old enough to start opting out of activities, us Caribous began to avoid almost all of them. It's hard to find an event that we're all enthusiastically invested in and even harder to corral an entire cabin of autistic campers to willingly do something that they're relatively neutral on, so we often stick to calmer activities and the outskirts of bigger events to keep the Caribou Crew from having to split up.

I'm a big fan of opting out. I come to camp to hang out with the people I like here, not to exhaust myself doing all the same crafts, sports, and activities that I've already been doing for almost a decade now. Things you got to experience as a child never manage to feel as exciting once you've grown up.

The Caribou Crew is down to seven members this summer. There used to be more of us, but the older we get, the more our numbers seem to dwindle. A camp accessible to the entire spectrum of autistic campers and their needs is a beautiful idea, but trying to cater to everything simultaneously inevitably means it falls short of other more specialized camps in several facets.

Corrain's campers with support needs low enough to attend mainstream camps often start disappearing once we reach double digits, opting to go to more interest-specific places with their friends from school. Our higher support needs population also shrinks with age as campers and parents find more specialized camps elsewhere where their children won't feel consistently frustrated by or left out of the freedoms that lower support needs campers receive. Having a sleep-away option for older campers whose needs allow it might help promote the normalcy and freedom that Corrain seeks to instill, but it also inevitably makes a lot of people feel left behind.

Sometimes, I worry that by the time we reach eighteen and switch over to CITing, Morgan and I might be the only Caribous left.

Anyway, there are supposed to be seven of us this summer, but there are only five Caribous taking refuge beneath our tree.

This alone isn't too big of an anomaly. Sunny and her support worker always split away from us for group events and celebrations because Sunny's the only one of us sensory-seeking enough to consistently enjoy the combined chaos of dancing, pounding music, and far too many bodies that such events typically entail. She never passes up a bonfire.

Faith always wanders as far from us as possible because Faith's a bitch.

But she isn't just wandering. We're some of the oldest people at camp now so Caribous are typically easy to spot, but when I scan the clearing, Faith's nowhere to be found.

Van notices me noticing. Van's extremely good at noticing things at often extremely inconvenient moments.

"Sunny's over there," he nods. Van was assigned to our cabin long before he came out, so luckily, we've managed to keep our claws in him. Autistic people are statistically far more likely to identify as genderqueer than allistics, so gender-based cabins are a lot more difficult to maintain here. They start out gender-specific, but the older we get, the more they seem to just be based off of friend groups and vibes.

"Yeah." I shake myself back into the present moment. "Yeah, I know. Where's..." I crinkle my forehead to show my confusion. Sometimes, giving other people facial clues can help facilitate communication, even when those expressions don't come naturally to me. "Is Faith back this summer?"

There's a moment of perplexed silence. There always is, when Faith's involved. For someone so overtly annoying, she's surprisingly easy to forget about. I used to think that it was just my ADHD, but it seems to affect everyone else too. Maybe it's actually an autism thing. It can be difficult to draw the line between which of my disabilities causes what sometimes.

The more I think about Faith, the more confused I become. I included her in my headcount: me, Morgan, Van, Gator, Brain, Sunny, Faith. I couldn't have gotten to seven without her. I can even practically hear her showing up at the cabin, finding out that there were only seven of us this year, and then complaining about Gator getting a bunk all to themself to help them mitigate OCD triggers despite Faith only having to share with Sunny who practically never sleeps in the cabin anyway and keeps pretty much all of her stuff in the main building. I distinctly remember trading the sign for "bitch" with Van and then exchanging eyerolls with everyone else. I can remember up to the moment that Janine showed up to summon us all to the bonfire but then, abruptly, I somehow lose track of Faith.

Brain normally has to type out most of the things she wants to say to me because I'm still the shittest person in our cabin at ASL (including Faith, which is extremely infuriating), but "Lots is obsessed" is a preloaded phrase on her iPad. I do not appreciate the mileage she gets with that one.

"Eh!" I kick her shoe. As I do, the sense of collective unease evaporates slightly. Or maybe I'm the only one feeling it. I've never been comfortable with the sensation of not-knowing, but something about the way that the air feels whenever I realize that I've lost track of Faith has always felt distinctly different. More wrong, somehow. Foreboding. The mood's light though, so I try to shake it off. "I'm not—she was here though, right? A bit ago? This is like, the one thing where attendance isn't optional?"

We look around. We look at each other. She's nowhere to be found.

Faith's up to something nefarious. I know she must be. The problem is, it's been years now, and I still haven't figured out what that "something" is.

"Maybe she had something," Brain's iPad dictates.

"What could—"

Van—who's sprawled out across Brain's lap in a way that's equal parts adorable for them and uncomfortable for everyone else—waves off the end of my question. "She'll show up. Always does."

"But—"

"If we tell Janine, she'll hunt her down then we'll have to deal with her," he cuts me off. "Let it go for one night?"

I sigh and give in. It's our first day back. We deserve at least one day free of Faith-related drama.

July 3

My dearest Alice,

Hideing in the washroom rn bcuz there have already been DAVELOPMENTS!!!!!

M wants to do Leadership. Which like obviusly M wants to do Leadership she brings a roll up whiteboard every summer to keep track of every1 elses skedules. She used to come over and rearange are dollhouses to make sure every room was properly habitable for a family of 4. She just wasnt supposed to addmit she wants 2 do Leadership for 2 more years. Thats wht we agreed on.

The thing is I dont know if Im aloud to be mad? Im pretty sure I cant be actually bcuz shes M so she obviusly gave me full veto powers but Im not aloud 2 actually use them right? Thatd make me a terrible friend? Thats just her being polight isnt it?

Hsbdkljgknfgkdfkjgjkdfgdfl its been less than a day and I already wish u were here to desifer social rules for me.

Talk at u soon,
Charlotte

Chapter 5

We don't get even one day free of Faith-related drama. I should have known that that'd be too much to ask for.

I somehow forget that I'm supposed to be watching out for her. We eat as many s'mores as we can handle then drop Sunny and Van off at the main building for the night (Van has to sleep close to admin because of how frequently he gets nocturnal seizures and Sunny only spends nights in the cabin once or twice a month when they overstaff support workers and can spare the extra supervision). We walk back to the cabin as a group of four. I think. But then I'm in the middle of setting up my bunk (the top one. I'm a much bigger fan of climbing than Morgan is), look up for half a moment, and spot Faith sitting on hers as if nothing's amiss.

I climb down my ladder and march right over to her. Faith always takes the top bunk. Technically it's because Sunny uses the bottom one when she's hanging out in the cabin during the day since she can't climb safely, but I'm certain Faith would've fought for the top one regardless. She's always made it extremely clear that she thinks she's above the rest of us.

I'm pretty sure Faith started coming to Corrain when we were nine. Morgan swears it was earlier, though, so I could be wrong. Brain's even fuzzy on the specifics, and she's the most detail-oriented of the lot of us. Photographic memories are a myth, but Brain has savant syndrome and an obsession with dates, so her memory's pretty much as close to infallible as you can get. What I do know is that at some point, Faith was suddenly added to our age cohort. And doing everything in her power to make sure it was expressly clear to the rest of us that she didn't want to be.

Autistics are allowed to not like our autism. We are capable of complex thought and sometimes, managing living with a disability is not as simple as slapping an "autism's my superpower!" bumper sticker over it. There is no such thing as a "good" autistic person, and even if there were, loving one's diagnosis would not be a prerequisite to that.

There is, however, such thing as a "bad" autistic, and Faith's been performing that role to perfection ever since she first infested the Caribou Crew.

When Faith first showed up (whenever that was), she was adamant that she didn't belong here. Corrain's big on self-empowerment and acceptance, but Janine's never forced it. No one was expecting Faith to show up proudly proclaiming, "I have autism and I'm completely fine with that!", and no one would have faulted her if she hadn't. I think I'm a fairly disability-positive person, and even I hate mine some days.

But it takes a level of assholeness that can only be intentional to sit in an introduction circle year after year, listen to a group of other children talk about their lives and hopes and dreams and their relationships to their autism, and then proudly proclaim that the most important thing about yourself is that you don't have it.

Being in denial is fine. Self-doubt is neutral when determining a person's tolerability and everyone goes through some level of it. Especially when you're nine-ish and potentially only recently diagnosed. But for some reason, Faith kept coming back summer after summer, year after year, to surround herself with autistic people while making it expressly clear that she fears nothing more than being lumped in with the rest of us.

I have no idea why she keeps doing it and if I think about it for too long, I start to drive myself crazy.

Morgan thinks that she's secretly wildly insecure and insists that Faith really does like the rest of us and is just hoping that one day, if she spends enough time around us, she'll finally learn to like herself too. Morgan is a sweetheart to an absolute fault. That's why she needs me to keep her a bit more cynical. We've always balanced each other out.

Van says Faith's parents probably keep forcing her to come back as some kind of punishment for also being a bitch in her home life, which is almost definitely closer to the truth.

But if Faith *is* hoping we'll somehow rub off on her, she's going about it in the least sensical way possible.

She sits as far from us as she can at all group activities and talks to the counsellors or other campers instead, steadfast in her attempts to pretend that we don't exist. She refuses to humour camp chants or traditions and is the only member of the Caribou Cabin to have never gotten a nickname despite the fact that she's one of its most consistent inhabitants. We tried out a few for a while too (though mine were mostly at least slightly vulgar), but she just refused to respond until we dropped it. She might be okay-ish at abiding by the rest of the cabin's needs, but even that's always seemed more like something she reluctantly forces herself to do to keep Janine from reprimanding her. I'm still fairly certain she only bothered learning basic ASL a few years ago to make me feel even shittier about struggling with it. Because that's just how Faith operates.

"What do you want, Lots?"

I jump and gasp audibly before I can stop myself. Faith was in her bunk a moment ago. I know this because it's what made me start thinking about her. Now, though, she's somehow behind me. Faith's inexplicably learned how to use my every moment of inattention to her advantage.

I don't want to give her the satisfaction of watching me turn to face her, but it happens on impulse.

"Geez." When Faith smiles, even that's unwelcoming. It happens so subtly that it doesn't form a single crease near either her eyes or cheeks. Her head tilts ever so slightly to the right, almost completely counteracting any curvature that her lips do gain. "Someone's jumpy."

"Well obviously when someone sneaks up on me, I'm gonna—"

"I wasn't sneaking." As a chronic interrupter, I don't take it personally when other people interrupt me. Unless that other person is Faith Harris. Something about the way she does it feels too much like an intentional silencing, even though she never fights to speak over anyone. Maybe that's *why* it feels so much worse. Faith sounds eternally bored. A lot of autistics can come across more monotoned, but I've known Faith since she was young and loud and dynamic. But now, she keeps her words short and uninterested and never above speaking level. Like she *knows* everyone else is going to stop and listen to her regardless. It's infuriating. "You just weren't paying enough attention."

"I'm—" I stomp my foot. "That's not—" I sigh. "What do you even want?"

Her head tilts slightly further. As it does, her long, near-black hair falls behind her shoulder and I resent myself for noticing. Linking visual memories to objects has always helped me encode them better. My hair is the trunk of an old dying tree: a thousand shades of brown twisting and tangling and never quite sure which direction they're supposed to go. Faith's is ink. It's always been ink. As full of life and story and as unreadable to me as written word. I quickly look away, moving my focus to just past her shoulder where Gator's setting up their bunk.

I don't know anything about Faith's personal life (she's made a very big point of never giving anyone her contact information at the end of the summer. Not that I've ever asked, of course), but every time I try to imagine how it might look, I can't see her being anything other than a textbook mean girl. Not the main one, of course. Despite her claims to the contrary, Faith's actually visibly autistic. She might put a lot of effort into masking, but she can't hold eye-contact for the life of her, occasionally gets so overwhelmed navigating conversations that she'll just abruptly shut down mid-sentence, and when she *is* talking, her verbiage is just off enough that something about it always feels not-quite-right. The biggest factor I could see preventing her from rising to ultimate popular mean-girldom, though, is how potently uncanny she feels.

The autistic relationship to the uncanny valley effect is a bizarre one. Some studies say autistics and allistics are equally susceptible to it. Others have found that autistics are less likely to identify things as "uncanny", potentially due to our tendency to get caught up in the individual components of something before focusing on the product as a whole. What all the literature appears to agree on, though, is that autistics are more likely to elicit a *feeling* of the uncanny in others. Especially those of us with higher abilities to mask.

I had never experienced the uncanny valley effect with anyone (autistic or otherwise) until Faith Harris. I've never experienced it anywhere else since. I usually struggle to identify even the most reoccurring of emotions and sensations within myself until re-examining them in retrospect, but the moment I met her (whenever that was), I knew with such unyielding certainty that what I was feeling was "uncanny", that I spent that entire week researching what that meant. Camp Corrain's pro-electronic stance and widespread Wi-Fi means that I get to pursue my obsessive need to know everything year-round. Research rarely solves problems, though. No matter how much work I pour into trying to determine *why* looking at Faith for too long makes my stomach twist and my skin flush, I've never figured out how to avoid that physical sensation of unease.

Anyway, Faith gets pretending to be allistic just wrong enough that it probably makes the allistics in her personal life uncomfortable around her, even if they can't pinpoint exactly why. Faith is also extremely traditionally pretty. Flowing ink hair and clear, tan skin with the faintest dusting of freckles. I note this not from a position of jealousy or infatuation, but one of practicality. I'm too awful at remembering physical characteristics to make any lasting personal value judgements on them, so I don't typically pay too much attention to that kind of thing. But being a lower support needs traditionally pretty autistic person is a vastly different experience to being an average-looking one. People never see disability in beauty. If Faith doesn't disclose her autism diagnosis in her personal life (which I'm almost certain she doesn't) she could spend years as some popular mean girl's righthand henchman and no one would bat an eye.

"Hello?" A hand is suddenly being waved in front of my face. Faith's nails are neat and even and covered in a clear, shining gloss. I could never do that. I'm in a constant state of picking at skin and cuticles, even with all the fidgets I've collected over the years to try and keep myself otherwise occupied. I normally don't resent others for being able to do the things that I can't, but something about Faith makes even the smallest of her actions seem intentionally offensive.

I stuff my fists into my pockets. "What?"

"Oh my god," she almost laughs. Faith exclusively 'almost' laughs. It sounds more like she's clearing her throat than any form of actual amusement. "Of course you weren't listening."

"I—" I am not about to tell Faith Harris that I got distracted thinking about her eyes. Even if I specify that I was simply pondering why they make me feel so uniquely unsettled, she'll somehow figure out how to take that as a compliment. "Where were you?" I remember to ask. "At the bonfire."

Her lips pull further upwards. It's almost a sneer. "Why? D'you miss me?"

"That's not— I just— if you wander off on your own, Janine might get—"

She rolls her eyes. "I was there. You've always been bad at paying attention."

"I'm... liar!" I spend far more time during the school year than I'd like to admit scripting out how I'm going to completely destroy Faith with witty insults and retorts, but interacting with her always sends all that work flying out the window. I've found that the people the least likely to follow my secret, preplanned scripts are often the ones that I want to follow them the most.

"Whatever. Believe whatever you want."

"That's not— you're the one lying!"

"Maybe." Faith shrugs. She pulls out her phone and unlocks it, clearly having already decided that I'm no longer worth her attention. It's part of why I know she's definitely used to being popular. You'd think her being an objectively horrible person would negate that even with her pretty privilege, but allistics are terrible judges of character whenever physical attraction's involved. Faith's clearly so used to everyone just throwing themselves at her in her home life that at camp, she's decided that nothing less than the entire cabin burning down could possibly warrant her attention. "Was that it then? Were you just creepily staring at me because you missed me too much earlier?"

"That's not—" I feel my skin go hot. "I wasn't— you're up to something! You—"

She rolls her eyes. "Not everything's a conspiracy, Lots. Glad to see you're just as paranoid as ever. Sometimes people just don't want to spend time with you."

I think up a comeback then bite my lip and swallow it back down. When Faith's insisting on acting unbothered, the only way to make sure you don't lose an argument against her is to do the same and pretend to give up. Even if I really, really don't want to. I'm clearly not mentally prepared for a conversation right now, and I will not give her the satisfaction of watching me flounder my way through one.

I storm over to Brain's bunk where everyone else has congregated to finish catching up. Faith silently returns to her bed and rolls over to scroll through her phone. She might be a popular mean girl the other ten months of the year, but here, bitchiness rarely translates into social currency.

This is going to be a good summer. I'm going to spend two months doing absolutely nothing with my friends and love every second of it. Maybe, I'll even finally figure out how to stop giving Faith the time of day.

Just right after I figure out whatever the fuck she's up to.

Chapter 6

I'm noticeably, obviously obsessed with exactly two people at camp, so when Gator yells my name while I'm brushing my teeth that night, I instantly know who it's about.

When things become yell-worthy with Faith, it's standard Caribou policy to keep me as far from her as possible. That only leaves one other option.

I drop my toothbrush onto the counter (both planning on returning to put it in its holder later and fully aware that I'll almost definitely keep pushing that back until I need to use it again tomorrow morning) and rush into the main room.

The entire contents of Morgan's suitcase have been strewn all over the cabin floor. I know everything must be hers because she's meticulously labeled each and every item with her custom, blue name stickers. Because Morgan is the most organized person I know and definitely wouldn't have destroyed the entire cabin without due cause.

My eyes instantly find Faith. She's sitting on her top bunk, watching Morgan tear through her sheets with nothing more than mild curiosity. Her legs are even swinging over the edge of her bed.

"What did—"

"She lost something," Gator fills me in. "A binder. Do you know..."

I do. Morgan showed it to me as we made the walk over to the cabin. She spent the last three months researching camp activities, management skills, and child-friendly conflict resolution strategies. Because of course she did.

"It's a... thick blue one." I scrunch up my eyes to try and remember it better. I do my best work when all of my muscles are so tense that I no longer have to worry about the movement of anything but my thoughts. "Her name's on it. Probably. Almost definitely." I rush to kneel down beside Morgan, knowing that I can trust Brain and Gator to do everything in their power to find it.

By the time I reach her, Morgan's already run out of things to pull apart and has resorted to clawing at her own skin.

"Hey!" I scoot closer. "Mor—"

Faith, (unhelpfully), is suddenly right in front of me. "I'll walkie the night staff," she deadpans, as if my best friend isn't in the middle of tearing herself apart less than 24 hours after arriving at camp. "They'll—"

Morgan's attention snaps to her. "No!"

Faith ignores her, keeping her attention on me. Her face is expressionless. "If she's spending the night there, I'm assuming you'll—"

"She said she's fine!" I yell.

Faith raises a perfectly-plucked eyebrow. The rest of her face remains entirely still. "She didn't, actually."

"She'll be fine!" I guess. I'm not sure if I'm right, but I do know that most of Morgan's anxiety stems from not being in control. Having an adult burst in right now when she clearly doesn't want them to definitely isn't going to help with that.

"Doesn't look like it."

"Will you shut up!" I catch myself and take a deep breath. I can't afford to also be freaking out right now. Faith's just an expert at getting under my skin. "Just... go do something useful. Help look for the binder."

"That'd be a waste of time. It's clearly not here."

"It is!" I yell over her, hoping Morgan somehow didn't hear that. "Obviously. It must be. Just—" I freeze. "Did you take it?"

I know Morgan brought the binder into the cabin earlier. There's no reason it wouldn't still be here unless someone's moved it. Maybe that's what Faith was up to when she disappeared during the bonfire.

For half a moment, the right corner of Faith's lips twitch. Faith's face never moves unintentionally. She has it. "It'd be pretty funny if I did, huh?"

I'm filled with a million responses I want to hurl against that, but I know yelling them right now is exactly what she wants. I'll deal with getting the binder back later. For now, I need to keep my focus on its owner. I push past Faith to get to Morgan and hear her sigh behind me.

"You're probably not going to find it any time soon. If she keeps us up much longer, I'm calling whoever's on rounds."

I ignore her. "Morgan." I inch closer. It's typically inadvisable to suddenly grab someone mid-meltdown unless they're at imminent risk of jeopardizing the safety of either themselves or others, but I also know that Morgan is the kind of person who needs physical pressure to help her regulate, so I want to be as close as possible in case she decides she wants that from me.

"Missing," she says. She's curled in on herself, rocking violently enough that her feet pound audibly each time they make contact with the floor. If Morgan can still talk while she's overwhelmed, her sentences almost always get shorter. There are tears on her cheeks.

I shake my head. "No, it's not. It's—"

She reaches for me, so I throw myself on top of her, careful to cradle her head as we both crash to the floor.

I do not know how to handle other people's emotions, but I've made myself an expert on Morgan's. She came to her first sleepover at my house when we were twelve and freaked out at bedtime when she realized that she'd left the weighted blanket she usually used at home. Naturally, in all of my twelve-year-old wisdom, I'd offered to become the blanket myself. I would give Morgan my entire being if she asked for it, if only because I already can't imagine mine existing outside of hers. It ended up being such a good idea that we created a protocol for it. If Morgan reaches for me and squeezes her fist twice, I'm supposed to tackle her as quickly as possible.

Safely, ideally.

She pulls me closer and cries into my shirt. I stroke her back. I wait for her shaking to subside before leaning up enough to scan the rest of the cabin, but Brain catches my eye and quickly shakes her head. Someone's fixed her bed, at least. None of us would ever dare interfere with the layout of Morgan's luggage, but even that's all been temporarily piled away in front of the chests at the foot of our bunk.

"Okay." I wrap an arm around Morgan's back and pull her up with me. "Let's get some sleep, okay? No point looking on half functional brains. It'll show up."

She lets me guide her into the bunk. The bottom one's technically hers anyway, but we end up sharing so frequently that it hardly would have mattered. Sure enough, she wraps her fingers around my arm and pulls me in after her when I start to move away, so I keep my body fused to hers as she gets comfortable. Morgan's bunk already has an actual heavy-duty weighted blanketed in it at all times, but she wraps my arm and leg around her for the added pressure. Someone gets up to turn off the light as her breathing settles, so I'm left to watch her through the moonlight.

"Sorry," she eventually whispers.

"Nope." I kiss her head. "That's extremely not necessary."

"I'm... I can talk to Janine. Tell her it's too much. I'm sure—"

"Morgan." I wiggle lower to press my forehead to hers. "You'll be fine, okay? We're going to find it, but even if we don't, I'm a thousand percent sure you already have it all backed up on your phone, right?"

"That'd look unprofessional," she says, which means yes.

"Then we'll get your parents to reprint it and drop it off. Or get admin to print it themselves or something. Whatever.

We'll figure it out. It's all here anyway, right?" I tap her temple. "You have one of the biggest, sexiest brains I've ever seen. I bet you've secretly had the whole thing memorized this whole time."

She's quiet. Then, "I'm having a meltdown over a missing book."

"It's Corrain." I kiss her forehead. "They're not going to expect you to suddenly stop being autistic."

"Do you think I should do this?" she whispers. "Seriously?"

I chew my cheek. I knew exactly what this summer was supposed to look like. Me and Morgan and the rest of the Caribous doing everything we could to avoid actual responsibility so that we could hang out all summer. And secretly, I am worried about it. I've never had to exist at camp without Morgan. I can't imagine her existing here without me. But the professionals around her apparently think she'll be able to, and if anything, they have a history of *under*estimating her. Morgan is built of the stuff of miracles and I am not about to be the person who stops her from proving that.

"I think you'll kick ass."

She sniffles. "Not the children's, preferably."

I laugh a bit too loudly and wait a beat to see if anyone'll yell at us to shut up, but even Faith isn't evil enough to demand absolute silence right now.

"See?" I kiss her nose. "You've already got all the important rules memorized and everything. No binder necessary. You're gonna crush this."

I truly believe that she doesn't need a book to teach her how to be a good leader, but I also know that with Morgan, the comfort of having a backup plan is normally more important than any of that plan's actual contents. So, after I'm sure she and the rest of the cabin are fast asleep, I gently ease myself out of the bed and tiptoe over to Faith's bunk.

She has it. I know she must. I haven't figured out the 'why' of it all yet, but Faith is the kind of person capable of being motivated by nothing more than the misery of others, so that doesn't dissuade me.

Since Sunny rarely uses her bunk, Faith's claimed it as her own personal shelf space. We let her, (if only to avoid more conflict), but right now that means she has twice as many hiding places as the rest of us.

I check beneath the bed. I check in both chests at its foot and then comb through Faith's suitcases under the moonlight. The binder's nowhere to be seen. It's not the kind of thing small enough to be hidden on her physical person, so she must have stashed it somewhere else just for the sake of being a bitch. I feel my body go hot. Faith has always been the worst, but intentionally doing something that she knew was likely to trigger a meltdown is a new low even for her.

I'm about to sneak back over to our bunk when I see it. Not the binder, but perhaps the next best thing.

As long as I've known her, (for however long that might have been), Faith's worn the same necklace. I remember it because it's never quite suited the rest of her. A small, rounded blue stone attached to a black chord. All the rest of Faith's jewellery is silver, so every summer I expect her to change it for something else, but it's the only constant. And now it's right there: laid out on her chest practically begging to be stolen.

I loop it around my ankle until it's tight enough to hold, then clasp it. Faith fiddles with it so frequently that I'm almost certain it's a comfort object so I have no intention of actually losing it, but if she thinks making my best friend panic is fun, then we'll see how she likes it when the pendant's on the other foot.

July 4

My Dearest Alice,

Debateing killing someone rn. If I haven't been arested by the time u read this I eether changed my mind or did a really good job hideing the body.

Talk at u later,
Charlotte

Chapter 7

"Gooood morning Caribous!" Janine finds us in our usual spot outside the dining hall the next morning, Faith in tow.

Gator's OCD already makes eating a lot more laborious and time-consuming for them, so we've been eating together outside for years now to try and get away from the added stress of having to listen to dozens of other campers chewing and chatting. A lot of us (myself included) have other sensory issues that make eating in group settings its own special form of hell, so no one's ever contested that.

Except Faith who physically jolts every time she hears a fork squeak, yet still refuses to admit that she'd probably also rather be eating elsewhere. It's all part of her never-ending quest to make herself feel superior to the rest of us, of course.

Even while just with our little group, I typically prefer to wear my headphones while other people are eating. Whoever invented the sound of chewing must have been personally trying to spite me, so I'm more than okay with doing as much to limit our contact with other campers as possible during meals.

Janine's a lot less hands-on now that we're older, but she's still our main point person at camp. She's the one on-call in case any of us ever need anything and the person that we're supposed to check in with twice hourly, so she gathers us together a couple of times a day to make sure she knows where everyone's going.

Which normally (ideally), is absolutely nowhere. Morgan's already off with the other Leadership kids, but I'm trying not to focus on that. I am perfectly capable of spending the day lounging around with our friends without her. Hopefully.

"Alrighty!" Janine crosses her legs as she sits down to join us. She's been working at camp far longer than any of us have been here, and she was clearly built for it. Forty-year-olds who still manage to maintain that level of pep all have to go into childcare fields. It's a universal rule. Janine is also my singular favourite adult on the planet, due largely to her being the only one I've ever met who consistently makes me feel like I belong on this one.

I'm constantly either doing too much or too little for the other adults in my life. Teachers are simultaneously shocked by my ability to function in classroom settings despite my IEP, and disappointed whenever they realize why said IEP exists in the first place. My parents are extremely good, (as far as parents go), but I am the first diagnosed autistic *or* ADHD person that they've ever been close to and there are a lot of expectations and stigmas that come along with that. Especially when you're told that the first autistic or ADHD person you're ever going to be knowingly interacting with is your own child.

I was far from the first AuDHD person Janine had ever interacted with when I first met her, but she also never used that as an excuse to stop treating me as an individual. She also had the background to know how to simultaneously do that without erasing or expecting me to erase any of my AuDHD traits. She might be peppy, but she's also never let that stop her from being remarkably cool. She'll answer any question to the best of her abilities and does it like you're actually speaking to her adult-to-adult. Even when you're an eleven-year-old gradually working your way through every question that's ever been thought. She fights higher-ups and even a few of our schools when she doesn't feel like we're being adequately supported, and even advocated against some parents the summer we all got very into swearing at fourteen after someone showed up with a "fuckity fuck" verbal stim and there was pushback against us programming it into AAC devices so that everyone could participate.

Janine's the best. Which also makes me extremely aware of all the ways that I need her to think that *I'm* the best every time we interact.

She taps her pen against her clipboard. "Are my Welcome Back helpers all still feeling up to it today?"

I frown at the pluralization. Sunny sometimes gets involved with that kind of thing, but Sunny's supposed to be the *only* one who does. Plus, since she has a one-on-one support worker, she doesn't have to rely on the buddy system. I'd obviously rather have all of us together, but at least when Sunny goes off to get involved in actual activities, it doesn't do much to hurt our usual numbers. Every year I feel pressured to volunteer because it seems like the kind of thing that I *should* be doing as a lower support needs older camper, but every year no one else does it either, so it's always felt fine to turn it down. When we'd talked at the end of last summer, it had seemed like we'd all mutually agreed to another blissful two months of nothingness. Morgan was supposed to be the only fluke.

I look at Faith in hopes that she suddenly felt so overcome with camp spirit that she signed up, but she's the only other person not nodding along. Which makes sense, of course. Brain and Van have been crawling all over each other ever since they started dating last summer and Gator and Van have been joined at the hip since long before that, so of course if one of them signed on to help, then the other two would have as well. I'd just assumed that they would have asked me about it first.

I can practically feel Janine's eyes on mine, even though she's not even looking towards me. Faith not helping out was a given. Me being the only one to join her in that is a disappointment.

My shock must be showing, because Van taps my knee and smiles sympathetically.

Didn't know M-O-R-G, he signs.

"Don't know" was one of the first things I got down in ASL. For a person obsessed with learning things, there's plenty that I'm still working on knowing. Brain's technically the only Caribou who uses Sign as their primary form of communication, but Van uses it so much at camp that it might as well also be his. Those of us with the capability to started trying to pick up as much as we could over the school year when we were ten so that Brain wouldn't have to bear the brunt of communication labour herself, and Van came back the next summer having realized that while he can speak verbally when need be, he much prefers Sign.

I definitely do not prefer Sign and have no idea how Van could possibly find it the *least* energy consuming method of communicating, but autistic people are not a monolith. If he says it's easier for him, then I have no reason not to believe that and try to adjust the way we communicate accordingly.

Janine (not noticing that I'm actively shocked because allistics are not, in fact, infallible body-language readers either) claps her hands. "Excellent! That should take up most of your free activity blocks this week, then. We'll tell me if anyone changes their minds there?" She points an accusatory pen at each of them in turn and waits for everyone to nod their assent before moving on. "That'll of course put the two of you together today."

Janine's all smiles when she turns to me and Faith, but even she's not chipper enough to have missed that neither of us would ever voluntarily spend time alone with the other. I'm not sure if I'm the Caribou that Faith dislikes the most or even the one who dislikes her the most strongly. I'm just the one impulsive and talkative enough to bring it up the most frequently.

Janine's smile is unflinching. She's mastered the art of cheer.

I smile back. I don't want to let her down twice in one morning.

"Have you girls gotten the chance to talk over what you want to do?"

"We'll head over to crafts," Faith says before I can respond for myself.

I keep a tangle on my wrist at all times for immediate fidget access. It's built of various different shades of pink links that I extracted from several deconstructed ones and sized so that it can sit there comfortably when triple looped. I slip off a loop as casually as I can and run it through my fingers to try and keep myself from glowering at Faith, even more annoyed that crafts was exactly what I was going to say. Spending the day there is the easiest way to get away with doing nothing while also avoiding Janine's awful attempts at hiding her disappointment whenever you declare that you're just planning on spending the whole day in the cabin. You can only get away with that a few times in a row before she puts her foot down and (politely) demands you become an "active camp participant".

Crafts was objectively the correct answer. Still, I wish Faith had at least had the decency to give me the opportunity to correct her.

"All day?"

"Maybe." Faith shrugs. "There are lots of crafts. We'll let you know if we change our minds, though."

Brain pulls me aside before we break up for the activity block of the day to show me something on her iPad. Brain's AAC makes her an expert secret keeper. All she has to do to achieve the perfect whisper is stop herself from hitting the "read-aloud" button.

You be okay?

As a rule, we always arrange our daily groups so that Faith never ends up in a pair. Leaving anyone alone with her has always felt too similar to a death sentence. But tomorrow, Morgan will be back again. And after this week, everyone else won't be busy doing whatever welcome back duties they decided to sign up for without consulting me.

Still, I have never liked change. I've always been terrible at it, actually. Spending time at Corrain without Morgan had already felt daunting, but doing that alone with Faith might be enough to push me over the edge.

I watch Faith in the distance, not oblivious to the way that her fingers keep tapping anxiously against her collarbone where her necklace would normally sit.

I roll my ankle and feel her pendant snag against my sock.

I take a deep breath. "I'll be fine."

Faith might be up to something (in fact, she almost definitely is), but for once, I have a secret of my own.

I'm pretty sure that means that I finally have the upper hand.

Chapter 8

"D'you take it?"

Faith and I spend a mind-numbing amount of time scrolling through our phones as far away from each other as possible at the crafts shed before giving up at pretended productivity and excusing ourselves back to the cabin. She waits until we've hit tree cover to confront me.

"I don't know what you're talking about."

Faith rolls her eyes. "That's just about the guiltiest thing you could've possibly said. Give it."

"I don't—"

"Morgan's too much of a pacifist for thievery and I haven't personally pissed off anyone else yet, so it's almost definitely you. Give it back before I tell Janine."

Even while accusing me, Faith manages to force her tone to remain bored. The calm façade that she's insisted on wearing ever since we became teenagers only enrages me further. It's a lot harder to justify hating someone despicable when they keep their despicability concealed.

Still, her threat gives me pause. She wouldn't have made it if it wouldn't have. Faith's had plenty of time to learn all the worst ways of getting under my skin.

Like most children who grew up getting yelled at for the simple act of existing, I do not fair well beneath adult reprimand. Luckily, I'm not the only one who's stolen something.

"I wouldn't do that," I call her bluff. "A lost necklace is a lot more believable than an entire binder. Maybe it just—"

"Oh my god, Lots. You're such a shit liar." Faith steps in front of me, blocking the path.

I stop moving. I am not about to give Faith Harris the pleasure of watching me awkwardly attempt to maneuver around her.

"Give it back."

"I don't know what you're—"

"Never said it was a necklace. You basically just admitted to it. Give it."

I loathe when logic decides to take someone else's side.

"Where's Morgan's binder?" I ask.

"I don't know. Just give me the—"

"Admit you took it first."

Faith rolls her eyes. "I didn't."

"So it just disappeared? Into thin air?"

"I don't know. Maybe she lost it."

I shake my head. "Morgan doesn't lose things." She doesn't. She can track a million different objects and thoughts simultaneously. She's so good at it, that sometimes she holds on to mine too.

"Or maybe she's not as perfect as you keep pretending she is." Faith sighs, pinching her brow. "Look, you know you have it, I know you have it, so just give it back before—"

"What if I don't anymore?"

Finally, Faith falters. "Excuse me?"

"Apparently Morgan's stuff can just disappear, right?" I remind her. "What if yours did too? To the bottom of a lake, maybe. Incredibly mysteriously, of course."

Faith freezes. I've got her. "Did you—"

"No," I admit, because I am not Faith Harris. I don't get off on the suffering of others. I want to make her feel shitty, not terrified. Once she's fully back to neutral, I let myself smile. "Not yet, anyway."

I'm expecting her to glare or to roll her eyes at me again. Maybe yell like she used to. I would have even been able to cope with her breaking character entirely and begging for the necklace back.

What I'm not ready for is Faith Harris lunging at me, arms raised.

I leap to the side. "Oh my god! Were you just about to—"

She tries to grab at me again before I've even finished the sentence, so I take off running.

"What the fuck!" Even if I wanted to give the necklace back, (which I definitely don't now), I don't think I'd be able to. Faith would claw my eyeballs out before I'd even finished undoing the clasp.

Luckily, when we were kids, I actually did participate in camp activities. Quite enthusiastically, actually. In my mind, Faith might be a cheerleader whenever I imagine her existing in the real world (movies have conditioned me to assume that *all* pretty assholes are cheerleaders), but as she chases me, it quickly becomes evident that she isn't one.

I've never been particularly agile, but anyone would be able to outpace Faith. She catches herself on branch after branch even though I've barely veered off-path. Her footfalls are so uneven that I'm convinced she'll trip over herself. I've never been more grateful for someone else's motor issues.

"Lots!" she shrieks.

By the time she does, I'm already full of adrenaline. Maybe I've missed camp games more than I'd realized. Or maybe I just really love bothering Faith.

This version of her is different, though. Gone is her desperate attempt to appear unaffected and unbothered by anything or anyone and in its place is a Faith who might actually kill me if I let her catch me. I don't know how I'm supposed to adjust to the sudden change.

Eventually, she falls so far behind that I have enough time to pull myself up a tree. I finally let myself catch my breath, confident that she won't be able to follow me. When you grow up playing manhunt with the same group of kids every summer, you learn to keep track of which ones can climb.

Faith stops beneath my tree to catch her breath. She huffs and tosses her knapsack to the ground. I've only risked climbing up a few branches, (I'm not agile enough to get much further either), but I'm entirely out of her reach.

I have the upper hand. Again. And it feels really, really good.

"You're being ridiculous," she says.

"What'd you do with Morgan's notes?"

"I already said I don't have them."

"Right," I nod, reaching down to unclasp her necklace from my ankle. "Then I don't have this."

She takes one step back then two steps forward.

"Lots."

I examine the tree and find a hole in its trunk. "Woah, it looks like this thing's pretty hollow, actually."

"Lots, I swear to—"

"If someone were to drop something down there, you'd probably have to chop down the whole tree to get it back." I'm lying. The hole's less than a foot deep. I might covet accuracy, but sometimes, lying's just more fun.

"Don't—"

I swing my legs, moving the necklace closer to the hole. I don't let Faith get a word in edgewise. "Where's the binder?"

"I don't have the fucking binder!" Her voice pitches up at the end. "Just..." she glowers. Faith's not used to having to negotiate. "Come down. I'll help you look for it, alright? Whatever. Just... stop acting stupid."

It occurs to me that this might all be futile. Maybe she really didn't take it. Faith lives to cause tiny disasters, (intentionally using up all the hot water, spilling paint on other people's work, stealing snacks, et cetra), but I highly doubt she'd ever prioritize that over maintaining her dignity. Faith is not the kind of person who offers to help other people. Ever. So maybe, for once, I'm the one starting problems. But Faith has ruined a lot of summers over things much bigger than binders, so I am not about to surrender until I get something out of her.

I try to think up what that could be, and the obvious answer comes instantly. "Admit you know you're autistic."

"Excuse me?"

"Say it. Admit you're full of shit and that deep down, you know you're not actually any different from the rest of us."

She fiddles with her hair. "Wow, Lots. Didn't realize you were a fucking psychiatrist. You don't get to—"

"*You* don't get to keep making everyone else feel like crap!" I exclaim. "People can have complexes about it. Whatever. You lost the right to have yours when you decided to keep coming back every year just to look the rest of us in the eye and make sure we knew you'd hate nothing more than admitting you have anything in common with us!"

Faith crosses her arms over her chest. She squeezes at her elbows. "Just—"

"Admit it." I move the necklace closer to the hole. Let it dangle a bit.

"Jesus, Lots! Just—"

"Say it!"

"You're being ridiculous! Just—"

I wind the necklace around my fingers once and tighten my grip before lowering it into the hole. Faith's clearly attached to it, so I'm obviously not about to lose it. Even if my fingers do somehow slip, it wouldn't be hard to reach in and pull it back out. Faith just doesn't need to know any of that until after I win. "Admit it!"

"I'm not autistic! I'm sorry if that hurts your fragile little feelings, but—"

I move the chain lower.

"Jesus, Lots! Don't—"

"Say you're autistic."

"I'm not!"

"Bullshit! Admit—"

"I physically can't—"

"Say—"

"I'm not even human, okay!" Faith finally yells.

I enjoy scripting my social encounters. I'd been thinking up dozens of different ways that this conversation could have ended.

That was not one of them.

Chapter 9

I could be a terrible person.

I'm not, but I'm constantly aware that I could be.

I know that autistic people are not innately good or bad, but I also know that because of my autism, I am much more likely to accidentally land on the wrong side of that particular spectrum.

When you can't read people, it's difficult to know when you're upsetting them until after you've already taken things too far. When people know you're disabled, they're less likely to tell you when you've messed up. So, (unless you remain hypervigilant and pour constant research into it), you're often doomed to mess up again.

Faith Harris is not a good person, but she still *is* one. My brain is wired to cope better with absolutes, so sometimes, it struggles to consider those two things in tandem.

"Fuck." Faith stumbles away from me. She's trained herself out of hyper-visible stims, but now her arms are crossed and her fists are pounding against her elbows. Because I've pushed her into some kind of crisis. "I'm—I just said that. I didn't mean to... *fuck!*"

My stomach rolls. I have not always hated Faith Harris. Or at least, I don't think I did. I'm not good at people not liking me. I can never make sense of it. Not because I think I'm a particularly likeable person, but because it's antithetical to my mental image of myself.

I know that I'm not a malicious person. In my mind, if someone's not a malicious person, then it's only a matter of time until people realize that it's nonsensical to dislike them. I wasted years trying to be nice to Faith, and once I'd finally been forced to acknowledge that that was futile, I'd promised that I'd never debase myself like that ever again.

I just might have gotten a little too good at upholding that.

I carefully slide the necklace into my pocket before lowering myself back to the ground a lot less carefully. I wince as my feet make contact with the earth and do my best to shake out the pins and needles that the drop sends shooting up my legs.

"Hey." I take a cautious step towards Faith. She's still backing further into the trees and mumbling to herself, as if she's completely forgotten that I'm even here.

And she's terrified. *Faith Harris* is terrified.

Sometimes, Faith does such a good job pretending to be unaffected by things that I forget that she can be.

I pull the pendant out of my pocket and fully extend my arm towards her as I approach. I don't know how Faith reacts to getting upset. I don't think she's ever let any of us actually see that for years now. I am far worse at comforting people when they've yet to provide me with explicit instructions on how to do so.

"I'm sorry, okay?" I say. "That was clearly... I don't have any right to try and police how you identify. Obviously. No matter how much of a bitch you normally are about it."

She just keeps whispering to herself, breath fast and frantic. She seemed desperate to get the necklace back a few seconds ago but now, she's not even acknowledging it. I shake the fist it's in to try and regain her attention. "Faith? It's right here, okay? Are you—"

All at once, Faith goes rigid. Her head jerks to the right. "They're already coming."

"What—"

Her focus snaps to me. She pounces again, this time to grab my shoulders. I flinch beneath the sudden touch. Faith's preoccupied enough to mumble a quick "sorry", but not to let go of me. "You need to lie, alright?"

"I..." I try to step away, but her grip tightens. "Listen, why don't I just call Janine and—"

"Lots!" She shakes me. "You need to—shit." Faith's eyes lock on something behind me. Her voice drops to a whisper. *"Shit."*

I hear a pop. I feel a gust of wind raise the hairs on the back of my neck. And then, I turn around and almost bump noses with an incredibly small, incredibly angry fairy.

Chapter 10

"What. The. Fu—"

A hand grabs at the back of my shirt and tugs hard enough to make me lose my balance.

I turn to find Faith already on the forest floor, bowed so comically low that she must be getting dirt in her hair. It's a weird thing to focus on after having just found out that fairies exist, but I don't have the mental bandwidth to process that bit quite yet.

I make it my personal mission to understand as much as possible about everything I encounter at all times. Other autistics have special interests that they spend lifetimes obsessively building knowledge bases around, but something about me (maybe it's the ADHD, maybe it's just run-of-the-mill scatterbrainness) makes it too difficult for me to focus on any one topic long enough for anything like that.

The closest thing I have to a special interest is a love of the physical act of researching and fact-sharing, though a lot of that might actually just be spurred by my deep-seated hatred of ever being wrong. I know a little about a lot of things, but it's normally enough to let me get by on at least appearing intelligent. My whole camp nickname is based around it.

Fairies are not the kind of thing that one can simply choose to understand, so I focus on Faith's hair.

She tilts her head up slightly and I watch it swirl in the dirt. Then, she notices me watching, hisses an angry *"Lots!"*, and tugs me the rest of the way down.

I hastily unfreeze and do my best to copy the bow.

Everyone is completely silent. Even the forest feels motionless. Animals typically only do that when there's a predator nearby. I am both desperate to look up and terrified of what I'll see if I do.

"You may rise." When the fairy I'd almost bumped into speaks, his voice is even higher and more nasally than I'd thought it would be.

Faith throws a dirt-smudged hand over my mouth. It's a smart move since I was definitely about to laugh at what's presumably some form of fairy royalty, but I bite at her fingers in protest anyway, because she's Faith Harris. She's known me long enough to know that I'd prefer a magical smiting to sudden, nonconsensual physical contact.

With my mouth concealed, I finally let myself take in the creatures before me. The high-voiced fairy (their leader, presumably. The other two hover a few inches back) has a bushy green beard, which I'd usually assume indicates some level of adulthood and maturity, but I haven't read enough reliable sources on fairy developmental stages to know that for sure. On account of not knowing that any sources on fairies even *could* be reliable until a few seconds ago.

His skin is light blue. This is not a universal fairy characteristic, evidently. The feminine-presenting fairy on his right is purple and the one on his left is pink. It's difficult to imagine why any species would evolve to be such a wide array of colours that so rarely appear in nature, but I try not to get too caught up on that. On account of having just realized that fairies apparently exist, and all.

The bearded fairy wears a small, vaguely crown-shaped, upside-down pink flower that I don't recognize on his head, so I try to commit as many of its characteristics to memory as I possibly can. I do not know how to research fairies. Flora is a lot easier to gain clarity on. The two fairies flanking the probable royal are brandishing porcupine quills pointed directly towards me. Which is more than a little concerning.

The king flutters over to Faith, getting so close that I can physically see her breath ruffling his leaf-sewn skirts. He's only about two-thirds the size of her head, but Faith looks terrified. She's physically trembling.

"Has this human outwitted you, then?" the royal asks. "Has she tested you in the ways of her ancestors? Were you too cowardly to bear her torment?"

There's something ridiculously hilarious about a tiny, pastel creature talking about torment, but Faith chooses that exact moment to remove her hand from my mouth, so I'm forced to physically bite my tongue to stop myself from snickering. I'm worried raising my hand to pop a charm between my teeth to chew on instead might be seen as some kind of attack.

"No, Your Excellentance." In all the years I've known her, I've never once heard Faith speak respectfully. It's jarring. And terrifying.

"Ah." The fairy turns slightly to look at me. Faith's fingers instantly fly to mine, as if she's already decided that I'm about to do something stupid.

She's overreacting. I wouldn't dream of squashing a fairy unless they attacked me first. I wouldn't be able to bear the thought of destroying that many opportunities for scientific discovery.

"She's your mate, then," the fairy says.

"No!"

I am only slightly offended that Faith's clearly more disturbed now that he thinks she might like me than she was when they were discussing torture. Mostly, because I found the royal's statement equally horrifying.

"I'm not..." Faith sputters. "She's not... that's just... Lots."

The fairy's face pinches. It bears a striking resemblance to a blueberry as it does. "You've several mates? Where are—"

"No!" Faith's entire head turns several shades redder. I don't know if I'm expending more energy keeping myself from laughing at the fairy or at her. "It's just... it slipped out. The fairy thing."

The king frowns. "You broke your one and only oath because it *slipped out*?"

"Yes?"

The fairy on the right raises her quill. Faith flinches and stumbles back. Notably, without pulling me away with her, which I'm more than a little offended at.

The royal sighs and gestures for the quill to be lowered. "No matter how this came about then, we've protocol to follow. I assume you were made aware of the consequences of revealing your true nature to a human?"

Faith swallows. She licks her lips.

I have never seen Faith Harris nervous before. Truthfully, I wasn't aware that she was capable of caring about anything enough for nervousness to even be a possibility. It's unnerving.

"I was," she whispers.

"And you've made your decision?"

"I have." Her voice is little more than a croak.

I'm suddenly hit with the sickening realization that I might be about to watch Faith Harris cry.

"Since it appears you do not have this human's alliance and unyielding devotion, then, I assume you—"

"Super devoted, actually," I interrupt. It would have been helpful if Faith had been more specific about what I'm supposed to be lying about, but Faith's never been willingly helpful about anything ever, so I should have seen that coming. Now feels as good a time as any to start lying. Besides, I enter most conversations only half aware of what's going on and have managed to escape those relatively unscathed, so hopefully this shouldn't be much different. "Extremely unyieldingly."

Faith blanches. "That's not—"

"What were these umm... consequences? Again, though?" I cut her off. Even if I did get her panicked demands wrong, Faith is not about to make me look stupid in front of the first fairy I've ever met. I normally take great care to ensure I never end up looking wrong, and that evidently also extends to when I'm speaking to magical creatures that aren't supposed to exist. "Faith never got around to explaining that bit."

The fairy frowns. "A hundred years of obscurity and damnation or a chance to win a pardon in a battle in accordance with current human customs. Followed by those hundred years of obscurity and damnation should she lose, of course." He pauses to size me up. "If you *are* her mate, surely she must have—"

"Oh, right!" I stop him. "That. Yes. We pick the second option, please. The one that's not all automatic doom-y."

"*Lots*," Faith hisses.

I ignore her again. She's evidently in no state to be useful here, and I am in no headspace to be caught in a lie. When you find out that everything you ever believed was wrong, it's helpful to hold onto the illusion that you're not.

I latch onto the fairy's vague wording and make an educated guess.

"Are you up to date on modern human battle mechanics, then?" Based on his casual use of "mate", I'd wager he hasn't been up to date on anything human for a very, very long time. Hopefully. I am not about to go to actual war for Faith Fucking Harris, but I'd feel guilty enough if she was sentenced to semi-eternal doom in my presence that it feels like I have to at least try to do something about it.

Sure enough, the king scoffs. "I do not concern myself with human conflicts," he says. "I've much more important things to occupy myself with."

"Of course." I bow again. He seems like the kind of person who would appreciate that. "Your... royalness. I'd only meant to umm... see if you knew where we are!" I decide.

"And where might that be?"

"Human battle training facility." I nod in a way that I hope passes for solemn. Vaguer expressions like that still baffle me. "If you send your people out to verify, you'll find lots of arrows and targets and... beachballs! Several human objects of mass destruction."

"Oh my." He turns back to Faith. "It seems you've misled me. You've been preparing after all."

"I—" Faith starts. She doesn't finish.

I sigh. She's really very bad at this.

"How many humans are in your fleet?" the fairy asks.

"Seven," I supply when Faith fails to. "Or... six. Plus whatever Faith is. Which all three of us obviously already know all about, so it'd be a waste of time to specify. Obviously. Would that be alright?"

The king nods. "You mustn't let them know the true nature of the battle, of course. But if they spend their days training to fight other human battalions, I'm confident that won't be an issue. We'll even glamour ourselves human when the battle arrives to better facilitate the deception."

I swallow. "Thank you for that um... charity. Your liege."

"We'll need more information on specific battle protocol, of course," he continues. "And time to train. Are your people still infatuated with that whole killing obsession of theirs?"

"Oh, no!" I shake my head emphatically. "We got over that years ago! Our newer strategies are much less... murdery."

"Ah, excellent." He nods once. "Always seemed a waste of resources. I'll send a representative down to iron out official rules in due time, then. How long do you think would allow for an adequate amount of preparation?"

"Ten years?" I suggest.

The fairy frowns for a moment before erupting into tinkling laughter. "Oh my!" He wipes a tear from his eye after finally calming down, clutching his stomach as he physically struggles to regain control of his breathing. "I've been told you humans jest, but I hadn't expected it to be so remarkable!" Instantly, his tone shifts back to serious. Or as serious as a squeaky-voiced fairy could possibly get. "Now, of course if your troops aren't prepared to fight before the end of the season, we'll be forced to take that as an automatic forfeit."

"Oh." I chew my cheek. "Right. Is umm... end of August? We leave for... different battle training. After that. We're all extremely scary and intimidating, actually, so I'd completely understand if—"

"As long as we've time to prepare, I'm certain you'll find our efforts more than sufficient."

I'm caught off guard by how gullible this fairy is. I've spent a lot of time prattling on, pretending I know what I'm talking about. I've spent far less talking to people who genuinely take everything I say this seriously.

Even if I'd humoured the possibility of fairies existing, I hadn't considered that they might also be stupid.

(Though, if this means that Faith's one, that would actually make a lot of sense.)

"I do not abide by human metrics of time, however," the fairy continues.

"Oh, right." I turn to Faith. "Faith?"

Faith continues to unhelpfully stare off into space.

I tense the muscles in my cheeks. "Faith will get back to you on that later, actually. Pleasure to meet you, Your Excellency. Forgive us if we need a bit of time to—"

"What do you call it?" he interrupts.

I falter. "What?"

"Your newfangled human battle mechanism. My people will want to begin looking into it before our next meeting, of course."

"Oh, right. It's umm..." I search my brain for something high stakes enough to be believable, yet safe enough to hopefully not end in any actual bloodshed. "The most vicious human sport of them all: capture the flag."

Faith sounds like she physically chokes at that, but before she can say anything, there's another pop, a flash of cool air, and then, all three fairies are suddenly gone.

I finally let myself take a breath. Now that my adrenaline's faded, I suddenly feel dizzy. "What the—"

Faith promptly turns and vomits directly into a bush.

Chapter 11

"Okay," I let myself pace for a moment, shaking out my shoulders to try and reorient myself. "That was... okay."

Faith's still busy spilling her stomach contents all over the forest floor, so I go and retrieve her bag from where she abandoned it a few feet away.

I grab her water bottle and roll it over to her. I prefer to keep my distance from both vomit and potentially magical bitches. "Here. You should—"

She chucks it at me.

I catch it with my face.

"What the fuck!" I stumble back, clutching my jaw. I should have seen something like this coming. This is what I get for trying to be nice to someone like Faith Harris. I dig through my bag for my own metal bottle and press it against my pulsing lip. I taste iron. I'm pretty sure it's busted. "Are you seriously that incapable of being a half-decent person? I just saved your ass, and you couldn't even wait two seconds before—"

"You just ruined my life," Faith deadpans.

"And then *saved* it!" I remind her. "Or... probably. Maybe. It definitely sounds like I got you a better shot than you would have had without me though, so if you really think about it, you should probably be thanking me, actually." I leave the '*instead of unhinging your jaw to devour me whole*' part unvoiced. If Faith actually can do things like that, I'm not about to start offering up suggestions.

Faith just glares. I search her for anything magical, but she still looks just as human and annoying as ever. Maybe slightly paler, actually, but that's more likely to be a side effect of the vomiting than of some kind of magical phenomena.

"If you would've preferred eternal doom and oblivion or whatever, feel free to call them back here, okay? At least now your options are still open, right? So... yeah. You're welcome." I accent this with a brief bit of jazz hands. Based on my research there's seldom a good occasion for such a gesture, but Alice has been using it to fill silences for years now and I caught the bad habit from her.

"You ruined my life!" Faith repeats, the jazz hands evidently having done nothing to calm her down. She stomps against the dirt as she says it. Her voice is slightly higher this time. More shrill. I've never heard her sound like this before.

And I am, perhaps, at least slightly at fault.

I do not like Faith Harris. I'm fairly certain I hate her, in fact. But good people don't get to ruin other people's lives. Even if those other people are awful and terrible and more annoying than anyone else you've ever met. I detest moral wrongness even more than factual inaccuracy.

"Look," I sigh. "If there's anything I can do to—"

"Shut up!"

"Okay," I shrug. "Whatever. At least I offered." I throw my bag back over my shoulder and pull out my phone. I have two missed texts. "Text Janine. We're a few minutes late for check-in and she's very politely freaking out about it." I start off towards the cabin.

Eventually, Faith falls into step beside me. "If you tell anyone, I'll—"

"Okay, sure. I won't."

"I'm serious, Lots. Ever. If a single other person finds out about this, I'll—"

"I said okay." I'm not eager to hear a list of all the ways that Faith could theoretically destroy me. I'll definitely become curious about that eventually, but right now, I'm prioritizing my sanity. I'm at an information overload.

Faith's quiet for a moment. "I can't lie," she says. "At all. That's why I told you to in case I had to. No faefolk can do that."

"Okay." I do my best to not react visibly to her overtly calling herself 'faefolk'. I don't want to get anything else thrown at me.

"Everything I say, no matter how small, has to be something I believe's completely true."

"Got it."

"Good." She nods. "Then I've met dozens of people. Almost certainly hundreds. You are the absolute last person I would have ever willingly told about this."

"You—oh my god! You physically can't stop yourself from being a bitch, can you?"

Faith smirks. She holds out her palm. "I need my necklace."

I sigh and hand it over. I'm not trying to force any more life-altering confessions. Faith visibly relaxes once it's back around her neck.

"I'm probably going to touch your face."

Faith going from insulting me to respecting my boundaries in a matter of seconds is simultaneously incredibly jarring and the most on brand thing I've seen her do all afternoon, so I nod on impulse. She wraps one hand around the pendant (confirming my theory that at least something about it must be linked to her fairy-ness) and presses two dusty fingers against my lip.

"Wha—"

"Shush," she mutters. She squeezes her eyes shut and whispers something under her breath. My mouth goes cold then hot then cold again and then, in a matter of milliseconds, the pain's gone. I run my tongue over where the break had been and find the skin entirely smooth.

I start to say something (though what, I can't be sure. I often start talking before I've planned out the end of a sentence and just hope I'll figure the rest out before I reach it), but Faith's already walking off again.

"I wasn't aiming for your face," she says when I start to follow, not bothering to look back at me. "Showing up with a mysterious injury would have been inconvenient." She pauses. Finally, she turns. "If you tell anyone about any of this, even if it's years from now, I will know and I will do everything in my power to find you and make you regret it."

I open my mouth to respond, but she's already turned away again. She's either magicked her hair to dramatically swoosh after her or put enough effort into moving her neck that I'm surprised she hasn't strained it yet. Faith might not be human, but she's still as covertly dramatic as ever.

For a moment, realizing that makes the day's previous events seem a bit easier to cope with. This might not have to mean much of anything at all. I've never been comfortable around Faith Harris, so in the grand scheme of things, finding out that she's not human shouldn't actually change much.

About our relationship, that is. Everything else has gone to absolute shit.

Chapter 12

Finding out that fairies are real, (and that your archnemesis is one), has a tendency to make the rest of the world fade away a bit. I forget all about camp until I follow Faith back into the cabin and find the rest of the Caribous waiting for us.

Almost simultaneously, everyone turns to stare. No one was expecting us to spend the most time out today. Under normal circumstances, Faith and I tend to spend as little time together as humanly (or whatever-ly) possible.

Morgan breaks through the stillness, hopping off her bunk to jog over to us. She's prepared two colour-coded cue cards.

Mine says,

Forgot I asked Janine to look over my notes last night! ~~Apologize~~
Say sorry to Faith if you've been giving her shit about it all day.

Faith reads hers then flips it around so I can see it too.

Found my notes! Lots is going to apologize for giving you shit about it all day.

They both watch me expectedly.

I sigh and roll my eyes. "Sorry I got one tiny thing wrong."

I say it for the sake of avoiding further conflict. In reality, I'm not sorry, I'm confused. It's hardly my fault that Faith decided to act incredibly suspicious about the binder for absolutely no reason. I'd gone with the most logical conclusion, and there's absolutely nothing wrong with that. If anything, Faith should be apologizing for clearly trying to make the situation worse just for the fun of it.

Morgan either doesn't notice my lack of sincerity or didn't care about the apology being real in the first place, because she instantly applauds then grabs my hand and pulls me to our bunk.

We sit down on her bed. She pulls out her pad of paper so that we can start talking. The entire perimeter of the top page is already covered in tightly packed spirals and stars.

I frown. Morgan's hypergraphia means that she's in an almost constant state of compulsive doodling, but it normally only amps up like this when she's stressed.

"Hey," I say before she's even started writing. "Are you good?"

She nods. *Tired.*

I start to say something else, but she quickly adds more in front of it and turns the paper back towards me.

Very good tired.

I pull the muscles in my cheeks taut. I'd obviously wanted her to be okay, I'd just also been hoping that she'd somehow have simultaneously decided that she never wants to abandon me ever again. I've only spent one day on my own so far, and I've already managed to get myself wrapped up in some kind of magical feud.

Knowing I'd have to exist without Morgan was nerve-wracking. Being stuck alone with Faith had been scary. Spending even more time alone with Faith now that I know she's apparently some kind of magical creature currently holding me responsible for ruining her life might actually be deadly.

How was your day?

"Good," I lie. "Boring," I lie more. "I missed you," I promise.

Morgan rolls her eyes. It's not an expression that comes naturally to her, so there's always some level of perceivable effort behind the action whenever she performs it. Morgan's non-verbal gestures are much easier for me to navigate than other people's because she always uses them obviously and intentionally.

It was only a few hours, she writes.

"Yeah, but I'm needy. Joking." I quickly add when she instantly starts to scribble away a response. I will not let Morgan offer up sacrifices on my behalf. "I think. How was yours?"

She flips the notepad around so quickly that I know my attempt at changing the topic definitely didn't work.

Faith?

"Weirdly quiet," I wave her off. "She's probably like, saving her energy for peak evildom. Or plotting. She's almost definitely plotting." I realize I might be laying it on a bit thick and quickly change the topic. "Your turn."

Morgan gives in and starts writing something longer, so I flop back against her pillow and stare at the underside of my bunk.

There's this quote credited to Dr. Stephen Shore thrown around a lot in autistic spaces: "if you've met one person with autism, you've met one person with autism".

I've found it quoted a few different ways over the years, which used to bother me immensely. When quoting something important, it felt crucial to get each and every word right. Misquoting was not the kind of oversight that I would have expected from other autistics. We're not exactly known for being lax when it comes to specifics.

Now, I try to remember that my anger at the frequency of misquotes was probably a good indicator that I'm exactly the kind of person who needs to pay attention to ideas like that.

I like when things are concrete and predictable. Sometimes, that means that I make logical leaps based on the assumption that things will be. I'm trying to get better at focusing on intent and impact over more trivial forms of accuracy, but it's been difficult.

It's important to remember that all autistic people are not me. If you meet one autistic person, you've met one autistic person, regardless of how you phrase it. And if you *are* an autistic person, it's important to keep in mind that that applies to all other disabilities, comorbidities, and support needs as well.

Morgan was the first AAC user I got close to, so for a while, I just assumed that every AAC user was exactly like Morgan. I learned and memorized the specific ways she communicated and automatically decided that that was universal.

For example, Morgan's selective mutism is directly tied to her social anxiety, so staring at her the entire time she's writing something out removes most of the benefits that written communication provides her with in the first place. She needs the safety net of knowing that she'll be able to reread and edit out her thoughts before sharing them sometimes, so the physical act of writing has to be private.

Brain's nonverbal and also uses AAC, but she's fully aware that she's right about most things and entirely confident about the things that she gets wrong, so she requires no such buffer time. It took months of her aggressively pointing, stomping, and squeaking at me whenever I'd look away or busy myself with something else while she was typing to realize that she'd been interpreting that as incredibly rude and needlessly inefficient.

When you learn how to accommodate for one autistic person, it's important to remember that that only means you've learned how to accommodate for one autistic person. Even if you're also autistic. Maybe especially if you are.

Talking to Morgan can go really slowly at times. Morgan's a relatively fast writer, but she's also a careful thinker. And I am far from a fast reader. I've been years behind in literacy my entire life and have enough of a working grasp on it now that conversational vocabulary should technically be fine, but that doesn't stop my brain from skipping over and rearranging words or syllables or entire lines at times, so even after she's finished writing (and oftentimes, finished editing anything too multi-syllabic out for me), I have to take things bit by bit to make sure I'm actually processing what she's written.

I am not a slow-paced person. I have too many thoughts to think and opinions to voice for that. My body requires literal medication to operate at a speed slow enough to pass for functional. So, when I'm reading things online, I set my screen reader to the fastest possible setting to accommodate that. With pen and paper, that's no longer possible. With pen and paper, I have to rewire my entire brain.

The allistic belief that all autistics will get along is sometimes fueled not only by the assumption that we are incapable of moral complexity, but also by the equally incorrect belief that our communication and activity preferences must all line up. Autism is a series of ever-shifting extremes, so in actuality, finding another autistic person who isn't a bit too 'hyper-' in at least one thing that you're 'hypo-' is incredibly improbable. I do not love Morgan because our brains work identically. In fact, Morgan and I likely have more opposing support needs than congruent ones. Morgan was not custom-built for me and I was definitely not custom-built for her, but I love her so deeply that I unwind all my neurons and reconstruct them to fit better with hers biweekly.

Loving Morgan has meant learning how to sit in a quiet and calmness that I didn't know I possessed. She's somehow figured out how to make me still enough to hear my thoughts.

Which is normally wonderful. When I'm not in the middle of trying not to visibly panic about one of our cabinmates not being human.

I count the grooves on the underside of the bunk. Focus on reading all about how great Morgan obviously was over in Leadership. I try to center myself by emptying and filling my lungs over and over again.

When we turn in for the night, I stay in Morgan's bunk.

Okay? she signs.

I nod. "Just tired."

Morgan knows how to read me far better than I usually do though, so she disappears up into my bunk and returns with my pillow. She waits for me to curl up against her before throwing her arm around me and I eventually drift off to the faint sound of her resting heart rate.

And the unshakeable feeling of a pair of eyes glaring at me through the darkness.

July 5

My Dearest Alice,

Yesterday was really boring and nothing intresting hapened what so ever.

Talk at u later,
Charlotte

Chapter 13

Morgan doesn't have Leadership on Wednesday, so I stick as close to her as possible the entire day.

Faith seemed pretty insistent that no one else finds out that she's whatever she is, (I woke up early to google, but it's exceptionally difficult to find concrete answers on things that aren't supposed to exist), so if she *is* planning on feasting on my life force or peeling all my skin off strip by strip, I'm fairly confident that she won't do that while there's anyone else around. Hopefully.

Luckily, I'm already an incredibly clingy friend, so no one seems to notice that anything's amiss. I'm pretty sure Morgan catches at least something based on the amount of, "you're sure you're okay"s she casually drops, but even she never gets concerned enough to actually push anything.

By Thursday, my curiosity's already overpowered my attempts at self-preservation. Lasting over 24-hours is still impressive for me, though. I've never been all that good at keeping myself alive.

I work up the nerve to confront Faith while we're trapped at the craft tent again. I'm so anxious about doing it that I actually get half-way through a lanyard bracelet before marching over to where she's helping a group of kids pick out colours for theirs.

Faith's always been uncharacteristically decent with children, which finally seems less paradoxical to me now. Maybe she's trying to coax them into giving up their souls or something. From what I've read, magical creatures tend to be *extremely* into prepubescent souls.

Finding out that fairies exist might have made the rest of the world blurry, but at least now a lot of Faith's Faithisms might actually make sense.

"Hey," I hover a few feet away from her. Faith might be fine around children, but I'm certainly not. They're creepy and needy and far too unpredictable for my liking. "We should talk."

Faith doesn't even look up at me. "Busy."

"In a bit, then. I—"

"No."

I lower my voice. "This umm... this isn't the kind of conversation you'd want to have in public."

Slowly, her eyes drag up to mine. I try my best to stare straight back. Generally, I don't have anywhere near as much of a problem with eye contact as some of the other autistics I know, but looking at Faith's eyes always makes mine water. I squint and try to keep looking anyway. Eye-contact is an important demonstration of dominance and bravery across several different species, after all. Eventually, though, I have to give up and look away first.

Faith sighs. She hands off her partially started bracelet to the nearest counsellor. "Lots and I are going on a walk. We'll check in if we end up at a different station." Her voice is ice. From a normal magical creature (if normal magical creatures could even exist) that might freak me out, but Faith's always been rude and standoffish, so I try not to read too much into that. Mostly. She walks off into the seclusion of the forest and forces me to awkwardly jog after her.

"What do you want?" Faith whips around so suddenly that I almost crash into her.

I slip my tangle around my fingers. 'You were acting ridiculously suspicious," I say. "Just... for the record."

"I haven't been doing anything different," Faith deadpans. "I've lasted sixteen years so far, so if someone's found out, it's—"

"No, I meant about the binder."

Her eyebrows curve. "Excuse me?"

"About..." I swallow, bouncing from heel to toe to give myself time to formulate a coherent sentence. Those are hard to make whilst alone in a forest with a magical creature. Or just anywhere around Faith Harris in general, actually. "You said you couldn't lie, right? Unless that was a lie. That actually would've been an excellent lie, now that I think about it. If I was a fairy and I *could* lie, I'd probably—"

"Lots." Faith stops me. "Focus. I don't need a whole monologue."

"Right, sorry," I say. "Or... not sorry, actually. Fuck you. Anyway, you presumably can't lie, right? And even if you could, Morgan said Janine had the binder the whole time so you clearly weren't, but you still... you were acting ridiculously suspicious about it! Like, so suspicious that anyone with half a braincell would've assumed you'd taken it. So accusing you was the most logical thing I could've done, actually. Just so you know. So... why'd you act like you took it?"

Faith stares. She cocks her head to the side, ever so slightly. "I'm probably about to tackle you."

"You absolutely are n—"

She shoves me up against a tree before I can even finish the sentence.

"Hey!" I try to push her off. "What the—"

Faith keeps her forearm pressed against my chest, locking my upper body in place. "What are you?" she demands.

"Currently? Extremely uncomfortable! And pissed! Stop shoving me places!"

Faith doesn't even flinch. She's so close that I could count each strand of her perfectly combed, eternally shining hair if I wanted to. Which, of course, I don't. Obviously.

"You knew what I was, right?" she says. "Before I told you. Were you trying to bait me into—"

"I still don't even know what you are!"

Her eyebrows flinch. "You negotiated with a fairy like it was nothing."

"Because talking to the majority of allistic people already always feels like talking to an alien species, so I've kind of gotten used to pretending I'm good at it over the years!"

Faith sighs, releasing me. There's nothing on my shirt, but I hastily brush out the area she'd been touching anyway.

Faith takes a step back and mutters something under her breath. She starts sucking on her hair as she paces the forest floor. She hasn't let herself do that around other people since we were kids. She's freaking out. Quietly and subtly, but she is.

"You're human?" She eventually turns back to me. "You swear?"

"Yes!" I consider. According to some sources, swearing to anything around fairies is incredibly risky business. "Or... as far as I know, at least. Don't hold me to that."

"And you're sure nothing sent you? No one—"

"Okay, no offense, but it kind of seems like you don't carry that much magical weight. Or... full offense, actually." It's been a lot more difficult to remember that I hate Faith now that I've seen her freak out in the forest. Twice. It's like there's a Faith-who-is-human in my head and a Faith-who-isn't, and I haven't properly consolidated them yet. I shake out my neck. "Fuck you. I'm pretty sure you got pine needles in my hair."

She doesn't apologize. "You're seriously expecting me to believe you didn't know anything about the fae until two days ago." Her face is frozen. Her eyes are dark and probing.

I ignore all of that and focus on the word choice instead. According to most sources, "fae" means something distinctly different from "fairy". It's another clue.

When I notice Faith's still staring at me, I give a quick shrug.

"And you're... asking me about why I didn't steal a binder?"

"Why you acted like you *did* steal a binder," I correct. "I don't like being wrong about things. It's important we both know you clearly intentionally misled me there. I came to the same logical conclusion that anyone would've if presented with the same scenario so... ha. Fuck you. Again."

Faith pinches her brow. She sits down and starts tracing circles in the dirt with her sneaker.

Slowly, I sit too. A few feet away, of course. I'm not eager to get hexed or anything. "If you wanted to tell me about fairy stuff—fae, actually? Or faefolk? Fairfolk? Or are they all right? Or is that faery with an e, actually. I've read it's different, sometimes, if it's with an e—I also would not be opposed. But I'm only officially asking about the binder."

"Sure sounds like you're asking about a lot more than a binder," Faith mutters.

"Not intentionally," I correct. "I'm really not trying to..." I sigh. "You're like, the worst. Objectively. Full offense, fuck you. But I also know that having to listen to a million questions and assumptions about your disability sucks. Not that magical creature status is like... a disability. Or a diagnosis. I just... I'm trying really hard to not be an asshole here."

"That must be really difficult for you."

"See, I know you mean that as an insult, but it actually has been so... thank you for acknowledging my efforts. Ha."

Faith abandons her dirt drawing and pulls her knees into her chest. "You're so fucking weird."

"Thanks. It's the AuDHD. Also, fuck you. Anyway, so. Binder. Suspicious. Why."

"Thought you just said you were working on not bombarding people with questions."

"Identity-based questions," I clarify. "So unless lying about binder-stealing's like, a core part of your being, I'm in the clear."

Faith sighs. She picks at the grass. "Sometimes I just like being annoying."

"Oh, I'm well aware. That's it, then?"

"That's it."

"Oh." I frown. "That's... inconvenient but also entirely plausible. And an incredibly stupid thing to accidentally start a... war? A feud? A whatever it is over."

"Fuck you." Faith starts to stand up.

I wince. "I wasn't being annoying on purpose. Just... observing. This time."

She sighs. She sits back down.

We're both quiet, for a while. Faith, because she might not have anything left to say. Me, because I know that whatever I do come up with, she'll probably take it the wrong way. And because a part of me is secretly hoping that if I let the silence sit for long enough, she'll offer up more information. It's not rude if I never technically pester her about it.

Eventually, it works.

"Have you figured it out, then?" Faith tugs a few blades of grass from the earth. "What I am?"

"I'm working on it. I have theories."

She's quiet again. Then, "You seriously not gonna share 'em?"

"I'm being respectful!" I remind her. "So respectful that I'm waiting for you to offer up information completely voluntarily." Then, I very respectfully stare in her general direction and wait for her to cave.

Faith sighs. "Fine, whatever. Guess."

"If you're gonna tell me anyway, you might as well—"

"Quit it, Lots. You don't give a shit about being respectful, you're just obsessed with convincing people you do. You're not asking questions because you don't want to have to deal with the embarrassment of being wrong. I'm not telling you until you guess it right."

I frown. "I care about respecting most people," I grumble. "Just not you."

"Fine, maybe. Guess. If I have to deal with this," She gestures so vaguely that I can't tell if 'this' is referring to my presence or her impending doom. "I'm not making it easy on you either."

"That's— you're so annoying!"

Faith shrugs and waits. The corners of her lips flinch upward for half a second.

I sigh. There's obviously a list of potential theories in my notes app, but I don't want to pull that out until I absolutely have to. "Okay." I relent. There's no point in trying to hold off, after all. We both clearly know I'll go crazy if I'm left in the dark much longer. "So I thought fairy, right? The 'i' kind, not the 'e' kind. Because that king guy—"

"Not a king."

"Not a—" I frown. An in-depth explanation of magical political systems sounds like it would be fascinating, but I know that I'm not likely to get that out of Faith right now. I force myself to stick to the more imminently important mystery. "Okay. We'll shelve that for later then, I guess. That whatever-he-was looked like one, right? But you don't. I mean, size-wise, obviously, but I also feel like if you had wings hidden away somewhere, you would've definitely shown those off the moment you gave yourself away so... changeling?" I guess. "On account of the humanness and secrecy and stuff? And the amount of time you've clearly spent here—unless that wasn't always you. Which might actually be more indicative of changelingness. But your mannerisms have always been fairly consistent so I'm pretty— oh." I stop. "I'm right. Yes. Excellent." I applaud myself.

Faith glares. "I didn't say that."

"You're playing with your hair," I explain. "That's an anxious or upset stim for you, not an excited one. You would've been excited if I'd gotten it wrong."

Her eyebrows shift. "It's creepy when you do stuff like that, you know."

"I know." I nod. "It's the AuDHD. So? Am I right?"

Faith doesn't respond. People normally do that when they're wrong. Or when you're right and they don't want you to be.

I grin. "You said you'd tell me if—"

"Fine," Faith grumbles. "Yes. Whatever. That was a lot less fun for me than I'd thought it'd be."

"Did you know most historians agree changelings probably came about as a means of explaining away disabled children to remove a parent's ownership over them and thus justify their abandonment? Which obviously isn't true because you clearly actually exist, but—"

"I'm a changeling stuck at an autistic summer camp, Lots." Even when she's interrupting me to talk about something earth-shattering, Faith speaks in eternal deadpan. "Obviously I'm well aware."

"Oh." I nod. "Right."

Faith picks dirt out from under her nails with the stem of a leaf. "Technically faery wouldn't have been wrong either. With an e. But that's a massive blanket term. It'd be like calling dogs and humans 'earthlings'."

"Oh, okay." I wasn't expecting Faith to offer up any additional information. It's suspicious that she has, but I'm more than willing to take anything I can get. "Good to know."

She sighs, dropping her leaf. "Changelings don't deal in magical trades," Faith says. "If you've read that anywhere, it was wrong. That's high fae. Or trolls. Or pixies, technically, but they pretty much exclusively offer deals for the thrill of trying to figure out how to mess them up. Or genies, kind of, but—"

"Genies are real?"

Faith frowns. "That's the part that gets a reaction?"

"I'm compartmentalizing."

She cracks her fingers one by one.

I wince at the sound of each joint popping.

"I can't make those kinds of deals. I don't have much of my own magic, so even if I could, I probably wouldn't. Offering to help a changeling benefits only the changeling."

"Good to know."

Faith waits. "Well?"

"Well?"

"Did you want to..." she gestures vaguely.

I comb through potential interpretations of the gesture. I do not do well with vagueness. "Was that... is this how you think asking for help works?"

Faith's face darkens slightly before she looks away to continue picking at the earth. "I wasn't asking," she mutters. "You already tried to offer. I'm just giving you the opportunity to do that again."

"Hmmm," I consider.

Faith wears her anxiety visibly, even if she seems mostly unaware of that. She rubs her thumb along the side of her finger so rapidly that I'm surprised it doesn't chafe. She has an extremely long skincare routine (though part of me's always wondered if that's partially just a ploy to let her hog the bathroom for longer), so maybe that's what counteracts it. She's constantly tucking and untucking and retucking her hair behind her ears. I wonder if that's how she's managed to transition away from the hair-sucking.

"Lots?" She says. I can't tell what specific aspect of her tone's abnormal, but it unsettles me. "This is partially your fault." Her pace is slightly above her typical slow drawl, but only slightly. "So—"

"Where's the human baby?"

"Excuse me?"

"If I'm about to sign up to help you win some kind of battle, I need to make sure I'm actually on the right side," I explain. "The fate of the human babies that changelings swap themselves out for varies drastically source to source. I need to hear it from you."

Faith's eyes narrow a smidge. I can't tell if it's because she's thinking or because she's about to try to lie. Supposedly, the second option should be impossible. Unless that really was an incredibly well-placed lie, but I don't think Faith's clever enough for that. "I'd assume she's in Faerie. I haven't been there since we were switched, though, so I can't say for sure."

"*Alive* in Faerie?" I clarify. I've read that even non-lying fae are tricky with their words, so follow-up questions are vital.

"I'd assume? If she isn't, it has nothing to do with me."

"Do you..." I look around. Lean forward to whisper even after confirming that we're alone. "Eat people?"

"No, I do not *eat people.*"

"Their souls?"

"No!"

"Life forces?"

Faith rolls her eyes.

"You didn't actually say no to life forces," I point out.

She sighs. "I don't eat life forces either. Obviously."

"I just learned magic's real! Unless you're planning on explaining how it actually works, I'm allowed to be cautious about it!"

Faith considers. "You've seen Peter Pan?"

"The Disney movie?"

"That should work. I haven't actually seen it. Too worried it'd give something away to my parents. Tinkerbell needs humans to survive, right? The fae operate like that."

I sift through vague childhood memories. "Attention?" I realize. "You feed off of human attention?"

"That would probably be the simplest way of explaining it." I can hear Faith's annoyance at having to walk me through all this, but I pretend not to notice.

Social cues are tricky for me. If I occasionally choose to interpret them incorrectly on purpose, I feel like that's more than owed.

"You're like... a literal magical attention whore." I typically don't use the word 'whore' as a matter of feminist principle, but it's too perfect an opportunity to pass up.

Faith pushes herself to her feet. "You're not taking this seriously."

"I met a magical talking blueberry wearing a flower hat a few days ago! All things considered, I'd say—"

She glares. "This isn't funny."

"Okay." I nod. "Okay. Fair. This is..." I hesitate. "You're in trouble, then? For real?"

She scoffs. "I wouldn't be if you hadn't gone and—"

"Okay. I'll help." I might have threatened to kill Faith once or twice or a few hundred times over the years, but that doesn't mean I actually want her dead.

Maybe Faith didn't know that though, because she frowns. "I won't give you anything for it."

"Okay."

"You don't like me," she reminds us both.

I roll my eyes. Of course Faith doesn't get it. She's never lifted a finger to help anyone but herself. "Right, but I'm a good person. It doesn't matter if you're not, I'm not just gonna sit back and watch you get sentenced to semi-eternal damnation or whatever." I consider. "If I help," I add. "You don't come back next summer. Or the one after that. That's what I get out of this. No magic or eternal life, or whatever, just two summers where I don't have to put up with you."

She considers for a while before nodding. "Sounds fair."

"Alright." I get up. "What do I have to do?"

Faith wraps a fist around her necklace. "Let's go lie to some faeries."

Chapter 14

The angry blue fairy (Faith says he actually *is* both a fairy and a faery which is wildly confusing in a way that seemingly only makes sense to the fae) is indeed not a king, but I'm still supposed to treat him like one.

Apparently, the fae found out about the way human royalty was treated a few centuries ago and found it so delightful that they decided to apply all the bowing and honorifics to even their most low ranking of officials.

From what I understand (Faith's never been exactly forthcoming with information of even the nonmagical variety), he's the magical equivalent of a public relations person. Just with the power to declare war and sentence people to damnation if they ever break the rules of how those relations are meant to go.

He's been Faith's point-person since she first became cognisant enough of her fae nature to start getting in contact with Faerie (that's where they're from. Once again, a confusing word choice that Faith treats as perfectly logical).

Despite that (or, in my opinion, because of it, though Faith didn't seem open to that hypothesis) he's never developed any level of fondness for her. Luckily, that probably won't matter. According to Faith, the fae are ridiculously rigid about rules. Those who don't spend any time in the human realm are also apparently unbelievably gullible, so as long as the rules we propose are relatively believable and we make sure that I'm the one delivering anything false, it should be easy to turn things in our favour.

If only anyone in our cabin was actually good at capture the flag.

Faith grips her necklace, mutters a quick enchantment, and then the fairy pops back into the forest. This time, he comes alone.

"You've decided to set your terms then?" The fairy
squeaks.

"I have," Faith says.

I wait for her to rise from her bow before standing up
myself. If I'm awful at judging the appropriate time to perform
human social rituals, I doubt I'll fare any better with faerie
customs (faerie's also apparently an adjective because of course it
is).

"I trust you've already begun your own research?" Faith
checks. If he hasn't, we'll be able to make up an entirely new
game. One that preferably does not involve any running. Or
chasing. Or any kind of physical activity whatsoever.

"I have."

Faith nods. She doesn't look disappointed. Not a single
muscle in her face moves. "I assume you've discovered that
capture the flag has many variations, then?"

The fairy nods.

"I propose we play by the standard rules used by my
human associates, then. We shall choose a battlefield and mark a
line down its center. We will both be given a pinnie—"

"That's like, a lightweight overshirt used in human sports.
And warcraft." I helpfully explain. "We use them as flags here."

Faith's jaw twitches. "Right. We will both be given a
pinnie," she repeats. "To hide as we see fit."

"It has to be hidden within the boundary line!" I add.
"And players can't leave the boundary during the game!"

"Thank you, Lots," She grimaces. "The surrounding
environment cannot be manipulated in the hiding of the pinnie.
No digging, branch breaking, or grass pulling. No placing it
somewhere difficult to retrieve it from. And at least two
centimeters of the pinnie must be visible from at least one angle.
Once both pinnies have been hidden, we will be permitted to
cross the line in pursuit of the other team's flag—"

"She means pinnie."

Faith tenses her shoulders. "Yes. I do. We'll be permitted

to cross the line in pursuit of the other team's flag, but if a member of either team is tagged whilst in their territory, they are to immediately proceed to the other team's jail—"

"Not an actual jail."

"Lots!" Faith squeezes her eyes shut and takes a deep breath. "No," she says, much more quietly. "Not an actual jail. Though Faerie doesn't have those, so I'd *assumed* it wouldn't have been a problem. That competitor is not permitted to leave the jail lest a teammate make it to them untagged, at which point the pair may safely walk directly back to their side of the battlefield and continue the game. The first team to find the other's flag and get it back over the line without getting tagged wins. Anything to add or change?"

This is supposed to be my cue to bring up magic, but I've been listening to Morgan go over safe-play rules for days now. I'm not about to let those go unaccounted for. "We should add no monkey guarding."

Faith's eyes cut to me. "I—yes." She grits her teeth. "Of course." She quickly explains the concept of 'monkey-guarding' to the very confused looking fairy and waits for him to nod his assent. "Any—"

"And the two-finger rule," I add.

"Excuse me?"

"The only physical contact allowed is one-or-two finger tags. It safeguards against injury."

Faith's ears start to go red, but the fairy nods eagerly.

"A very sensible stipulation," he says. "If that's all then, we'll—"

Faith stomps on my foot.

"Wha—oh," I say. "Right. It'd only be fair if you either use human-shaped and abilitied fae folk or use a umm... spell? To make your competitors equal in strength and speed to ours? Also obviously to keep the whole," I lean forward to whisper. "*Faerie thing* secret from our battalion. And no magic from either side can be used during the battle, obviously. To level the playing field." I make sure not to look at Faith as I say it. She's annoyingly elusive about what kind of magic she does possess (though it clearly comes from her necklace), but she seems to think that at least some of it could be helpful. It's imperative that she doesn't verbally agree to not use any.

"Sounds adequate." The blue fairy nods. "I agree to your terms and shall get my champions to swear by them."

That's all there is to it. There's no contract or need for Faith to pledge to follow terms as well because apparently, creatures that can't lie don't need written records. We set a date for the end of the summer then the fairy pops back out of existence.

The moment he's gone, Faith's shoulders slump. We'd been stationary the entire conversation, but suddenly, she's breathless.

It makes me uncomfortable.

"So umm..." I try to fill the air. "That went—"

"You didn't have to keep interrupting me," she snaps.

"Right, but it still—"

"No!" she says. "No! We came up with a script and then you went and—"

"They were important things to add!"

"Or you just love listening to the sound of your own voice. God, you could've ruined my life *again* just because—"

"I didn't ruin it the first time," I remind her. "Technically. I didn't force you to—"

"Shut up!" Faith takes a deep breath. She fixes her hair. "I'm telling Janine we're spending the rest of the afternoon at the cabin," she mumbles. "I need to be anywhere I can pretend this all isn't happening. Don't talk to me."

"Wasn't planning on it."

Faith storms off. I wait a beat to give her space before following. We might be technical allies in the eyes of a few Faerie officials, but we are clearly never, ever going to be friends.

July 6

My dearest Alice,

If some1 keeps blowing up at u even tho ur doing them a masive favor, that means ur aloud to stop helping with that right?

Even if you'd kinda be a terible person if you did?

Talk at u soon,
Charlotte

Chapter 15

Faith is not the first changeling to blow her cover.

I learn this gradually and tediously. Talking to Faith about anything is always like pulling teeth, but she's especially quiet about faerie stuff and I'm trying my best to not be too pushy there.

A battle with the fate of her entire existence hanging in the balance feels like the kind of thing that definitely justifies sacrificing a bit of decorum, though.

Changelings have apparently been revealing their true natures to humans since time began. It's difficult for creatures that privilege truth above all else to enter into long-term relationships without feeling compelled to reveal their truest selves to their partners. Still, changelings going around revealing themselves all willy-nilly would obviously ruin the whole secret-child-swap operation, so penalties had to be put in place.

Punishment for breaking codes of secrecy are cumulative. If a changeling were to let an entire army in on their secret, then they would be expected to win an individual battle for each and every person told.

As a result, a changeling typically doesn't reveal themself until they've amassed enough allies who would willingly follow them blindly into battle for them to feel fairly confident that they'll be able to win their absolution.

Faith's far from the first changeling to blow her cover, but she is, perhaps, the first to do it accidentally. Without a friend in sight. Faith has exactly zero allies at Corrain, which means I'm now her closest one by default. Through shared responsibility, of course, not genuine tolerability.

If this is going to work, I'm going to have to completely reform Faith in the eyes of the rest of the Caribou Crew. That might be harder than the actual battle.

"Hear ye, hear ye!" I stand up on my bunk Monday morning. The beginning of the week is one of the rare times when we're all practically forced to exist in close proximity. The counsellors have their weekly check-in meetings right after breakfast, so all older campers are sent back to their cabins regardless of the activities we've selected for the day since there isn't enough staff free to adhere to our differing wants. It's the perfect time for recruitment. Hopefully.

I press a palm against the ceiling to help balance myself and stare out at my audience.

The blue fairy—who I'm supposed to call 'His Excellentance Squirge', apparently—supposedly put a spell over the cabin so that anyone who enters it will instantaneously acquire false memories of a rival camp across the lake so that we can explain the battle more easily, but I don't want to be the first one to bring that up in case it didn't work. His Excellentance Squirge doesn't exactly inspire confidence.

"I umm..." I make eye contact with Faith and gesture her over.

She doesn't move.

I bite my cheek and try to stop myself from rolling my eyes. Letting the others know that I'm just as fed up with Faith as I've always been will not help the plan. "Faith has something to say!"

Faith (who apparently doesn't care at all about pretending that we're on goodish terms) sighs and sits up slightly straighter in her bunk. "I umm..." She still doesn't move.

"Up here!" I hope I sound good-natured. I'm pretty sure I'm smiling, so hopefully that makes up for any annoyance that sneaks into my tone.

Audiences are much more likely to side with you if they believe you to be an authority, even if both parties know that that authority is only imagined. Higher ground provides an excellent mechanism for establishing this. So do lower voices and suits, but I don't have access to either of those right now.

Faith waits a beat before reluctantly dragging herself up to my bunk. I step to the side to give her more space and she hesitates again before standing up. At first, she seems to think she's too cool to require ceiling stabilization, but she begins to topple almost instantly and throws her palms up.

Some autistic people are incredibly athletic and coordinated.

Most of our cabin is not.

I glance over at Sunny's support worker to make sure she's not about to tell us to sit down, but she looks relatively unbothered. I hope they keep getting paired together. Having support staff who won't narc about smaller things will make this all go considerably more smoothly.

Everyone's watching us and waiting. Brain signs something that I can't mentally translate quickly enough to comprehend that results in Van throwing a hand over his mouth to smother a laugh. Which probably isn't the best sign.

"Faith?" I prompt.

She rolls her eyes. "You're the one who wanted to make a big announcement."

I'm about to push back on that (one of the best parts of having to work with Faith Harris was supposed to be forcing her to work with *me*) before remembering that there's a very strong possibility that she physically can't do this part. Faith and I aren't supposed to be impacted by Squirge's spell, so if she tries to make up a story about a fictional rival camp, her body would probably process it as a lie.

It's hard to remember to attribute Faith's faerie traits to her being a faery when a lot of them already align so well with her being a bitch.

"Right!" I make myself smile. "So, Faith had a run-in with the umm... Antelope Cabin. From across the lake. And—"

"Boooooo!" Gator hisses, which is hopefully a good sign.

I nod a little to myself, words picking up speed as I gradually become confident in the lie. "Right!" I point. "Yes! Exactly! And they were all like, 'I don't even know why they'd even *have* an autistic summer camp. I bet all those losers can't even do any camp stuff." I don't decide to make the still-unnamed camp ableist until I'm already in the middle of doing it, but supposedly whatever spell His Excellentance Squirge cast on the cabin should work around anything I feed it, so I decide to play into it. It gives us a fast, believable motive for hating them. It is exceptionally easier to rally a group around a cause if you all share a mutual hatred for the enemy. "And Faith was all like, 'umm actually, we're all super capable and great at camp', which..."

I can see myself losing my audience and quickly realize why. Faith would never defend a single one of us.

"Or... okay, not that exactly, actually," I backtrack. "It was more her just kind of passive-aggressively insulting them, actually. Anyway, she pissed them off and they pissed her off and things escalated and then Faith accidentally made a bet. She said we'd have a big cabin versus cabin capture the flag game at the end of the summer and if she loses she has to give them..." I pause. We hadn't actually come up with that part yet. Probably because I'd just assumed Faith would be doing the talking while she'd figured that I'd somehow know that coming up with a false explanation would have to fall upon me. Even though I only found out faefolk exist a week ago, Faith seems to get consistently annoyed whenever I don't magically intuit everything about them.

I search for something big enough to inspire urgency yet small enough to be something another teenager could feasibly hold her up to. Luckily, we shouldn't have to worry about anyone running off to tell any authorities about any of this. His Excellentance Squirge says that if they try to mention it to anyone outside of our chosen champions, they'll abruptly forget what they were going to say.

(Secretly, I wonder if I've already run into any fae who've cast similar spells on me. I'm exceptionally bad at seeing a thought through to completion.)

"Five hundred dollars," I decide. "Which obviously means she needs help because that's an insane ask."

I see Faith wince.

Gator raises their hand.

"Yes?"

"Faith's stupid rich."

"I umm..." I turn to Faith.

"My parents are definitely stupid rich," she unhelpfully confirms. I realize for the first time that that was probably a large contributing factor behind why she was placed with them. Count on the fae to only willingly experience humanity through its most privileged perspectives.

"Right," I nod. "Right, okay, but that's her parents' money, right? So she'd have to withdraw it and she'd get grounded forever and stuff. And..." I sigh. "And Faith's not out as autistic at school so he said if she doesn't follow through he'll tell everyone, which is BS. No one else gets to decide how open we are about our diagnoses." It's exactly half of an apology because I'm exactly half sorry about the argument that started this all in the first place. "Plus, don't we want to kick Antelope ass?"

"Kick Antelope ass!" Sunny cheers. Sunny's echolalia is far more likely to kick in when you use a more charged or taboo word. Swearing's an excellent way to get her on your side.

"Exactly! See? Fun. Tons of fun. The game's scheduled for the end of August, so if we all sign up for more athletics-based camp stuff until then to prepare, then—"

Gator raises their hand again.

I chew on my cheek. "Yes, Gator?"

"You don't like camp stuff. In general. Especially athletics."

"Good point, but—"

They raise their hand again. Gator does that to keep themself from interrupting others since they also struggle with turn-taking. Since I'm much worse at navigating that and *don't* go through the added effort of trying to come up with that kind of buffer, it's always felt fairest to let them interrupt me whenever they want. "Yes?"

"You don't like Faith."

"Even better point. But. Okay. Consider. I hate Camp... Joshua, that camp we all hate, a lot more."

Everyone looks at each other. The cabin is tense and silent.

You might assume that asking a group of people to help you with something has a greater possibility of success than asking a series of individuals, but you'd be wrong. You might be increasing your possible targets, but the odds of any of them stepping up to volunteer decreases drastically.

Through studying the public stabbing of a woman in the mid-twentieth-century, social psychologists concluded that bystanders felt less compelled to step in and do anything to stop it because of two main contributing factors. Firstly, groups allow for responsibility diffusion amongst their members. There's less of an urgency behind "I have to do something" when "someone has to do something" is such a more appealing option. Secondly, humans (even autistic ones, sometimes), often seek to mimic the social behaviors of the people around them. If no one else immediately steps forward while they're still in the responsibility diffusion stage, everyone else begins to think "maybe there's a reason they're not doing anything. Maybe I shouldn't do anything either."

That stabbing case that first popularized the bystander effect has actually since been debunked due to gross misreporting (in some aspects, it seems, for the specific purpose of creating a clearer case for the very effect it originated), but it still provides us with a logical rationale behind how bystanders are made. Since similar responses have been observed elsewhere time and time again, it would be reckless to not pay that any kind of mind.

Targeting someone one-on-one typically makes them more likely to go along with whatever you're asking them to do. Whether or not that's the reason that no one intervened in a specific historic stabbing.

I scan my audience and try to decide who would be the ideal initial target.

Morgan would be the easiest, of course. I'd follow her into anything and I'm fairly certain she'd do the same for me. That also makes her one of the least effective instigators. It's practically already a given that if I'm about to spend all summer training to beat some non-existent rival campers, Morgan'll be right there beside me. That assumption hasn't swayed anyone yet, so confirmation of it likely won't do much.

Sunny would probably be an even less helpful choice. She already signs up for far more events than the rest of us and long ago established herself as the bravest physical activity-wise. That's yet to convince anyone else to become more ambitious.

That leaves Van as the obvious choice. He's dating Brain and best friends with Gator, so it'd be good to single out someone who has a lot of pull with other people I'd likely have more trouble converting. Van's also the only person I wouldn't be able to push back on if he said no. While several of us are less-than-sporty, Van's a lot more hesitant about strenuous activity, and for good reason. He has both epilepsy and POTS, so his ability to partake in camp sports is significantly diminished. Most of the time, Van prefers to avoid the possibility of having an episode or flare-up altogether rather than starting something and having to stop in the middle of it. If I single him out and he says he doesn't think he'd be comfortable helping, the plan's dead in the water. If I ask Brain or Gator, they'll almost definitely check in with Van before confirming and everything'll come crashing down just as quickly.

I've been told that I shouldn't do this: spend so much time watching pop psychology videos and skimming actual psychology papers so that I can think through how best to shift conversations in my favour. Apparently, it can come off as creepy and manipulative. I've only ever been told that by the kind of neurotypicals who would likely also get frustrated if I *hadn't* done enough research to develop the limited understanding of emotional expressions and reactions that I currently possess though, so I try not to pay those complaints much mind. It's extremely easy to vilify someone for studying how to predict and manipulate social interactions when you were wired to do that instinctively.

Anyway, there's no clear way to break the stalemate. Even if there were, these are my friends, and I don't want any of them to have to feel responsible for this inevitably making our summer miserable. So, I throw the one person in the room that I'm not friends with under the bus instead.

"Faith also promises she'll do anything anyone asks her to all week as like, a thank you for helping. And an apology for being such a bitch literally every other summer."

Faith removes one of her palms from the ceiling to presumably whack me, but then she teeters and has to press it back up again before she can enact any actual violence.

"Like as a servant?" Van checks.

"Yes!" I snap. "Exactly! And she's super on board with that, right Faith?"

She takes a deep breath. I can physically see her nostrils flare. "Yes," she spits out. "Only for people who agree to help."

I grin. "So? Who's—"

I don't even have to finish the question. Every single hand is already in the air.

July 10

My dearest Alice,

Thru sircumstances completly beyond my control and that absolutly werent my falt Im helping FH w something right know.

Ud think thatd modivate her to b less annoying but nooooooooooooooooo thatd be 2 much 2 ask.

Talk at u soon (if 1 of us doesnt kill the other 1ˢᵗ),
Charlotte

Chapter 16

"This is useless."

Faith insisted that we should start running drills right away, but I made sure to veto that. No one likes her enough to put in any actual effort on her behalf yet, so we have to at least get through this one week of her pretending to be semi-decentish first. Faith doesn't seem to think that getting people to like her should matter. I don't think she'd be able to comprehend the concept of teamwork if it whacked her in the face. Repeatedly.

Luckily, I have a best friend who's spent months researching all the best ways to elevate camp-specific comradery. Morgan's tragically too busy with Leadership to help in person at our first official team meeting, but she still helped me go over her notes ahead of time.

I've planned this perfectly. I scheduled our first meeting for Friday so that everyone would have an adequate amount of time to prepare themselves. I managed to talk my cabinmates into giving up the entirety of their free activity block for the day, which was no small feat. I even ran things by Janine to ensure we'd have enough supplies and to confirm that the counsellors running the official Corrain activities on the recreation field would be fine with staying out of the way and supervising us from afar.

Faith's done nothing but mumble and complain, but I've mentally prepared myself for that too. I'm obviously going to have to carry the bulk of the workload here myself. I'm far from fine with that, but I've come to terms with it. It's a small price to pay for a clear conscience and a Faith-free summer next year.

All Faith was supposed to do was stay in her own fucking lane for a few hours. I should have known that that'd be too much to ask for.

I strain the muscles in my cheeks. "This," I correct, shaking out the shirt in my hands before laying it down on the grass amongst the others. I've corralled everyone into a circle to debrief before getting started. Faith couldn't even wait for me to get into the actual instructions before reverting back to insufferable. "Is scientifically proven to help bolster feelings of comradery, actually. Teams statistically tend to perform better whilst playing in matching uniforms, so making group tie-dye'll—"

"Like the matching shirts we all already wear every day?"

I frown. I hadn't considered that. I haven't done any reading on it yet, but surely something solid and thus more identical would work even better than the shirts that I'd been planning on having us make. I've been so busy trying to come up with ways to get a leg-up on our competition that I've completely missed the one we already have.

"Right," I try to regain my footing. "Okay, but have you considered that umm... tie-dye's umm..."

"Tie-dye fucks!" Gator whistles.

"Excellent point!" I snap my fingers at them, glancing around to make sure no counsellor's about to storm over to protest our use of curse words in an all-ages space. Sunny's current support worker either didn't hear them properly or has spent enough time around teenagers that it doesn't faze her. "Tie-dye *does* fuck. And is therefore an excellent form of team building. So we'll—"

"You know what else is an excellent form of team building?" Faith leans back against the grass. As she does, her hair almost sparkles in the sunlight. I file that observation away. I'll have to keep an eye out for it; It might be magic-related. "Actually practicing."

I blink. We've already talked this over privately. I have no idea why she's insisting on being difficult right now. I slip my tangle around my fingers and make myself smile. "Now, I fully recognize that some of us might not feel super comfortable with tie-dye," I continue with my script. "That's super fine. Because I've also brought this," I pull the container of assorted beads and string out of my bag. "Anyone who wants to make team bracelets can do that instead. I made sure to grab a bunch of different materials, so feel free to work with whatever you're most comfortable with."

Faith scoffs. "How are bracelets supposed to—"

"The exchange of gifts strengthens bonds in both directions," I raise my voice to cut her off before she can derail things even further. I will not allow her to continue to undermine me while I'm actively trying to save her ass. Maybe a century of obscurity isn't as serious as the not-king made it sound. Or maybe Faith's just incredibly dedicated to getting under my skin, no matter the cost. "Since our brains associate gift-giving with people we like, giving someone something or helping them with a task's more likely to trick us into assuming that we like that person. Gift receivers also tend to feel some level of indebted to the person who delivers the gift, obviously. Which makes homemade ones an excellent way to get people to agree to help you with something, since they demonstrate an extra level of effort. I'm assuming you'll be making six then, Faith?" I exhale slowly. Pop psychology is my domain. Not even Faith can set me off balance here. I slide the bins of beads and string towards her, then turn to address the rest of the group. "Anyway, if everyone wanted to choose a station, we can—"

I hear something crash behind me and spin around.

"What the fuck!" I drop to my knees to try and catch as many beads as I can before they disappear into the grass, but I'm too slow. Because Faith's somehow decided that the appropriate response to me trying to *help* her was dumping the supplies I've borrowed all over the field. Everyone else scrambles to help. Except Faith, obviously, because of course she doesn't.

And me, whose fingers have inexplicably decided to stop functioning.

"That— these aren't even ours!" I exclaim. "I'm supposed to return the leftovers! Why would—"

Faith shrugs. "Guess now we can team build over cleaning it all up."

"You're... ugg!" I give up on words and look over to Sunny's support worker for help. Said worker (one who looks less than half a decade older than us, which would normally be great but is presently a lot less than helpful) doesn't meet my eye which is fair because she's just supposed to be invisibly nearby until Sunny needs help with something or tries to elope, but still. I don't feel like being the adult here right now. Especially while knowing that the *actual* adult I got to trust me with this is probably going to be pissed when I inevitably have to tell her that not only did my cabin bonding idea fail miserably, but that I also lost over half the supplies she entrusted me with in the process. Janine had been so proud when I'd first floated my team-building ideas by her. She's going to be devastated.

I slip my tangle all the way off my wrist so that I can move it around my fingers more rapidly.

Van gets up. *Let's go*, he signs. *She cleans up. We're done.*

Finally, for half a moment, Faith looks down. It's an indicator of embarrassment or regret. I resist the urge to roll my eyes. Faith's gotten so used to getting away with being a dick 24/7 that she's clearly somehow genuinely forgotten that she wasn't supposed to be doing that right now.

I wait for her to apologize or defend herself, but maybe I just imagined that second of panic. Faith doesn't even start picking up the beads.

I take a deep breath. If Faith isn't going to fix this, then I'm the only one left to. Just a few more weeks of hell, then I get to shittalk her to my heart's content.

"No," I sigh. "No, we should... we promised we'd help, right? So... might as well. At least for today."

"Faith not doing everything we tell her to," Brain's iPad dictates.

This time, I'm certain I see Faith flinch. And with good reason. I hadn't known it when I'd made her do it, (though based on all the angry whisper-accusations she's hurled at me since,

Faith clearly doesn't believe that), but apparently getting any kind of faefolk to agree to a deal is instantly binding. If any of my cabinmates tell her to do something this week, she's physically incapable of not complying. If only I'd thought to add 'and stop being the worst' to our stipulations.

Faith glares at me. I pretend not to notice. She's made it incredibly clear that listening to *me* wasn't part of that deal, so I don't want to risk escalating things even further right now.

Eventually, Faith sighs and looks away. "Fine," she finally sits up properly. "Whatever. I'll help clean up."

Van shakes his head. *Apologize to L-O-T-S.*

Faith rolls her eyes. "I'm sorry I told you your stupid plan was a stupid plan. There." She looks back at Van. "Are we good, then? Because—"

"I'm not stupid," I interrupt.

Van starts signing something else, but I'm too preoccupied to process it.

"I'm not stupid," I repeat.

Faith has never shied away from insults, so I learned long ago to never put much stake in them. I just never used to know that she actually had to mean them.

"Whatever," Faith waves me off. "I apologized, okay? So everyone—"

My skin goes hot. My stomach rolls.

I am a smart person. I know this about myself. I've put so much time and energy into *ensuring* that I'm a smart person that I'm finally at a place where I'm comfortable acknowledging that I am, most of the time.

I'm also likely learning disabled. I know intelligence is not the end-all-be-all factor that determines a person's worth, but it's become an integral part of mine.

Faith and Van are arguing in rapid-fire ASL and I am processing absolutely none of it because no matter how much time I've poured into attempting to learn it and how many different methods and expensive programs I've tried, my brain can barely even grasp basic Signed English.

"I'm done," I realize. I'm not sure if I say it more to alert Faith, my friends, or myself. It comes out a bit too breathy to be a fully conscious proclamation. "With this. I think. The... I don't know why I agreed to help in the first place." My conscience is absolved too, at least. If the consequences of losing are really as serious as I'd initially assumed they were, surely Faith would've sucked it up for a couple of hours.

"What?" Faith stops signing. Because everyone knows that most of it's useless around me. "You can't—"

I turn away from her to start folding the shirts back up. I can feel my face going hot and don't want to give her the satisfaction of seeing that she's affected me.

This was a stupid idea. I don't know why I thought making t-shirts together would do anything to help anyone. You can't possibly erase years of animosity that quickly. "Clean up the fucking beads."

Sunny's support worker helps me fold the shirts while Sunny helps with bead collection. I move slowly to stall from being expected to join the rest of my cabinmates. I can see the continuation of Faith and Van's argument in my peripheral and I'm not in the mood to be confronted with all the things that I'm incapable of understanding right now.

"Lots." I'm dimly aware of Faith eventually saying from somewhere behind me. "Lots!"

I ignore her.

She sighs. "I'm probably going to touch your—"

"No." I move away before she can grab me.

"Fine, whatever," Faith shoves her fists into her pockets. "Just tell your friend that he needs to—"

"Why would I keep doing things for you?"

Faith stares at me. Her eyebrows move marginally closer together. "Okay," she says. "Fine. Fuck all of you then, I guess."

She watches me for another long beat, then she turns around, dramatically swishes her hair, and walks off.

Everyone is quiet. Everyone is watching me. I've forgotten how to be a person.

"Booooo!" Gator eventually declares, flopping back onto the grass.

"Boooooooooooooooo," Brain types. It makes her reader glitch and comes out as a series of 'oh's.

Van signs something. I miss it.

I must be wearing my ineptitude visibly because Gator translates, "he says we should still make the shirts. One for Morgan too so Faith feels all left out and upset once she realizes she's the only one without one."

I smile. I breathe. "Alright, then." I dump everything back out and get to work explaining the potential rubber band configurations that I spent last night looking up. As I do, my gaze drifts across the field. I frown. "Did no one... where'd she go?"

What? Van signs.

"Faith. She's not..." I scan the field again. "Did they just... let her walk off? On her own?"

There's a moment of confused silence, then Sunny's support worker steps aside to start frantically whispering into her walkie. I don't know how we managed to lose her. She was just right here.

Van signs something. It looks like *jump maybe* to me, so I assume I've mistranslated something because that makes absolutely no sense.

"What?"

"Kidding," Van vocalizes. "She wouldn't have actually done it. She probably just found a tree to sulk behind or something."

"Done what?"

Van frowns. "Jumped off the pier."

I rush to my feet. "Fuck."

He laughs. "Lots. She wouldn't have—"

"You said that?" I double-check. "You told her to go jump off the pier?"

He shrugs. "It felt like a much more creative way to tell her to fuck off."

"Fuck." I reach for my tangle again. "Fuck."

I accidentally got Faith to agree to an apparent binding oath of servitude a few days ago. She hadn't been trying to smooth things over with me before storming off, she'd been trying to get me to save her. "Fuck. Does— can Faith even swim?"

It feels like something that I should know. I never do much swimming since Morgan gets absence seizures and isn't allowed to swim without an aid, but after going to camp with Faith for so long, I surely would have noticed if she joined the others in the water at beach trips.

No one else volunteers any answers either. Which almost definitely means she can't.

"Fuck." I repeat.

I do not like Faith Harris. In fact, it wouldn't be much of a stretch to say that I despise her. But I am not about to let her turn me into a manslaughterer. "Okay," I shake out my wrists to try and gather my thoughts. It doesn't help. "Okay, I—"

I take off sprinting towards the lake. Voices call after me as I go. A whistle's blown somewhere, but I'm moving too quickly to wonder how Faith managed to slip away without causing anywhere near this level of commotion. I just run.

By the time the pier's in sight, Faith's already almost all the way down it. Her steps are awkward and jerky, as if not entirely of her own free will. Because, I realize in horror, they're not.

"Faith!" I call.

She doesn't turn. It's windier by the water and the air catches her hair and swirls it around her head. Only Faith Harris would manage to look so cinematic while doing something so incredibly stupid.

"Faith!" I'm not sure what my plan is. Wrestle her to the ground, preferably. It's not the first time that I've considered doing that, but contemplating attacking Faith to *help* her is a foreign sensation.

She takes another stilted step. I heard at least someone take off after me when I started running. I'll tackle her then hold her down until someone capable of taking back whatever Van said gets here. "Faith!"

I'm too slow. I'm only halfway down the pier when she takes one final step and plunges beneath the water's surface.

"Fuck!" I glance back to the other end of the pier then to the water then back again. There's no one in sight. "Okay," I whisper, shaking out my arms as I move further down the dock. "Okay. Alright. Fuck. I... fuck this."

I don't know what I'm supposed to do here. There's only one thing *to* do. I toss my jacket, knapsack, and lanyard aside, plug my nose, and race towards the water.

Chapter 17

I don't like the sensation of becoming wet.

Being submerged itself is relatively fine, but the moments that lead up to it are always unpleasant.

Even if you manage to land in the exact same spot every time you enter it, water never feels the same. It's constantly moving and tides are constantly meeting and changing and rearranging, so any one place is a mess of conflicting temperatures and densities and mineral compositions. Entering water means navigating all of that while simultaneously adjusting to all the ways that your limbs above and below its surface now feel misaligned. Coupled with the varying speeds at which your various body parts acclimate to all those changes.

I have never enjoyed the sensation of becoming wet, but that dislike is exacerbated even further when it also means dealing with a kicking, splashing, screaming changeling who seems completely ungrateful for all the sacrifices that you're making to try and save her life. This feeling of discomfort is further intensified when you're unceremoniously yanked from the water by a disappointed lifeguard and then made to sheepishly wait dripping and shivering on shore, wrapped in nothing but your thin, rapidly dampening jacket.

"This is your fault," Faith mutters the moment the lifeguard steps away to walkie someone else down to deal with us. Her teeth chatter as she wrings out her hair. She doesn't have a jacket, and I'm not about to offer to share mine.

I don't respond. I don't have the mental bandwidth to deal with her right now. I'm too busy trying to figure out how I'm supposed to explain this to a counsellor.

My brain has never understood how to best protect me. It often opts to block out anything it reads as an imminent threat, despite that refusal to act almost always leading to more problems down the line. My brain perceives a lot of things as imminent threats.

I'm fucked. I've spent years convincing the staff here that I'm trustworthy enough to be left relatively on my own, and then I went barrelling into a body of water fully clothed and unsupervised. I don't know what kind of freedoms they'll take away for something like this because I've never witnessed anyone else doing something so *stupid*. And I can't even explain why I did it without pissing off a bunch of magical creatures.

Janine's going to kill me. Or worse, send me home.

A counsellor I vaguely recognize arrives to collect us and I'm supposed to be explaining myself as well as I can to try and get ahead of things, but the disappointment on her face is so potent that my brain decides to shut itself off instead.

I am no stranger to getting in trouble. When you grow up with an invisible disability, it's pretty hard to avoid it. I'm in a constant state of letting down the adults around me so I should be good at dealing with it by now, but if anything, my experience has worn away any tolerance I might have once possessed for it. Being labeled as 'disruptive' or 'inattentive' or 'difficult' or even just as a problem in general is an inherent part of my existence. It just isn't supposed to happen at camp.

The counsellor talks, but I barely hear him. Faith responds, but by the time she does, I'm not hearing anything at all. And I *know* I'm supposed to be responding or listening or at least paying enough attention to gain some semblance of understanding of what's going on, but my brain refuses to reboot. Not being able to lie should make it more difficult for Faith to throw me entirely under the bus, but I already know that she's had plenty of experience figuring out the perfect way to twist things in her favour.

I'm not fully aware of anything at all until I'm suddenly back on Morgan's bunk. I wrap the towel that's inexplicably appeared around my shoulders tighter and blink back into the present just in time to watch Faith storm out of the washroom and dramatically shove her blow-dryer back into her trunk.

She takes one look at me and sighs. "I'm not wasting magic on healing shit you did to yourself."

I examine the undersides of my nails. They're covered in already-crusting blood. I pick at my skin when I'm anxious or bored. Or breathing. I run my fingers over my cheek to try and find whatever I've been picking at so I can get back to work.

Faith stomps back into the washroom and returns to shove a wad of damp tissues into my fist. She fishes my fidget lanyard out from the pile of my belongings that someone must have retrieved from the dock and throws it at me.

I slip it over my neck then wrap my fingers around my tangle instead. "Thanks."

"You're not supposed to thank the fae," she mumbles. "It implies you owe us something."

I frown. "Are you... threatening me?"

Slowly, her eyes slide up to meet mine. "Would that work?"

"I don't think so."

"No then, I guess." She moves her hair from one shoulder to the other. " 's not like I'm powerful enough to do much to follow through anyway. Clean yourself up. I need us to plan out a lie before Janine gets here."

I freeze. "Janine's coming?"

"Yes? Because you decided to jump into a body of water fully clothed? That kind of thing tends to draw attention."

"You jumped too," I remind her.

"Yeah, well, *I* would have been able to cover for myself. This one's on you."

Faith sits down. She drums her fingers along the edge of Morgan's bunk. I want to tell her not to touch it (Faith being remotely close to anything of Morgan's is something I'm deeply uncomfortable with), but I'm too tired to do much of anything right now.

"Give me your hand," Faith eventually says.

"What?"

"I can only stall her if we're making physical contact. I'm a changeling. Attention-based magic's kind of my whole thing."

I hold out my arm. Faith stares at it for a moment before limply wrapping her fingers around my wrist. Her nose crinkles slightly and her eyes unfocus as she presumably casts something.

"There," she breathes. "Unless she's like, unhealthily obsessed with you, she won't remember she's supposed to come check in until I let go. That gives us plenty of time to come up with an explanation that doesn't fuck me over."

"Right," I nod. I don't know what I was expecting. I *like* Janine. It's not like I would have wanted Faith to poof her off into some unreachable other dimension. Delaying the problem just definitely wasn't the kind of magical solution I'd been hoping for.

"This is fully on you, for the record," Faith continues. "If you'd just let me handle it myself, I could've erased myself from all nearby staff's attention, popped in, popped out, then—"

"You don't get to get mad at me for not magically knowing how your powers work when you refuse to fill me in on them!" It's shocking how quickly I've started seeing Faith's magic as more of an annoyance than a curiosity.

She cocks her head to the side. "Alright," she acknowledges. "Fair. Still not my fault either, though. And even though it's not, I'm still not gonna hold it against you or try to kill you or anything, so it's really only fair if—"

"You're seriously already trying to threaten me again?"

"No," Faith rolls her eyes. "I'm actually very overtly *not* doing that. Even if it would be a lot easier to. I need you functional enough to help me, though, so—"

"I'm obviously not helping you anymore!"

Faith frowns slightly. "Because I didn't want to make a bracelet?"

"Because you're a massive bitch!"

Her frown just deepens. "Yes. Which you were already well aware of. I don't see why you'd change your mind over—"

"You're ridiculous," I realize. Faith is not some redeemable victim. She is and always will be a self-centered monster, and if even *she* can't push aside her ego long enough to see this through, I don't see why I should. I get up to try to move away from her but her grip on my wrist tightens. "I don't know why I ever thought—"

"You're the one who just tried to *kill* me!" She follows me to my feet. "All things considered, I'd say I'm—"

"What?"

"So I'm not your favourite person. Whatever. I was never trying to be. But at least I—"

"Faith!" I stop her. "No one tried to kill you. Unless bracelets are some kind of weapon of mass faerie destruction, but even if they are, that's on you for not—"

"Stop playing dumb!"

"I've literally never once done that!"

Faith sighs. She pinches the bridge of her nose. "I can hear all the fucking podcasts and articles you've been listening to, you know. Which, for the record, are mostly bullshit. I mean sure, stabbing a changeling through the heart with an iron dagger might hurt them, but only because that'd also kill just about any other living thing too. I just didn't think I'd have to worry about it because I'd assumed you hadn't smuggled a dagger into camp with you and I'd thought you'd at least be competent enough to realize that the burning or drowning options are typically only suggested when babies are involved because anything stronger would just *not* let you throw them into an open flame then wait to get burnt up, but—"

"I'm not even the one who told you to jump in!" I remind her.

Faith crosses her free arm across her chest. "I'm just supposed to believe you followed to try and drag me down for

114

what then? Fun?"

"I'm... oh my god," I realize. "You're actually insane."

"Attempted murder can do that to someone. You—"

"I didn't know if you could swim, Faith," I say slowly. "I was trying to rescue you."

"Oh." Her eyes widen slightly. Then, they narrow. She's instantly back to normal. "Well, that was useless then. Counterproductive, actually."

"So I've heard."

"You could've just told the lifeguard too. 'S not my fault you didn't think it through enough to—"

"Stop doing that!" I cut her off. "I know. It's over, I fucked up, I'm obviously not going to try and help next time you're in trouble so... there. Congrats."

I feel her watching me. I don't meet her eye. "So you... don't think I'm about to try and take some kind of murderous revenge, then." Faith confirms.

I sigh, "Not until you started bringing it up, no."

Her mouth twitches. "You were freaking out, though. Still are. I can hear your heartbeat."

I roll my eyes. *Of course* she has to have creepy hyper-perceptive powers. "Not everything's about you. I'm worried about what Janine'll say."

Faith blinks. "Our counsellor."

"Yes."

"Who's like fifty-something."

"She's forty-nine."

Faith fixes her hair. "If I ask you to talk about your feelings, will you change your mind about—"

"Nope."

"Alright then." She tugs me towards her bunk and starts rifling through her chest. "Plan b, I guess."

"What are—holy shit!" I try to jump away, but Faith's fingers dig into my wrist. "Is that a knife?"

Faith relaxes her grip on what is indeed some kind of half-rusted ornate dagger. I keep my eyes locked on it. It's pointed towards the ground. For now. "Don't—"

"I'm weird for reading about magical weapons yet you've had one on you this whole time?"

"You're supposedly non-magical. Obviously I have—"

"Does Janine know?"

Faith rolls her eyes. "No, Lots, I haven't told Janine about the ancient weapon I sleep beside every night."

She raises the dagger again and takes a step towards me. I stumble back, but can't break free of her grasp.

Faith sighs. She releases my wrist. "Stop being so dramatic. It's not for you." She readjusts her grip so that the dagger lies flat against her palm and holds it out to me. "Here. Do it."

"I— excuse me?"

"We both know you did your research. Iron through the heart, right? So, take it."

"That's not..." I don't know how she's managed to hide a weapon in the cabin for this long, but I'm definitely not about to be the one caught with it. Maybe she's even planting it for when Janine gets here. "I'm not going to forget I hate you just because you've given me some—"

"I know." Even now—even while she's *waving a knife at me*—Faith still sounds bored. "Stab me, then."

"Sta— what the fuck!"

"I'm probably going to touch your hand."

"You are absolutely not!"

Faith sighs, extending her open palm further towards me instead. "Then grab it yourself and stab me."

"I'm—" I take the handle. Not because I'm planning on murdering anyone or anything. Letting the person raving about getting stabbed continue to wave around a weapon just feels inadvisable.

"Well?" Faith shakes the dagger. "Are you gonna do it, then? Surely even you're not stupid enough to not know where the heart is."

"I'm—stop insulting me while I'm holding a weapon!"

"Stop being such a coward, then!" Faith steps closer. "You might as well either help me or stab me right now, okay? It'd be practically the same thing either way."

"I'm not—"

"I'm not letting you feel guilt-free about giving me a fucking death sentence!" There are several strands of hair in Faith's face. It's an odd thing to focus on, but I've never seen her hair there before. Streams of spilled ink slicing her expression apart. "Either get over yourself and get back on board or man up and do it with your own two hands! Either—"

I try to step around her to put the dagger somewhere out of reach and she flinches, stumbling back. "Faith." I back away and slowly lower the dagger to my side. "I'm not... you don't actually want me to stab you, do you?" I realize.

"Of course I don't want you to fucking stab me!" Her words are loud and shrill. Her chest is heaving. "You were supposed to—" Her attention snaps to the door. "Fuck." She snaps her fingers and the dagger flies into her palm. She stares at me, eyes wide and frantic. "Don't mention it."

"Wh—"

The door to the cabin creaks open.

I freeze. However mad Janine might have been about the pier, getting caught with a weapon is infinitely worse. Slowly, Janine looks from me to Faith. She scans us each from head to toe and I'm holding my breath and biting my lip in anticipation of how she'll react, but then she just sighs and puts her hands on her hips.

"Alright," she says. "What's going on here?"

My eyes instantly dart to Faith's hand. I'm expecting the dagger to have disappeared into some kind of pocket dimension but it's still in her fist, as corporeal as ever. Faith catches me looking and subtly angles her arm away from me. "Lots?" Faith says slowly. Pointedly. "You want to tell her?"

"Nothing."

Janine frowns. "I was already filled in, Charlotte."

"Right." I remember the thing that I'm actually in trouble for and my entire body instantly goes hot. "Right. That..." I reach for my tangle. "I didn't mean to... you don't have to..." I find myself wishing Faith could lie just so I wouldn't have to be the one talking right now. Even if she'd use it to pin everything on me. "I um..." I squeeze my every facial muscle taunt, but I'm having trouble focusing on the present. Janine's mouth is straight and her eyes are flat and her tone is cold. I am an expert at identifying disappointment and presently, I'm crumbling beneath the unfamiliar weight of hers. "I don't know," I look down. I feel my eyes water and I hate it. It's just another thing I can't control as well as I should be able to. "I'm sorry I just... I don't know."

Janine sighs. "Faith? Or do we have to—"

"I jumped off the pier," she says.

Janine takes a deep breath. "I'm aware, yes. Do I get to know why?"

Faith turns to face me. I'm already falling apart under one person's gaze. I don't know how to cope with that doubling. "Lots?" Faith prompts.

There isn't a single thought in my brain.

Faith sighs. "It was like, a dare," she mumbles. "Felt like I had to do it."

Janine frowns, watching me. I'm normally the forthcoming one. "Wh—"

"Not from Lots," Faith regains her attention. "She's too annoyingly rule following for that. It's not... in hindsight, I don't even think the person who said it thought I'd take it as a dare so it's not like... I'm the only one who fucked up, I guess. No one else was being malicious."

Janine keeps watching me. I keep watching the floor. "Charlotte, were you also—"

"Lots realized I was taking it seriously and for some reason thought it would be helpful to jump in and physically try to drag me back to shore. Which, it wasn't, obviously, but... you know. Technically wasn't her fault. I guess."

Janine seems confused. I don't blame her. I am too. "Are you sure that's—"

"Why would I lie to protect someone I don't even like? It's also incredibly unprofessional to try and have this conversation in public, by the way," Faith adds. "Especially while one of your campers is clearly too freaked out to actually participate."

"Two people's hardly—"

"Two people count as public if they're not comfortable around each other. Lots hates me. You know that, yet you still thought this would somehow be productive. Is that what they taught you to do when they declared you an expert on autistic children? Publicly shame and interrogate—"

"Stop it!" I remember how to form a sentence.

Faith's lips twitch. "Of course that's what gets your attention. We done here?" she asks Janine. "Because—"

"Can I trust you to wait outside for a moment, Charlotte?" Janine interrupts.

"Yes." I eagerly take the chance to flee. "Of course."

I rush out the door then sit down directly beside it. I am not about to do anything else that'll make me look like a flight risk. I stuff my chewlery between my teeth and try to focus on getting control of my breathing. But the time Janine reappears across from me, I'm semi-put together again.

Janine sighs as she sits. "I take it team building didn't go well, then?"

"No," I admit.

She fishes through her fanny pack and holds out a lemon lollipop. I'm sixteen years old. Most sixteen-year-olds don't need pity candy when they're upset and right now I desperately want to be exactly like most sixteen-year-olds, but I'm the kind who'll gnaw my cheek past infection if my mouth isn't otherwise occupied. I flinch against the sound of the wrapper as I open it. Things always seem so much louder when I'm worked up. Janine leans forward slightly. "You're not in trouble, Charlotte."

"Okay." I nod.

"If I didn't handle that well and upset you—"

"You didn't," I make myself smile. "You're fine. Perfect, actually. Faith's just stupid. Or— I didn't mean that in like a mean way even though I guess there's no other way to... shoot. Sorry. Again."

Janine smiles slightly. "It's okay. You're allowed to be a teenager. Just preferably a safe one."

"Right," I nod. "Got it."

"I think it's really awesome that you've decided to put such a big effort into helping out your cabinmates. Just because this didn't work doesn't mean the next thing won't, alright? If you're looking for more leadership opportunities, I could talk to—"

"It's too late to switch into Leadership." I remind her.

"I'm sure if I talked to—"

"No," I interrupt then instantly regret it. I wind my tangle tighter. "I didn't mean... it wouldn't be fair. To everyone already in it. Morgan says they've been putting in a lot of work."

The truth is, I am incredibly aware that I'm the kind of camper who's *supposed* to be doing leadership. I'm fully verbal, fully mobile, and don't have any major autistic traits or comorbidities that would make assisting with programming too difficult for me. Most of the CITs we had growing up *had* my presentation of autism. Plenty of them had far more complex needs than I do.

I just don't want to do it.

Janine taps her pen against her wrist. She does that when she's thinking. "Unofficially, then. I've let Faith know I want her shadowing me this next week just to stay on the safe side and it seems like you two could use some space, but if you wanted to test the waters, Numaan should be running field games with the five through eights right now. I could walkie in and see if he wants some help?"

    I bite down too hard on the lollipop. It splinters in my mouth. "Sure. Sounds fun."

Chapter 18

The five- through eight-year-olds are sticky. I don't know *why* they're sticky (Janine's lollipops notwithstanding, Corrain is far from overflowing with sugar), but their little grabby hands manage to leave some kind of residue on everything they touch regardless. Which just makes the stickiness even more alarming.

By the time I've done an adequate enough job pretending to be helpful and get to return to the cabin, I'm exhausted, uncomfortable, and confused. Faith had the perfect opportunity to throw me under the bus, but instead, she twisted her words to my benefit. I know her too well to read that as any form of remorse or sudden humanity. And as I've been learning these last couple of weeks, an unpredictable Faith Harris is far from a good thing.

Luckily, Faith's jump off the pier made Janine worried about her being a potential flight risk, so at least for the time being, she's sleeping in the main building. When I finally get back to the cabin, her bunk's empty. I'm the last one to return so everyone else gets up to ask me about what the hell happened today, but I mumble some excuse about needing a shower and go straight to the bathroom. I stand under the water until my skin's red, raw, and sticky-handprint-free, tie my hair up since I'm way too tired to actually dry it, then force myself to go face the rest of the world.

"What—"

"Faith's staying in the main building tonight," I explain. I'm not ready to answer less predictable questions. "I think Janine's worried she might jump off another pier or something."

Gator raises their hand. I bite my lip and hope it keeps me from grimacing visibly. "Yeah, Gator?"

"Are you staying here?"

"Yeah." I grind my heel into the floor. "Yeah, Faith... made it clear that none of that was on me."

They raise their hand again. I take a deep breath.

"Yeah?"

"Doesn't sound like her."

"No, it..." I rub my palms against my leggings. "I think she's desperate?" I try to segue into the conversation I've been dreading all day. "And trying?" I lie. "In her own weird nonsensical way?" I sit down on Sunny's bunk since I suddenly feel unsteady and it's the closest. "Look, I think we might as well give it another shot. Her taking the blame's a good sign, right?" I'm not naïve enough to think that it is. I haven't changed my mind because Faith decided to correctly make it clear that something wasn't my fault, I'd made it up already when the thought of giving up led to her waving a knife in my face. She's either come completely undone, or this really is as serious as I initially thought and she's just going about it in the worst way possible. Proposed violence (even against oneself) typically doesn't inspire confidence or strengthen alliances. I'm going to have to make it extremely clear to her that several things are going to have to change if she wants another chance at making this work.

Gator looks at Brain. Brain looks at Gator.

My heart rate increases. "What?"

Gator keeps looking at Brain.

"What?"

I look to Morgan, but she either doesn't know what's going on or doesn't want to tell me either. She shakes her head slightly.

Slowly, Brain starts to type something. "Van says say no."

I frown. "Then we're just down one. And he might change his mind. That doesn't mean—"

Gator raises a hand.

"Yes?"

"He said he doesn't think any of us should. And he doesn't get why you'd want to."

I reach for my tangle. I consider possible solutions that don't have anything to do with faeries or magic or semi-eternal damnation. "We made a deal," I remember. "As long as we help, she swore she won't come back next summer. If we don't, she'll be back and probably even more annoying than usual."

People tend to lean forward when they agree with what you're saying. No one's doing that.

"We don't have to actually win," I realize. If we lose, it sounds like Faith won't have the option to come back at all. "Just convince her that we're actually trying. We just have to give up a couple of hours once or twice a week to make her think we're actually on board. And... and then we can throw it on purpose at the end. Just not super obviously of course, but then Faith's down five hundred dollars, we get to watch her lose at something she's really invested in, then she never comes back again. Ultimate revenge."

I know Gator's hand's going to go up before it does. "Gator?"

"How do you know she's being serious?"

I shrug. "I don't see why she wouldn't be. She's willing to lose five hundred over a bet with someone she could easily just ignore. She clearly takes stuff like that seriously. Probably on account of her being incredibly annoying."

I wait. There are no more questions. No one's looking directly at me either which tends not to be a good thing, but also isn't necessarily a negative indicator when dealing with a group of autistics. Ironically, other neurodivergent people are actually some of the hardest for me to psychoanalyze.

"Can we be in?" I check. "Please? I really, really need us to be in."

Gator licks their lips. "I can... probably get Van on board with that."

"Yes." I clap. "Excellent."

I have over a month to get these people serious about winning. For now, all I have to do is trick them into getting prepared.

Chapter 19

I've already crawled beneath my covers when Morgan gets back
from brushing her teeth and knocks against the underside of my
bunk to signal that I should come join her, but I eagerly climb
down our ladder regardless. Other people drain my energy,
especially when I'm already on edge. Morgan's one of the few
who gives me more of it.

She takes one look at me and scrunches her eyebrows
together. "Your hair's going to dry weird."

"I have weird part-curly part-straight white person hair. It
always dries weird."

She clicks her tongue and crawls down to the edge of her
bed to go through my trunk. I wait for her to find my comb and
return to fix me. She leans against her backboard then tugs me
closer and starts working away at a knot. It's best for people with
my curl pattern to comb their hair right away while it's still damp
to keep from damaging it. Sometimes I think ending up with both
ADHD *and* curly hair was the universe personally trying to spite
me.

"Big day," Morgan says. I can't quite tell if it's a question
or not. Morgan's vocal pitch never shifts as obviously as allistic
people's do with those.

I also can't tell if it's angry. I'm the one who's spent years
insisting than I'm nowhere near ready for Leadership and yet I
went and spent most of my day essentially CITing. If anything the
experience confirmed that I'm not ready for it, but Morgan
doesn't know that part yet. I wince. "Janine asked me too," I try to
explain. "It was mostly last minute. I think she secretly just wanted
an excuse to have someone supervising me."

"Janine asked you to jump off the pier?"

Today feels like it's been going on forever. I'd forgotten
all about that part. "No, that..." I sigh. "Is also not happening
again."

Morgan finishes my hair then turns me to face her. I do not do well with external physical guidance, much to the dismay of my childhood therapists. It's always felt less demanding, somehow, coming from someone my age. Morgan's not only allowed to move my body for me because she used to not be able to give me directions as readily as other people could. That might have been part of it at some point, but it was definitely never the biggest reason. She just always seems to know exactly where I'm meant to be before even I do.

"Are you okay?" She whispers.

"Of course. Are you?"

"This summer you've seemed..." she taps her fingers together. "Different."

"You've barely seen me this summer, Morgan."

Her face changes.

"That wasn't angry," I panic. "Or whatever else you're worried that was. It... I'm fine," I lie. "Seriously. I just meant that if I do seem different, it might just be your brain compensating for not seeing me as much as usual."

She frowns. "You jumped off the pier."

"One time temporary loss of judgement." I wave her off. "I'm fine."

"I could still drop out of Leadership. If—"

"No. Don't."

Her eyes flit around my face. Morgan typically spends as little time on faces as possible. She's looking for something.

"I actually did leadery stuff on my own today," I make myself smile. "Helped out with the five to eights."

"Did you like it?"

"Sure. So you just... keep doing your thing and maybe I'll see if I could do that a few more times this summer then we'll be extra ready to do it together for real, okay?"

She keeps watching me.

"Morgan," I lean forward to kiss her forehead. "I'm good, okay? Everything's fine."

"Okay." Her chest shakes as she exhales. "Good. Great. If you liked working with the five to eights and wanted to try and switch into Leadership—"

"Already tried," I stop her. It feels less like lying if I don't let her get too far. "It wouldn't be fair to the others. Next year, okay? You were right. We probably should have always planned on doing it earlier."

Morgan beams, throwing her arms around my neck. "Love you," she whispers against me.

"Love you too."

That's true. It's always been one of the truest things about myself, so I know without a shadow of a doubt that I mean it. But something about saying it directly after lying to her face makes me feel awful. Morgan and I are honest with each other about all big things as a rule. Neither one of us is good at determining when someone's lying to us, so we've promised not to do it around each other. Despite that, I'm convinced she'll somehow hear the betrayal in my voice.

She doesn't. She lets go of me, whispers a quick, "good night", and lets me escape back up to my bunk. I stare at the ceiling until I somehow manage to fall asleep, something like nausea beginning to stir in my stomach.

Chapter 20

I awake to the cabin on fire.

By the time I do, things must have progressed so far that there's nothing left to burn.

I squint my eyes against an all-encompassing brightness, but even when I close them entirely, the light penetrates my eyelids and makes my head hurt. I risk opening them a sliver again and try to seek out any form of escape route, but there's nothing left. Just light and flame and fire and nothing beyond it.

I blindly throw off whatever remains of my blankets and try to scream, but the flames must have already begun to eat me alive. Maybe that's why I can't feel the heat. My pain receptors have all been burned through. My lips are fused together.

When you have an attention-based disorder and a penchant for panic, you learn to prepare yourself for fires. They're always only one forgotten hair straightener or abandoned stove away, after all. But now, my limbs are too useless to move and my lips are too stuck to shout so all that preparation's left me with is the inexplicable certainty that my friends are burning alive and it somehow must be all my fault.

Then, all at once, the light fades away. The cabin is still and silent. A long, glossy-nailed hand hovers above my face and waves slowly, one finger at a time.

I try to scream again to alert the rest of the cabin to the fact that Faith's somehow broken in to kill us all, but my mouth still refuses to move. She's undoubtedly the cause of that, but she raises a finger to her lips anyway, jerks her head towards the door, and holds out her hand.

There are many different regional fighting styles that all claim to be the best and I've done extensive research into exactly none of them, but I at least know this: having the element of surprise on your side is almost always considered an asset when challenging an adversary. If I want to stand any kind of chance against Faith before she decides to permanently turn my skin to barbeque, I need her to think my guard's down.

Even if that means accepting her hand and letting her lead me all the way past the camp property line where no one'll ever find my body.

"Okay." Faith finally breaks her eerie silence to turn to face me once we're so far away that I'm not sure how I'll ever find my way back. " 's probably best to keep holding on. Doubt anyone'll— what the fuck!"

I've attempted to valiantly charge her. In my mind, I headbutt her in the stomach and send us both toppling to the earth for a dramatic fistfight that only one of us'll end up walking away from. In reality, I slam into her, she takes a grand total of three steps back, then easily steadies herself.

"What the hell was—"

It's too late to backtrack now. I no longer have the element of surprise on my side. I take five steps back to give myself leverage, emit a sound that's half grunt, half battle cry, and charge at her again. I've almost made contact and then, all at once, Faith pops out of existence and there's nothing I can do to stop myself from hurtling face-first towards the earth.

Chapter 21

Hearing someone who doesn't even like you start swearing aggressively after you've fallen is never a good sign.

"Fuck," Faith's saying. "Fuck, fuck, fuck, fuck—"

I tune her out and force my body to roll over. It hurts, (falling over always hurts, especially when you thought you were going to have an entire person there to break your fall and end up with no time to brace yourself once they poof into a cloud of nothingness), but I can't feel anything that would warrant that amount of cursing.

"Fuck," Faith's still saying. She's leaning over me, so close to my face that her hair tickles my arms every time the wind catches it. Her eyes are far too large for comfort. I quickly look away.

"Charlotte," she says. "Lots. Fuck, sorry. Don't... just don't look at it, okay?"

Like most kids with ADHD, I was given the less than helpful 'why don't you try out meditation?' advice pretty consistently throughout my upbringing. None of the podcasts I was suggested ever actually helped me relax, but they did leave me with an excellent technique for checking to make sure my body's still in order when my brain wanders a little too far. I start in my leftmost toe and test out each and every joint, working through my body limb by limb.

My right arm aches. My entire body aches (I did just fall directly onto my face, after all), but my right arm is especially sore. And based on the way Faith's freaking out right now, it's definitely more than bruised.

I groan. "Is it broken?"

I risk looking at Faith again and she hesitates before nodding, hair already trapped between her teeth. "Only a bit of it's actually in your skin," she says. "Just... I can't fix it. I can't—"

I instantly push myself up with my good arm. "Only a bit
of it's—"

"I said not to look!" Faith exclaims.

Once I do, though, I finally calm down. The tip of a
branch has embedded itself in my arm, just above my elbow. I
must've landed right on top of it when I fell. I'd much rather have
nothing lodged in my arm, but as far as injuries go, a tiny little
stick thinner than my pinky that looks like it can't possibly have
actually gone that deep is the least of my concerns. Sure enough,
as I rotate my wrist to try and test out my mobility, the piece of
branch falls out and disappears into the grass. I throw a hand over
the cut to try and keep my blood on the preferable side of my
flesh.

"You're actually the worst!" I exclaim, turning to find
Faith. "You seriously made me think—" I freeze. I'd expected her
to still be sitting down somewhere in my general vicinity, but she's
moved a few feet away to pace the forest floor, running her hands
through her hair so rapidly that I can't believe she's not hurting
her scalp.

Of course Faith would be tangle-free even mid-midnight
freakout.

She senses my attention (likely in more ways than one)
and looks up at me for half a second before continuing her
pacing. "I can't fix it right now."

"Okay." I nod. "Fine, whatever. We'll go back and—"

"I don't let myself hurt people!" she ignores me. "I wasn't
trying to hurt you, I don't—"

"Okay," I repeat. "That's fine, it—"

"I don't let myself hurt people!" she screams.

I truly don't understand why she's more freaked out than
I am about me getting a minor injury that'll probably heal itself
entirely by the end of the week, but she clearly is. She paces and
mutters to herself and every few seconds she gives up on the
muttering entirely and shouts something at the sky. Or at me. I'm
not sure which.

"Faith," I try to take a step towards her. She doesn't seem to notice. "I'm not mad. I'm not going to—"

"This isn't about you!" she screams.

I blink. "Okay, wow. Rude. Of course even me getting stabbed has to be all about—"

"I'm not supposed to hurt people!"

I feel for my tangle, but I didn't have the chance to slip it on before getting dragged out of the cabin. I play with my pajama top instead, trying to decide what I'm supposed to do next. A few minutes ago, I was sure Faith was about to kill me and then magically pin my corpse to the bottom of the lake or something just to make sure my family never gets any form of closure. Faith Harris is evil and terrifying and almost gave me a heart attack just for the fun of it less than half an hour ago.

But now, she just seems scared.

I am no stranger to thought spirals, but that doesn't mean that I have any idea how to stop them for someone else. Still, Faith's seems to have manifested as a physical spiralling motion, so I decide that breaking her path will be the best way to snap her out of it. Probably. Hopefully.

"Faith." She doesn't so much as flinch as I move to plant myself in her way. She stops a hair away from running me over, staring at the earth. Her muttering stops, but her lips still move around words I can no longer hear. "Faith," I try again, bending my knees slightly to try and meet her eye. "You're okay, alright? You didn't... if there's some kind of anti-violence changeling rule or something, you didn't even break it. I fully launched myself at the ground, you just... something'd yourself out of the way. You didn't even touch me."

"I don't let myself hurt people," she whispers, which makes absolutely no sense because Faith absolutely lives to torture others, but I nod anyway.

"Okay," I agree. "Of course you don't. I believe you."

Finally she looks up. "Liar."

I shake my head. "Not if you're this worried about it. People who hurt people on purpose don't tend to freak out immediately afterward. I actually *was* trying to hurt you a few minutes ago. If that helps."

She snorts. "It does, actually," Faith mumbles. She takes a deep, rattling breath then steps away from me. I'm worried she's just going to alter her route slightly and start the pacing back up again, but she sits down against a tree and folds her knees into her chest.

"I scared you," she says after a long silence. "Earlier. In the cabin."

"Oh, when you blinded and restrained me? Yeah. That was less than comfortable."

"I was just trying to wake you."

"BS. You could've like, lightly shaken my shoulders. But instead you—"

"I'm not supposed to touch you," Faith shrugs. "Without announcing it first. Didn't know how to do that while you were unconscious."

"That's..." I gape, momentarily releasing my wounded arm to lower myself to the ground. "You get that that's ridiculous, right? I'm pretty sure anyone on the planet would've preferred a few seconds of questionably consensual shoulder shaking to waking up in the middle of an actual nightmare come to life."

"Well I know that *now*," Faith grumbles, breaking off a twig to dig at the earth. "I'm sorry I scared you," she says. "And inadvertently got your arm semi-impaled."

"Scratched," I correct. Then, something occurs to me. "Does that 'no thanking the fae or you'll owe them' thing also apply to apologies to, because—"

Her eyes cut to mine. "You're figuratively holding my entire future in the palm of your hand, Lots. I don't really have space to give a shit about calling in a favour over a half-assed apology."

I swallow. I'm supposed to pretend that there's no way I'll continue helping her until she agrees to my updated terms, but Faith just seems so scared. And regretful, maybe. About accidentally hurting me.

"I made you your stupid bracelet," Faith digs through her pocket and tosses it at me.

I pluck it up from the dirt and turn it over under the moonlight. It's a terrible bracelet. The beads are all different sizes and textures, and though it's entirely pink, there's no rhyme or reason to how she placed the beads. It's quite possibly the most obviously low-effort bracelet I've ever seen. I spent a good portion of my day hanging out with five-year-olds with coordination issues.

"Kind of anti-climactic after the whole, force you from your bed, got you injured thing, but you know. Thought that counts and all."

"It really doesn't look like you put any thought into this at all, actually," I accidentally say out loud.

Faith doesn't seem offended by that though, because I'm clearly right. "Doing it that counts, then."

I don't know how to respond. "It's pink," I decide. That, at least, seems intentional enough to pretend to appreciate. "That's my favourite colour."

Faith instantly ruins any goodwill I was trying to establish by rolling her eyes. "Yeah, no shit. You practically never shut up about it. I would've had to put actual effort into not knowing that."

I frown, flipping it over to read the white letter beads on its back. *sOrY.*

"You didn't even bother finding an actual o," I observe. "Or a second r."

"You're shit at spelling. Maybe I thought you wouldn't notice."

My skin goes hot. I *am* shit at spelling. That's an objectively true fact. I'm normally a very big fan of objectively true facts. It's even one that I'm usually the first to point out.

But Faith thinks I'm stupid. Faith can't lie and she knows that I know that and she doesn't even hesitate a second before making sure I know that she *knows* I'm stupid.

Faith's head snaps up from the dirt she'd been poking at. "What was that?"

"What?" I squeeze my sleeve between my fingers. "Nothing. What?"

"Your attention just—"

"Can you read my mind?" I realize. I'm already halfway to my feet. If Faith can read minds, I need to be as far from her as possible.

But she just rolls her eyes. "Obviously not. I can feel your attention, though. It just like... spiked."

I sit back down. "I don't know," I lie, scratching at my arm. "Maybe I was just thinking about how unbelievably ugly the bracelet is."

Faith squints at me for a moment before shrugging. "Okay, whatever." She holds out her hands. "Arm, please."

I frown. "You said you couldn't fix it."

"I couldn't," she agrees. "Only attention magic's actually mine. The rest I have to trade excess energy to Faerie for. I'd used all mine up already. Luckily for you, you're ridiculously obsessed with me."

"That's not— I wasn't—"

The corners of her lips curve. She arches an eyebrow. "Do you want to keep bleeding out?"

"Well like, not particularly."

Faith starts to reach for my arm then hesitates. "I'm probably... I think I have enough energy left," she admits. "I'll probably be too tired to do anything for like... a while. Afterward."

I start to move my arm away. "You don't have to—"

She shakes her head. "I do. It'd be suspicious. Just... if I pass out and you abandon me alone this far away from camp, I'll make sure you—"

I roll my eyes. "I literally just stopped watching you freak out about hurting me, Faith. Stop trying to threaten me to avoid asking for help. It wouldn't have worked anyway."

Faith squeezes her eyes shut. She takes a long, measured breath. "Just... don't leave me alone here," she whispers.

"Okay." I nod. "Sounds easy. Fix me, please."

I remove my hand from the wound again and watch her grimace as she moves hers to take its place. Then, Faith closes her eyes, grabs her necklace, whispers impossibly quietly once again, and swoons backward.

Luckily for her, my arm patches itself up quickly enough that I'm able to catch her before her head crashes into the tree.

Being gentle around Faith is something I would have considered impossible a few hours ago, but she's surprisingly less terrible unconscious. Just flesh and bones and slow, steady breath and dark, inky hair spilling over my skin. Once I lower her to the ground, I double check my arms, half convinced that they'll be stained. Faith feels like the kind of thing that should leave some kind of mark.

But she doesn't. Because right now she's just flesh and bones against the forest floor and I'm left with nothing to do but watch, wait, and try to cope with how incredibly, vulnerably human she looks beneath the moonlight.

Chapter 22

"God, you're so creepy sometimes," Faith manages to insult me the moment she starts to regain consciousness a few minutes later. Quite literally the moment it happens, too. She hasn't even opened her eyes yet, sensing my presence before even witnessing it.

I quickly look away. "Thank you, Lots, for remembering I live off attention and diligently staring at me until I got enough of it to stop being unconscious."

"I didn't ask you to stare at me," Faith mutters, easing herself up and dragging her body closer to the tree so that she can keep leaning against it. She's clearly still drained, but if she's going to act like me trying to fix that is inconvenient, then I'm not going to keep helping. I have a lot of practice looking literally anywhere but her.

Faith sighs. "What'd you do with the bracelet?"

"Threw it somewhere, probably?" I can hardly remember. It was so obviously a non-gift that I probably accidentally dropped it at some point and didn't think anything of it. "It was really ugly."

"You still took it, though."

I frown. Some sources caution against accepting any kind of gift from the fae, but I'd interpreted that as more of a politeness thing than anything. If Faith can't convert me thanking her into some form of eternal servitude, then I don't see why any other niceties would be dangerous either. "I'm not a faery, Faith. I don't—"

"You're the one who said giving people things makes them help you with stuff. By your own logic, you have to—"

"I'm not a faery!" I repeat. "That's not how people work!"

"Whatever, then." She scoffs. "Just... go back. Whatever. I'll head back later."

I turn my attention back to her. Luckily this time, she's the one avoiding my eyes. "Is that... was that why you woke me up? To give me a shitty bracelet, insult me, then somehow use all that to make me want to keep helping you?"

She doesn't respond.

"You're ridiculously bad at apologies, you know," I inform her. "Like, unbelievably terrible."

"Shut up," she mutters.

I sigh. "Everyone's already back in," I admit.

Despite her sagging shoulders and obvious exhaustion, Faith momentarily straightens. "What?"

"Or I mean... not Van yet," I add. "But Gator thinks they can handle that. And I guess I didn't technically ask Sunny, but she loves camp games—especially if they involve chasing people— so I'm sure she'll—"

"What?" Faith repeats. "When did you..."

"I talked to them earlier." I feel myself blush and am momentarily grateful that the darkness is likely hiding it before remembering that Faith apparently has incredibly heightened senses.

If she's noticed anything though, she's too confused to comment on it. "You were pissed last time I saw you," Faith says. "Why would you..." She trails off, leaving a silence for me to fill.

Normally, I'm quite good at filling silences. I have thoughts on all the things all the time. The difficulty comes in deciding which of those things the other person would consider an appropriate silence filler.

People ask you to lie to them constantly, even if they don't fully realize that that's what they're doing. I've learned this over the years through the vitriol I've received after answering people's "why"s with the truth. Faith Harris does not want to hear that I decided I'd have to keep helping her while she was small and scared and shaking and pretending to be strong. Faith Harris definitely does not want to know that she is the kind of person capable of evoking pity.

So, I shrug and search for another answer instead.

"I'm autistic," I say.

Faith rolls her eyes. "Yes, Lots. Believe it or not, you've made that extremely—"

"That means I don't do well with change," I stop her before she can say something else that'll make it difficult to keep helping her. "Or, for me at least, it means I don't do well with change. I think... complaining about you's a pretty big part of my daily routine, actually. One of the few consistent parts of it, in fact. That'd probably be a lot harder to do if I knew you were off... somewhere. That you're clearly terrified of. For the rest of my life."

"But you didn't—"

I scoot closer to catch her shoulder when she starts to swoon again. "I'm all in, okay?" I keep my hand on her arm, just for a moment. Faith is not the kind of person who'd ever let anyone comfort her, but I feel like I'm supposed to at least be doing something. "Obviously."

Faith just blinks. "You're... going to battle a bunch of faeries for someone you can't stand just because you have a change aversion?"

"It's a pretty big change aversion," I shrug. "But," I remember. "If this is going to work, I'm gonna need some stuff from you too."

Faith scoffs. If she had enough energy to, I'm almost certain she'd stomp off, hair swooshing all the while. "I knew it," she says. "This was useless. I have next to no magical abilities, Lots. I already warned you I wasn't going to—"

"Faith." I stop her. "Not a trade, just... information."

She groans. "Somehow that sounds almost worse."

I ignore her and push through. "I need to know what happens if you lose."

"You already heard. A thousand years of—"

"I need to know what that means."

She looks away, playing with her hair.

"I'm not... I need to know how serious this is, Faith. Half the time you act like it'd be the end of the world, but then you go and throw a temper tantrum over—"

"It's serious." She stops me.

"Okay," I force my tone to do what I hope comes off as softening. "Okay, I know. I believe that. But you refuse to tell me stuff until it's too late for it to be helpful and I need to know more right now."

Faith sighs. She crosses then uncrosses her legs. Then, she straightens them entirely and leans back to stare at the sky. "Earthside faefolk are sustained by individual human attention," she relents. "Which.... see, I do tell you things. You knew that." Only Faith would be so dedicated to reminding me that I'm wrong. "It's different, though," she continues, "for the ones faeside. They live off more generalized faerie notoriety. Which is why revealing your identity to a human's considered theft since once you do—if the humans as a whole ever figure out the fae are real—Faerie itself inevitably crumbles. Might cause a surge in attention for a while, but it'll eventually wane and then once the fae are known enough to become mundane, the majority of humans would probably only focus on the ones they've personally met." She swallows. Fixes her already perfect hair. "Obscurity's... in between. Like a personal little pocket dimension. You get locked away with just enough attention allocated there to keep it from outright killing you since the fae are squeamish about murder, but unless you've somehow made enough of an impact that humans are also going to be sending energy your way for an entire century, you spend all of it too drained to even pull together a thought. Then you finish your sentence and they release you and you're inevitably so weak that you almost definitely die instantaneously and they get to act like that was somehow your fault since you technically had a chance to save yourself, so... yeah. Not exactly looking forward to an entire fucking century of..." Her breath catches. She pushes herself to her feet and instantly starts to wobble. I have to jump up to stabilize her. "This is stupid," she mutters, doing such a poor job at pulling away from me that I can't tell if she's just too weak to put any real amount of effort into it or if she knows she won't be able to support herself if she does. "I don't know why I even—"

"You're going to be okay."

She turns her neck to glare at me. "It's a lot harder to find lies comforting when you can't tell them yourself."

"Well." I nod, gently pulling her back to the ground. "Then we'll just have to make sure it isn't one. Easy. We literally don't have to follow the rules, Faith. If we wanted to, we could just fully not even hide a flag. Or... would that piss them off? I don't want to like, accidentally get a massive curse place upon the entire camp. No offense."

"I agreed to hide one," she mutters. "We have to."

"Oh." I frown. I try to remember the conversation more clearly. "I said the in bounds part, right? Would they like, wage even more war if we hid ours on the other side of camp?"

"The fae love liars," Faith admits. "They'd probably find that delightful."

"Excellent!" I clap my hands. "Easy."

"You're underestimating how much they also love winning. Not hiding a flag in bounds just means they won't win. Or— we forgot to ban outside help, actually, so if they find out we're cheating they might call more faefolk in to help find it. It doesn't mean we won't lose."

"Well then, we'll just have to get really good at running and seeking." I hesitate. "That's where my one absolutely non-negotiable rule comes in. There's what? Seven weeks until the end of the summer? You have to play nice for all seven of them. I'm fine with slightly deceiving my friends into helping you if there's like, an actual life on the line, but I'm not letting you make their summer miserable."

I watch her tongue trace a complete circle along the inside of her lips. Then I realize that I'm alone with Faith Harris in a forest, watching her tongue, and quickly look away again. Other people have a penchant for reading far too much into me paying attention to their non-verbal cues.

"I can't," Faith eventually says.

"Umm, you very much can, actually. And you will. It's just a couple of weeks. You basically won't even have to do anything. Honestly, if you did too much it'd probably look even more suspicious. Just act apologetic for a bit, then—"

"I *can't*," she repeats.

"What?" I frown. "Isn't making people like you supposed to be like, your main thing? Why would—oh." I finally realize. It feels ridiculous that it took me this long to. "Oh my god. You're *literally* acting out for attention, aren't you?"

Faith doesn't laugh. Or even smile. She also doesn't contradict me, though, so I know I'm right.

"Oh my god! Is that why there are so many stories about the fae bothering people? Is it like—"

"I'm not evil!" Faith blurts.

Blurting is so completely contradictory to my mental image of Faith that it makes me freeze.

"I'm not evil," she repeats, much closer to her normal volume but still far too full of strain and emotion to match her typical tone. "I'm not... I don't let myself hurt people. I don't... I'm so careful. I'm not... I'm annoying, not harmful. I pay so much attention to everything all the time to make sure... I'm not evil!"

"Yeah." I nod slowly. "Yeah, of course. I know that. I believe you. I never thought— okay well I've like, jokingly called you evil like, a ton, but that wasn't... you're just a shitty teenager, Faith. I know that."

She takes a rattling breath. "I don't deserve to suffer."

"Okay." I put my hand on her knee to try and calm her down but then she doesn't shove it off and it'd feel too awkward to remove it, so it's just stuck there. "I know that too. Of course." I swallow. My throat's abruptly gone very, very dry. I must not have drunk enough water today. "Is that... that's how it works, then?

Negative attention or annoyance or..."

"Positive attention tends to be more sustainable," Faith admits. "Obviously. It's also more fragile. Most fae advocate for diversifying for safety reasons."

"And you decided the best people to intentionally be an asshole to were a bunch of disabled kids?" I ask. "No offense," I quickly add, worried she'll get all sad and emotional and worthy of empathy again. "Or I mean, full offense. Fuck you," I throw in on impulse. "Or... I don't know. Fully neutral question, I guess."

"I was eight," Faith shrugs, fixing her hair. "It's not like I'd even fully realized..." she sighs. "Whatever. Point is I decided to siphon negative energy here, I've put years of work into it, and if I lose, it's not like I'll get the chance to go feed off of a new group of people instead. When I lose, I'm gonna need every bit of magic I can get. I'm not playing nice just to fuck myself over even more in the end."

I don't know the most morally correct way to respond to that. I'm not about to subject my friends to over a month of someone intentionally doing their best to upset them, but I also know I can't ask Faith to sacrifice that much potential attention now when she'll apparently need a lot of it really soon.

Faith watches me search for solutions and misreads it as reconsideration.

"Lots," she whispers, voice smaller and shakier than I've ever heard it. "Just... please, okay? Please."

I lick my lips. "I'm helping," I confirm. "It doesn't matter that you're not a particularly good one, you're still a person, so obviously... I can't ask them to, though. What if... I could just promise to hate you like, especially hard. Then you could—"

"I doubt it'd be physically possible for you to spend much more time obsessing over me than you already do. You're my biggest energy source here. Especially whenever I'm not actively talking to you. It's kind of pathetic, actually."

"Okay, so, rude," I say now that she's clearly feeling more like herself. "Again. That's exactly what..." It finally hits me. "You should pretend to be nice."

Faith rolls her eyes. "I already—"

"No. Just for the summer, though."

"I might not *have* any more than this summer. Geez, Lots. Have you even—"

"Stop interrupting," I interrupt. "I think... I don't think any of us actually hate you," I realize. "We might think we do—or, me, mostly. I think that's mostly me, actually—but I think that's more just being worse at identifying in-between emotions? Unless someone's like, ridiculously, obviously evil you have to like someone before you hate them, right? At least a little. I don't think any of us have ever liked you." I pause, waiting for her to catch on. She doesn't.

"So?"

"*So* you get everyone to. For one summer. Then, at the end of it, if you win you can just like, say something super rude, reveal you were using everyone the whole time, then disappear forever and leave everyone extra angry that they not only had to spend years sharing a cabin with you, but that you also managed to trick them into liking you for a bit at the end there. Or worst-case scenario you disappear into obscurity, and I tell everyone we had some kind of confrontation privately where you told me you were so tired of having to pretend to tolerate everyone that you're just taking the win and leaving for good. That way you still get more people thinking about you than you probably would've if you'd kept doing things your way. *And* everyone else gets to have a semi-decent summer. Minus one last minute betrayal, obviously, but at least the whole thing won't be ruined that way. Win-win."

Faith frowns. "And you'd be... fine? With me intentionally pretending to be nice just so I could hurt people more when I go?"

I shrug. "Not like it'd make much of a difference in the grand scheme of things. You'll be annoying either way, right? At least now it'll be with a purpose."

She considers. "I'm not agreeing to be nice to you. In private. 'S not like pretending'd work on you anyway."

"Okay, fine. Whatever." I push myself up and dust off my pajama pants. I'm already going to have to come up with some way to conceal the blood stain on my top, I don't need to worry about looking even more disheveled.

"Lots." Faith reaches for me but remembers to stop herself before making contact. "Promise me you're never going to like me, okay?"

I roll my eyes. "Trust me. You definitely won't have to worry about that. Are you okay enough to hobble all the way back to the cabin?"

Faith groans. "We're so far."

"We are," I agree, grabbing her hand and pulling her up. "Which means you're going to need to ask for my help and I absolutely get to be ridiculously annoying about it now that I know we're bothering each other on purpose. There's absolutely nothing wrong with being a little amoral to someone who's literally asked you to be."

"I'm probably going to touch your shoulder," Faith mumbled quickly, which is definitely an under exaggeration considering she proceeds to throw practically all of her body weight onto it. Then, at her normal volume, she adds. "You're telling me you can get even more annoying than you already are?"

I beam. "Just you wait."

Chapter 23

Janine's apparently decided to keep Faith under supervision for an entire week which Faith seems incredibly irritated by, but in a way, it's exactly what we needed. It's hard to start off with a clean slate when the person you're actively trying to get people to forgive was antagonizing them just a day ago.

Faith spends her days with Janine and her nights in the main building, so beyond the occasional intense staring during breakfast or moments where Janine needs my help with something and we overlap (I'm pretty sure Janine's been trying to find excuses to ask me to help her ever since we talked about Leadership which *would* be an incredible honour if I wasn't already busy trying to covertly save a changeling's life), I get a much needed break from her too.

I'd been concerned that Faith spending her nights in the main building could undo some of the "she's actually not as terrible of a person as we thought she was guys, I swear" work I've been trying to subtly implement all week since it puts her alone with Sunny and Van away from my supervision, but surprisingly, (despite being the Caribou I thought I'd have the most trouble converting) Van hasn't had any complaints so far. He hasn't said anything positive about Faith either, but a lack of vitriol anywhere he and Faith are concerned is always a good sign. I told Faith it'd probably be a good idea to try and get people to warm up to her, but I'm far more comfortable with her just keeping her distance if that's what she's decided to do. There's a lot less room for disaster that way.

Even without Faith's constant presence, my week has been less than relaxing. It turns out, there's no rule book on how to train a group of people for competitive capture the flag. (On account of competitive capture the flag not being an actual regulated sport). We could just get right into running actual games like Faith clearly wants us to, but I don't think that'd be a good idea either. There are only so many times you can get a group of people to play the exact same thing over and over again before they get bored and lose interest. I need to find activities similar enough to help prepare us yet different enough to span six weeks of camp. While also trying to convince everyone that Faith's worth practicing for. While also spending half of my time helping run activities that have absolutely nothing to do with any of my goals, because apparently, I did such a good job helping Numaan with the five through eights last week that I'm now a sought-after camp assistant commodity. But it's fine. It's probably good to be productive.

Once Faith's finally released back into our custody on Friday, I decide to organize something right away. It's a risky choice. I had to let Janine know I'm planning something ahead of time again to make sure the staff would be fine with it and she strongly cautioned me against trying to jump right back into team building after it went so poorly last time. Which is Janine speak for "I really don't want you to do this, but I'm incredibly dedicated to respecting your autonomy as a budding adult so I'm not going to explicitly say no." We're already a third of the way through the summer though, so waiting any longer is not an option. And besides, Faith's agreed to act more on board this time, so everything's going to go perfectly. Hopefully.

"Welcome to our second first official training session!" I once again take my place in the middle of the circle.

Circles are excellent team-building shapes for a variety of reasons. People typically seek out those that they're already close to or familiar with in group settings, but when sitting in circles, they often don't consider that the people they're likely going to spend the most time looking at aren't the ones beside them, but the ones across from them. This helps foster more subconscious positive connections and increases feelings of unity. It also provides everyone with more equal access to the speaker, decreasing the likelihood that people might feel less willing to contribute based off of their lack of proximity.

"Since we're a week closer to the big event, we've decided it's best to jump right into activities!" I haven't actually given up on my original team-building idea, I've just adapted it. Faith was right to point out that we don't actually need to construct any form of uniform since we all already come pre-equipped with those, but that doesn't erase any of the psychological benefits of gift-giving. I've had her make actual, non-half-assed bracelets for everyone, but decided at the last minute that it'd be best she hold off on handing them out. You never know when you might need an olive branch, and in Faith's case, my guess would be sooner rather than later. "We're gonna start with a warm-up activity to get us into the groove of things and then transition to something a little more intense," I finish.

Faith opens her mouth to protest yet another non-capture the flag related activity, but I'm anticipating it this time. I catch her eye instantly.

"We good, Faith?"

She sighs and kicks at the grass. "Yeah," she says. "Fine. Whatever."

Our first activity goes relatively well, but I also took enough precautions to ensure that it would. Elephant ball only has a couple of rules and I know we've all played it before, but I go over them again before starting anyway, just to avoid any potential confusion or conflicts.

The game's intentionally simple. You get your players to stand in a circle with their feet touching their neighbors' and their fists clasped together to swing like a pendulum between their parted legs. Then, you introduce a ball to the middle of the circle and use your fists to try and push it away from yourself and through someone else's legs. If it slips past yours, you're out. Then you just keep going until there's only one person remaining.

I've talked things over with Morgan and then again with Janine to prepared for any potential complications too. Getting someone with a disability exacerbated by posture change to play a game entirely dependent on practically bending your body in half is obviously an inadvisable idea, so I've made sure to acquire a chair for Van that's both wide enough for balls to fit through (the bar on his rollator was too low for most of them) and narrow enough that he's not at a disadvantage. I also ran my activity and accommodation ideas by him a few days ago to make sure he'd be comfortable with them. From personal experience, I know that accommodations (even good ones) can sometimes feel embarrassing or isolating to use. They should be put in place to increase the comfort of the person using them, not just everyone surrounding them, and I've found nondisabled people often forget that physical and mental comfort do not always go hand in hand.

Typical elephant ball often involves incorporating new rules and additional balls to make the game more intense as it progresses, but since I only want to use it as a warm-up, I've brought a bag of different colour and sized balls to swap out instead. Sunny generally gets really invested in any game that involves some level of physical activity, but she also tends to get bored and wander off frequently, so if it seems like she's about to, I figured swapping in a new stimulus might help hold her focus for a few more minutes. It turns out, I didn't even have to worry about that.

We get through fifteen minutes and six rounds without a hitch. Sunny's by far the most enthusiastically athletic of our group so she wins half of them, then Morgan, Faith, and Van win a round each. But, most importantly, it seems like everyone's actually having fun. People laugh when they get out and cheer when someone else does (particularly loudly if that someone is Faith, but for now, I've decided some level of light-hearted, common enemy based bonding is beneficial). As the rounds go on, everyone (even Faith, though maybe that's part of her act) starts to play more competitively, getting genuinely invested in the outcome of the game.

According to multiple online camp handbooks that likely were never supposed to become public access and one conversation with a verified camp counsellor, stopping or adapting an activity at its peak is a crucial part of creating a lively, engaging camp atmosphere. If you stop too early, people don't feel involved enough for an activity to seem worthwhile. If you stop too late, their energy and attention wane and they'll approach any following activities with less enthusiasm. I decide the end of the sixth round is the perfect time to adjust.

"Alright!" I tuck the ball under one arm and straighten to address the group again. "We're gonna switch things up to start working on team building! Instead of trying to get the ball out of the circle, the goal's now to keep it in. Say the name of the person you're passing to before you pass the ball so they know to expect it." I model with Morgan a few times to make sure the instructions are clear then we run a much less exciting round, but a productive one nonetheless. Multiple members of our cabin (myself included) struggle to hold on to multi-step instructions, so I want to make sure we adapt things slowly. I'd originally planned on explaining that Brain'll be pointing at people instead since she's nonverbal (Sunny doesn't have a ton of speech either, but she's *really* enthusiastic about names), but when I ran that by her, she declared it redundant and apparently talked to Gator ahead of time to let them know she'll always be passing there so that Gator'll know to always expect the ball shortly after Brain's name's been called. Not having to explain that makes introducing new steps go even more smoothly.

It's not until I've gotten us to all sit down on the ground and switch to tossing the ball then added a second that Faith starts to cause problems. Which, all things considered, was honestly longer than I'd thought she'd last.

"Is this all we're doing all day?"

I tighten my smile. "It'll help with team building, learning to read each other, and—"

"Is this all we're doing?" she cuts me off.

"Well," I smile tightly, trying to psychically force her to shut up. "Depending on how we do, I was thinking we'd keep making it harder until—"

"This isn't gonna work."

I don't know what she thinks she's doing. It should not be this difficult to convince someone to work in their own best interests. I can feel the mood souring.

"Faith." I try to inject a bit of "what the fuck are you doing" into my tone. I'm not sure if it reaches her. "Just..." I sigh. "We're doing this for you. The least you could do is—"

"We're wasting time."

"Yeah? How much more do you want to waste on this conversation?"

Faith sighs and sits back down. "Add the ball," she mumbles.

"What was that?"

She just glares at me, but it's response enough. She's been managed. At least for now.

But then, the next time one of the balls is tossed at her, she doesn't catch it. And then it happens again. And again. After the third miss, I make sure to keep my eyes on her, and sure enough, she isn't even making an attempt at reaching for them.

I gather up the balls at the end of the next round and glare at her.

"You have to try, Faith."

She shrugs. "Who said I wasn't?"

"You're obviously not! It'd be physically difficult to even intentionally be that bad at this! If you keep letting them fall, we can't work up a rhythm and there won't be a point to—"

"I never asked to play your stupid game!" she explodes.

I want to take it back. At least when Faith was just stubbornly sabotaging things, everyone else was less likely to remember why we don't like her.

"It's helpful. It—"

"Yeah? Where exactly in capture the flag do you play fucking catch?"

"It's a team-building game," I reiterate slowly. "And increases our ability to read each other and strengthens perception and awareness, which you would've already known if you'd just listen to—"

"This is so stupid."

I bristle. "Stop saying that!" I feel Morgan tug at my sleeve, but I don't let myself turn. I already know we're freaking everyone else out. I don't need to also see it. "You don't get to keep saying stuff like that one second then ask us to help you the next!"

Faith stares at me. I stare at her. For once, she breaks contact first. "Fine," she mumbles. "Whatever. Add the third ball."

She's already ruined everything, though. Whatever good energy we'd built up earlier is entirely gone. And then, to make matters worse, just a few tosses into the game, she fully gets up and walks away.

"What the heck!" I exclaim once she's gotten far enough to make it clear that she has no intention of storming back over to apologize.

All three balls drop.

Okay? Van signs.

"Yeah," I force myself to breathe. If Faith's going to throw a tantrum, then I have to act coolheaded until I figure out what the hell she thinks she's doing. "Yeah, sorry. We can... we'll play without her. This was fun. There's no point letting her ruin things."

There's a beat of silence and then, Gator raises their hand.

"Gator?"

"When did Faith go?"

I frown. "What? Like, a minute ago. How did you not—" I take in everyone else's confused expressions. No one else saw

Faith go. Because she was doing some kind of weird attention magic again.

I just don't know why. What's the point of staging an outburst if you're not planning on sucking up any of the attention it causes? Now that I've had time to think it through, I don't understand why she would have walked off calmly in the first place. Faith is very good at dramatic exits.

Unless this isn't her acting out and something else is going on.

"I umm... right." I clap my hands together. "Right, sorry, didn't want to interrupt the game, but I umm... cabin!" Faith might've escaped everyone's notice, but I'm pretty sure I've ruined that by bringing her up. Even if I hadn't, *I* can't disappear without anyone noticing and she'd at least started off in that direction, so it's a plausible cover. "Faith forgot her water bottle. I told her I'd go with her to get it because like, buddy system and all so..." I pull over the bag of balls. "Keep practicing! Excellent work team! Be right back!"

I rush to go find a potentially pissed-off changeling.

Chapter 24

Faith's long gone by the time I leave to follow her, but luckily, my hunch was right.

The moment I step foot in the cabin, Faith pulls her blanket over her head, rolls over to face the wall, and says, "Go away, Lots."

I check to make sure I haven't been followed before closing the door behind me. "How'd you know it was me?"

"You mean apart from you being the only one insufferable enough to follow me when I clearly wanted to be left alone?" She deadpans.

I don't respond.

Faith sighs. "You're loud."

"I barely even—"

"Not you specifically, just... humans in general. Your bodies refuse to shut up."

I scrunch up my nose. I do not like the idea of my body having a distinct noise *or* Faith knowing what that noise is. I take another step then hesitate. On the walk over, I'd hyped myself up for a fight. Faith's been actually engaging in those, recently. But yelling at her feels a lot more absurd now that she's hiding in her bunk, doing a very poor job of pretending that I don't exist.

I sit down on the ground and look up at her instead. "You're really, *really* bad at trying to get people to want to help you with stuff, you know."

"Shut up," she mutters.

"Like, incredibly bad. Like, I keep having to remind myself that just straight-up letting people get future-killed isn't a morally acceptable option. And even then, it's still—"

"Shut up, Lots!"

It's because she's shouted it—because she suddenly sounds so *real*—that I do.

I climb up my own bunk, scroll through my phone, and pretend to be perfectly fine doing absolutely nothing. I don't know what comes next. I do know that whatever kind of magic Faith must have used to slip away doesn't seem to extend to other people or objects when she's not making physical contact, though, so after a few minutes, I slowly lower my phone and risk peeking towards her bunk.

She's still lying down, facing the wall. She's completely still. She's a magical creature in the middle of some kind of emotional episode and she very clearly doesn't want to be disturbed, so I probably shouldn't disturb her.

It takes three more minutes for me to become bored enough to fast-track my own destruction. Again.

I climb up Faith's ladder to ensure she's not actually asleep before I let myself say anything, pausing at the top to try and discern whether or not she's faking. Her eyes are closed, but she goes a little too still when the ladder creaks beneath me for it to be a believable act.

I freeze.

Faith stays too frozen.

Then, slowly, she rolls over and opens her eyes. It's only when she blows a clump of my hair off of her face that I realize how close I am.

"You're being creepy again," she says.

I'd already deduced that she was awake, but the sudden noise still startles me enough that I lose my balance. Faith grabs my wrist after it slips off the rung and I take a moment to catch my breath. Once I'm stabilized, I climb the rest of the way onto her bunk. Sitting next to a potentially angry changeling is hopefully less fatal than falling several feet.

Hopefully.

Especially considering the fact that said changeling's already in the process of crossing her legs to make space for me. And just saved me from that aforementioned death plummet.

"Would you have preferred I announced it before or after letting you break a bone?" Faith says.

I blink, looking up at her. My focus had been locked on the wrist she'd grabbed as I'd tried to puzzle out why she'd done it. When she healed me in the forest last week, she was actively about to ask me for a favour and needed to cover up evidence. This time, I can't find the motive.

"'m not apologizing for not politely getting your consent before stopping you from hurting yourself," Faith continues. "Especially since you definitely would've tried to blame it on me if you'd ended up breaking anything."

"I... yeah." I nod. "Right. I... you should touch me, actually. My wrist. Or hand. Or wherever or— not literally wherever, obviously, but you know. So the others don't come looking."

Faith uncurls her fingers and waits for me to place my palm in hers.

"How does the attention thing work anyway? You used it on the field just now, right? So no one but me would notice you leaving?"

She rolls her eyes. "You weren't supposed to notice either. I don't want you here."

"Oh."

Faith waits a beat. "You're still not gonna leave me alone?"

"I don't think I actually care all that much about what you want right now," I admit. "All things considered."

Faith sighs, pressing her back against her headboard until she's sitting up straighter. "I run on attention," she says. "I can't target whose I erase myself from, just how much I do it. It's more like... making people forget for a little. Unless I erase myself entirely, I can't stop them from re-remembering if they're putting enough thought into it and obviously if they're looking right at me, they'll be at least dimly aware that there's someone there, but unless the other person's putting a lot of effort into it, their mind should just kinda skip over me."

I frown. "So I was... paying too much attention to you."

"Yeah," Faith's lips twitch. "You do that a lot, actually."

"I do not!"

She rolls her eyes. "You're arguing with someone who literally can't lie, Lots."

"That's—" I scrunch up my nose. "I think I hate that a lot, actually."

"Yeah." Her smug grin grows. "Figured you would."

I consider. "Could you do that for the actual game, then? Pop all the way out of everyone's attention and—"

Any half-smiling she might have been inching towards instantly vanishes. Faith pulls her blanket up around her shoulders. "No."

"I'm just saying, it'd be smart to—"

"I *run* on attention, Lots. I cut it off all the way, I die."

"Oh," I nod. "Right. That umm... sounds inadvisable then."

Faith fixes her hair with her free hand. "Are you here to tell me you're backing out, then? Just because I didn't want to do your stupid game?"

"Depends. Do *you* respond well to threats?"

Faith doesn't respond, but she also does. Her eyes dart down. She runs her tongue along the inside of her gums. I might not be good at most people's non-verbal cues, but I've been studying Faith Harris's for almost a decade.

"Oh," I realize. I weigh my options. It would be easier to try and use this to add in some more concrete stipulations to our arrangement now that I know that if I get her to promise to them, they'll apparently be binding. Threats and ultimatums are generally morally frowned upon, but I decided years ago that Faith was the one person I didn't have to bother being morally upstanding around. If anything, I'm doing her a massive favour right now, so I'm more than entitled to a little bit of wrongness. I sigh. "I don't think threats would suit me," I admit. "I've kind of already got the biggest built-in one of all anyway, right? If you don't stop messing stuff up, we lose and you're future-dead." I lean towards her. "Why'd you sabotage today? We had a plan, there was no reason to—"

"I like attention," she mutters.

I shake my head. "You didn't take any, though. When you left. It sounds like you used some of it up, actually, since you had to divert it to slip away, right? Why—"

"Maybe I didn't want to play some stupid fucking—" Faith straightens. "What did I just do?"

"Besides freak out and storm off again?" I try to play it off.

"No." I've somehow forgotten that Faith's hand's wrapped around mine until her grip tightens. My skin suddenly feels too hot. "Not earlier, just now. Your attention..." she gestures vaguely. "Did something. Again."

I swallow. I've been realizing with alarming speed that Faith Harris might not actually be the evil, conniving mastermind that I'd built her up to be in my head, but that doesn't mean that I think she's a decent person either. Whatever she is must just be a lot more confusing. I *do* know that I'm absolutely not handing the girl who's made it expressly clear that she has every intention of antagonizing me for as long as she possibly can the key to my biggest insecurity.

"Nothing," I say. "Or... I don't know. Maybe you imagined it. Or your brain's subconsciously trying to distract you to change the topic. Who knows. What happened today?"

Faith watches me for another half a second before looking away. "I didn't like your game."

I frown. "That can't possibly be it. We're running out of time here, Faith. You can't blow up about every single—"

"You think I don't know that!" she blows up. Only for a second, though. Almost as quickly as the outburst begins, Faith takes a deep breath and looks down to study her sheets. Her free hand flies back to her hair.

It draws my attention to her face. To the faint glossy sheen just beneath her eyes.

I frown. "Were you... crying?" That doesn't make any sense. Faith might not love team building, but that's hardly worth crying over. Especially for someone like her.

She scoffs, but not so subtly angles her face away from me all the same. "You wish."

"That's not... does that mean you genuinely think I do? With the no lying thing and all? I'm—I'm not a bad person, Faith. I wouldn't... I don't. Just for the record."

She doesn't respond.

"In fact, if you're like, about to start crying again or something, I'd actually really prefer it if you didn't. Other people crying around me always makes me really uncomfortable. I never know what I'm supposed to do when that happens."

She rolls her eyes. "You're terrible at comforting people."

I feel my eyebrows draw closer together. "I'm not... is that what you think I'm supposed to be doing right now?"

"Shut up."

"I'm trying to help you!" I remind her. "I've been trying to help you for weeks and all you do is treat me like crap for it and... and refuse to tell me anything and— there's not even a point! I *saw you* last week, Faith. I know you're terrified. I know you're full of shit. You don't get to keep acting like you don't care about any of this or—or like it's my fault I can't read your mind!"

"I'll do the next game," Faith deadpans. Right back to neutral, just like she handles everything. It makes me want to scream.

And then, I realize that that might actually work. The only way I've ever gotten any answers out of her is by riling her up.

As a rule, I try my best to never intentionally upset anyone. My rules have never technically extended to Faith, though, and definitely don't now that I've promised to keep hating her. With her life in the balance, that feels like an adequate one to bend a bit.

"That's not good enough!" It's easy to keep my tone loud and angry because that's exactly how I'm feeling right now. I just normally try to hide it a bit more. "Why do you keep messing everything up!"

She sighs. "Maybe I just—"

"No more maybes!" I stop her. "Give me the actual fucking answer!"

"Just forget it. It's—"

"What happened today!" I tug her hand closer to my chest.

"I already said I'd—"

"Tell me what happened!"

"I'm not—" She tries to pull away again, but I refuse to let her.

"What could have possibly been so important that you couldn't pretend to be tolerable for one fucking—"

"I couldn't do it!" Faith screams, finally shaking my hand free to throw hers over her ears. Then, she stares at me, chest heaving. She hastily redirects her fingers to run them through her hair, down her neck, and eventually beneath her legs. "There," she mumbles. "Happy?"

"Not really," I admit. "That was actually incredibly vague."

"I should probably take your hand again," she says. "If you're still not planning on leaving me alone."

"Alright," I hold it out and wait for her to grab it, sorting through potential interpretations of what she just said. "Could you not... pretend to be having a half-decent time?" I guess. "Because that seems implausible. It's not like you would've had to lie, you could've just like, been quiet."

She doesn't look at me. She also doesn't respond.

"You obviously could've done the game too," I continue thinking aloud. "You did, for a while. I don't get why that'd suddenly change unless—oh." I suck on my lip. "You can't get mad at me for not accommodating you if you don't tell me how to, Faith."

She rolls her eyes. "I didn't say I needed—"

"But you do, right? That's why you can't say you don't?"

She studies her bedsheets.

I sigh. "I yelled at you, just now. I shouldn't have done that. I didn't realize... okay, full disclosure I absolutely realized yelling at you makes you more prone to accidentally blurting things out and I was definitely trying to manipulate you, but I hadn't processed that it was because of like, an actual debilitating sensory thing."

"I don't think you're supposed to tell people when you're manipulating them," Faith mumbles.

I shrug. "Maybe I'm just trying to get you to lower your guard next time I decide to." I slip my tangle around my fingers. "Still, though, if you have auditory processing issues or sensitivities, you could've just—"

"I don't."

I frown. "You can apparently hear me listening to things across the room with headphones on and like, enough body noises—whatever those are. I think I'd actually you rather didn't tell me anything else about that particular faeryism—to identify a person based off of them and you somehow—"

"I'm not autistic," Faith interrupts.

"I didn't say you were," I say slowly. "Is that why you stopped playing? Because the names were too difficult to track?"

"Possibly," she admits.

"And you have trouble processing auditory stimuli?"

"Yes, but—"

"Then you have auditory processing issues. Congrats. Next time say something instead of just blowing up at everyone about it. Or if you don't want to, just let yourself look bad at something for once. You're literally surrounded by disabled people right now, Faith. Obviously no one'll judge you for not being able to—"

"You did." She looks at me and almost instantly, my eyes start to water. I look away.

"That's different. I thought you were just being annoying. If I'd known you were just self-conscious because you physically couldn't play, I would have—"

"You would've what, Lots?" she demands. "Been fine with it? Come up with a workaround and then patted yourself on the back for being such a good person for only getting mad at people *before* you've decided they might be disabled?"

I frown. "That's not fair."

"You love pitying things," she spits. "You *need* to pity things, because if you don't, how are you supposed to feel like a good person, right? What's the point in being a decent fucking person if you don't get to applaud yourself for it?"

"That's not—" her fingers are still on my wrist. I suddenly need them to not be on my wrist, but I can't make my muscles work properly. "I don't—I'm helping you!" I remind her. "I'm the one—"

"And you wouldn't be if you didn't know I'd die if you didn't!"

Her fingers are still on my wrist and I need them to not be on my wrist and all of a sudden, every single one of my muscles comes alive at once. "That's not fair!"

I'm just trying to push her arm away. Later, I'll swear to myself that I was just trying to push her arm away. Because I might be a terrible person, but even as my palms slam against Faith's shoulders and send her shooting toward the edge of the bunk, I need to believe that I'm not.

Chapter 25

"I'm sorry."

Faith does not go hurtling to the ground. She grabs onto the headboard to stabilize herself before I've even finished pulling away. She presses her back against it so I shouldn't be able to knock her down even if I do get worked up again, but I hug my arms around my stomach anyway, just in case.

"I'm sorry, I didn't... that wasn't... I didn't do that. Or... I didn't *mean* to do that." I risk releasing my left arm for half a second to shove my chewlery between my teeth.

Faith just shrugs. " 's whatever."

I shake my head. "I didn't mean to... I wasn't trying to—" I thought I'd trapped my arms but somehow, they've freed themselves to smack against her mattress. I quickly shove them under my arm pits. "I didn't mean to do that!"

"Lots." Faith raises her voice over mine. "It's actually fine. I was trying to manipulate you too. Guess that's what I get."

"I still shouldn't have—"

She leans forward. "Nobody's hurt, nobody's angry at you."

"But I—"

Faith shakes her head. "Nope. Stop wasting time, they'll notice we're gone and come looking soon. Nobody's hurt, nobody's angry at you. Repeat it back to me."

I take a deep breath. "Nobody's hurt, nobody's angry at me."

"Good." Faith nods.

"But I'm still—"

"I know," she stops me. "It's fine. Make it up to me by pitying me a little more and fixing this, yeah? I've actually kind of been banking on that."

I suck on the charm. "We could..." I scrunch up my face to try and think, but my mind's in none of the right places right now.

"I'm probably going to touch your hand," Faith interrupts my lack of thinking.

"You've always said that wrong," I realized it years ago, but I started tuning it out at some point. "Is that like, somehow a faery thing too?"

She shrugs. "Most of the time I don't know if you'll actually let me."

"Maybe you shouldn't." I scratch my wrist. "I just—"

"You're fine, Lots," Faith leans forward to look at me. I squirm under the sudden attention and crane my neck to look at the wall instead. She sighs. "That was my fault, okay? I knew what I was doing. I could literally feel myself riling you up. I've literally given you no other reason to want to help anyway, I just... I'm not used to being seen," she admits. "Made me uncomfy, so I figured flipping it would... just don't do it again, yeah? Hand."

I hold it out. "You don't wear headphones," I say.

Faith exhales forcefully instead of laughing. "Took you eight years to—"

"I realized," I stop her. "I just figured you weren't sound sensitive. Do they bother you? Alice—that's my sister—"

"I'm very aware."

"She hates them," I ignore her commentary. "She's not even autistic or anything and most sensory stuff doesn't bug her, but she says they make her ears feel all squished. But if sound stuff's that bad for you, maybe you could try—"

"I'm not autistic, Lots," she repeats. Faith seems to really like repeating that. "I don't need headphones."

I frown. "You very clearly—"

"Drop it."

I normally wouldn't. I did just try to maybe hurt her, though, so I give in. For now.

"Okay," I nod. "Right. Sure. We'll just switch to less auditory-based activities then, deal? Anything else I need to keep in mind?" It would probably be more helpful to just get her to plan out all future activities with me to make sure they're faery-friendly, but every time I've tried to get Faith's input, it's just turned into an argument about how much time I'm wasting on easing us into things.

She shrugs. Because *of course* Faith's just planning on continuing to expect me to read her mind.

I sort through ideas. I have to bite my cheek to keep from grinning when I find the perfect one. "If I have a backup plan that'll help smooth things over *and* be good capture the flag practice, would you do it? Like, go along with it completely no matter what?"

The corners of her lips turn down slightly. "What would—"

"Nope." I cut her off. "It'll have a better impact if it doesn't look like you know it's coming."

"Believe it or not, that doesn't make me any more eager to—"

"Faith." I take her other hand and lean forward. My eyes still refuse to look at hers for some reason, so I stare at her hairline instead. "I'm going to help you," I promise. "I've been trying to help you for weeks now. But that's never going to work if you keep refusing to trust me."

She's entirely still for a long beat before letting go of my hands. "Okay," she starts making her way down the ladder. "Let's go."

I grin and giggle to myself, which likely doesn't help make her any less suspicious, but in my defense, I grin and giggle about a lot of non-nefarious things too.

"It'll involve running!" I decide it's safe to mention. "Are you good with that?"

Faith sighs. "Let me grab my shoes."

Chapter 26

Removing people from someone's attention doesn't seem to have any impact on their perception of how much time's passed since said people disappeared, so when we return to the recreation field, I'm immediately greeted by Gator raising their hand to ask, "what took so long?"

"We were busy," I say. "We had a very long, very lovely heart-to-heart in which Faith told me she's really, really sorry about how she reacted earlier and revealed that she actually cares a lot about everyone's opinion of her and desperately hopes that you'll all forgive her enough to play another game."

Van raises an eyebrow. "Seriously?"

"Yes," I nod enthusiastically. I'll have to ask Faith if not being able to lie extends to gestures. "In fact, Faith was *so* ashamed and insecure that she also said she'll probably feel uncomfortable saying any of this in person, which is why she asked me too. But she's like, super sorry. And made apology gifts for everyone that'll be distributed after we get a bit more work done so they're not a distraction. Anyway, I told her I was sure it'd be no big deal because we've all reacted a little too strongly to something once or twice before and it would be wildly hypocritical to hold a grudge over that, right?" I take a page from Janine's book and slowly and deliberately look at everyone until they all (mostly reluctantly) nod in agreement. I can feel Faith glowering beside me, but hopefully no one else has noticed. True to her word, she's at least not vocally contradicting me right now.

"Excellent!" I clap my hands together. "Alright then. Faith got frustrated earlier because we weren't doing obviously capture the flag related drills, so we're gonna switch gears and do something a bit more physical." It's a carefully curated excuse. True enough that Faith should be able to go along with it if asked follow-up questions, but different enough that I'm nowhere near divulging her actual reason for giving up on the previous activity.

Whether caused by a disability or by literally being a different species, other people's limits and insecurities are not mine to talk about. "Now, Faith also told me in our super long super sincere heart-to-heart that she's worried about her capability to function in a team right now, so on the walk over, I came up with the perfect solution!" I march over to the bag of balls and reach all the way to the bottom to pull out a bean bag. 'We're gonna spend the rest of today practicing protecting a flag! Our job." I toss the beanbag in the air. "Is to protect and guard this. Faith's is to steal it." I turn to her. "We don't have enough space for two full sides and it's not like you're hiding your own flag, so is taking like a foot of space near the edge of the field to be your safe zone big enough?"

She stares at me. "Are you serious?"

"Maybe two feet?"

"One versus six is ridiculous. It—"

"I thought you were super eager to get to more capture the flag stuff," I feign innocence. "Unless you're not willing to do whatever it takes to win?"

She sighs. "Fine, whatever." Faith trudges over to the other end of the field. "Hurry up and hide your stupid beanbag."

You might assume that "make Faith try and run fast enough to retrieve a beanbag while the rest of our cabin monkey guards her" wouldn't be an activity that we'd be able to burn much time on. That assumption would demonstrate a complete lack of understanding of how desperately a lot of us have been waiting for the opportunity to get back at Faith for something. And of how fun messing with her is.

Our first few rounds are relatively normal. We place the beanbag near the end of our zone, Faith attempts to retrieve it, then she inevitably gets caught almost immediately and we reset. Quickly, though, everyone begins to catch onto the fact that it's much more fun to let Faith think she has the upper hand. Round after round, we seem to somehow come to the unspoken, unanimous decision to let her get closer and closer to the beanbag before someone swoops in to ruin it for her.

(The ability to make unspoken, unanimous decisions is incredibly beneficial when trying to construct a team. Even if those decisions are made at someone else on that team's expense.)

Then, once people start getting bored with that, the game shifts again. We start taking the hiding part of capture the flag more seriously, sending someone (usually Van) over to guard Faith to make sure she doesn't peek. Pretending to guard fake flags just for the joy of watching Faith think she's finally made it to one only to realize she's been deceived becomes a game in and of itself.

I wanted to avoid going right to a running-intensive game both to accommodate Van's support needs and other people's tendencies (mostly mine) to give up on activities early on, but the six versus one format ends up circumventing a lot of that for me. It's hard to get frustrated when you're pretty much guaranteed to always win. It's easy to take shifts and breaks when there's a ludicrous number of people on your side. The six versus one model doesn't build in much time for Faith to take breaks though, so I call an official one about forty-five minutes in. I don't actually want to kill her, after all. Most of the time.

My team gathers to laugh about the previous round's antics and to hatch future schemes, so I take the moment to peel away and check in with Faith.

"Hey." I make my voice as chipper as I can manage as I plop myself down beside her. She's a mess. Her hair's in disarray and clinging to her neck and cheeks with sweat, her temples are dotted red with effort, and her leggings and camp shirt are splattered in mud from one particularly over-zealous attempt at stopping her by Sunny (which, if anything, proves that Faith should've been extremely grateful that I'd remembered the two-finger rule with His Excellentance Squirge. Even if I forgot to mention it today). "Having fun?"

"You're enjoying this way too much," Faith mutters, somehow managing to even make the act of unzipping her backpack look violent. " 're you enjoying torturing me?"

"Yes! A lot!" I grin. "I can't stand you. It turns out it's considerably easier to help you with things if I get to make you miserable while doing it."

Faith rolls her eyes.

"I brought you extra water," I pull it out from my bag. "Or... I stole the extra bottle Morgan stocks for me because I always forget to fill mine from beside our bunk before we left the cabin. So technically I guess Morgan *and* I brought you extra water. You're welcome."

She snatches it from me and downs half of it in a matter of seconds.

"You can take my hair-tie too, if you want," I pull it off my wrist.

Faith waves me off. "Don't need it."

"You do, actually," I correct her. "You look terrible."

She just glares.

I slowly slip the hair-tie back on. "Is," I drop my voice. "Magical energy."

Faith rolls her eyes even though my whispering's for her benefit.

"Like actual energy?" I continued. "I figured it was. You seem extra tired and short-fused when you're low on it. So like, you should really be thanking me for coming up with an activity that puts all focus on you."

"I'm still actually running," Faith complains. "Forcing someone to exercise then handing them an energy drink doesn't erase—"

"Thank you, Lots," I sing over her.

She just keeps glaring.

I sigh. "Thank you, then. For genuinely trying. For once. Even though it's definitely more to help you than me since I'm only trying to do this to help you in the first place. I know trying must be hard for you."

Faith snorts.

"*And* I'm not just trying to annoy you, for the record. This is a hard thing to make feel serious to anyone else. Especially if you're not ready to genuinely beg for help. I know it's serious, obviously, but spending this much time on something you're clearly not enjoying'll help everyone else realize that too. Plus, working against a mutual enemy? Great bonding tool."

"I thought I was the one we were supposed to be getting people to bond with," Faith grumbles.

I shrug. "This'll help that, too. The heroes never let the villains join their team when the villain's at peak power. They need to celebrate how much better they are than them first."

"And a lot of pity."

I nod. "An abundance of it." I stand up and hold out a hand to help her do the same. "You ready to come look pathetic for a bit longer?"

Faith sighs. "As I'll ever be, I guess."

Chapter 27

Faith is annoyingly bad at looking pathetic. She does for a while, of course. Trying and failing and failing again. It's all incredibly entertaining and going exactly to plan. But I've miscalculated slightly. Faith is far more invested in success than anyone else is, and the more she loses, the more confident we become in the certainty of our inevitable triumph. Plus, she's the only one regaining her energy magically as we continue to play.

Technically, it's not a proper win. It happens once I'm already close to wrapping everything up and attention's waning. I'm still playing because I know the moment I stop everything'll fall apart, Sunny's more invested than she was when we first started playing because her energy somehow never seems to fade, and Morgan's still doing her best because she's brilliant and would never even consider leaving my side, but Van stopped entirely and switched to cheering from his rollator on the side sidelines ages ago and Brain and Gator are hanging around more to be obstacles in case Faith happens to go their way than to actually chase her. Our numbers and energy are depleted and we're all only half paying attention so somehow, before I even know it's happening, Faith's suddenly a foot away from me with the beanbag already in her hand, rushing towards the boundary line.

I sprint off after her, but I'm too slow. She might be more tired than I am, but she's already built up momentum. I take off clumsy and slowly and even after making one last-ditch leap to get her before she can cross the line, I barely manage to touch to ends of her hair.

She could have cheated, of course. Found a moment where absolutely no eyes were on her and blipped herself to the back of everyone's minds for a few seconds. I decide that that must be what happened. My ego can't take actually losing.

"Faith!" Sunny yells.

I cringe. I'd introduced cheering for whoever tags Faith as a way to boost comradery and keep anyone sitting out engaged. It wasn't supposed to be used to inflate Faith's ego even further.

But then Van decides to take his role as cheerleader seriously and joins in and suddenly *Van's* even cheering for Faith, so everyone else is too. I've done my job a little too well.

I look up from where I've less-than-majestically hurled myself to the ground to find Faith's lips curled up, ever so slightly. She bends towards me and holds out an arm to pull me up. I am not a fan of how quickly our positions have switched, but I'm not about to look like the unsportsmanly one, so I wrap my fingers around her wrist and let her drag me to my feet. She pulls a little too hard and I'm suddenly a little too close. I can feel her ragged breath against my forehead. "Can we be done now?" She murmurs as the chanting continues behind us.

"Wait!" Gator yells. "Nickname!"

The chant shifts to "nickname, nickname, nickname!" and Faith looks off-put enough by it that I regain enough confidence to think clearly. I skip over the first few less-than-chant-friendly ones that pass my mind before I finally hit it: the reason that she's probably always refused nicknames in the first place.

"What about Fay?" I turn to the rest of the cabin. "It's kind of the only option, right? Unless Faith suddenly decides to tell us enough about herself for a proper one? -th doesn't have the same repeatability."

"Fay can be another word for fairy," Brain's iPad reads.

"Can it!" I feign surprise.

Faith kicks the back of my shoe. Which, considering it's one of the only places she could have chosen that doesn't involve actual physical contact, I realize is an acceptably considerate form of violence.

"Well then," I continue. "It's perfect, right? It can be like, ironic. Since Faith's just about as far from sparkles and whimsy as you can possibly get."

There's a beat of silence, so I start up the chanting myself. "Fay, Fay, Fay, Fay!"

I turn around to find the fae in question glowering at me.

"Now," I grin, "we can be done."

Chapter 28

Attending a giant campfire is far from my ideal way of ending a day well spent. I prefer to celebrate my productivity through sweet treats, naps, and YouTube documentaries. But Corrain throws an end of week bonfire every Friday and when Sunny's aide announces it's time for them to head over, Gator spontaneously suggests that the rest of us go too to celebrate our first official day of Antelope annihilation training. A good leader knows when to sacrifice their own wants for the betterment of the group.

Plus, Brain and Van instantly agree to accompany them and Morgan says she'll go too moments later because Morgan's never been able to say no to something someone else is excited about, which means my only remaining options are giving in or being left alone with the changeling who's not so subtly been glaring at me all evening.

I never hate anything as much as I think I'm going to once I actually get there. Knowing this has done nothing to stop me from the aforementioned premature hatred, of course. It's almost a form of coping mechanism. If I decide something's going to be awful, then even the smallest bit of joy I get from it somehow feels bigger.

Still, I don't think I end up having a surprisingly good time because I've suddenly developed a miraculous love for Corrain bonfires (though I'd always welcome the s'mores served at them). My love of Corrain and all of its various activities and quirks has always come from other people.

We stick by the fire for a few campfire songs and chants before scattering becomes more socially acceptable and we all slowly begin to migrate our way over to our tree. Brain finds a pad of origami paper somewhere and sprawls out on her stomach on a picnic blanket.

Brain's Caribou name has nothing to do with her memory, savant syndrome, or ability to instantly look up the answers to any and all questions that might arise in a given conversation. It's from how entirely she dedicates her mind to each and every thing she does (and because Briana's not super nicknameable, but mostly the dedication part). She'll sit down somewhere, catch the tip of her tongue between her teeth so that it's poking out ever so slightly from the left corner of her mouth, and won't move or notice anything around her until a task's been completed.

I've often heard autism and ADHD described as lists of traits that you just have to check off enough of to be diagnosed, but I think framing them as that is incredibly misleading. A lot of those so-called traits only become disabling in their muchness. Being able to focus is not a disability, until it is. Being unable to focus is just a regular part of every human experience, until it isn't. We are disabled not because we have a trait, but due to how extremely it affects us.

I want Brain's. Which makes me feel ableist and awful and like a terrible human being because I'm sure getting so lost in a thought that she genuinely forgets that the world exists beyond it must be debilitating, but I'd love to feel disabled by an attention difference that people see as a strength for once.

Anyway, Brain is making flowers and I'm trying my very best to pretend that I'm not jealous that she gets to be so focused on something as inconsequential as paper flowers until suddenly, I realize I'm not upset at all. Because Brain is making flowers and Gator is attempting to teach Van some kind of handshake-based camp song that I'm almost certain they're making up as they go to try and distract him from said flower-making (we all know Brain'll inevitably give them to him and that Van only accepts softness when you catch him off guard with it) and Sunny is doing an absolutely ear-splitting job playing the bongo that one of the counsellors near the fire handed off to her under the foolish assumption that they'd be able to get it back before Sunny falls asleep. And we are happy. And for the first time this summer, a day feels like it's truly gone right.

Morgan returns with an extra blanket and throws it over me before sitting down. She leans her head against my shoulder and relaxes against our tree and I know, somehow, that she's thinking the exact same thing I am: that we're perfect. And maybe, possibly, that we're going to have to start savouring all of these perfect summer nights now that we're running out of them.

Eventually, she raises her head to kiss my cheek. "You did so good today."

I roll my eyes. "I barely even came up with anything new. Just adapted games that already existed slightly to—"

"You problem-solved," she corrects, squeezing my arm. "Enough to make people like *Faith*. For hours."

"Like is probably a strong word," I admit.

Morgan shifts to look towards me, angling my shoulders so that I'm facing her as well. "You liked it though, right? Leading? You're a natural at it."

"Of course. Love bossing people around."

Morgan grins, waving her hands in front of her face. "Perfect," she clasps them together, tapping along her knuckles. "Next year's going to be... I'm so excited! I've been talking to Janine about after we graduate? My CIT feedback's been great so far. She said if I applied to work here, I'd probably have a really good shot at—"

"We're only sixteen." I stop her.

Morgan frowns. "Right, but after we're eighteen—"

My pulse goes too loud for me to focus on anything else. I don't want to be an adult. I don't want to have to think about anything more consequential than this summer and this night and origami flowers.

"Lots?" Morgan's saying. "Would you not want to..."

"I'd love to." I'm not sure what I'm agreeing to, only that I'm supposed to be agreeing. "Sorry," I try to shake my head clear. "I just..." I'm more surprised to spot Faith sitting alone near the edge of the firelight than I've ever been to notice her missing. Ever since figuring out how she's been disappearing, I've just been assuming she's only fully visible whenever she needs someone for something. "Sorry." I push myself up. "I should probably... I'm gonna go check in on Faith. Make sure she's not planning on killing me in my sleep for spending all day kicking her ass."

"She kicked yours at the end there," Morgan reminds me.

"One point!" I stomp. "That hardly—" I giggle, bending down to fix the blanket around her shoulders. "Love you, very excited to do Leadership with you, but first I have to survive the night. Wish me luck!"

"Good luck!" Morgan calls after me. "I'll be sure to avenge you if it comes down to it!"

I grin, breathe in the campfire air and the sight of my friends in their most natural habitat, and try to use that as fuel to keep grinning. The thought of talking to Faith alone makes my heart beat too quickly and my skin feel too warm. I'm clearly terrified. Maybe she's been threatening me in some way so covert that I haven't caught onto it yet.

Hopefully, I won't actually have to take Morgan up on her promised vengeance.

Chapter 29

"Hey, Fay!" I try to make myself sound as cheery as I possibly can as I approach.

Faith doesn't so much as flinch as I sit down beside her. I like that I finally know how she's always able to seem so calm and put together. She's not immune to shock, she just heard me coming from several feet away.

"I could hex you if I wanted to, you know." Faith digs a stick into the dirt, sending tiny clumps of mud flying near our shoes. Most of the crowd's either gathered around the campfire or far enough from it to make talking easier over the barrage of drumbeats. The edge of the pit is the perfect place for secret, private conversations about things that aren't supposed to exist.

"I know," I feign confidence. "Which makes it extra sweet that you haven't yet."

Faith doesn't respond (or follow through on the threat), so I stretch out my legs and slip my tangle around my fingers. "I hurt your feelings today," I admit. "I'm sorry. I didn't mean to do that."

"'s whatever," she shrugs.

"It's not, though," I say. "I don't want to... I shouldn't have just assumed you were just trying to be difficult. Even if you really *are* just trying to be difficult like ninety-nine percent of the time."

Faith rolls her eyes. "This is kind of a shit apology, you know."

I laugh. "You were right," I continue. "You shouldn't have to announce every single thing you can or can't do for me to be a decent person about them, but I want to make sure it's super clear that if you do tell me something, I'm going to try a lot harder not to suck about it, alright? I'm not... I didn't mean to make you feel like shit."

"Is that why you made me spend ages running around?"

"That's completely different. You're an incredibly annoying person." I poke her shoulder. "I'm more than entitled to be annoying back. Speaking of, actually, today went really well. Van was talking strategy for the actual game afterwards—or battle or war or whatever it is, but he thinks it's a game, obviously—and I figured he'd be the hardest one to win over, so..."

I hold out a fist.

Faith just stares at it.

"Ptchoooo!" I bump my own knuckles. In the moment, it had felt a lot less awkward than just leaving my hand hanging there. I immediately realize that it definitely wasn't. "Anyway, I, for one, think I did an excellent job, so instead of being all mopey and angry about a silly activity and sillier nickname—"

"A potentially dangerous nickname," Faith interrupts.

I roll my eyes. "Faith, I promise no one in the history of the universe has ever met someone named Fay and assumed they had magical powers because of it. If anything, it'll make it less obvious. A faery named Fay is way too on the nose."

"You're not calling me that," she grumbles. "Or... only around them. The nickname thing's probably an okay idea. For team building."

"Fine. Yes. Whatever. Point is, I did a good job today. You could at least try to act grateful about it, you know."

"Sure," Faith rolls her eyes. "I'm *so* thankful you forced me to spend the day exhausting myself."

"You're welcome," I grin.

"That was sarcasm, Lots."

"It sure sounded like it," I acknowledge. "If only I didn't already know you can't lie."

"That's not—" Faith sputters. I think it's the first time I've ever heard her sputter over something. I enjoy it immensely. "Stop grinning like that!"

I keep grinning like that.

Faith raises her arm to swat at me then stops herself. "I'm going to hit you," she says before waiting a beat and smacking my shoulder.

"No probably this time," I observe afterwards.

Faith glares. "That one wasn't optional."

I laugh. "It'd probably be best strategy-wise if you didn't act like you're immediately back to hating everyone right now? Come over, bring the bracelets, and—"

"No."

"I knew you'd say that," I inform her. "So," I slip my backpack off my shoulder and onto my lap. "I've come prepared." I pull out my spare headphones and hold them out to her. "Luckily for you, I'm very good at breaking things, so I always bring two extra pairs to camp every summer just in case. These are—"

"I said I don't want headphones, Lots."

"Right, but you made it sound like you've never even tried them. Which is kind of ridiculous given the amount of people you know who benefit from them. Like, I get it's not for everyone, but—"

"I'm not autistic."

I try not to react visibly, but I must because Faith sighs.

"I'm not... that's not an insult. It's great that they help you, but I'm bad with sound because I have faerie senses and I'm worse at tuning things out than other changelings. Not... I have nothing against autism or you being autistic or whatever, I'm literally just not. I'm not even human, so I physically can't be. It's genetic."

"Oh." I lean over to inspect the headphones more closely, turning them over and over again in my hands to make sure I'm exploring every possible nook and cranny.

"What are you doing now?" Faith eventually gives in.

"Looking for the 'autistics only' label," I squint. I hand the headphones off to her. "They must've forgotten to include it on this pair."

She sighs. "You know what I mean."

"I don't, actually, because no one has ever once said that noise-cancelling headphones are just for autistic people. And it sounds like you could really use a pair."

Faith wraps her hair around her fist then lets it fall. "I'm just not... I don't need to take resources away from actual disabled people just because I still haven't figured out how to regulate my own senses."

"Ah yes." I nod gravely. "Allistics paying top dollar for fancy headphones *has* historically discouraged manufacturers from making them. I don't know how I and my six ears would ever function without having three whole pairs all to myself."

"I could still hex you," Faith mutters. "If I wanted to make that a reality."

"Nope." I lean towards her. "You're too sleepy, remember?"

It's weird, now that the discovery phase of finding out that Faith's a changeling has passed. She's always felt far more intimidating to be around in person than she does when I imagine arguing with her in her head, but any fears I have about her actual magical nature seem to disappear the moment I'm close enough to remember that she's Faith. Awful and annoying and terrible, but ultimately harmless. And maybe even a little insecure.

"You don't have to keep them if they're not helpful, but I think it's actually ridiculous you haven't tried them yet."

Maybe it's only because she actually *is* exhausted, but Faith finally relents and pulls them over her ears.

"Hold the longer button on the side to turn them on," I instruct. "There should be a switch beside it. You can flip between transparency and noise cancelling mode, but for you specifically, I figured noise cancelling would probably already let in more noise than transparency's supposed to anyway. You can just tell people they're on transparency. Or I guess you can answer vaguely then I can say that bit for you. Not that anyone'll ask, I just like to overprepare."

I watch Faith fiddle with the dial. As she lowers her hand, she takes a deep breath and squeezes her eyes shut.

"Well?" I prompt. "Do you like them?"

Slowly, her eyes reopen. "They're... very pink."

"Yes," I nod proudly. "You're welcome."

"Incredibly hot pink."

"The best of all colours."

Faith takes another long breath. "I'll... try them out. Since you'll probably keep bothering me if I don't."

I bite my lip. Maybe even a lot insecure, actually.

"It's you calling me stupid," I say to try and balance things out a bit more between us. Vulnerability is always so much more difficult to bear if you're the only one wearing it.

"Excuse me?"

"Right," I nod. "Right, obviously you wouldn't have the context for— sometimes I forget that other people don't see all the connections in my brain. Sorry. Or... not sorry. Fuck you. Or... not fuck you, right now. Maybe fuck you. I'm not sure, I'm—"

"Lots," she stops me. "You were saying?"

"Right." I slip my tangle between my fingers and try again. "It's umm... the thing you kept catching? My attention spiking and then me pretending it isn't spiking? It's... I don't like it when you call me stupid. It's an ableist adjective, you know. I mean, a lot of things originated as ableist adjectives, unfortunately, but that doesn't mean people shouldn't make an effort to—"

"Lots." Faith interrupts my rambling again. "You call things stupid. All the time."

"Well, maybe I'm trying to turn over a new leaf." The problem with deciding to be vulnerable is that my mouth rarely follows through with it.

Faith frowns. "I'm supposed to believe you've been getting abruptly, noticeably angrier because I sometimes use an adjective with an ableist origin that you haven't even stopped using yet?"

"I mean, preferably, yeah." I sigh. I wind my tangle tighter. I scrape my sneakers against the dirt. "Okay, no, it's... a lot more self-centered, actually. I think I just don't like you saying it about me."

"You call yourself stupid," Faith refuses to let me off the hook. I can't believe I thought being vulnerable to try and make her feel better was somehow a good idea. "And me. Regularly."

"Well, maybe you just imagined—"

"I didn't. I'm going for annoying, not evil, Lots. I keep track of the insults people are just mildly bothered by."

I consider. "That's... actually oddly sweet."

"Shut up."

I think I almost catch Faith blush, but then my attention's momentarily drawn to the fire, and when I look back, she's pulled her knees to her chest and her face is half covered. I don't even know if my momentary lapse in attention was her or my ADHD.

"It's mostly annoying," Faith mutters. "And really smart of me."

I fold my tangle into a tight spiral before talking again to give myself time to gather my thoughts, but they still don't come out as clearly as I'd wanted them to. "I don't like that you do it," I say. "You specifically."

"You never used to—"

"I never used to know you had to mean it!"

I'm expecting her to apologize to try and keep exploiting my help or to try and change the topic entirely if apologizing's impossible, but instead, Faith just blinks and shifts her head slightly. "Why the fuck would I think you're stupid?"

"You said it!" I remind her. "And you can't lie! You're the one who—"

"I also say 'fuck off'. A lot. I definitely don't mean that one literally either."

"But you said you can't lie!"

"I can't." Faith shrugs. "But words are... I don't know. Messy. A lot of them mean different things in different contexts. I mean, you said it yourself. Stupid *originated* as an ableist adjective. It means something else now. Like, a lighter curse word, I think. To me. I call objects stupid all the time and I'm obviously not making some kind of judgement call on their intelligence."

"I still don't like it," I say.

"Okay," Faith nods. "Very okay with just swearing around you more. 've also never called you stupid, though."

"I literally just said—"

"And I said I didn't. Geez, Lots. We've already established I can't lie. Try to keep up." Faith sighs. "I think it still definitely means at least some kind of unintelligence when I say it about people," she admits. "So I know for a fact there's no way I've ever been able to say it about you."

"But—" I sputter. "I *know* you've—"

"I mean, I've probably called some of your ideas stupid," she acknowledges. "And your belongings. Like, these headphones? Stupid colour. Extremely annoying. If I buy my own, they'll be as different from these as possible. You're obviously smart though, so I wouldn't have been able to call you that." Faith says it in the same way she says everything: like it's such a given that it's ridiculously redundant and inconvenient that I'm making her explain it at all.

"I can't read," I remind her.

"I'm not overly invested in world literacy or anything, Lots. Believe it or not, your inability to read has basically no impact on my quality of—"

"The intelligence definition," I try to explain. I obviously hadn't wanted her to double down and list off all the ways I actually am stupid, but her pretending that there aren't any is somehow making me doubt my intelligence even more.

Faith rolls her eyes. "Congrats, you have like, one of the most common learning disabilities."

"I'm not dyslexic." Most sources report that twenty-five to forty-percent of ADHDers also have dyslexia, with others placing that statistic as high as fifty or sixty percent. Even only considering the low-bound there, though, that's a far larger likelihood than the five to ten percent chance estimated for the general population. But I've never been diagnosed with it.

"Oh," Faith looks genuinely confused for half a second, but it quickly disappears. "Guess I should've realized that if you were diagnosed, you would've been just as insufferable about that as all the other identity labels you never shut up about."

"Saying 'just as' is an excellent way of alluding to an insult without having to actually make one," I observe.

Faith's eyes widen, but she's quick to shift that expression into confidence as well. "Yeah. It took me a while to figure that one out, actually. If you were a faery, you'd probably be super impressed right now."

I snort.

"Anyway. Point is, struggling with something that people with one of the most common learning—"

"I'm still learning disabled," I correct her. "Technically. Or... depending on who you ask. I consider myself learning disabled, sometimes. ADHD isn't a learning disability, technically, but it's actually lumped in with them in a lot of resources. And my IEP treats the way it makes me worse at reading as a literacy disability which would fall under learning disabilities so... yeah. ADHD's more common than dyslexia, actually. I think. I'd have to double-check."

"Okay," Faith nods. "Right. So anyway—"

"And it's not that I'm saying I couldn't possibly *be* dyslexic," I amend. "Or that my struggles are as bad or the same as a dyslexic person's. I mean, it's come up, obviously. But since it's difficult to tell what's my ADHD and what isn't and the vague 'ADHD linked literacy difficulties' on my IEP get me pretty much all the same accomodations I'd get if I *was* diagnosed with dyslexia, it'd be a waste of time to try and pursue. But—"

"Geez, Lots, I'm trying to be nice."

"Oh." I frown, momentarily thrown. "Well," I roll my shoulders. "A nice person would've let me infodump my entire medical history so... ha."

Faith rolls her eyes. "If I thought being an expert at reading was the only way to prove you're not an idiot, then I'd be the stupid one. That's all I was trying to say. I think..." She sighs, leaning back to stare at the sky before finishing her sentence. "I know you're smart, obviously. I wouldn't have spent most of my afternoon practically running in circles if I didn't think you were smart enough for that to somehow be a good idea. Plus you literally just clocked me trying to twist my words. You're very clearly very smart."

Something in my chest tightens. I unwind and rewind my tangle. "Judging a person's value by their perceived intelligence at all is also ableist, actually. People aren't worth the things that they can do for others. Implying intelligence is somehow linked to—"

"Let me be nice, Lots!"

I bite my lip. "I don't think I know what to do with that," I admit. "It feels... weird. Plus, being nice to me isn't part of the plan, actually. In fact, you made it expressly clear that I'm supposed to keep hating you."

"Genuinely hurting people wasn't part of mine either, though," Faith mutters. "I fix my mistakes."

"Most children can read better than I can," I whisper.

Faith groans. "We're seriously still on that?" She sticks out her leg. "Look at my feet."

"I'm not into that. Even if I was, believe it or not, I don't think staring at your feet would fix any of my—"

"Shut up, Lots. Just..." She kicks her heels against the ground. "Look."

I do. Then, I frown. "Are those— have you been wearing water shoes all day?"

"You said there'd be running involved and I only brought these and my sneakers. I can't tie those."

"You outran me in *water shoes*?" I reiterate.

Faith blushes. "I think it's a changeling thing. That my fingers refuse to cooperate. I think... I mean technically my body wasn't supposed to be quite this shape, so that might make it hard to do things that require precision sometimes."

It doesn't *sound* like a changeling thing, but it's obvious that Faith needs to believe that it is, so I nod. "They make Velcro shoes, you know. I'm sure you could—"

"It's a lot less draining to risk someone noticing they're undone and divert their attention for a bit so they don't notice me not fixing them then masking an entire pair of shoes constantly."

"You could just... not do that?" I point out.

"No," Faith presses her tongue against her lip. "I can't."

And I realize. This is something she's insecure about. This is something she's insecure about, so when she noticed that I was feeling uncomfortable, she turned it around on herself to try and make me feel better. She's doing the exact same thing that I was trying to do.

I don't know what to do with that realization.

"Anyway," Faith says. "Obviously the majority of children can do that too. Probably way more than can read, actually. And that doesn't mean... I mean, I'm so smart that I've managed to trick a bunch of people into believing I'm a human for years."

I take a deep breath. "Thank you."

"For being bad at tying knots? I don't see how—"

"Faith." I gently bump her shoulder with mine. "Thank you."

She stares at me for a long moment. Her lips even part, so for half a second, I think she's about to accept my thanks. Then, her expression instantly reverts back to her blank default, and she flies to her feet. "Let's get over there, I guess," she mumbles. "Bracelets to hand out. We'd better umm... I'll go do that."

She leaves me alone. And more confused than ever.

July 25

My dearest Alice,

Everything continues 2 b terible & awfull.

Jk but also maybe actually not.

As part of the thing Im helping FH w shes been trying 2 get closer 2 are cabinmates and shes wierdly good at it? 2 good at it. It makes me uncomfortable. She eats w us evry day now & sines up 2 do stuff w ppl ON PURPOSE and even stayed up a few nights just to socialize. Its suspishus and I don't like it. Accept also I really really do which is even more suspishus and awful.

A series of questions 4 u 2 desifer.

1) *Being scared of & having a crush on some1 r both supposed 2 make your palms sweety. How do u know which is which?*
2) *Same question 4 increesed heartrate*
3) *Same question 4 atypical breatheing*
4) *If u find urself always acidently making eye-contact w some1 it must mean there looking at u a lot 2 right? What does that mean?*
5) *If some1s teknikly using u 4 help but also keeps hanging out alone w u whn ur not directly helping them does that mean they like u?*
6) *If ur teknikly helping some 1 w something & r pretty sure u cant stand them but also keep finding excooses 2 hang out w them whn ur not directly helping them w something does that mean you like them?*
7) *What does it mean whn u cant look some1 in the eye even if youve nevr had a problem w that w anyone else?*

8) *What does it mean if u felt someones hair agenst ur arm days ago but keep imagining the way it tikled evry time u let ur mind wander 2 far?*

(maybe I know the answer to those last 2 and am jst not ready 2 comfront them yet)

Talk at u soon (PLEASE hurry up and do smthn terible enuf 2 get sent home from camp so u can help me out here), Charlotte

Chapter 30

My very genetics reject the concept of plan-making.

ADHD has been associated with forgetfulness practically since it was first identified, but calling myself forgetful has never seemed that accurate. It's not that I'm not, necessarily, more that memory is often the least of my problems.

It's difficult to maintain an impressive working memory when your brain is jumping in a thousand different directions at once, but I'm actually exceptional at remembering things. It's just that I often only do it at the most inopportune times.

I know August is getting closer (though I can rarely guess the specific date without checking). I know that that means that I'm rapidly running out of time to turn our rag-tag group of less-than-athletic teenagers into a battle-ready war machine. I also know that I'm supposed to be planning out all the little steps that will get us there.

The issue is that I spend far more time remembering that I'm *supposed* to be constructing and abiding to a plan than actually *doing* any of that.

In my home life, I'd never be able to even begin to pull something like this off. Even plans that I'm looking forward to often result in me sitting in bed for hours at a time, feeling guilty about not starting whatever activity I'm excited about. And I'm far from excited about devoting yet another day to fixing Faith's problems.

(Or at least, I think that's right. I'm not so sure anymore.)

Being around other people doesn't make the dread of plan-making any easier to manage, but it does make it a lot more difficult to wrap myself up in a safe little executive dysfunction bubble and do nothing all day.

I've found that the best way to hold myself accountable is to involve as many people as possible in my plans and hope that my fear of letting them down will beat out my nervous system's rejection of productivity.

Having a changeling constantly breathing down my neck demanding to know what I'm planning on doing next (though I'd never tell her this, obviously) has actually been an excellent motivator.

Still, planning is not my strong suit, so I scatter half-baked games, drills, and team-building exercises throughout the week to try and save up all my true productivity for another big Friday activity. And then, I get Janine's permission to run it days in advance to make sure it all goes off without a hitch.

Involving Janine had seemed like the perfect idea ahead of time. If neither Faith nor her impending doom could snap me into serious action, then the notion of letting Janine down was my only remaining option. I would've needed counsellor assistance for this activity anyway, so it had seemed like a win-win.

But now she's here and watching and I'm supposed to try and get everyone to participate willingly and peacefully despite my less than stellar track record there so far, and suddenly asking for her help seems like the worst decision I could have possibly made.

"Okay!" I shake out my wrists, pacing at the entrance to the trail.

Since we worked mostly on defensive skills last week, today's big activity will focus on the offensive part of capture the flag. I got Janine to help me hide fifty coloured ping pong balls all along the path since we're not allowed in the forest without a partner and I wanted to make sure everyone had the chance to participate. Faith keeps reminding me that the fae will undoubtedly hide their pinnie in the most difficult yet rule-abiding location possible, so hopefully working on attention and retrieval skills will prepare us for that. I can't explain any of that, of course. Even if we got Janine in the cabin to enchant her, there's no way she would ever encourage any kind of camp versus camp battle, capture the flag or otherwise. Everyone's been briefed on not mentioning the fight overtly though, so we should be fine. Hopefully.

"I want to thank you all again for giving up your activity blocks to um... team build. Today." I shoot a glance at Janine and she nods in encouragement. "I've—*we've*," I correct, "hidden fifty ping pong balls!"

I hold one up for absolutely no reason because my brain's somehow decided that my cabinmates might not know what a ping pong ball looks like. I quickly slip it back into my pocket and rub my palms against my jeans.

"None of them are more than a foot off the path, but some of them are really well concealed, so make sure you're paying attention! Janine'll stay at this side, I'll go to the end of the hiding range to make sure no one gets confused and wanders too far, and you'll have an hour to find as many as you can! Feel free to work in teams and divide the balls amongst your baskets at the end, but whoever finds the most gets to keep the super special golden ping-pong ball forever! You have—"

Janine discreetly raises her hand. My stomach flips. I've literally spent the past half hour talking over the best way to introduce the activity with her and somehow still managed to skip a step.

"Any questions?"

No one provides any.

"Right!" I nod. "You have forty-five minutes then! On your marks, get set, go!"

I sprint off to take my place on the other end of the section of path we marked off. I don't think I start breathing again until I'm at my post, far from any prying eyes.

I've never enjoyed public speaking. I don't think any kid who grew up with a (potential) reading disability has ever enjoyed public speaking. So many of the earliest ways we're expected to demonstrate mastery of it involve reading words someone else wrote which was obviously always a nightmare for me, but even when I got a bit older and got to choose my own words, they always came out too fast or too loud or too flat. I get anxious and then I get anxious that people can tell that I'm anxious and then I'm suddenly flipping syllables and swapping out the end of one sentence for the beginning of another.

I know that explaining a game is nothing like delivering a speech. I know that the small remains of the Caribou cohort are far from a 'public'. But Janine is an adult and an authority figure and most importantly, an authority figure who's spent an immense amount of time trying to make me confident about all the things I'm terrible at, so her mere presence never fails to make everything feel a lot bigger.

I'm supposed to be watching my side of the path to try and assess how the game's going so that I can intervene and sneakily move a few balls to more visible locations if it seems like people are getting discouraged, but I spend at least the first third of the game so in my own head that I can't even manage to do that right. Luckily, it seems like most of my cabinmates decided to stick near the beginning of the path for a while. When I finally escape my brain enough to exist in the present, Faith's the only one nearby enough for me to effectively watch. Which is incredibly inconvenient because I've spent all week trying to let my eyes wander towards Faith as little as possible.

I watch her spot three balls in what can't possibly be longer than three seconds and immediately realize that I hadn't properly thought through even the one proper activity I did bother to plan this week. Faith has the obvious advantage. She's been as tight-lipped as ever about how her heightened senses work since we last talked about them, but her sight's clearly also impacted. At this point, I wouldn't be surprised to find out that she found some of the ping pong balls based off nothing but a slight change in airflow.

I watch Faith spot three balls. I know I do. I've been mentally chanting where each one is hidden to make sure I don't lose any, so when her neck shifts slightly, I instantly know which ones she's noticed. In the time it takes her to walk over to a bush and dislodge a blue ball from its branches, I watch her spot five more. But she just slips the single ball into her basket, straightens, and turns to me as if she's noticed me for the first time despite the fact that we both know she's probably aware of the exact position of every breathing thing in the trail. It's infuriating.

Her lips curve slightly. She tilts her head to the side. Despite her refusal to ever overtly thank me for them or to even admit that they're helpful, Faith's been wearing my spare headphones pretty much constantly and I hate how quickly she's made even those look like they belong with her. When I wear mine they always manage to get tangled in my hair, but Faith's just give hers more volume, as if each strand perfectly reshapes itself to spill over them. As smooth as ink.

"Hey, Lots." I hate that Faith refuses to give me anything to work with. I'm far from perfect at reading other people's tone, but at least there's normally enough there to give me something to occupy myself with attempting to decipher. Faith's words come out deceptively flat. Her expression isn't even blank. Blankness itself can be telling. It's just nothing. Just a greeting and my name and absolutely nothing else behind it, which forces my brain to run through every possible thing that could have been. The Faith of last summer would have found some subtle way to get under my skin. The Faith of a few years ago would have tried her best to insult or enrage me. The Faith who *should* be trying to suck up to me right now would have thanked me or complimented my hiding spots or done at least *something*.

But this one's just said "hey".

I do not like it when people's motives are unclear.

Then, before I can respond, she does something even more baffling. Faith turns around and leaves. At least seven balls that I *know* I saw her see abandoned between branches and under leaves. She wanders back into my section a few more times as the game goes on, but I only watch her grab a fraction of the balls I watch her notice.

She's up to something. Faith's always up to something and I've always been better at noticing that than most other people, but it's especially unnerving to realize that she's up to something now that we're supposed to be on the same team. She's a terrible co-conspirator.

My cabinmates do better than expected and we meet at the entrance of the trail a few minutes before the forty-five minutes are up after Janine declares all the balls found. I was too busy puzzling over Faith to pay attention to the actual gameplay, but it must have gone well because Janine pulls me aside while everyone's counting up their balls and whispers, "This was a great idea, Charlotte!"

I blush. My chest feels warm, but it's a good warm. I think. "Thank you."

"I'm thinking I might actually adapt it and run it again for some of the other cohorts? Would you want to help with that?"

I bite my cheek. "Sure. Of course. Sounds fun." I've been helping pseudo-CIT more and more every day now and still had enough time to pull today together, so taking on more responsibility should be fine. I do well when I'm productive anyway. If I don't have enough time to think, then I don't have enough time to fall into dysfunction.

"Perfect!" Janine smiles. "I'm really proud of you, Charlotte. It's great you've been finding so many innovative ways to take on initiative."

I beam. My throat abruptly feels so thick that I forget how to respond. Luckily, Janine's attention's already moved elsewhere.

"Do we have a winner?"

"Morgan got seventeen!" Gator announces. Morgan is not the kind of person who announces her victories.

"Excellent!" Janine applauds. "Then this," she dramatically pulls a sloppily spray-painted ping pong ball out of her fanny pack. "Is for you."

Morgan blushes as everyone claps and slips the trophy into her pocket. She catches my eye and mouths an over-dramatic, "save me!"

I laugh and jog to her side to envelope her in a hug.

The game might have been distressing for me, but as we walk back to the cabin, it at least seems like everyone else had a good time. I nod and smile and pretend I'm paying attention as people brag about their most difficult finds and joke about the balls that they passed by countless times before finally spotting. I laugh when Van lightly teases Faith for only finding two despite apparently swearing up and down that this would be easy for her, because over the course of this past week, Faith has somehow become the kind of person that Van lightly teases.

But mostly, I'm focused on the fact that Faith clearly lost on purpose.

It was a smart move. If I'd had the foresight to realize that her enhanced perception would make it too easy for her to win, I would've advised her to do exactly that to boost everyone else's morale.

I wait for her to reveal that she intentionally lost for everyone else's benefit. The only way any of this makes sense to me is if it was part of her plan to make the rest of our cabinmates like her. But when asked about how she could've possibly done so poorly, Faith just feigns embarrassment and shakes her head in supposed shame.

Very little about Faith Harris has ever made sense to me and I've already learned several things this summer that have completely shaken my outlook on the world, but Faith doing something nice in secret—Faith doing *multiple* somethings nice this summer and then not holding it over anyone's head—is so earth-shattering that I have no idea how I'm supposed to proceed.

Chapter 31

Since I'm not particularly looking forward to waking up to a nightmare hellscape again any time soon, I connect my headphones to my phone, type out a message, and turn on the screen reader.

Meeting at 11pm.

I watch Faith's bunk carefully, but she doesn't react.

If your hearing this say code word tomato to confirm. I even take the time to click through all the spell-check suggestions before getting the reader to run through that second one because I'm incredibly considerate and accommodating. And possibly because I'm still a lot more insecure about typos with Faith, but mostly that first thing.

Slowly, Faith rolls over to face me. "Good night, Lots," she sighs.

My skin feels too warm. I understand that tomato might not have been the easiest code word to seamlessly integrate into conversation, but addressing me directly is infinitely worse. I can practically feel everyone wondering why she said it. I pull my blanket up as high as I can get it without making it too obvious that I'm trying to hide from the rest of the universe, close my eyes to pretend that my heart rate is anywhere near resting, and wait until eleven.

Faith has permission to touch me without announcing it first if doing so is necessary for a nighttime meeting. She hasn't done that yet, though, because Faith Harris is annoyingly, paradoxically careful about other people's boundaries.

Tonight, I make sure to stay awake so I can physically watch her climb up my ladder to collect me. There's something about awakening to Faith and her story-coated hair leaning over me that makes it exceptionally difficult to regulate my breathing.

Wordlessly, she holds out a palm, waits for me to take it, and we awkwardly descend back down the ladder together. I'm the one who called the meeting, but I haven't figured out how to put my thoughts to words quite yet, so she's the one who talks first once we're hidden away beneath the trees.

"Today went well." Faith slips her headphones off her ears and lets them rest around her neck. She does that a lot when we're in or near forests. I wonder if the sound of nature entices the fae part of her brain. She dusts off a stump and sits down on it. She's done no such dusting for me, so I'm forced to sit down on the forest floor to keep our hands conjoined. "Finding the actual flag'll probably be the hardest part. That was a really smart idea."

She's been doing that a lot, recently. Making a point of calling all my ideas 'smart'. I am deeply uncomfortable with how warm it makes my skin.

I have a complex with being perceived as intelligent. I hate that I have one because I know it's spurred by internalized ableism and I don't like having to consider that I could be harbouring *any* form of ableist ideology, but I still have to admit that I have one. I don't even think that's why it keeps affecting me, though.

Faith's been casually mentioning how smart I am ever since we talked about it, not because she's suddenly realized that I'm a genius, but because she knows that I don't think I am. Despite her making it extremely clear that she has no intention of trying to endear herself to me, she's going out of her way to subtly try and boost my confidence. Which is, annoyingly, endearing. And completely antithetical to my mental image of her.

I do not like having to change my mental images of things.

Faith frowns. "What'd I do this time?"

I suck on my lip. "Nothing."

"Felt it, though," she insists. "Your attention spiked again. What'd I—"

"Are you nice?" I blurt. It's far blunter than all the speeches I'd been planning out, but it'll have to suffice.

Faith laughs. *Actually* laughs. Loud and long and nasally. I think it surprises us both.

"No." She quickly pulls her tone back to flat. "Definitely not."

I slip my tangle into my free hand and try to collect my thoughts. "You lost today. Like, it would have actually been difficult for anyone to do worse than you."

"Maybe I just—"

"I saw you see them! I saw you take more than two!"

"You might've—"

"Sunny found fourteen." I try to look right at her, but she doesn't react. "Janine was worried that long of an attention based activity would be too difficult for her, so we gave her aid extras to plant in case she didn't find any to make sure she wouldn't feel left out when we counted them up. Somehow, she ended up with fourteen."

"Good for her," Faith shrugs.

"Faith!"

She sighs. "What do you want me to say here, Lots?"

"That you're terrible," I admit. "That you're terrible and that you've been pretending not to be these last few weeks as part of some secret, nefarious plan that I haven't quite figured out yet. That you lost on purpose. Not because you didn't want anyone else to have to get last, but because it somehow now means we all owe you our souls for the rest of eternity."

Faith cocks her head to the side. "You *want* me to steal your souls?"

"I don't know!" I realize my arm is flailing only when hers jerks against it. I do my best to calm down, but that's a lot more difficult to do when I can't do anything to keep that hand busy without pulling her along with me. "You just can't be nice! You— are you? In your home life? Are... that's where you get positive attention from, right? I told myself it was all just pretty privilege but... I *need* it to all be pretty privilege, actually. Tell me—"

Faith smiles lopsidedly. "You think I'm pretty?" she teases.

"Faith!" I exclaim. Luckily, I'm too worked up for any actual embarrassment. "That's not... You can't be nice! Because if you're nice then this has to be my fault and if this is my fault then I might have ruined a nice person's life over a fucking binder you didn't even steal!"

Faith sucks on her teeth. She takes so long to respond that I almost give up on waiting. "I'm not nice," she says quietly.

"But even saying that's you trying to make me feel better! Which just means you actually might be—"

"Not if I can't lie about it," Faith stops me. Her voice is low and quiet. She must have forgotten that my senses don't work the same way hers do. "I'm not a good person, Lots. You have nothing to worry about."

"Good," I take a deep breath. "That's excellent." My eyes widen. "Not that I'm gonna start helping less or anything. I'm still trying. Just as hard."

"I know," Faith nods. "Of course you are."

I clear my throat. I search for literally any way to change the topic.

"Janine said today went well," I fill Faith in. "She's going to have me rerun it with a bunch of the other cohorts next week."

Faith sighs. "You shouldn't be wasting your time on—"

"Helping people's never a waste," I interrupt her. "In fact, you're very, very lucky that I'm so devoted to it."

Faith groans, rolling her eyes. "Right. Forgot you're in love with Janine or something."

"Just because I'm pan doesn't mean I'm in love with every woman I come across!" I scoff. "You'd never say that about a straight person, you know. It's queerphobic. If I saw you talking to a guy counselor, I'd never just assume—"

"You think I like guys?" The corners of Faith's lips curl in a way that tells me I'm definitely wrong.

"That's irrelevant," I wave her off with my tangle. It's extremely relevant, actually, but for some reason it suddenly feels vital that I don't find out anything else about what Faith does and doesn't like right now. "Queer people can be homophobic too, obviously, so—"

"I'm a lesbian," she says. "Some would say that makes me twice as gay as you, actually."

"That's—acting like bi and pan people are half gay is extremely reductive! You can't just—" I stop when I finally notice that Faith looks entirely too pleased with herself. "You're doing that on purpose!" I swat at her knee with our shared hand. Involving her in hitting herself feels more cathartic, somehow. "You're trying to piss me off!"

"It's just so fun," she grins.

I roll my eyes. "I normally don't assume people's sexualities," I realize. "That's also queerphobic. It's normally based off of stereotypes or assuming that straight's the default. How... why was I so sure you were straight?"

Faith shrugs. "Over half our cabin's some kind of queer. You're obsessed with identity politics. Felt like an easy way to keep you disliking me."

"That's not—I don't hate straight people!"

"Possibly," she acknowledges, "but you're also way more willing to assume you'll get along with people when you know they're queer."

"That's not—that is a completely normal human phenomenon," I rationalize. "We seek out people who remind us of ourselves and are more likely to relate to our experience. If... I might have a few subconscious biases, but so does everyone. It doesn't make me a bad person if... I'm not a bad person just because I get more excited about meeting other queer people."

"What?" Faith frowns. "Yeah, obviously. I wasn't saying you suck, just answering your question."

"Okay." I nod. "Right. Yes. Of course. But just for the record, I wouldn't—"

"I know you're a good person, Lots," Faith rolls her eyes. "No need to keep reminding anyone."

Because she knows all the things that make me the most insecure, and she's actively trying to soothe them. Which is confusing. And terrible.

"We should umm... strategize!" I decide. "For the battle. Have you come up with any magical ways we can improve our chances?"

Faith's expression darkens. "Not since last time you asked. Or the time before that."

"Right." I pop a charm into my mouth to try and help myself think. "Well, there could still be—"

"If I try to use anything from Faerie, they might think it's smart, but they'd almost definitely cut me off immediately and start trying to find ways that they can cheat too. It won't help."

"We don't have to hide a flag in bounds," I remind her.

"Then how long until our team forfeits?"

"That's not going to happen," I lie. "We could—"

Faith's head snaps towards camp. She flies to her feet, awkwardly jerking me up alongside her via our clasped hands. "Faith?" My pulse spikes. "Did something happen? Are you—"

"Someone's awake."

I stare. "Can you hear that all the way from here?"

"No, they're—" she releases my hand and shakes out her palm before shoving it into her pocket. "I'm getting attention from someone again. Someone must have noticed you're gone."

"Or they noticed you were."

She smiles tightly. "People don't notice when I go missing. Probably realized your bed's empty then looked around to see who else's is. We should get back before they send a search party."

"Right." I nod, starting off towards camp. "Good idea. We could..." I hold out my hand. "If you make us fade away again, could that—"

Faith shakes her head. "It won't hold if they're already paying this much attention to you. Not much left to discuss anyway."

"Right."

We walk in silence for a while. As we do, I think through our conversation.

"Faith." I stop moving to look at her.

She ignores me. "Trying to hurry back, Lots. Don't—"

"I notice, don't I? When you're missing? I mean, I have an entire attention-based disability, but somehow... I've always noticed."

She slows for half a second, turning to watch me in the moonlight. "Yeah." She licks her lips. "Yeah, you..." She shakes out her shoulders then turns back around. "Let's go."

Chapter 32

In hindsight, I should have known that Morgan'd be the one to notice that I was missing. We return to the cabin to find her sitting up in her bunk, face illuminated slightly as she frantically types on her phone.

I'm immediately overcome with guilt. I should have known she'd worry. I should have figured out a way to explain my mysterious nighttime absences weeks ago. I've been keeping so many secrets from her this summer that they're getting impossible to manage.

Right now I have to be in damage control mode, so I make myself smile, hold a finger to my lip, and tiptoe over to sit down beside her. Faith breezes past me to her bunk and disappears into the darkness.

"Hey," I whisper, slowly lowering myself onto the mattress. All sound feels catastrophic right now. I wince as the springs squeak. "Did you need me for something? Did you—"

"Faith," she whispers.

I wince. "Yes, right. We umm... strategy meeting. We were talking game day strategy and trying to plan out activities and... we figured we'd step out so we wouldn't wake anyone."

"Midnight," Morgan calls me out.

I shrug. "I had a good idea. Didn't want to forget it before the morning." I kiss her head then immediately become far too aware that I'm actively trying to manipulate my best friend. My stomach rolls. "Sorry," I wince. "Sorry, that's not..." A floorboard creaks somewhere. I jump. "Can we talk in the morning? I don't want to wake anyone."

Morgan smiles, grabbing my hand and pulling me down to lie beside her. "Love you," she curls up beside me.

For the first time in years, I hesitate before wrapping my arm around her. I swallow, trying to clear the lump in my throat. "Love you too," I whisper.

Chapter 33

"Lots and I are going to go have a secret meeting!" Morgan stands up to announce the moment she's done her breakfast the next morning.

I, for my part, was intentionally eating as slowly as possible to try and keep said meeting from arriving.

Gator raises their hand and waits for Morgan to nod in acknowledgement before pointing out, "it's not secret if you announce it."

"Except it will be," Morgan bounces on her toes. "Because you're all going to very respectfully keep your distance and refrain from interrupting us now that you know about it, right?" She waits for everyone to nod before giggling and clapping to herself. "Excellent. Lots?" She extends a hand towards me.

I swallow, risk one quick look at Faith (whose gaze seems to be attempting to convey 'tell her anything and I'll kill you', but I like to think that we've made enough progress by now that if she does end up following through on that, she'll at least be gentle about it), and let Morgan drag me to an empty picnic table at the edge of the field.

"So?" She sits down across from me and rests her clasped hands in the centre of the table, staring at me expectantly.

I take a deep breath. 'Breakfast was good." I attempt to stall. "The eggs could've been a bit less runny, but—"

"Are you dating Faith?"

My eyes widen. "Absolutely not! Why would—"

Morgan taps her fingers together, eyes drifting up to the clouds. "I haven't said anything about Brain and Van asking to have the cabin to themselves. If you're sneaking out at night to have forest sex, it'd be more hygienic to—"

"Why does everyone keep thinking I'm having sex with Faith!"

Morgan frowns. "Who else—"

"No one," I quickly stop her. Because I'm a terrible liar. "Or... Alice. We were texting about this summer and—"

"Alice doesn't have her phone with her."

"Right, no. Of course not. I meant... before this summer she said something about it then I've been texting her during— the point is no. Absolutely not. Never in a million years."

The truth is, I'm always slightly baffled every time I remember that people our age *are* having sex. It's not something I'd ever voice, of course. Disabled people are ridiculously desexualized so admitting that I also can't comprehend anyone doing that would feed into several different harmful biases. That's not because I'm autistic though, it's because I'm sixteen. I've had exactly one non-strictly platonic kiss my entire life (though it was with Morgan and purely done to try and see if there was any merit to everyone around us assuming we were a couple, so I'm not sure if that even counts as non-platonic) and even that seemed like more than enough excitement for now.

"I can't stand Faith, remember?" I continue. "Why would—"

"You've spent all summer saying we should all give her another chance."

"Right," I remember. "But—"

"And you spend a lot of time alone with her. Apparently even more than—"

"We're strategizing!"

Morgan blinks. "It's no big deal. We've all always thought it would happen eventually. You're always talking about how pretty she is and—"

"Pretty privilege is a real thing! It's important to make sure people are aware of how it might be influencing them!"

Morgan giggles. "I don't think you have to spend hours trying to find someone's Instagram account and even longer rambling about how pretty you think their hair is to prove that point, Lots."

"That's—" I suddenly and mortifyingly become aware of the fact that moving far enough to get privacy from our cabinmates might not be far enough to escape Faith's hearing. I quickly turn around, and sure enough, she's staring right at us, hand over her mouth and shoulders shaking slightly. She notices me looking and winks exactly once, which causes my stomach to do something that I'd rather not examine right now. Or ever. "Okay, new idea." I turn back to Morgan. "We should finish this conversation over text!"

Her eyes drift back towards mine. "You don't like to do that."

"Exactly!" I snap my fingers. "It'll help me practice."

"There's really not any situation where I'd need you to text instead of—"

"Let's practice!" I scramble to pull out my phone. If my face is flaming, Morgan at least isn't looking closely enough to notice.

> Me: Not sexing F. 4 the rekerd.
> Morgan: Okay.
> Me: Or kissing.
> Me: Or crushing.

Morgan's response takes a few minutes to come through. She's rewording things.

> Morgan: If you were, I'd want you to be able to tell me.

"Of course," I accidentally say out loud.

> Morgan: Not that you'd have to.
> Morgan: If you didn't want to.
> Me: Ud b the 1ˢᵗ or 2ⁿᵈ prsn id tell.

208

Morgan takes a deep breath. She looks up at me for half a moment before returning to her phone.

>   Morgan: *What were you doing last night, then?*

I hesitate. I'd been planning out lies all night, but now that I'm sitting across from her, they all feel impossible to deliver.

>   Me: *Stratiguysing. 4 real.*
>   Morgan: *At midnight?*

I type then delete and try again. I have to be careful with how close to the truth I get.

>   Me: *F's really nerviss abt it*
>   Me: *it's higher steaks than we made it seem*
>   Me: *I'm not aloud to tell u y*
>   Morgan: *Okay.*

I risk looking up at her. "Okay?"

"Sure." Morgan shrugs. "As long as you're okay."

I beam. I don't know why I let myself get so worked up. I have the single greatest, most understanding best friend on the planet.

I round the table to hug her shoulders. "Thank you," I say. "A lot."

She just nods, as if her acceptance was always a given. "And if you ever do want to ramble more about how pretty you think Faith is," Morgan gets up to return to our group. "I can still listen to that too." She pops up on her toes to kiss my cheek. "Friends let their friends stay in denial," she whispers.

"That's not— I never—"

Morgan giggles, jogging off to escape my reply.

I wait a beat before following her, noticing Faith watching me. I turn my head slightly to hide my mouth from anyone else.

"I think you're only slightly above average, actually," I mutter. Which is of course an excellent comeback.

Somewhere, I hear someone laugh.

July 29

My dearest Alice,

If every1 around us apparently thought u had a crush on the same person for almost a hole decade theres still a chans they could b wrong right?

Asking 4 a friend.
(the friend is me)

Talk at u soon,
Charlotte

Chapter 34

I've always found summers difficult to grab onto.

Time and its passage are a struggle for me to navigate on even the best of days, but summers exacerbate those issues tenfold. The days are too long and hot and unstructured to keep from bleeding into each other. There aren't as many deadlines to meet or big events to count down to, so my ability to track the days diminishes greatly.

There is, of course, *the* big deadline. August 31ᵗ: the second last day of camp and potentially the last day I'll ever see Faith on this plane of existence. The second last day I'll see her regardless of the outcome, actually. That's a very hard thing to forget, even if you are predisposed to forgetting.

But still, it feels far off enough that the days begin to bleed. Or maybe, I'm just too tired to staunch them.

Being alive is exhausting when your brain works the way mine does. My body doesn't do a lot of the things that it's supposed to do intuitively. I have to pour constant effort into following conversations or remembering what I should be doing or even just into staying in the present moment most of the time.

What abled people seem to constantly misunderstand about living with a disability is that just doing that—that simple act of living itself—makes it feel like the world is constantly pushing down upon you, waiting for you to crumble. My ability to function requires long stretches of what others might look at and call laziness because my body never *gets* to be lazy. The energy that I expend lying in bed all day might be an able-bodied person's baseline level of exhaustion after a full day of work.

This summer, lying around all day is no longer an option. I have a never-ending stream of activities to plan or to rework and rerun for the younger cohorts. When I'm not doing that, the counselors always find somewhere else I can be useful. In the rare moments I do get a second to myself, I consider hiding away in the cabin and staying perfectly still in my bed until someone else needs me for something, but I always feel too guilty to actually do that. This is my third last summer here. Since I've apparently told Morgan I'll do Leadership next year, it's also my last one as a normal camper. If I throw it away, I'll hate myself forever.

So, I socialize. And plan. And run activities and socialize more and plan even harder. I consider climbing up to my bunk to brainstorm lying down at least bi-hourly, but I know it's a trap. Once I stop moving, my body will come up with a million reasons that I shouldn't start again. I'm having the most productive summer of my entire life.

And everyone else loves it. I thought we all hated being pressured to do activities every summer, but maybe my friends just didn't like having to repeat the same ones over and over again. My games are custom-built for us. My cabinmates compliment each and every thing I do and provide suggestions and requests and I do my best to honour every single one of them because these are my friends and a lot of them are more disabled than me and I want them to have the best possible summer ever.

So, I socialize and plan and run activities and socialize more and plan even harder until it no longer feels like I'm doing any of it. Like I'm there listening to them laugh and play games and joke around and watching Faith Harris of all people managing to genuinely laugh and play games and joke alongside them, but *I'm* not there. Present physically, but not there. But I socialize and plan and run activities and socialize more and plan even harder anyway because my friends' happiness and my something's life hang in the balance, so it's the only option.

It's just one more month. I can get through one more month. A lot of people would be able to do this no problem.

Our next big Friday training day goes perfectly because I've put every single fiber of my being into ensuring that it'll go perfectly. Janine loves it and asks me to meet with her Monday to talk about how we can adapt it for the other cohorts because I've put every single fiber of my being into ensuring that she'll think

I'm doing a good job. Faith catches me alone as we walk back to the cabin to quietly inform me that she'll be collecting me again for another midnight meeting because I've been putting every single fiber of my being into ensuring she gets out of all this alright, and she probably wants to thank me.

Then, after walking past the camp boundary line in silence, she turns to face me. And instead of 'thank you' or 'you're incredible' or 'wow, seeing how good of a job you've done has miraculously made me realize that I'm actually a very nice, chill person who it'd be incredibly fine to have a maybe-crush on', Faith says "you need to stop wasting time doing shit for other people."

And I explode.

Chapter 35

"What's wrong with you!"

Faith transforms instantly. Her eyes go a little rounder. Her lips go a little too straight. "Lots," she starts. "I didn't—"

"You were supposed to thank me!" I scream. "You should've—"

She takes a step back. She begins to release my hand for half a second before thinking better of it and tightening her grip instead. "Okay," she says. "Thank you. I didn't—"

"No!" I stop her. "It's too late! It doesn't count if I have to ask, it's—" I can't find the sentence's end. I'm not sure there ever was one. I hit the side of my head to try and realign my thoughts.

"Lots," Faith repeats. "I was just—"

"You were just being terrible!" I finish for her. "Again! I'm... I've wasted my whole summer on this! I'm... I'm so tired! All the time! For you! I spend all afternoon coming up with an activity or running an activity or doing clean up because you fucked up something with someone and you're apparently incapable of fixing things yourself! Then you wake me up in the middle of the night anyway just to exhaust me more, then I have to get up early to help Janine or some other counsellor with—"

"You don't have to do that part, though. You—"

"I have to do everything!" I shriek. "All the time!" I jerk my arm so hard that this time, she finally does let go of me.

"Lots," Faith repeats. Again. It does nothing. Again.

"You don't get it!" I tell the entire forest. "I don't get to say no! When you're disabled, you don't get to say no!"

"That's not—"

"You don't get it!" I try to shake my brain again, but the wind tightens around my fist and holds it in place. I stare at Faith. Notice the fist clasped at her chest. "Let me go!" I try to pull my arm back in the other direction, but it won't move there either. "Let go of me!"

"I'm not..." she whispers. "I don't let myself hurt people."

"I *want* to hurt me! I'm—let me go!"

Faith shakes her head slightly. Her voice comes out hoarse. "I'm sorry."

I scream. I scream until it hurts too much to keep going. I press my fist against nothingness until the entire thing goes numb. Then, slowly, I let myself collapse to the forest floor.

Chapter 36

I can physically feel Faith watching me.

She walks around me in slow, wide circles, as if I'm some kind of dangerous creature that she's trying to figure out the safest angle to approach from. Or maybe, actually, as if I'm the prey.

I came undone. I've been doing such a good job not coming undone this summer, and yet I did it alone with her in the middle of the night.

Eventually, Faith gives up on pacing and sits down across from me.

"Are you okay?"

The thing that no one tells you about being disabled is that it's *hard*. Not the limitations of the disability itself, of course, (other people seem constantly aware of that), but the knowledge that you *are* disabled and that everything you do will always be in some way, shape, or form influenced by your disability. There is no such thing as a "good" disabled person, but I've been trying to be that my entire life. A good disabled person takes up space and knows that they're entitled to it and feels empowered instead of destroyed every time their disability manifests. A good disabled person would not sit atop dying leaves, desperately trying to scrape their breath back up their throat, feeling so incredibly ashamed that they've given in to their disability that it compresses all the air back down again. A good disabled person does not spend this much time hating the fact that they're disabled.

I turn away from Faith. I lean over until I'm lying down, trust the leaves to catch me (I don't feel whether or not they do. I don't feel much of anything right now), then curl my knees into my chest. Not for the added compression, but because I need to hide.

"Lots." Faith gets up to relocate my face and crouches down in front of it. "Are you okay?"

I am not okay. I am a wild thing—the kind of creature who screams at leaves and trees and insects.

The Good Disabled Person conquers every challenge. The Good Disabled Person is not supposed to feel this easily conquered.

"Lots," Faith repeats.

I don't respond.

She either sighs or breathes or whispers something that I can't quite catch. "Is there someone I'm supposed to go get? What—"

It's that—her eagerness to run away after I've spent over a month weathering her every outburst and demand—that snaps me back out of my head. "You don't get to leave," I say.

"Okay," she nods. "What—"

"Of course you'd try to do that! *Of course* you'd cause another problem and then try to run away and let someone else clean up your—"

"Lots," Faith stops me. She doesn't yell. *I'm* yelling, and yet the sound of my own name spoken as calmly and evenly as pretty much everything Faith's ever said conquers me once again. "I want to stay. Just thought you wouldn't want me to."

"Oh," I realize. "Well, I do."

"Well, okay."

Faith waits a beat before sighing and getting down on the ground. She presses her cheek onto the earth half a foot from mine, lying upside down so that her legs point out past my head.

"You're going to get dirt in your hair," I whisper. My voice catches as I do and I quickly decide that the wisest course of action is to never speak again.

"Don't care. Fuck the dirt."

We're both quiet; me because I've decided to be silent for the rest of eternity, Faith because I can't tell her what to do next. I can't swoop in and fix all her problems when I'm the one she has a problem with.

"Are you..." she tries anyway. "What was that—"

"I shouldn't have yelled." My eagerness to stop her from asking any further questions beats out my short-lived abstinence. "I forgot. About your hearing."

Faith shrugs the shoulder that isn't actively pinned against the floor. " 's fine. Someone gave me headphones." She taps them exactly twice. "Even if you didn't..." she sighs. "I've been making your life hell for weeks now, Lots. Longer, actually. You deserve to yell a bit."

I shake my head. "That wouldn't be right. Now that I know it's painful for you, I wouldn't be a good person if I—"

She tilts her face closer to mine. "If you need to yell at someone—right now or ever or especially right now—I'm very okay with that being me."

I suck on my lip. "That wouldn't be... I can't."

"You can, actually," Faith corrects. "Literally just did. I don't give a fuck about whether or not you've proven you're the best person in every single room, Lots. You deserve to make people uncomfortable too, sometimes."

I squeeze my eyes shut. I take a deep breath. And then, I scream directly in Faith Harris's face.

"Holy shit!" She rolls out of the way before jumping to her feet, wiping what could only be my spit off her nose.

"Sorry." I shake out my legs until they feel semi-solid again and force myself to stand. "Sorry, I didn't... in hindsight, I should have realized screaming that close to someone's face would—"

Then, something remarkable happens. I stop in my tracks (it isn't every day you get to be the sole witness to a never before seen phenomenon). Faith's eyes widen, her lips tug further upward than I'd previously thought her face was capable of moving, and she bursts into a wheezing, all-encompassing bough of laughter so powerful that it sends her back down to the ground.

All I can do is stare.

"I'm not—" even over a full minute later, when Faith tries to speak, she has to keep gasping to catch her breath. "I'm not making fun of you, Lots."

"I know." I back into the nearest tree and hesitantly sit back down.

"But your attention's..." she gestures vaguely.

"You're laughing," I say. "You don't do that."

Faith rolls her eyes. Her chest is still heaving. Also, I should probably start looking at literally anything but her chest. "I laugh."

"Not around me."

"Well," Faith scoots towards me to share my tree-backrest. "Maybe you're just not that funny."

I smack her arm. "You're—"

"Hand please," she interrupts, holding out her palm. "One of us just screamed at the top of her lungs."

"You're so annoying!" I finish.

Faith beams. "I know." Then, she hesitates. "I didn't mean to... you're helpful, Lots. You've been so, so helpful. I didn't mean to... I'm grateful for that. Seriously."

I nod. "Okay."

"I didn't mean to make it sound like I wasn't," she sighs. "Repeat this to anyone and I'll... passive-aggression you extra hard, I guess. Or overt-aggression you. I don't know." She takes another long breath. "I think I'm just scared," she whispers. "I think... I know trying to get everyone to spend every second of every day preparing won't work if I can't explain *why* I need them to do that, but I think I still... spending more time training wouldn't even make sense. You have every right to spend your spare time helping whoever you want I just... I feel like I'm in an impossible situation right now. And I need that to be anyone's fault but mine."

"I don't want to spend my spare time helping other people," I admit. I throw a hand over my mouth slightly too late to catch the confession. "Not that—that sounds terrible," I correct.

"If people need help, obviously I'd—obviously I'm—" I sigh, giving up. Faith wants to dislike me. I'm supposed to want to dislike her. There's no point trying to lie my way into being better than I am. "I'm autistic," I say.

"Yes, Lots, I—"

"I am, though," I stop her.

Faith goes absolutely silent. Maybe she's worried I'll start screaming again.

"You act like it's annoying that I keep bringing it up or making everything about it or whatever, but everything is *always* going to be about it because when you're disabled, that's all anyone's ever going to let you be. I could cure cancer and that'd just make me the autistic girl who cured cancer, it's not..." I slip my tangle off my wrist. "I don't hate myself. I don't hate that I'm autistic or at least if I do, I'm trying really hard not to. But I loathe that that's all I'm ever going to be. Which means I have to be good. Which means if someone wants me to do something or try something or succeed at something then I *have* to do it, because I have to be good."

Faith sighs. "No one's entirely good, Lots."

"I have to be though," I inform her.

"You're prone to black and white thinking, right? So maybe—"

"I have to be!" I take a deep breath. I loosely slip my tangle around my free wrist for a moment to grab for my chewlery, but then I let it go. I need to be able to speak clearly right now. "Sorry," I mumble. "I didn't mean to... the volume."

Faith just squeezes my fingers.

I take a deep breath. "I know people are rarely ever entirely good or entirely bad," I admit. "In theory, I know that. Most of the time. But it's not... I don't get to be the in-betweens! If I was neurotypical, I could grow up and work some kind of unremarkable middle management job and have an unremarkable middle management partner and like, a dog and a house and that would be enough for most people. Not phenomenal or noteworthy, but enough. But when you're disabled that is always going to be the first thing people think about and that is always going to be devastating to other people. People like me can only ever grow up to be tragedies or success stories and being disabled and mediocre is always going to be treated as disastrous and I am not going to let myself be someone else's sob story! I need... I don't get to be the in-betweens!" I try to take a deep breath, but it doesn't work properly. "I'm able-bodied and fully verbal and not even technically learning disabled, depending on who you ask. I'm supposed to be the *textbook* for autism success stories and it makes me feel like shit every time I don't live up to that because like, is it wasted on me? I know so many amazing people with so many more struggles and limitations than I have and it's like... I know they'd do such a better job living in my body. Every time I say no to something or turn something down or can't get something quickly enough, I have to sit in that and know that I'm wasting opportunities that other neurodivergent kids would die for. And I know other people know it and I can physically hear it, sometimes. The eagerness that I'll try something new and love it and the disappointment when I can't or don't because yeah, I bring up my disabilities a lot, but other people are thinking about them *constantly* and are just too polite to mention them verbally. But I can still... that sucks! That sucks so much!"

I pause to pick at an acne scab on my chin. Faith stays quiet.

I sigh. "It's fine. It's whatever. I'll still—"

"I'm literally not the child my parents are supposed to have, Lots." Faith snaps a twig from the earth and tosses it in front of us. Most sources describe some form of kinship between the fae and nature, but I don't think I've ever seen anyone destroy as much of it as Faith Harris. "You don't have a monopoly on feeling like you're supposed to live up to all the things that someone else would've done if they were in your shoes. You know how I cope with it, though?" She stands up. Her hand's wrapped around mine, so I'm forced to do the same. She starts guiding me further away from camp and I'm so tired and emotionally worn out that I follow her almost mindlessly.

By the time it occurs to me that Faith might have paused after that question because she was looking for a genuine guess, she's already answering it herself. "I remind myself that there's just as big of a chance that she would've been a massive bitch."

I laugh in surprise.

"Probably an even bigger chance, actually," Faith adds. "Our parents are like, ridiculously wealthy. And very eager to spoil me at any given opportunity. Imagine a version of me that didn't have to also deal with having a body incompatible with this realm and the constant threat that if I don't get enough attention any given day, I might have to spend the entire next one feeling super sick and weak. She'd be a nightmare. The world's lucky we switched."

"Good job making all of my problems suddenly about you," I say.

Faith stops dragging me forward, pausing briefly to turn to face me. "Sorry, was that not—"

"No." I go to make myself smile to try and make her feel better then realize I already am. "I actually meant that. Responding to other people's problems with your own to show you empathize is actually incredibly common amongst autistic people. Not that you're autistic," I quickly correct. "I know you're not. Just... I am, and I appreciate it when people communicate in ways I can understand."

"Oh," Faith says. She clears her throat. "Right, um..." She pulls me a few steps further until we reach a small creek that I had no idea existed. Faerie senses can clearly be debilitating, but they definitely also have their perks.

Faith crosses her legs and sits down beside the water. I awkwardly crouch to keep our fingers locked together.

"Lie down, Lots," she instructs.

I scrunch up my nose. "It's probably muddy."

Faith sighs dramatically before reangling her arm to lie down first. "I promise I'll save enough magic to un-muddify any clothes you destroy." She tugs at my hand. "Lie down."

You don't realize how much moving from standing to lying forces you to rely on your arms until one of yours is busy connecting itself to someone else's. Eventually, I manage to lie down on my stomach and lean over the water's edge like Faith is, smearing my knees in what'll hopefully only be a small amount of mud in the process.

"Okay." Faith props up her chin with our joined hands and wraps the other around her necklace. After a bit more of her undistinguishable whispering, light somehow seemingly originating somewhere beneath the water illuminates our tiny patch of forest.

I frown. "Is this wasting—"

"No way I'm saving magic long enough to use it for anything more useful anyway," Faith stops me. "This is fine." She nods towards the water. "Look."

So, I look. At nothing. Any tiny fish or bugs that might've inhabited this section of the creek must have fled at the sudden unnatural light.

"What—"

As I speak, like something ripped out of every cliché horror movie ever made, my rippling reflection's mouth stays entirely still.

"Oh my god!" I instantly try to roll away from it. Since I can't get far with Faith holding onto me, all that accomplishes is smearing more mud all over my back.

As I try to catch my breath and search for any possible conceivable explanation for what I just saw, I hear Faith laughing to herself. It's a night of impossibilities.

I glare, kicking at her with my sneaker. I do it lightly, but I'm not trying to hurt her anyway. Just hopefully getting a bit of mud on her clothes as well.

"Sorry." Faith takes a moment to catch her breath for completely different reasons. "I should have—"

"Freaking out when your reflection doesn't move with you is a perfectly rational thing to do!" I remind her.

She just laughs again.

"Lots." Faith tugs me back towards the water once we've both calmed down. "Look again, okay? Should've warned you ahead of time, but no more surprises. Promise. I'm being helpful."

"By taking over my reflection!"

"By doing a little light illusion magic. Look." Faith pitches up her voice. "Hello, my name may or may not be Lots."

I watch in amazement as the reflection's mouth moves along with hers. Then, I process what she actually said. "That is not what I sound like!" I protest.

Faith shrugs. "Maybe it's what you would've. If you were someone else." She gestures at the falsified reflection. "This may or may not be Other Lots," she pauses to look at me. "Full disclosure, I'm terrible at metaphors and thought exercises. Kind of impossible to do those properly when you can't lie. But we're probably going to take turns having Other Lots tell us all the things she'd be worse at, if you were anyone other than you."

I frown. "You want to make me feel better by... insulting me?"

"It's not you though."

"It very much looks like me! The degree to which positive affirmations work is debatable study to study, but I'm sure almost everyone agrees that negative affirmations—"

Faith pitches up her voice again. "If I were another version of Lots, I probably wouldn't know so many occasionally useful facts about things," the reflection mime's her words. "Do positive affirmations work for you?" Faith returns to her normal tone.

"Well, no, but—"

"Let's try something else then. Your go."

I think about it. "If I were another version of me—" I turn to stare at Faith when the reflection copies me as well. "It looks like it's saying the things I'm saying."

She smiles slightly. "Yes, Lots. That's the whole point—"

"But with you I thought—" I take a deep breath, shaking myself out. "Okay, cool. Magic. Creepy. Or cool. Or..." I swallow. "If I were another version of me, I might not be as close to Alice—that's my sister—"

"Still very aware."

"As I am now." I look away from the water. "I really wouldn't like that, I think."

Faith nods. "If I were another version of Lots, I probably wouldn't force a far more powerful being to pinky promise not to be mean to my friends."

"You're not *that* much more powerful than me," I mutter.

"I'm actively manipulating your own reflection!"

Which is an excellent point that I truly hadn't considered, but I'm not about to admit that I was wrong. "Yeah, well you'll probably need like, a really long nap after. So it's not actually all that impressive."

Before she can insult me back, I return my focus to the water. "I'm other Lots. I probably don't have as many pink things as you do. Which would be very sad for everyone involved."

Faith rolls her eyes. "If I were another version of Lots, I probably wouldn't spend nearly as much time trying to help people I can't stand."

It feels like I'm supposed to say something to that, but things already feel far too serious, so I whisper, "I really do like Janine, actually."

It's the correct response, because Faith instantly says, "I'm going to kick you," (no probably, there are rarely probablies when she's warning me about attacks) then follows through on the threat.

We take turns controlling my reflection and gradually, I realize that they're not negative affirmations after all. Having a freaky mirror version of me list all the things they'd be terrible at is just a thinly veiled way of forcing me to list all the things I'd never want to change about myself. And to allow Faith to compliment me without having to admit that's what she's doing.

I typically resent being tricked, but I'm fine with it when it involves boosting my own ego.

Eventually, Faith clearly begins running out of magic and starts yawning at least once a minute, so I put a stop to things.

"We're good," I say instead of taking my next turn. "I... feel strangely better. Thanks."

"One more," she insists. She yawns again before continuing. "If I were another version of Lots." Her hold on the reflection begins to waver so she turns to face me instead. "I probably wouldn't even care about other people thinking I'm a good person. Or about whether or not I actually am one. If I was another version of Lots," she pauses to yawn again. "And I met the real one, I'd probably be amazed that someone that good could actually exist."

Faith's the one whose body's physically battling exhaustion, but I suddenly find myself incapable of speech.

"That's ummm... thanks for—"

"You know, if I were her," her tone and expression instantly go back to default. "Which would obviously be impossible."

I smile. "Let's get you back before you fall asleep all the way out here."

It's weird. You'd think making physical contact with someone you've sworn to dislike—someone who already made your heartbeat quicken and your skin heat with rage long before swearing to do that—would be uncomfortable, but I think the amount of hand-holding we've had to do to keep our meetings a secret has desensitized me to it. I wrap my hand around Faith's waist, she throws hers around my shoulder, and it feels more natural than anything I've ever done.

"Charlotte, wait," she stops me when we're about to recross the boundary line.

I wait. But then she doesn't say anything.

Faith sighs, scratching at the back of her head. "I umm... I know you're exhausted. I know you feel like you can never turn anything down and that fucking sucks and I really hope you learn to stop doing that soon, but I also... I know I'm supposed to tell you that you don't have to keep helping me but I really..." Her voice breaks. The rest of her sentence comes out a whisper. "I can't. I'm sorry, I just... I really, really can't."

I frown. "What? Obviously I didn't mean—I'm pretty sure you're the only person I'm usually not trying to impress at all, actually. I'm helping because you need help. There's a very big difference between assistant counselling and saving someone's life, Faith."

"Right." She looks away. "Obviously. Of course."

"And I also..." I bite my lip. "I said I couldn't imagine a world without you in it."

I don't say 'my world' even though it's the first thing that comes to mind, because that'd be ridiculous. Besides, even if we do win, Faith'll still be out of my life for good at the end of this summer. Even if I maybe don't want her to be, since faeries apparently have to keep their word on all promises, deals, and oaths. Not that I regret making her agree to that, obviously.

"I meant that," I continue. "You don't... you deserve to be okay. I really, really want you to be okay."

"That's umm..." Faith watches me a moment and I try so, so hard to read her expression, but I get absolutely nothing. Then, her tone shifts. "I'm the only person you're not trying to impress?" She checks.

"Usually, yeah."

"Cool. We're having a meeting with Janine tomorrow."

I panic. "That's not—"

"Lots." She looks right at me. "Trust me, okay? I wouldn't... I don't hurt people."

"You don't hurt people," I echo.

But then we reach the cabin, Faith disentangles herself from me and disappears up into her bunk, and I lay awake for hours. I replay each and every pseudo-insult she fed the other me at the creek. I fail to forget the feeling of my hand around her waist and realize that at some point, I've memorized the way her fingers feel wrapped around my own.

And I remember our deal. That one way or another, three weeks from now, I'll leave camp and then never see Faith Harris ever again.

She *can* hurt people. And no matter what, I know she's going to end up hurting me very, very much.

August 12

Alice,

*What does it mean whnn u cant stop thinking abt some1 even
whn ur 2 tired 2 think abt litrally anything else?*

Chapter 37

Janine normally only does admin stuff on the weekends since the staff switches out then, but she still agrees to let us stop by her office in the main building for a meeting after Faith texts her about it.

Because Janine's the best. And I've somehow decided it's a good idea to let Faith say something to her on my behalf. I've come a long way this summer. The me of a year ago would be losing her mind.

The me of the present is also losing her mind, but moreso over how Janine'll react. Faith's asked me to trust her. And she's had to put a *lot* of trust in me these last few weeks, so I'm trying to actually do that.

Mostly. I've thought up approximately two dozen questions to ask, but that has a lot more to do with me being me than Faith being untrustworthy, so I've kept them to myself.

"Alright, ladies!" Janine sweeps into the office. She's not wearing her camp clothes today, opting instead for a loose, bright, flower-speckled dress. Her hair's pulled up in a scrunchie. "What've you got for me?"

I should have insisted that Faith told me what this meeting was for last night. Trust aside, I should have realized that blindly following her lead would make me look ridiculous. What kind of person schedules a meeting without knowing what it's about?

My knee shakes against the floor so rapidly that I'm convinced it's all anyone'll be able to hear, but I'm the only one staring at it.

Faith leans back in her chair, stretching out her legs. "Lots doesn't want to help out with things as much this week. Or at all, maybe."

Janine frowns, looking between us. I'm normally the last person to go along with anything Faith proposes. "Is that what you wanted to tell me, Charlotte?" she checks.

"If that's okay," I say a little too quickly. I'm terrible at controlling my pace even when I'm not stressed. "If no one needs help. Or if— if anyone does it'd obviously be totally fine if—"

Faith groans dramatically. "She means yes. She just doesn't know how to say it because she thinks you're a half-decent counsellor or whatever, and she doesn't want to let you down."

"Was that you calling me half-decent, Faith?" Janine smiles.

"It was me saying Lots thinks you are," she deadpans. "Don't get a big head about it."

Janine looks forward to speak directly to me. I try very, very hard to make my leg stop shaking. "I wouldn't get mad at you for not wanting to do something, Charlotte," she says, because of course she wouldn't. I already knew that. That's never been the problem. "You can tell me yourself next time, okay? No big deal."

"Okay," I agree.

"She's lying," Faith says.

"Faith!" I spin to face her. Trusting Faith has historically always been a bad idea. I don't know what I'm doing. But when I look at her, her expression's entirely serious.

"Aren't you?" I feel her watching me.

And I am (of course I am), so I just shrug. Faith turns back to Janine. "Lots would probably want me to say it's not personal. She just doesn't like letting people down. But she doesn't give a shit about what I think, so for the rest of the summer, any and all favours or activity suggestions go through me first so she actually has a shot at saying no."

Janine nods. "Would that work for you, Charlotte?"

I don't know what the right answer is.

Faith sighs. "Lots. Is that going to help?"

I nod.

"Okay," Faith shrugs. "That's settled then. Do you want to do any camp assisting or activity prep or whatever this week?"

I don't let myself look at Janine. I don't want to watch her react. "No," I whisper. "I'm not— I don't— I know that's supposed to be fun or uplifting or fulfilling but it's just... it just makes me tired."

"Cool." Faith nods again. "Glad we sorted that out, then. You're not doing that."

"What about next year?" Janine checks.

I freeze. I watch Faith's brow crease. She doesn't know about the promises I've already made.

"I'm..." I lick my lips. Janine holds out another lemon lollipop and I instantly accept it. "I'll be fine by next year."

"Do you still want to do it?" she checks.

"Sure." I nod. "Of course."

Faith frowns. "What's happening next year?"

"I'm CITing with Morgan," I fill her in. "We're gonna do Leadership together. We have it all planned out."

Faith squints at me for a moment before sighing. "Go," she tells Janine.

"It's her office," I protest. "You can't just—"

But Janine's already on her way out the door. She smiles before closing it. "Holler if you need me."

We both nod.

"Lots." I can feel Faith looking at me. I can't bring myself to look at her. "You very obviously don't want to do Leadership."

"I told Morgan I would," I whisper.

"Then tell Morgan you won't. She's obsessed with you, I'm sure she'll—"

"Morgan's straight," I correct.

"Okay? And also very obviously in love with you? She's not gonna be pissed if you tell her you don't want to do something."

I take off my tangle. "I promised, though. I don't get to—"

"You're human. You can break those. Being able to and acting like you can't around me might be considered incredibly rude, actually."

"I didn't mean to—"

"Lots," Faith's voice softens. "Joking."

I take a long breath. I finish off the entire lollipop while I collect my thoughts. "Morgan's so smart," I say. "Like, so, so smart. Like I call her to explain concepts to me from classes she's never even taken. But I'm somehow in gen. ed and she's not which means once we graduate, I'm the only one of us with a shot at going to uni right away— which like, not a super big one because a lot of my grades are terrible, but that just makes it worse that I'm the one who can do that. I don't need a Leadership camp on my resume or a shot at getting a job here one day anywhere near as much as she does which isn't at all fair because she'd be so much better at most degree-requiring jobs than I'd ever be so it's not... even if she didn't like Leadership, she'd probably still make herself do it to have at least something to point to on resumes and applications and stuff."

"Okay," Faith says slowly, "but she very clearly likes it?"

I shake my head. "That's not the point, though. She'd have to do it which means it's not fair if I don't have to do it. And I mean—it *should* be easier for me. There are so many more barriers there for her and I'm technically capable of doing it so how can I... how do I go 'hey I actually don't want to do this at all, actually, just because it sounds less fun than relaxing all summer?"

"Probably by going 'hey I actually don't want to do this at all, actually, just because it sounds less fun than relaxing all summer?" Faith suggests.

I swat at her. "I'm serious."

"Me too." She shrugs. "Morgan's cool. She'd be fine with that."

"But *I* wouldn't be."

Faith sighs. "What if I say maybe for now then, okay? Or you can, if you want to—"

"I definitely don't want to."

"Okay." She nods. "At some point, you've got to talk to Morgan about this, though."

I chew my cheek. "Yeah," I admit. "I know."

We summon Janine back in, Faith gives her my non-answer, then we head back to the cabin.

"Pretty smart," I say, because it feels like I'm supposed to be saying something. "Putting yourself in charge of whether or not I spend any time working on stuff that doesn't benefit you."

It was the wrong choice. Faith bristles. "If you don't trust me to tell her what you actually want, you can go back in and say that."

"I didn't mean—"

"You did, though," she speeds up. "That's fine. Probably for the best."

"Faith." I catch her arm.

Slowly, she turns to face me.

"Thank you," I try again. "Seriously. This'll be really, really helpful, okay? I just didn't know if you'd want me acknowledging that. Sworn hatred, and all."

"Sworn disliking," she whispers.

"Disliking, then," I nod.

Faith sighs. "I don't know what I want," she admits. "I just..." she kicks at the dirt. Twists her hair around her fists. "Don't visibly react," she warns me. "That'll... I don't think I'd be able to deal with that right now."

"Got it," I nod. "I can do that."

She sighs again. "I think you're okay, Lots. Alright?" She looks anywhere but at me as she speaks. "I think... I want you to be okay. Which feels gross and icky and has been incredibly distressing and unnerving," she picks up volume again. "But you know, whatever." She gestures vaguely. "Not like I need to not care about you to keep siphoning. Just need you to keep getting annoyed with me. I'm... you're... you're a really hard person to not like, Lots."

I'm not supposed to be reacting but my eyes instantly try to widen and my lips instantly try to grin so I put every ounce of energy I can into trying to squash that all down. "That's..."

"It's fine." Faith spins on her heels and starts walking again. "I can physically feel that making you uncomfortable. 's not like I'm gonna abruptly start acting differently or anything. I'm annoying to the people I tolerate too. Just... I'm probably gone for good in a few weeks, yeah? You're not always gonna be able to rely on having someone you don't give a shit about around to deliver disappointments on your behalf. Try to get a little better at being selfish."

"Faith," I swallow. "That umm..."

"I really don't want to talk about it," she stops me. "Just... it's fine. Pretend I didn't say anything. You're doing great."

I follow her back to the cabin, bite my tongue, and remind myself that she needs me to keep disliking her.

August 13

My dearest Alice,

Wht does it mean whn some1 tells u they fisicly cant stop themselves frm liking u?

Wht r u suposed to do if u promised thm u wouldn't like thm eether but r pretty sure ur in the same bote?

And also how much harder is that if u think u might have a crush on thm? And also how tf do I know whn I have a crush on some1?

Talk at u soon,
Charlotte

Chapter 38

Faith Harris is an incredibly difficult person to not like once you've begun to get to know her.

She refuses to ever admit that she's trying to help you or make you comfortable outright, which unfortunately makes it a lot more difficult to try and assign her ulterior motives.

I like Faith. And she finds me tolerable, which seems like Faith-speak for liking someone too. And there's nothing I can do about it because the moment she finds out that I actually like her, she'll jump straight back to hating me.

Let alone if she finds out that I'm becoming increasingly confident that I might like-like her, but that's a problem that I'm not prepared to even begin to grapple with.

I insist on still running most of the drills and activities we space out throughout the week since I've fallen into a pretty good rhythm with those, but she occasionally takes over the ones we've already run before. And everyone lets her because *everyone's* starting to like Faith. She's started genuinely joining us for meals and no longer goes to hide away every activity time. If you saw how seamlessly she talks to or laughs with or even just exists around the rest of the Caribou Crew, it'd be difficult to remember that she only recently became an integrated part of it.

Everyone's starting to like Faith. And in a few weeks, one way or another, I'll be taking her away from them.

During our next Friday block where I'd normally organize a longer activity, Faith kicks everyone out of the cabin and declares she'll be doing it herself. I'm expecting to re-enter to overturned bunk beds and elaborate, rigorous obstacle courses, but when she comes to collect us from the recreation field, I'm met instead with streamers, copious amounts of popcorn, eight folding chairs, and a borrowed projector cued up to play a movie against the wall. As everyone rushes to stock up on the best snacks, I pull Faith aside.

"This doesn't seem very capture the flag centric," I whisper.

She rolls her eyes, but her cheeks flush pink. "Something, something, benefits of team morale boosters," she mutters. "Figured you deserved a break for once."

I'm filled with the inexplicable impulse to hug her, but since I'm not allowed to do that, I suck on my chewlery instead and search for some other way of telling her how much I appreciate this.

"I ummm... last week. When I freaked out. You tried really hard to make me feel better, but I didn't..." I wring my fingers together. "I *know* you're better than the other you. Your real life friends are all probably really, really glad they get to have you in their lives."

Faith fixes her hair. "Okay," she says. "Thanks." She nods at where Morgan's already claimed a seat in the back row. She's put her snacks on the chair beside it to save it for me even though everyone already knows that that's where I'll be sitting. "Talked to her yet?"

"Soon."

"Today."

I swallow. "Today, probably."

It'd feel wrong to let Faith down in yet another way, so I ask Morgan to go on a quick walk with me between movies. I might trust Faith now, but I'm still not comfortable with someone being able to listen in on every conversation I have near the cabin. Once I've decided we're far enough, I stop walking. Morgan's been gushing about the movie night the whole way, but I've retained exactly none of it.

"Lots?" She taps my shoulder with hers, realizes I haven't been listening, and doesn't so much as sigh. Because she's wonderful. "I was saying you've done a really good job, with team building stuff. I can't believe—"

"I might not want to do Leadership next year!" I exclaim. If I don't say it right away, I know I never will.

Morgan frowns. She takes a step back. Her hands move towards the pocket she keeps her cue cards in because I haven't even started explaining yet and she knows I'm about to make her anxious. "What?"

"I'm not..." I stretch my tangle to the point just before breaking then start weaving it through my fingers. "I don't want to, I think."

"Oh," she says. Then, she shakes out her neck. "Well you might though, right? It's been a lot of fun. And you'd be great at it. I was actually just saying—"

"I don't want to!" I accidentally scream.

Morgan starts to hum beneath her breath. I feel like shit.

"Morg." I hold out my hands and she takes them instantly. I try to count out the way her fingers tap against my knuckles to guide my way back to tranquility, but right now, they're just a reminder of all the ways that I'm letting her down.

Morgan leans forward to kiss my head. "Okay," she says. She shifts my fists into one of her palms and wraps the other around my back to pull me closer to her. "Okay, that's fine. Why'd you change your mind?"

I don't know how to say it. That my mind was made up years ago. That nothing about leadership seems scary or intimidating or impossible to me beyond the fact that I just don't want to do it. "I don't think I'd be good at it," I mumble, hating myself for the lie even as I deliver it. "It's probably not a good idea."

"Oh!" Morgan giggles. "You'll be fine, Lots. You're perfect. You've practically been practicing for it all summer and you've loved that, right?"

"Right," I echo. My mouth feels numb.

Morgan pulls away. "After the Antelope game, I'm sure you'll feel way more confident."

"Right," I repeat.

She kisses my cheek. "I think you can do anything you put your mind to," she says. "But especially this. You'll be great at this."

I make myself smile. "We should probably get back before they start the next movie without us."

Maybe Morgan's right. Maybe I'll feel so good after winning that I'll have proved to myself that Leadership's the perfect fit for me after all.

Chapter 39

When I have a deadline approaching, time only ever seems to move impossibly quickly or painfully slowly. Normally, whichever speed'll be the most inconvenient.

Summers feel like they get shorter and shorter every year, but now that I've realized that I desperately don't want Faith to leave at the end of this one (whether to go back home or to go spend a century in a torturous pocket dimension), it seems to speed up even more. In the blink of an eye, it's a week later and we only have seven days left until the end of camp. Six days until the big battle. And even still, I likely wouldn't have noticed how little time's left until the day of the battle itself if something eventful didn't happen to mark it.

Last Friday we might've taken a break, but that just means that we have to work twice as hard this one. Faith and I plan an entire day of activities, just to cover our bases. Since the battle's on a Thursday, this is our last big Friday training day. I can afford to go a little overboard this time.

We've mostly planned out who'll be best on offense or defense, but we've decided to keep running activities as a group anyway, both for numbers reasons and since most of the skills they'll help with are transferable.

We're in the middle of a warmup game of camouflage when Faith loses it. It's Brain's turn to be 'it'. (She uses a horn instead of actually yelling out 'camouflage' because like most camp games, this one's incredibly easy to adapt for people's specific needs if you put more than two seconds of thought into it). The goal of camouflage is to hide from the counter then run from your hiding spot, high-five them, and find somewhere new to hide before they finish counting down and open their eyes. If they see you, you're out. If they don't, they start counting again but this time, you have one less second. We're surrounded by trees and only at the 17 second round so logically, it *should* be hard to find people right now. But when Brain doesn't spot anyone and sounds the horn to start the next round, Faith bursts into the clearing.

"You seriously couldn't see anyone?" she demands.

Brain just shrugs.

"There are six full-grown people hidden within a few feet of you! How the fuck are you supposed to find—"

"Fay," I rush to cut her off. I can't let her ruin this. Not when we're so close. "You can't—"

She whirls around at me. "None of you are good enough at this!" she screams. "You can't find *people*! How the fuck are you—"

"Stop yelling at people!" Van interjects.

"Shut up!"

I plant myself right in front of Faith. Mostly because I don't want anyone else to get there first. "Faith," I try again. "I know you're—"

"You don't!" she yells. "You don't know! You're not the one who has anything to lose next week! You're all hardly even trying! You're not—"

"We're trying." I put my hands on her arms, trying to will her to understand. "Just because something's easy for you doesn't mean it's easy for everyone else. Everyone's trying. If you keep yelling. You'll make it a lot harder to want to, though."

Faith sighs. She tugs herself out of my grip and wraps her arms around her chest. "Water break," she whispers. "I need..." She glances at Brain. "Sorry. I just need a second."

Brain nods in acknowledgement. Faith grabs her bag and stomps all the way back to the entrance of the trail. I ready myself for damage control as Gator gathers up the rest of our water bottles and deposits them in the middle of a slowly forming circle. I sit down.

Good you? Van signs to Brain.

She just shrugs. All things considered, she was probably the best person for Faith to temporarily lose it at. Brain's exceptionally good at not letting herself dwell on things that don't matter.

"Sorry," I say, because Faith's no longer here to be apologizing and that means that I'm supposed to be her spokesperson. "She's just... worked up. Big days coming up. She'd obviously never admit it, but I think she's really nervous."

No problem, Brain signs. I know she means it too, because Brain never lies for other people's benefit.

"We're not still supposed to lose, right?" Gator checks just as I remember that Faith can definitely hear everything we're saying. "We never checked back in on that."

"Whaaaat?" I make myself laugh. "Why would we do that?"

They frown. "Because you said we should."

I spin around to do something, but by the time I do, I've already forgotten what. I shake out my shoulders and turn back to face my friends. Sometimes having ADHD feels like a constant slew of preparing yourself for tasks and then forgetting what they are the moment you're supposed to execute them.

I take a few more sips of my water before standing up and clapping my hands. "Right then, let's get back to— where's Faith?"

"What?" Van signs.

"Where's Faith? Fay, I mean. Where's—"

It's exceptionally difficult to forget someone when you're in the middle of an entire day of activities you've planned out on their behalf. Even if they're trying really, really hard to make sure you do.

"She said she needed a second," Morgan reminds us all after a beat of awkward silence. "Maybe—"

Then, I catch it. Not sight of her, exactly, but of a patch of the path that suddenly feels impossible to look at. I think I might even spot a flash of black hair. "I need to..." I lower my water bottle. "Right," I say. "Sorry. I totally forgot that we're supposed to go have a umm... game strategy meeting. You guys keep running camouflage."

I jog off before Faith can disappear herself entirely again.

It's exceptionally difficult to follow someone who's using actual magic to keep themself from being seen. Faith's not invisible so much as she's impossible to look at. As I jog after where I'm pretty sure she's gone, I catch the occasional glimpse of her, but it feels like my body's physically rejecting it. Whenever I do spot a sign of her, my eyes start to water and my heart starts to race. My head turns away without me even being entirely conscious of it.

Whatever Faith's doing right now is a lot more powerful than her typical attempts at slipping away. It must be. I consider trying to mentally chant her name to keep myself from forgetting her entirely, but my brain is an ever-shifting maze of hallways and trap doors leading to absolutely nowhere, so I physically whisper it under my breath, just to be on the safe side.

"Faith, Faith, Faith, Faith, Faith," I mutter.

Once we're further away from the rest of camp, I let myself start to chant it louder, evolving into physically yelling it out every few seconds even though she obviously has no intention of responding. I'm worried I'll lose the trail entirely and then have to find my way back on my own, but then I take a few steps off the path where it looks like someone's left some kind of vague footprints in the grass and suddenly not paying attention to her's impossible.

Leaves, twigs, and small stones twirl in a spiral so rapid that it's almost impossible to pick out any individual object. At the vortex's center sits a single girl, knees pulled into her chest and long, dark hair spinning up into the wind.

Faith's turned herself into the eye of a tornado.

Chapter 40

There are still a good several feet between me and the whatever-that-is, but I jump back impulsively anyway. Faith's hair's dark enough that I can tell when her head shifts to face me, but everything else is too obscured for me to make out any kind of movement.

"It's not going to hurt you!" she screams over the wind. Her voice sounds too uneven. The pauses between her words sound too long. The whole world sounds too much like I've made Faith cry.

I put up my hands. As if tornado's give a shit about surrenders. "Okay."

"It doesn't hurt other people!"

"Okay," I repeat. There's not much else you can say when the girl you have a maybe-crush on becomes a mini natural disaster. "I know. I trust you."

"You should go!" Faith yells. "You should... leave me the fuck alone!"

I hesitate. There might not be a clear, correct way to handle this, but I'm fairly certain that running away would be the wrong one. I lick my lips. "I will!" I yell. I'm not sure how well super-human hearing holds up over what are presumably deafening winds. "If you tell me you want me to!"

Faith doesn't answer. That means that she can't.

I sit down, cross my legs, and watch her.

"I'm mad at you!" she announces.

I nod. "I know!" I yell back.

"I'm really, really mad at you!"

"That makes sense!" I acknowledge. I feel the air nip at my nose, but I don't let myself back up. "But if you let me—"

"I didn't threaten you!" Faith screams. "I made it so clear I wasn't going to! You could've just said no!"

"That's not—"

"I could've come up with something else! If you hadn't pretended you'd help, I might've... I deserved the chance to— what the fuck did I do to make you hate me this much!"

"Faith!" I fight to shout over her, pausing to glance around to make sure no one's come running after us. We're far away enough that we won't draw attention. Hopefully. "No one's actually planning on losing! We just... that was a misunderstanding. I can—"

"Stop lying to me!" her voice splinters. "You weren't supposed to actually hate me!" Faith keeps screaming even though her voice already sounds well past raw. "You're the one who said that! You said you'd never cared enough to actually hate me!"

I frown. "You made me promise to—"

"You promised not to like me! That's— I knew you were lying!" she says. "I could *hear* your heartbeat change every time I brought it up. But I still... you were supposed to be too nice to do something like this! You weren't supposed to be able to hate me enough to spend an entire summer trying to ruin my life!"

"That's not what's happening!" I try to explain. "I don't... no one hates you!"

"Liar!" she accuses.

"I'm not!"

"I can hear it! Even now, I could *hear* you get anxious when I said you were only supposed to dislike me!"

"That's not—"

"Stop lying to me!"

I might just be imagining it, but for half a second, the wind seems to engulf me. I'm suddenly freezing. When I blink and try to look at it more closely, though, it's still contained to Faith.

"You're doing it right now!" Faith's still yelling. "I can hear you freaking out! I can—"

"That's not what's—"

"You were just supposed to be annoyed!" she says. "You weren't supposed to hate me enough to—"

247

"I like you!" I scream. "Okay?" I pause to lick my lips. My entire mouth feels far too dry. "I like you so, so much that I'm actively sitting beside a mini active tornado and I'm less scared of that than saying this so yeah, maybe I seem stressed whenever you bring up me not liking you, but it's because I've been failing at that for weeks!"

Faith doesn't say anything. The storm rages on.

"Faith?"

She's completely silent.

I sniffle, swiping at my dampened eyes. "I'm sorry!" I yell. "That's why I didn't... I need you to know I tried really, really hard, okay? I need you to... you're so important to me! I know that's the whole problem, but it's not... you're so important to me and we're not gonna lose so you have nothing to worry about, but if something goes wrong, I swear I'm gonna think about you constantly, okay? I'll set calendar reminders and... hourly alarms, honestly, if that works better! But I'm pretty sure I won't even need them because I've been spending all summer trying really, really hard to not think about you, and it turns out I'm terrible at it! Like, completely, pathetically awful! So you have nothing to worry about, okay?"

I can barely see her at all anymore.

"And— and if we win," I continue. "*When* we win, you can just be a bit more dickish to some new person instead, okay? Because I don't... I can't! I know I said I would but I really, really don't think I'm ever gonna be able to go back to not liking you at this point and I'm so, so sorry but I just... I can't!"

I don't think I can see her at all, actually.

"Faith?" I hear my own voice crackle. "Say something? Please?"

I hear nothing but wind and then, quietly, "I want this to be over now."

"Okay." I jump to my feet. "Good. That's umm... assuming you mean the storm, I mean, that's good. Great. Why don't you umm... come out! Get mad at me face to face!"

"I want this to be over!" she repeats. "I want this to be done!"

"Okay!" I say. "How do you—"

"I want to calm down!" Faith screams. "Why can't I calm down!"

"Oh." I chew on my lip. "I umm... don't know."

"Fix it!" she demands. "Fucking fix me!"

"You never told me how!" I take my tangle all the way off and let myself pace. I need to think. "Alice— that's my sister—"

"Everyone knows!" Faith says.

"When I piss off Alice or someone else pisses her off or she's just genuinely sad," I push forward, "she absolutely doesn't want to deal with people! So she— when Alice is upset, I'm supposed to stay out of her way for a couple of hours and make sure our parents leave her alone!"

Faith just screams. It sounds more frustrated than pained though and from what I can see, it seems like none of the spinning objects are physically hitting her, so I continue. "And Morgan— you know Morgan, obviously." I take another step towards her. "When she's upset, she always wants to talk it over after, but she likes it when I just hug her in the moment until she's ready to do that. Or tackle her if she's like, full meltdown-level upset, but that one obviously doesn't work for most other people!"

"You're not fixing it!"

"I don't know how to!" I admit, I feel moisture on my cheeks even though I can't pinpoint when exactly I started crying. "I want to so badly! I spend so much time researching all the best ways strangers and psychologists say to help other people but that never... people don't work like that in the real world! You have to learn the exact way their exact brain reacts to each and every emotional stimulus and even then, sometimes they contradict themselves! I don't—" I try to make myself breathe. "I want to help so badly, but you never told me what to do when you're upset!"

"You think I know!"

I swallow. This time, I actually do breathe. Faith doesn't know what she needs and I don't know either, but I do know that she didn't want me to leave, so I stick with that. I sit down so close to her that I can physically feel the revolving air tugging at the hairs on my arms.

"I'm not—it's stolen magic," Faith eventually says. She must know I've moved closer because she's started just projecting her voice instead of screaming everything. "It's not naturally mine. I'm—I always get too tired to keep pulling it then it stops. Eventually."

Now that she's no longer yelling, it's so, so much easier to hear the tears in her voice.

"Okay!" I say. "That's good!"

"You can go," she says. "I'll be fine. Might be dangerous."

"Do you want me to leave?" I double-check.

She doesn't say anything.

I take another breath and try to settle in. "Sounds like I'm staying, then. You told me not to leave you alone and exhausted, remember? So I'm not doing that. Obviously."

Faith stops talking, switching to quiet sobbing and the occasional frustrated shriek.

I stop talking, switching to pretending I can't hear any of that.

Then, what could be anywhere from five to fifty minutes later, the air stops all at once. The stones fall first, giving me enough warning to spring into action. I catch Faith before the first leaf touches the ground.

"Hey," I carefully lay her head down on my lap. She's torn a perfect circle of grass up from the earth where her tornado'd been, and I'm not about to lie her down on a bunch of dirt and twigs. "You're okay. I've got you."

Faith just pants silently, trying to catch her breath. Her left hand grabs at the air so I hold mine out above it, just in case.

"Special one time no announcement needed deal," I try to smile. It doesn't work. She does grab my hand. At first, I tell myself that it's to use her magic and buy us a bit more time, but then I realize she's already making physical contact. Maybe she's just too delirious to have caught on to that, though.

Faith's quietly slipping in and out of sleep and I'm terrible at sitting still, so I text Janine to check in and then message Morgan an excuse about leaving something at the cabin to buy us more time in case Faith's too tired for the attention magic to hold. I busy myself with picking grass, leaves, and sticks out of Faith's hair. With my hands physically in it, it's impossible not to notice. The large patches of missing and newly growing hair behind her ears and just beneath the crown of her head and the smaller ones scattered around her scalp. I remember her constant hair fidgeting and her refusal to put it up and the almost shimmery, otherworldly quality it takes on sometimes that I've been starting to mistake for crush-lenses, and all at once, I understand.

I carefully remove the rest of the debris from Faith's hair, smooth down as many wind-swept tangles as I can, then move on to dusting down her shoulders.

"You can mention it," she eventually croaks.

I shake my head. "None of my business. Unless you want it to be."

Faith inhales deeply. She starts to try to sit up on her own.

"I mean, not because I think it should be a secret," I instantly overthink it. "I'm a chronic skin picker. Not that I think it's as noticeable as skin-picking, obviously. I just—" I bite at my lip. "I was doing so good for two seconds there, wasn't I?"

"I honestly wasn't expecting you to last that long," she whispers.

"Hey! If you weren't like, one blink away from falling asleep, I'd insult you back so hard right now!" Instead, I carefully help her scoot her way over to a tree. "I'm sorry that... whatever that was happened," I say. "It looked really scary. You don't... you didn't deserve that. You must've been terrified."

Faith somehow manages to make even shrugging look sloppy. "Happens, sometimes. When I get worked up. Always ends when I'm..." she yawns. "When I'm too out of energy for it to keep going, though, so I shouldn't have had much of a reason to be scared."

"Were you, though?" I lean forward.

She looks away.

I sigh. "I'm really sorry."

"It's ridiculous." Her hands move to her hair, then she shoots a panicked look at me and quickly traps them beneath her thighs. "I know I'm fine. I know I'm the one doing it but it's like... my body just doesn't listen and the more I try to force it to the worse it gets? I shouldn't have to wait to be exhausted for it to stop. I don't... it's ridiculous."

"Not really," I shrug. "Sounds kind of like the way some autistic people's meltdowns, work. Not that you're autistic," I correct. "Not that... it's like a faerie thing. Probably. A faerie meltdown."

Faith grimaces. " 's not a faerie thing," she says. "Or at least, not a common one according to any of the faeries I've asked about it."

"Oh."

She reaches for her hair again then opts to retrap her hand between her back and the tree trunk instead.

"Here." I shake off my tangle and hold it out to her.

Faith glances at it. "I shouldn't need that."

"Okay." I don't put it back on my wrist.

She sighs and takes it. "It's not... I wouldn't hate it. Being autistic. I'm not offended when people assume I am because I get if I was a human and acting like this that'd be the obvious explanation, it's just..." She rolls my tangle against her knee. "I'd feel guilty claiming to be something as some kind of excuse for— not that it's an excuse," she corrects before I can. "When other people actually are. I'm just... people have been mistaking autistic children for changelings for centuries, Lots. I'd *love* to have an actual explanation to point to, but I'm just a faery."

"A faery who apparently has significantly more sensory and emotional regulation issues than the majority of other faeries," I point out.

Faith shrugs. "Maybe I'm just really bad at being a faery, then."

"That's not—"

"Lots," she stops me. "I'm exhausted, okay? Drop it."

"Okay." I nod. "I umm... I'm sorry, then. About what you overheard earlier. And about what I admitted a bit after that. I umm... I know that all seems scary, but I swear it isn't—"

"Do you like me?" Faith interrupts. "Or were you just trying to calm me down?"

I swallow. "I do. And I know I should've told you earlier, but in my defense, I don't even know when—"

"I think I'm about to hug you," Faith whispers.

"Oh!" My eyebrows shoot up. "I'm... okay, then? That's... very good. Extremely okay."

She proceeds to not hug me.

"Faith?"

"I really, really need you to tell me if I can't." Her voice shakes. "I know I'm not supposed to be asking permission, but if you're about to—"

"You can." I nod, opening my arms to her. "Of course. I just very rambly declared that I'm like, physically incapable of not wanting to be friends. Obviously you can—"

Faith sobs exactly once, drops my tangle to the side, and launches herself around my chest.

And maybe she didn't actually let go of all the air when she thought she did, because as she finally relaxes against me, I swear the world feels a little more kind.

Chapter 41

Faith's still too drained to hug me properly so I hold on tightly enough for both of us and let her quietly shake against me.

"There aren't any friends," she eventually whispers. "At home. There've never actually been any. I just... you..."

"Said that there were and you just went along with it?" I guess.

She pulls away to stare at me, but not far enough to save me from blushing. We have to keep our knees pressed together so she can keep using her magic, after all.

"I think I pieced it together a few minutes ago," I admit. "People don't typically react that strongly to me saying I find them tolerable. Not that— oh my god, not that I was like 'yup, Faith's totally and absolutely friendless' or anything like that. I didn't mean to—"

Faith laughs. "You're fine," she says. "Just too smart."

My throat goes dry. "And you're a lot more than tolerable," I admit. "I'm just... I've been actively trying really hard to pretend I don't know that for weeks now, so it's not like I can just... it's a lot."

Faith nods.

"But I swear I'm taking this so, so seriously, okay? So is everyone else, I think. I threw out pretending to prepare weeks ago because it felt faster than convincing everyone to actually get on board, but I swear I only did it because it felt like the most time-effective decision," I try to explain. "I'm like, ninety-nine percent sure if you'd stuck around a bit longer before making everyone forget what we were talking about, you would've heard everyone else confirming they're definitely trying their hardest too, okay? I'll double check, though," I promise. "Just to be safe."

"Okay," Faith says. She wipes her face against her sleeve then picks back up my tangle. "You're not gonna ask more questions, then?" She says after a beat. "'bout... basically everything I've said or done today?"

"I'm evolving," I nod proudly.

Faith smiles and rolls her eyes. Then, her smile falls. She wraps the tangle around her knuckles. "I'm really bad at pretending to be a person, Lots," she whispers, looking nowhere near me.

"You're not—"

"I am, though," she stops me. "I'm... you didn't ask if it's because positive attention doesn't work, because *of course* it works better. People give so much more of a shit about the things they like. But even if they didn't, obviously I'd rather..." she sighs. "I can't do that," she says. "It doesn't— shit." Faith pulls a bit too hard and a link on the tangle disconnects. "Shit, sorry," she instantly hands it back to me. "'m actively talking about how bad I am at friendships while destroying your property."

I laugh, separate another link halfway down the chain, and hand one of the halves back to her. "It's supposed to do that. Now we can share."

"Right," Faith nods. "Right, I... thanks." She runs her tongue along her gums and moves her eyes back to the tangle. "I can feel it, you know? The way people react to me? How much attention they're giving me, yeah, but I also eventually caught on to the way their physical bodies react to me and it's not... I tried?" She says. "To make friends? For a while? And sometimes when I was younger, I'd be able to convince myself I'd gotten really, really close but then I'd say something a little too wrong or react to something a little too much and... I could physically *feel* it. It's so exhausting to try and convince people to like you when you can physically tell the moment they decide there's something wrong with you instead."

"You get it wrong sometimes, though," I try to correct her. "A lot, actually. With me. If you can't feel specific emotions, how can you be sure—"

"I'm sure." Faith's voice goes hard. She pulls two links apart again. "Sorry." She glances up at me.

I shrug. "It's literally a fidget toy. Fidget however you want."

"Right," she reattaches them. "Yeah. I'm... I notice things, Lots. I can *hear* things, even when people think I can't. I'm not... it might make me a shitty person, but I *know* people are going to inevitably decide that there's something wrong with me and it feels so much less terrible when they eventually reveal they can't stand you if you can tell yourself you did it on purpose. I don't..." She takes a deep breath. She reaches for her hair again then winces and puts both hands back on the tangle. "And I need to do it, you know? Because if people aren't going to like me, then I *need* them to dislike me. And I can't even get that right most of the time. Because I'm so bad at passing for human that I got diagnosed with a fucking disability— no offense," she quickly looks up at me again. "Obviously."

"Obviously," I nod.

Faith cracks her knuckles. "It's like, even when I *am* trying to be an ass at school, people assume it's not voluntary? Like... I'm too weird to be anything but a nuisance but they think I'm too obviously disabled for anyone to feel okay holding any kind of actual grudge without getting judged for it, so I can't... I don't just not have friends at home, Lots, I don't have enemies either. I have fucking nothing. I spend all school year physically feeling like shit and barely being able to get out of bed most days, have to spend whatever energy I can muster up being disruptive or annoying or embarrassing enough for the brief attention boost, then repeat it all over again the next day. I let my parents keep sending me to a fucking disabled summer camp every year just so I can antagonize genuinely disabled kids because they're the only ones who actually care enough to get genuinely upset at me!" Faith breaks and reconnects her half of the tangle again. "How pathetic is that!"

"Well," I search for any possible comfort I can provide, feeling even worse for barring her from coming back next year. I've been doing my research, though, and I haven't been able to find anything on how to break a faery's oath. "Luckily for you, I'm extremely good at focusing on all the wrong things while I'm supposed to be learning. Plenty of school-day attention bound to come your way once we go back home."

Faith snorts. "Thanks."

"And for the record, I very obviously think you're a very difficult person to not want to be friends with, Faith. Maybe this school year you can try to—"

She shakes her head. "You could think about me 24/7 and I still probably wouldn't have enough energy to risk focusing on that instead." She pauses. "Thanks, though. Seriously."

"Right." I nod. "Okay." I have a probably-crush on someone who physically has to try and annoy everyone in her life in order to keep her body functional. I'm pretty sure there's no guide out there on how to figure out what that says about my moral principles. "Let's go find our friends here, then? Before they send out a search party?"

Faith sighs. "I just yelled at them," she says. "Even if they were about to say they're all on board, there's no way—"

"Friends lose it at friends, sometimes." I shrug. "Especially friends with pre-established emotional regulation issues. As long as it doesn't become like, a regular malicious thing and you apologize, I'm sure it'll be fine."

"What if it isn't?" Faith whispers.

"Only one way to find out, right?"

Faith still low on energy as we make our way back to our game site, so once she gets me reoriented on the trail, I have to do most of the guiding. When we get back to where we left the rest of the Caribou Crew, they're all sitting in a circle talking.

"Hello!" I wave as we approach. "We've returned! How about we—"

Gator raises their hand.

"Yes, Gator?"

"Cabin's the other way."

"Right," I laugh nervously, trying to cover. "Right, well..."
Everyone's focus seems to be somewhere near my hip, for some
reason. Autistics might be more likely to avoid eye-contact, but
that normally doesn't involve a whole group of us staring in the
same direction.

I look down, realize I've forgotten to let go of Faith's
hand, and quickly jump away from her.

"Right, I umm..." My face flames as Gator and Van
exchange a knowing look. "Faith!" I throw her under the bus.
Again. "Faith wanted to say something."

Faith rolls her eyes and walks forward to stand across
from Brain. "I'm sorry," she says.

Okay, Brain signs.

"That I yelled," Faith continues. "And was less than
polite, I was... obviously I didn't actually—"

Brain holds out a hand to stop her and pulls out her iPad
to type something.

"Waste of time," it reads. "Hurry and play?"

"Yeah," Faith's shoulders physically lower. "Yeah, I
umm... good. Thanks." She takes a step back and stumbles
because she clearly hasn't caught back up on all the energy she
expended yet, and an idea hits me.

"If you're okay with other people hugging you, nod." I
whisper so quietly that even I can't fully hear it, but the moment
the sentence is finished, Faith's head moves.

"Right," I clap my hands together. "Just to finish up our
previous conversation then, we were talking about whether or not
we're genuinely playing to win next week. No offense, Fay," I
pretend to tell her for the first time. "We were very much
planning on potentially screwing you over a few weeks ago."

"Understandable," she nods. "I was very annoying a few
weeks ago."

258

"We're not doing that though, right? Everyone? Vote?" I try to summon my very best Janine impression and look at everyone one by one to acknowledge their raised hands. "Excellent. Fay was just telling me that she's very worried about that, actually, which I told her was ridiculous because like, obviously we're all in. She also told me she loves and appreciates you all very, very much and thinks it'll make her a lot less stressed if we do a big team group hug." I consider. "Without me, actually. Too many hands," I shudder.

I watch Faith get swarmed then swallowed alive by a mass of limbs and hair and texture. It hardly looks comfortable, but being the centre of a group hug seems like an excellent way to get a much-needed energy boost. When the hug dissipates, Faith walks back over to me.

"I need to talk to you for a second," she says. "We should probably rearrange plans now that we've wasted time." She turns around briefly. "Sorry!" She calls out again.

Shut up, Brain signs.

"I'm probably going to grab your elbow," Faith says before dragging me a few feet away.

"What—" I start.

"If you tell anyone I hugged you and *cried* about it," she lowers her voice so no one else can hear. "I'll..." she frowns, drawing her eyebrows together. "Come up with an actual end to that threat," she decides.

I laugh. "I'm glad we're friends too, Faith," I squeeze her arm.

Her lips wiggle as she fights to control them. "Yeah," she mumbles, finally giving up and letting herself smile. "That's pretty cool, actually."

August 25

My dearest Alice,

Im ofishally friends w FH now!!!! Crazy. Wild. Unbelevable.

Just friends tho obviusly. And know that were friends its perfectly aceptable 2 spend this much time thinking abt her & comeing up w reesons to b alone together and stareing at her and such.

New problem know tho shes leeveing @ the end of summer. In a week. How does 1 ask for some1's # w/out making it sound like they dont want 2 just b friends? Which I obviusly do. Obviusly.

Talk at u later,
Charlotte

Chapter 42

The battle's scheduled for Thursday afternoon (the fae apparently are not morning people), but I'm still expecting Faith to try and get everyone to spend every second leading up to it either getting in some last-minute practice or trying to sleep for like twenty hours straight (which would've actually made us more lethargic, but Faith is far from immune to misguided ideas).

Instead, as we finish off going over strategy ideas and perfecting our battle cries Wednesday evening, she catches my eye, jerks her head dramatically to the side three times (I miss what she's trying to convey the first two), then steps just past the doors to the cabin to wait for me to meet her.

"Can I wake you tonight?" she whispers, staring out at the tree line. "Around twelve-thirty?"

"Sure?" I say. I want to ask more, but she instantly disappears back into the cabin.

Knowing I'm meeting with Faith has the annoying habit of not letting me sleep at all, so when she creeps up my ladder hours later, I'm already wide awake. I slip on my lanyard, grab a sweater and my tangle, and follow her into the night.

"Are we training?" I guess once we're out of earshot of any patrolling counsellors.

"No."

"Boobytrapping the battleground?"

"Do you *have* any booby traps?"

"Going over magical options again?" I guess.

Faith sighs. She turns to face me. "I think..." she pauses to study the sky. "I think I just want to have fun. If that's okay. Figured we could sleep in tomorrow, so..."

I beam. "I love fun."

Our first half-baked plan is to try and break into the kitchen and gorge ourselves on whatever leftovers we can find, but the kitchen has the unfortunate downside of being attached to the main building where the majority of Corrain's counsellors and campers are actively asleep, so we redirect to the art shed. Not because the art shed has anything particularly appealing in it or anything. It'd just be ridiculous to pass up the opportunity to do a little harmless breaking and entering when you have an accomplice who can physically make people uninterested in catching you.

Especially if it's also the last night that said accomplice might ever be able to use that ability, but I don't let myself dwell on that.

The lock that holds the shed's doors shut is never actually latched, so we just slip it off and let ourselves in. I awkwardly feel around for the pull switch to the singular light bulb only for Faith to find it instantly. I try not to take that too personally, though. She has an unfair advantage.

There are no chairs and only a single table in the shed, so Faith moves half-finished felt puppets to the ground and sits on the table. There's just enough space for me to join her if we press our knees together, which is a very normal thing for my heart rate to increase at. I have a minor touch aversion, after all.

"So," Faith says.

"So," I echo. Breaking and entering is a lot less exciting once you get past that 'entering' bit. "We could umm... destroy the place?" I suggest. "Graffiti all the walls and destroy all the material and... we could carve our names into the wood, if you want." I realize. "That'd definitely get you a lot of attention for years after this."

Faith smiles. "I can already physically hear you freaking out about that."

"Oh," I bite my lip. "Right. Well... we could write *your* name everywhere, then."

"It's fine," she says. "I'm not feeling very destructive right now."

"Right," I nod. "Good. What umm... what do you want to do then?"

"Dunno." Faith runs her fingers through her hair. "I think I might not know how to have fun, actually."

I laugh, pushing myself off the table to search through the shelves for something usable. "Ta-da!" I pull out a box of baking soda. "We're making volcanoes. Or... just the explosion part, actually. Paper mâché would take too long to dry."

Faith frowns. "When's the last time you did that?"

I roll my eyes. "You just mix vinegar and baking soda together and then it explodes. How hard can it be?"

It isn't hard at all. It also doesn't explode. I find a beaker to pour everything into, but it just fizzes extremely anticlimactically, then leaves a patch of goo on the ground that we have to clean up with scraps of felt.

"That was more exciting in my head," I say as we scrub. "I thought it'd be more time-consuming. And explodey. Sorry."

"It's fine," Faith says.

"It's actually really hard to come up with something fun to do when you're actively thinking about trying to make sure it's fun," I admit. "And all you have to use is a bunch of art supplies you've already had access to for months."

Faith throws her felt in a box and hops back onto the table. "It wouldn't be smart to use any magic right now," she reminds us both. "I should probably be saving it."

"Of course," I nod. "That makes sense. I wasn't trying to imply you should—"

Faith sighs. "Turn off the light and get up here."

I frown. "You just said you should—"

"'s worth wasting a little," she shrugs. "I feel like I haven't shown you anything actually cool yet. Waste a little now, give you something that'll make you remember me forever. Easy trade."

"You don't have to... I'm already going to remember you forever, Faith," I whisper.

She throws back her head and groans. "I just want you to see the cool shit I can do, Lots. Stop being all nice and selfless and let me."

"I... okay." I turn off the light and carefully climb back onto the table. Our knees are pressed together again. I take one of her hands for her attention magic and the other for... something.

Faith stares at me through the darkness. "Ready?"

I nod.

She grins. "Look up."

It starts as tiny pinpricks of light so small that at first, I convince myself that they're just odd-coloured eye-floaters and try to blink them away. But then, more and more appear, and suddenly the ceiling of the shed is covered in dots of pulsing pink-ish light. They dance and shift and twirl amongst themselves. Our own personal Milky Way.

I start to look down at Faith again, but she senses it and shakes her head. "Keep watching."

Slowly, one by one, each ball bursts and sprinkles down to the ground. A thousand tiny fireworks except far better than any firework ever could be, because these don't burn, they light. And they're all ours. I keep my eyes glued to the ceiling until each and every one's gone out, so I don't notice that their shimmering dust hasn't disappeared until looking down at my arms. At the glowing grains of sand on Faith's hair and cheeks. And eyelashes. I might spend a little too much time staring at her eyelashes, actually.

"Holy shit," I whisper.

Faith laughs, reaching out to touch my arm. "Can I?" she checks.

I usually hate it when people make me answer questions about physical contact, but I'm too amazed to care.

She traces her finger against my skin. It sends shivers up my spine that I'm fairly certain have nothing to do with the magic I'm currently coated in.

Faith draws a smiley face which is so unlike her—or maybe so much like her, actually—that I know it'd make me laugh if there was any oxygen left in my chest.

"Is this..." I eventually manage, "pixie dust?"

Faith gasps. "I am *not* a pixie!" Her voice goes so uncharacteristically high as she admonishes me that this time, I really do laugh. "It's magic," she says. "Faerie's covered in it. This realm less so, unless there's a faery nearby enough to be drawing it out of you."

"Magic's a physical thing?"

Faith considers. "In a way," she decides.

"And it's *pink*."

She smiles. "For you, yes. It's pretty much any colour you can think of. I only pulled over the pink stuff this time, though. Figured it'd be more effective."

"This is so, so much better than a half-assed friendship bracelet," I whisper.

Faith laughs. "Didn't like you enough back then to full-ass that one."

Faith likes me. I know she means as a friend, but right now we're alone in a tiny shed with our knees pressed together and our hands clasped and it might be her last night in this entire realm and she practically just pulled entire constellations over from an entirely different realm just for me. I know she means just as friends, but right now, she's all but covered in stardust and my heart refuses to stop hammering and I *know* she must hear it too.

"Faith," I whisper, voice so thick that I'm surprised I manage any sound at all.

"Lots?"

I take a deep breath. "I want to take a picture of you!"

Chapter 43

I do not want to take a picture of Faith. Well, I do (in all my internet sleuthing, I've never been able to find one of those), but right now, I'm extremely preoccupied with wanting to smoosh my face against hers. Because I've had the misfortune of being cursed with both hormones and an apparent crush on the very girl who'll inevitably break my heart.

I don't want to have my heart broken though, so I blurt out the first other proposition I can think of instead.

"What?" Faith says.

"There's none online," I explain. "So—"

"You've been looking me up online?"

"*You* eavesdrop on all my googling! Don't pretend you didn't already know that."

She smiles. "Seems like you probably don't use the screen reader for that."

If my skin wasn't already far too warm for comfort, I know my cheeks would start burning at that. "Oh," I say. "Right." I clap my hands together. "Well, I still should take one. I'm pretty sure I don't have a visual memory. Or if I do, I'm very bad at it. If I take a picture, that'll give me another way to remember you. Not that—we're going to win, but you can't come back next year, right? Because you promise? So if I have a picture, I can help out more after we go home."

(And she's gorgeous and her face is less than two feet away from my face and she's covered in *literal magic*, but those parts don't need to be voiced right now).

"Don't like taking pictures," Faith mumbles. "That's why you didn't find any."

"Oh," I say. "Right." The mood is shifting and she explicitly asked me to make her happy and I need to fix it. "I could draw you, then?"

Faith frowns. "You can draw?"

"I'm terrible at it," I beam. "That's why it'll be perfect. There's nothing to worry about if you're gonna come out looking like scribbles anyway. It'll be fun. We'll draw each other."

"Okay." With the light back on, the dust on our arms is a lot less sparkly, but still just as pink. I find a glitter crayon to dot her portrait with anyway. It might end up looking like chicken pox, but I'll know what it is. I want to remember this night for the rest of my life.

I draw her from the head down so when I realize I can't remember what colour Faith's eyes are, I assume it'll come back to me before I'm done. I spend so much time thinking about them (and getting so giddy and overwhelmed every time I even come close to seeing them) that I *must* know what colour they are. But then I finish outlining and colouring in her entire body, and I'm still drawing a blank. I try to sneak a glance at her for colour confirmation, but she's too focused on her own paper for me to get a clear view of her eyes.

I admit defeat. "What colour are your eyes?"

"Make 'em whatever colour you want," Faith mumbles.

I frown. "Do you not know? Are they one of those weird in-between colours? I'm very good at deciphering weird in between colours, actually. I love putting things in boxes. Let me look."

"Busy."

"You can't look up for one second?"

She sighs and does. Like always, looking straight at Faith instantly feels too overwhelming and my own gaze darts back down, but I force myself to hold it. I have a mission to complete. My eyes water and my heart hammers and then, just when I'm starting to consider that I might have actually been an 'eye-contact's painful' autistic this whole time and just somehow unaware of it, I finally see it.

Faith's eyes are black. Not just dark or so brown that the pupil and iris are indistinguishable, but entirely, completely black. There are no irises at all. Or whites.

"You could do brown?" she says, voice as bored as ever. "Lots of people say—" She meets my eye and scoots back so quickly that her back slams into the wall. "You're looking at me," she whispers.

"What—"

"How the fuck are you looking at me?"

I instantly look away, shielding my eyes for good measure. "Sorry," I say. "I didn't mean to—"

"I'm not evil, Lots," she says. "I'm not evil or— or some kind of demon or... you don't have to be afraid of me."

I suck on my lip. "I'm not afraid."

"You're actively hiding!"

"I'm being respectful!"

Faith sighs. "It's... the one thing we can't match right," she says. "The eyes. Window to the soul and all that. But it's... I don't even have to divert attention myself with them. My body's supposed to do it naturally. We evolved to. No one's ever supposed to— you're sure you're human?"

"Unless someone's been doing like, a really, really good job lying to me, yeah."

Faith just keeps staring. "How'd you do that?"

"I'm really good at hyperfixation when I want to be," I shrug. "Or actually mostly when I absolutely do *not* want to be, but you know. Maybe it's that. Can I look at you again? Or is that—"

"Try."

I do. This time, my eyes don't even water.

Faith blinks at me. It's bizarre. I never would have guessed that Faith's (or anyone's) eyes would look like that, but now that I've seen them twice, they're the only thing that make sense. They complete her face. "Does it... hurt?" she says. "Your body should be rejecting it. You should—"

"It used to," I admit. "I think. But now it's... I don't know. Maybe now that I've already seen them, the magic's chill with me."

268

"Maybe," Faith whispers. She looks away first. She has to. Now that I've finally fully seen her, I never want to stop looking. "Sorry," she says. "If that scared you. I should've warned you. But I figured—"

"I've always imagined your hair as ink," I tell her.

Faith's brow furrows. "Way to kick me while I'm down, Lots."

"Not like that," I quickly correct. "Not in a bad way or even because it actually looks like ink, I just... I like to link concepts together. It makes them easier to keep track of. I've always imagined your hair as ink because it's dark and mysterious and— I know hair can't be mysterious, obviously, but you always felt like you were and now I know why, so it always fit, you know? And I think... not like grease, like stories. I think as long as I've known you, I've looked at your hair and known you were full of millions of stories that I wanted to understand one day and—"

"My hair's a mess, Lots," Faith says.

"Shut up. You know you're hot. That's like, an objectively true thing."

She smiles slightly. "According to you."

"Which is why I should be in charge of everything all the time." I nod. "I have excellent taste." I put my hand against her jaw, gently tilting up her head so that I can see her eyes more clearly. "You have the kind of eyes a person could fall into and spend an eternity exploring," I tell her. "That's pretty cool, I think."

Faith blushes. "You're ridiculously calm about faerie stuff, you know."

I shrug. "I already told you. Humans scare me in general so I'm kind of already capped out there. I don't like things I don't understand and new people always mean navigating a lot of that but you're... I've known you too long for anything about you to feel scary," I reconsider. "Or, okay, I get you can like, literally hear when I'm scared, so full disclosure, you're also one of the most terrifying people I've ever met, but not in that 'ahh! I need to run away!' way. In the... you're intimidating. Or—again, not like scary intimidating, you're—oh my god, I'd been blaming that on crush stuff! Not being able to look right at you! Not that it's necessarily *not* crush stuff, but part of me was like, 'oh my god have I liked Faith since I was a little kid and I'm just now—"

"You have a crush on me?" Faith stops me.

I bite my lip. "I umm... I was kind of hoping you'd tell me that, actually. But then you hadn't yet, so I figured if I casually slipped it in somehow you'd..." I watch her. "I don't know. Which I know sounds ridiculous but I genuinely don't. You can like, hear my... body noises," I grimace. "Right? So can't you... do I?"

Faith snorts. "I can't diagnose you with a crush, Lots. It doesn't work like that."

"Right." I take off my tangle. "Yeah, of course. Obviously." I sigh. "I'm not... it's not that I don't like you enough," I say. "Or I don't know. Maybe it is. I just really like to intellectualize my own emotions and it turns out that's a really hard one to intellectualize."

Faith considers. "What if I said I have a crush on you too? That I also think you're really pretty. How does that make you feel?"

"Warm?" I guess. "But that kind of means absolutely nothing. Pretty much every emotion makes me warm. It could also mean I'm planning on murdering you."

"Oh."

"It also makes me feel like you absolutely could've made that way fancier of a reveal," I realize. "I practically wrote a whole monologue about the colour of your hair!"

"Don't do monologues," Faith says. "Or mushy emotions at all, most of the time. Fair warning, throwing in an extra 'really' or two before pretty's probably the best I'm ever gonna get."

I laugh.

"'s that okay?" Faith suddenly seems almost timid. "If I can't do fancy? Or..." she gestures vaguely. "Lengthy compliments."

I nod. "I love talking enough for other people."

"Good," Faith nods. Then she leans forward even though we both know she can hear what that's doing to my heart. Which is really very rude of her, all things considered. "What do you want to do right now, Lots?" she says. "Now that you know."

"I still don't know how I feel," I admit.

Faith laughs. "Neither does like, the majority of the population most of the time. Take a break from trying to figure everything out for a bit. What do you want to do?"

I swallow. Her eyes are on mine. Solid and wide and fathomless and cold and yet not the least bit uninviting. "I think I want to kiss you," I whisper.

"Oh, thank god," Faith giggles. "Good. Me too. Let's do that, then. Extremely memorable idea."

She closes her eyes and leans forward. I close mine too (partially because hers are closed, partially because I've read that you're supposed to), and do the same.

I am about to kiss Faith Harris.

I am about to know what it feels like to kiss *Faith Harris*.

I keep leaning what seems to be impossibly far and then all at once, her hands are slamming into my shoulders to stop me from falling off the table. My eyes fly open.

"Sorry." Faith quickly releases me. She's scooted over and pressed herself against the wall. "Didn't have time to warn you."

I frown. "What happened?"

"I umm..." She cracks her knuckles. "Maybe we shouldn't do that, actually. Right now."

My confusion just deepens. Faith can't lie and *said* she wanted to. Unless something major happened in the last few seconds, I don't understand why that's suddenly changed.

Maybe I should've kept my eyes open.

"It's alright. Is it a faerie thing?" I guess. "If I kiss you, do you like, claim my soul or something?"

She doesn't respond.

271

"Or the reverse? I claim yours? Or we're bound together for all of eternity which like, no offense, very much would not want that. If I do like you, I'm pretty sure it's only been for a few weeks and an eternity's a long— or does it turn me into a faery? I might be okay with that, actually. Depending on the kind. Or—"

"Lots!" Faith stops my rambling. She sighs. "I swear I was trying to come up with a nicer way to say this. You're really good at not giving people time to think."

"Oh," I nod, trying my very best to appear completely understanding. "You *don't* like me. That's... a perfectly reasonable—"

"I like you," Faith corrects. "A lot. You just also..." She tugs at her hair. "You smell."

My jaw drops. "I *smell*?"

"Not you specifically!" She rushes to defend herself. "Humans in general. You're all... everyone's breath's always..."

"I'm too *stinky* for you?" There were a lot of things I thought would keep me from kissing a girl like Faith Harris. That was not one of them.

She presses her tongue against her cheek. "Are you offended?"

I laugh. "I mostly think that's hilarious, actually. I could brush my teeth?" I suggest. "Would that—"

"Even your toothpaste smells too strongly," she says. "Unless you use the exact same brand as me. Which you don't," she adds before I can offer up brand names. "I checked."

I grin. "You *checked*."

"I'm..." Her entire face goes bright red. "Shut up!"

I laugh.

Faith fixes her hair again. "I wanted to kiss you," she reiterates. "I just... it's one thing to be around humans, it's another to physically put my mouth on theirs."

"Can I hug you instead?" I suggest.

"Oh my god, please," she says instantly. "I really need an excuse to not look at you right now."

I laugh again, pulling her against my chest. "Is the top of your head fair game?"

"Very fair," Faith whispers.

I kiss it exactly once. "You liked me enough to try to kiss me," I giggle. "Even if I am all disgusting and human."

"Shut up."

I grin. Then, I catch myself stroking her hair and stop myself. "Okay?" I check.

"Okay," she nods.

I consider keeping my thoughts to myself for once, then decide against it. Tonight's one of the last times I'll ever see Faith. If there was ever a time to be direct, it's right now. "Trichotillomania's nowhere near as genetic as autism," I say. "Just... so you know. Which means it's extremely possible for anyone to have it."

Faith doesn't respond.

"That's a hair pulling disorder?" I explain. "It's sometimes anxiety linked, but sometimes more of like, a boredom or compulsion thing. It's—"

"I know, Lots. Heard you googling."

"Oh." I chew on my lip. "Crap, sorry. I didn't mean to... if you don't want to talk about it that's totally fine and I definitely should've put like, more than two seconds of thought into where I was googling stuff, but it's not because I'm being like, judgemental or anything. I think research is just my love language?" I process what I've just said and quickly move away from her. Or as 'away' as you can get on a tiny little table. "Not that I *love* you or anything, obviously. Or even that I have a crush on you. It—"

"Didn't you just say you thought you did?" Faith reminds me.

"Right." I nod. "Yes, yeah. I do. I think I'm still freaking out about that, actually, and haven't fully entered 'this isn't a big giant secret' mode so... fair warning I might keep doing that for a bit. I extremely think I have a crush on you, actually. Like, for sure now. I think I'm... I tried to tell myself it was lust, for a while?

I try to explain. "On account of you being incredibly hot and me being a teenager? But I think I'm way too okay with you not wanting to kiss me—and like, straight up calling me disgusting—"

"I said it wasn't just you!"

"For that," I finish. "I think I just really, really like you."

Faith smiles. "I really, really like you too."

"Awesome." I take off my tangle. "That's great. Good for me. I umm... how's your day been?"

Faith rolls her eyes. "You can talk about my hair, Lots."

"You're sure?" I check. "Because I think... I need to know everything. All the time. If I don't it makes me physically uncomfortable so when I care about someone, obviously I want to know as much as possible about them too. But I also know that some people apparently *like* remaining oblivious which is... frankly ridiculous and completely nonsensical to me, honestly, but also very fair and I would be totally fine and respectful about it if you didn't want to—"

"Lots." Faith never has to raise her voice to speak over someone and I'm gradually beginning to realize that maybe that's not because she's entitled or abrasive or rude, it's because her voice is so gentle that you can't help but want to listen to it. She's not just monotone, she's steady. Cozy. Home. "I'm sure."

I lick my lips. "I think you like to come up with reasons you don't deserve help, then," I admit. "I don't think anyone *needs* to be disabled to accommodate themselves, but I know you think you don't deserve to just because autism *might* be entirely genetic and changelings *might* not have those genes—which is ridiculous, by the way. The majority of the rest of your genetic makeup is clearly similar to ours, so I don't get why that one thing wouldn't be, but I'm not mentioning that because I don't want to be annoying about it and—"

"You just did."

I pause to make sure she's not angry, but if anything, the curvature of Faith's lips looks vaguely smile-esque.

I roll my eyes. "I'm terrible at not being annoying. You should know that by now." I take a deep breath. "You've literally already been diagnosed with autism because you meet the criteria. Maybe when you go back to Faerie that'll be different, but right now even professionals agree you're living life as an autistic person, so I don't see why you shouldn't get to find ways to accommodate that. But I also get that identity and disability are messy and that's not up to me. But plenty of non-autistic people have trichotillomania. And it's also likely not entirely genetic. Just for the record."

"Okay," Faith says.

"And like, there are therapies and treatments and stuff, but a lot of people say using fidgets and other things to keep their hands busy is helpful and I have so many back with my luggage. Way too many, actually. I always overpack the things that I'll need the least. So if you wanted to go through my stuff on Friday," I don't let myself add 'if you're still here by then'. I need to believe that she will be. "then you can try them out and figure out what might work for you. If you want," I add. "Obviously."

Faith cracks her knuckles. "I... yeah," she breathes. "Okay. That'd be really helpful, thanks." Then, her eyes narrow. "Can you see that too?" she checks, hands flying to her head. "I don't control the eyes, but my hair should be—"

"I can't," I confirm. "Still makes my stomach all squiggly whenever I try to look too closely. Only partially for crush-related reasons, I think."

Faith nods, pulling out her phone to check the time. "It's late," she says. "It'd be smart to get back soon."

"Probably," I acknowledge.

"I'm probably gonna put my head on your shoulder." She scoots closer to me to do so. "Can we pretend everything's normal?" Faith asks. "Can we pretend I'm a normal sixteen-year-old human girl and you just told me you liked me and then we got to kiss and celebrate and stay up all night without a care in the world because we're normal and nothing terrible's coming?"

"Okay." My throat squeezes around the word as I wrap an arm around her. "Of course."

Faith relaxes against me and lets her eyes fall shut. There's still magic on her lashes.

"Everything's going to be okay, Faith," I squeeze her arm.

"Shhh," she whispers, turning to bury her face against my shoulder. "Just let me play pretend."

August 30

My dearest Alice,

Wht does it mean whn some1 says they have a crush on u & asks 2 kiss u BUT u said u have a crush on them 1ˢᵗ and they hvnt actuly kissed u yet? Is there an allistic social rool whr u pretend to have crushs on ur friends to spare there feelings? That feels like a thing that probly defently exists.

Anyway in very related news Ive decided I DO have a crush on FH & she knows about it know which is sjhbdeflisikdjblskdf.

Talk at u later,
Charlotte

Chapter 44

I don't know how Faith's managed to pretend to be human for over sixteen years. I can barely manage a morning of it.

We didn't make our way back to the cabin until a couple of hours before sunrise (Faith so tired that we had to lean against each other the entire way while I politely pretended not to notice the tears steadily rolling down her cheeks) so it at least hopefully seems believable when I insist that I'm exhausted and need to sleep in, but I don't know how I'm supposed to fill the rest of the time until the battle.

Because to everyone else, today's supposed to be exciting. The moment we finally claim victory over our arch-rivals. One final hurrah before summer ends. None of them know it's actually the end of the world. I don't know how many jokes or battle chants I'll be able to take before breaking down and ruining everything, so when I realize Faith's opted to sit away from the rest of us while we hang out on the recreation field after lunch, I take the out and join her.

"Hey." I slip in across from her at the bench she's claimed. "Are you like, magic-ing right now or am I just getting freakishly good at working through it?"

Faith doesn't even look up at me. " 'd be a waste." She picks at the table until a tiny piece splinters off. "Need to save it right now."

"Right." I nod. "Smart. I umm... you can join us." I wince even as I say it, but it still feels necessary to offer. My momentary discomfort at having to put on a happy face doesn't outweigh Faith's potentially last chance to spend time around other people for the next hundred years. "If you want. Honestly, the others are probably wondering why you're not—"

"If I talk to anyone right now, I'm gonna end up snapping at them," Faith deadpans. "Can't afford to burn any bridges right now."

"Well," I say slowly. "Luckily, I'm extremely bad at getting the hint when people are trying to snap at me. No burnable bridges here. Extremely unflammable. Or nonflammable, actually? I think that's it. Anyway, our bridges are made of like, steel."

Faith just keeps picking at the table.

I frown. "Are you... wait, am I doing that right now?" I realize. "Are you mad about something? Was it— I should've made it clearer you didn't need to use any magic last night. You're trying not to waste it, and I still let you—"

Faith looks up at me instantly. "That wasn't a waste." Her eyes are still wide and black and brilliant. And unfortunately for my heart rate, I can still see them perfectly. Faith sighs. "Sorry, I'm just... stressed. And not used to having to let people see me be stressed. Can we go be anywhere but here?"

I beam. "That sounds great."

The fae could arrive any moment now (they're rarely exact with times), so we don't let ourselves wander too far from the field. Instead, we walk loops around the trails surrounding it in silence for a while.

"I'm probably about to hold your hand," Faith eventually warns me.

"There's no one here," I remind her. "Don't waste more until—"

She cracks a knuckle. "Not for magic. I just..." she cracks another. "I'm probably about to hold it."

"Oh." I feel my skin go hot. "Right. Okay. Of course."

Faith wraps her fingers around mine and lets our arms swing between us.

"I've been thinking," I finally make myself say. "You said... they're probably going to cut any magic you can get from Faerie right away, right? But you can still do attention stuff, can't you?"

"Which doesn't work if someone's looking right at me." Faith sounds annoyed at having to repeat it, but despite her promise to snap at someone today, she doesn't mention how many times she's already told me that.

"But it does sometimes, right? When you put more magic into it? After camouflage, I had to put constant effort into chanting your name, and even that wasn't foolproof. And with your hair and your eyes most people supposedly can never get a close enough look to properly see them, so if you—"

"They're faeries, Lots. They'll figure out what I'm doing right away. Unless I erase myself entirely, they'll know to put extra effort into looking out for me and all that'll do is make you guys less likely to remember why we're playing in the first place."

"What if you did?" I suggest. "Erase yourself entirely?"

Faith freezes.

"I don't know how it works," I quickly add. "Not entirely, so I get it might not... I saw your eyes," I remind her. "I can see them right now, even though that's supposed to be impossible right? I focused on them enough that I could see them. So what if—"

"No."

I push forward. I *need* to push forward. If there's any chance at saving her that we've overlooked, we need to think it all the way through.

"Not as our plan A," I say. "Obviously. But what if—"

"I said no."

"Right, but what if we play it just like we were going to—"

"Lots." Faith lets go of me.

"We keep the actual flag wherever you hid it in the trails so it'll be impossible to find, you use your heightened senses to try and find theirs as quickly as possible, but then if—"

"Stop it!"

"If we can't," I keep going. "If it looks like people are going to start forfeiting, we try it. There's no point not—"

"Shut up!" Faith screams. As she does, she summons a wind so strong that it makes every branch within a few meters bend.

And me go flying backwards to land not-so-gracefully on my ass.

"Sorry," Faith gasps, instantly rushing to crouch down beside me. "I'm— I wasn't trying to—"

I squeeze her arm and make myself smile. "You're okay. Stressful day."

Faith sighs. She shifts to fully sitting and pulls her knees into her chest. "I know you're just trying to help," she admits. "It's not going to work though, Lots. If I do that, it's not just harder to remember me, your body'll physically try to make you forget. And if you do, for even half a second, then I'm completely severed. I'm not... it's too risky."

"That's why it's a backup plan," I remind her. "Which we won't need because you can use faerie senses and they can't and we're literally not even hiding a flag in-bounds so obviously we're gonna win, but if worst comes to worst—"

"I'd rather spend a century slowly wasting away than spend my dying moments knowing I wasn't memorable enough for you to save me." Faith stops me.

"What if you are, though?" I press.

"What if I'm not?" Obsidian eyes, it turns out, also shine when they're tear-logged. "It's a really, really smart offer, but I can't deal with that. It's... we'll just have to win."

"Okay." I open my arms and Faith all but collapses against my chest. "Okay. We will then."

I don't know how to comfort Faith Harris. She is not the kind of person who comes with clear instructions, and I don't usually fare well without those. So, as she softly cries against me, I'm forced to give up on intellectualizing and just improvise. I squeeze her not because I necessarily know it'll help, but because I want to be as close to her as physically possible. I slowly rub my hands along her arms and back not because I necessarily know she finds that soothing, but because I want to memorize every inch of her skin. I don't hold Faith because she or some book or article told me that it would solve all of my problems, because nothing can right now. I hold her because in this moment, she's absolutely everything and she's crying and I want to pull her soul into my chest and tuck it safely away until the storm passes. I hold her because I can no longer fathom *not* holding her.

I'm thinking about how real and solid she feels in my arms when I suddenly realize how real and solid she *looks* in my arms. I'm staring straight down at Faith's scalp and nothing's making me look away.

My pulse spikes. "Faith?" I try to keep my tone as calm and even as possible. I don't think I'm that good at that. "Do you... they can't mess with attention magic, right? That's all yours? Are you sure—"

"I know you can see it," she murmurs. Her eyes are closed. Her posture's still relaxed. "Saving magic, remember?"

"Right." I nod. "Good."

"Are you staring?"

"No?"

I feel her exhale. "I can feel you staring, Lots."

"Well then... that was entrapment! So you're in the wrong. Ha. Fuck you." I kiss her head. "I can stop," I offer. "If you want. But I swear I'm just... I can finally fully see you. It's really nice to finally see you. But I can stop."

"'s okay," Faith says. "Feel free to keep obsessing over me."

I laugh. "You're so pretty it's actually unfair. But like, big win for me." I smooth back her hair and kiss her scalp again. "Because *I'm* the one who tricked a ridiculously pretty person into liking me which means I must also be insanely hot. Maybe even hotter, actually. The fae probably have elevated taste, right? With the enhanced perception and all."

Faith snorts. "Whatever you wanna tell yourself."

I'm ninety-nine percent sure she's joking, but it hits me all at once regardless. Faith *is* amazing. Maybe a little too much so. After all, I'm the one who told her she should get close enough to people to hurt them this summer. She'd made it sound like that hadn't extended to me, but maybe, I've been her biggest target all along.

My grip on her goes slack. "Is this... do you actually like me? I don't think— you didn't say it, did you?" I realize. "*I* said it, but you just went along with it again, didn't you? Do you—"

Faith backs up to stare at me. Maybe she's trying to figure out if I've ruined her plan. "Why wouldn't I—"

"I told you to pretend to get close to people!" I remind her. "I— shit, don't tell me, actually. You shouldn't... I'm really good at wondering about things. So if today doesn't go well and I'm left to keep wondering about it forever, that'll—"

"I like you, Charlotte. A lot. For real."

I thought the confirmation would make me giddy, but instead, I'm devastated. "You weren't supposed to say that!" I sob.

"I know." Faith nods. "But I needed you to know you're really, really easy to like, okay? Especially when you're not trying to be."

"Thank you," I sniffle.

Faith takes a deep breath. "Keep your mouth closed, okay?"

"I... what—"

"Just..." She runs her fingers through her hair. "Do it? Please?"

I nod.

Faith shakes out her wrists before leaning towards me. "I'm going to kiss you, I think," she says. "I hope."

It's impossible to sit still after hearing that, but I make myself do it anyway. She leans in closer. I feel her hair tickle the tips of my ears. Then, for a fraction of a second her lips are on my cheek and then gone again and she's staring at me, waiting. "Okay?" she checks.

'Okay' is far from the proper descriptor for something that's turned all my bones into fizzy drinks, but it's all I can manage. "Okay. I umm..."

Faith's pendant lights up and all at once, the moment's over. She gasps and jumps away.

"Are you okay?" I rush to my feet. "Did it—"

"They're coming," she says. "Shit, I thought I'd..." She scrambles for my hands then realizes she's grabbed them and quickly lets go again. "Shit, sorry, I didn't mean to—"

I wrap my fingers back around hers and kiss the back of her hand. "You're fine. Very valid reason to forget for a moment."

"Right." Faith nods. "Thanks, I..." She takes a deep breath before looking right at me.

I try my very best to stay in the present moment instead of diving head-first into her eyes.

"I had a really good summer, okay?" Faith's voice shakes. "Best one of my life. Best anything of my life, actually. No matter what happens, I need you to know I'm so, so glad I knew you."

"I might've ruined your life," I whisper.

"No," Faith shakes her head, squeezing my fingers tighter. "That was me, okay? You saved it, no matter what happens. And I'm the only one of us who can't lie, so you have to take my word for that, okay?" She tries to laugh but her nose just bubbles snot. "This isn't your fault. I was always inevitably going to mess up and tell someone and I'm so, so glad it was you, okay? I don't... promise me you'll remember this wasn't your fault."

I swallow. "I can't... I can try," I decide.

"Okay." Faith nods. "I can take that." She lets go of my hands. "I need to go check on the actual flag, are you good to go gather everyone and get them ready?"

I don't feel myself nod, but I must, because she keeps talking.

"You're amazing, Lots," she says. "I hope you get to keep being amazing for a really, really long time."

"You too," I whisper.

Faith turns to go.

"Wait!" I cry out.

She does.

"Your shoes," I manage. "I need to—"

"Right." She waits for me to kneel and tie them. I don't know what I'm supposed to say as I do. I've bought myself more time, but I can't think of a single word to fill it with.

It'd be selfish to tie her shoes slowly on purpose, but my fingers feel so useless that it takes longer than usual anyway. When I stand back up, Faith's staring at me and I'm staring at her and I've run out of words in the dictionary, so I throw my arms around her instead and let myself cry into her chest for a moment

"I'm really glad I knew you," I finally manage to say as she pulls away.

Faith fails to smile and nods exactly once. "You too."

Then, we race off in opposite directions.

I fix my smile and try to pretend everything's alright.

Chapter 45

"Friends and enemies!" My legs feel like jelly as I stand in the middle of the field to address both teams. "Welcome to the final battle!"

My friends hoot and cheer because they have no idea what's actually going on. After observing for a few seconds, the faerie team does the same. I never knew whistling could sound so sinister.

"Both teams should have hidden their flags by now. Caribous?" As far as the rest of my cabin knows, our flag is a green tennis ball that Van hid between the roots of a tree near the far left of our side's boundary lines. I wait for him to nod before turning to the faeries.

"Antelopes?"

They nod their assent as well.

It's odd. I'm the one who proposed a capture the flag game and I knew we'd given the fae specific instructions to make themselves look human, but I was still kind of expecting glowing, muscle-bound super-humans with swords and machetes. Instead, our competition looks like a bunch of incredibly average, incredibly scrawny teenage boys. Faith must've done an incredibly accurate job describing what the kind of people who *would* challenge us would look like to His Excellentance Squirge.

I scan my team one more time for Faith, just in case. Ideally, we'd been hoping they wouldn't think to cut off her access to Faerie's magic supply so that she could just instantly figure out where the flag is, but when she meets my eye, she just shakes her head slightly. I try not to let my disappointment show. We still have the rest of the plan. Faith's the only person on the playing field with access to both heightened senses and the ability to make herself more difficult to track right now, so we still have the upper hand. And an actual in-bounds flag to find, presumably. We've got this in the bag. Hopefully.

I roll my shoulders and look away from her. If everyone's attention's on me, Faith might be able to disappear herself and scope out the flag before the game even officially begins. I re-explain the rules as slowly and pedantically as I can, but eventually, I run out of ways to say 'no cheating' and she hasn't returned to declare our early victory yet. I swallow.

"Well, then," I smile at the players, "the battle begins in three, two, one!"

Instantly, everyone takes off running. I rush to take my position.

If you've ever played capture the flag recreationally, you might assume that there's no real strategy behind it. You'd be assuming wrong. Anything can be strategized, if you're obsessive enough to think about it deeply enough.

For instance, if your team's fastest player *loves* chasing people but despises having to stay on task, you position her near the front of your side of the field. Further back she might not feel surrounded enough by the game to engage fully and could wander off and leave the flag unguarded. On offense, she might decide that something more interesting's happening mid-attack and would almost definitely lose interest the moment anyone tries to get her to wait around in jail. Near the middle line, Sunny easily outpaces anyone who even attempts to get by her. If the faeries want a shot at getting far enough into our zone to start to look for our non-existent flag, they have no other option but to send another assailant to distract her, inevitably bringing down their numbers. And giving us even more of an advantage.

If another of your team members is ridiculously good at reading people but also might need to take a lot of sudden breaks to make sure he's pacing himself properly, he needs to be entirely on offense. That way Van can scout things out whenever he feels alright enough to and doesn't have to worry about anyone sneaking by him if he has a sudden flare up.

Brain also takes offense so we can have our biggest sign-users together since the fae (and of course, the incredibly ableist fictional Antelope cabin) apparently don't know any ASL, providing our team with an excellent way of planning out attack routes in secret, and we keep Gator as close to the center line as possible in case they need to use them as a decoy runner since they're a lot better at being loud and disruptive than most of the rest of us.

Neither Morgan nor I are particularly good at offense or defense, but we also don't technically *need* a good defense, so we each take a back corner and pretend to guard it. The ball we've hidden's near me, but hopefully, the fae won't even consider that it's a decoy flag we planted to fool our own team. Ideally, they'll pass over it and just keep looking.

And Faith's a floater. Or at least, that's what we told the rest of our cabin. She thought it'd be best if she was the last person anyone would consider a part of their team so that she'd be able to disappear more effectively, so telling everyone that she could be anywhere at any given time should hopefully help with that. She's actually entirely offense, obviously. If she's right, the fae would've chosen a hiding spot too difficult for anyone else to notice. We need her searching and invisible.

Capture the flag might not technically require strategy, but I've never met a social encounter that I couldn't find some way to overthink, and I've overthought this one perfectly.

Except for the way it's supposed to make me feel.

I like to prepare for the unpreparable, so I've been running through all the ways I'd react to today since the moment I proposed it. I knew there was a very big chance I'd freeze beneath fear and pressure and prepared myself for it accordingly. I'd been ready to find it shockingly similar to a typical capture the flag game and find myself feeling competitive or excited. I'd even prepared for sadness in case it instantly became obvious that we were going to lose.

What I hadn't accounted for was boredom.

For a while, it feels like we're winning. The fae might've spent months training for this as intensely as they would for an actual war, but they spent those months preparing for typical human competition. Not a cabin multi-lingual enough to plan out how they're gonna destroy them right in front of their faces and aware enough of all their weaknesses to have every player with speech stage whisper about a fake hiding spot whenever a faery's within earshot. The fae are ridiculously gullible and for the first thirty minutes, we send them on such a wild goose chase that the win feels a shoo-in.

But we still haven't found the flag yet. I spot Faith a few times (mostly once she's already in jail and waiting to slip away again), but if she's figured out where it is and is just waiting for the moment to strike, she certainly doesn't seem confident about it. We said it had to be partially visible. One of us will inevitably find it. Eventually.

There's only so long you can fool even the most gullible of creatures into falling for the same tricks over and over again, though. As the afternoon wears on, the fae gradually start becoming a lot more skeptical of our fake-outs until they eventually stop listening to them altogether. There are also only so many ways you can sign variations of 'run!' before your competition starts catching on to what that looks like, and only so many attack patterns you can attempt before they memorize them all.

It's not a typical 'nothing to do' boredom because I know exactly what I'm supposed to be doing. It's not a low-stakes one either because the stakes are as high as they possibly could be. It's paralysis. It's helplessness. It's being forced to acknowledge that at the end of the day, no matter how much time and planning I've poured into today and how enthusiastic I try to appear, most of this is just a waiting game. You can't logic your way through a waiting game. The fae will keep trying to find our flag until they eventually realize it's not here, we'll keep trying to find theirs until we become too bored or tired to keep trying, and Faith (the only one of us with an actual shot at finding it at all, judging by how impossibly, perfectly hidden it seems to be) will keep blipping in and out of everyone else's awareness, desperately trying to find the other team's pinnie before one of those first two options happens.

A weapon-fueled, physically intensive battle with the fae would've been terrifying, and avoiding that was the objectively safest option, but in a weapon-fueled, physically intensive battle, at least I'd be able to feel like I'm *doing* something. At least I'd be able to see who's winning.

Instead, the girl I like's life hangs in the balance and all I can do is wait, try to avoid catching sight of her no matter how desperately I want to, and pretend to guard a flag that isn't actually hidden anywhere near here. I planned and trained us as close to winning as I could get us, but now, there's nothing left for me to do. And that's terrifying.

I've known Faith for most of my conscious life and we only finally got to start becoming friends a few weeks ago and if we don't win, she'll be gone forever just when we're finally starting to get things right. And there's absolutely nothing left for me to do about it.

If this was a normal capture the flag game we would've won ages ago, but clearly, the fae have also found some way to bend the rules in their favour. I'm sure we said the flag had to be hidden within the boundaries and had to be visible, but the longer the game wears on, the more holes I start to poke in my own rules.

Maybe someone's wearing the flag. Maybe they've been moving it. Maybe the fae can see into some extra fifth-dimension that the rest of us can't, so it's *technically* visible while being entirely unseeable for the rest of us.

I don't know the exact moment when the game stops feeling fun, but I'm pretty sure it's around the thirty-five minute mark. No one's started talking about giving up by that point yet (or at least, they haven't around me), but our triumphant "ha!"s after tagging someone start sounding a bit less triumphant. Our sprints out of our safe zone have a little less bounce to them. I do my best to smile and cheer to compensate, but people are losing interest quickly and I don't know how to convince anyone that a capture the flag game's important enough to waste hours on. We need to find their flag. And soon.

Around the fifty-minute mark, Brain sits down on the sidelines. I instantly jog over to meet her. Once people start to leave an event or activity, it almost always starts a trickle effect.

"Are you okay?" It's hard to pretend to be happy and energized while I'm actively panting. "Are you—"

Tired, Brain signs. Then, she signs something I can't understand.

"What?"

G-I-V-E-U-P, she spells.

I panic, glancing around. "Five more minutes," I beg. "Just give me..." I jog to the middle of the field and raise my hands in the air. "Water break!" I yell. "We're pausing until—"

"Pausing was not in the rules," a boy with pimply skin and war paint on his cheeks informs me.

"We all must be thirsty," I try to reason. "Why don't we—"

"Pausing was not in the rules!" He stomps his foot. I'm not sure if he's a particularly important faery, but now is probably not the best time to test any of them.

"Right," I sigh. "Yeah. Carry on, then."

I run back over to Brain.

"Fifteen more minutes," I try. "Please. You don't have to... just pretend to look busy so no one gives up. This is really important to Fay."

F-A-Y not here, she signs.

"Yeah," I nod. "No, yeah, she is." I squint at the field until she finally comes into focus near the edge of the faeries' domain. "See? She's just like... really good at being sneaky. Please. Fifteen minutes."

Brain squints at me. *Fifteen.*

I clap. "Thank you! Oh my god, thanks so much!"

I jog back to the far end of the field to find Morgan.

"I need something," I pant.

She nods instantly.

"Don't stop playing, okay? Even if everyone else does. I can't tell you why, but please just don't—"

Morgan gathers my fists together in hers and squeezes them. *Okay,* she signs.

That's enough. With Morgan, that's always enough.

I switch myself onto offense. Now that we're running out of time, there's no point keeping up appearances. Someone needs to find the flag. I don't even make it past the boundary line before someone grabs me. "Hey," I whirl around to face them. "Wrong side! You have to—"

Faith stares at me, eyes wide and shining. She jerks her head to the side and holds out a hand.

"Okay," I whisper. "Let's..."

We go.

Chapter 46

Faith keeps her finger on her lips until we're completely hidden by the trail.

"What—"

"They're sending back up," Faith says instantly. "To use magic to find the flag. Since the players can't use any or leave the playing field."

"Crap," I whisper. "Brain's about to give up anyway," I admit. "I think—"

Faith lets go of my hand. "Plan B."

I frown. "What? We didn't—"

"Plan B," she repeats, starting to pace. She pulls a cue card out of her pocket and hands it to me. It's Morgan's. I *instantly* know it's Morgan's. Spirals and stars and all.

"When did you—"

"Plan B," Faith says again.

I flip over the card and read it.

What ever you do, don't stop thinking about Faith. <u>*Not even for a 2nd!!!*</u>

It's not Faith's handwriting, though, it's Morgan's. I stare.

"She's very confused. You're gonna have to come up with a better excuse after all this is over. Asked her for it right before the game started." Faith continues to pace, somehow simultaneously ignoring me and answering all my unvoiced questions.

"What am I supposed to do with this?"

She finally turns to face me. Her cheeks are tear-streaked. "They know I'm still using my senses and magic to cheat. The second I cross that line, all eyes are on me," she whispers. "I can't... you were right. I need to be able to disappear completely."

"You said that was dangerous."

"You were right, though." Faith tries to smile. "Obviously. Too fucking smart. 's the only option. If you're still okay to try. Are you?"

"Of course." I nod, despite my hammering heart and my shaking hands. "What do I have to do?"

"Sit," Faith instructs.

I do.

"I don't know exactly what happens," Faith admits, sitting down across from me. "Obviously. People don't tend to..." She swallows. "But I do know your brain's probably going to do everything it can to make you forget I even exist, okay? So you need to... you keep your mind on me and your eyes on the cue card, alright? No matter what."

I feel like I'm about to vomit.

"Lots?"

I swallow. "I have ADHD," I whisper. "This... I'm probably the worst person to—"

"No," Faith shakes her head. "No, you're not. You're the only person who can, okay? I'm probably about to take your hands." She holds hers out. "Please."

I place mine in hers.

"I'm not scared," she squeezes my fingers. "Okay? I'm not—"

"You're actively crying," I correct her.

"Not because I'm scared." Faith just keeps shaking her head. She raises our joined hands to her lips and waits for me to nod before kissing my fingers. "You're loyal, and selfless, and so, so hard working, so I know I don't have to be, alright? I know I don't have to be. Because even if you forget how important this is or why you're supposed to be thinking about me in the first place, I know you're going to keep trying your hardest, just because you think someone you cared about asked you to. No questions asked or explanations needed. That's just how you work."

"What if I can't?" I remind her. "What if... you said..."

"Then I'm still not scared because I'll get to know you cared enough to try. I'm not scared, Lots," she repeats. "If this goes wrong it's absolutely not your fault, but neither of us will remember enough to be hurt by it anyway, okay? So right now, all I need you to know is I'm still really, really happy, okay? I'm not afraid."

"I am," I admit.

Faith laughs. "That's just 'cuz you don't know yourself as well as I do yet." She lets go of my hands then hesitates. "I should go, in a moment. Before their backup gets here."

"Okay." I nod.

"I want to... I think I'm going to try and kiss you again. Just to... not to try and be more memorable just... potential final moments and all that. 's that okay?"

I can barely breathe enough to manage a quick "very".

Faith leans forward. She gently moves my hair off my cheek. I close my eyes. I can practically feel the hairs on her skin brushing against mine.

Then, she gags, manages a quick "nope", and bails to the left at the last second. She starts to apologize and I burst out laughing and pull her into my chest instead. I watch my tears fall onto her scalp as she laughs against me.

"Everything's going to be okay," I say.

Faith kisses my neck. Possibly because she can't repeat the sentiment. "I've got to go," she says, getting back up. "Look at the cue card."

"Okay." I cross my legs and stare straight at it.

Faith takes a step then hesitates. "Charlotte?"

I start to look up and she instantly stops me.

"You can't look. Keep your eyes on the card."

"Right." I nod. "Okay."

I hear Faith take a long breath. "I just wanted to... just so you know, as far as potential final moments go, that was a pretty great one."

I open my mouth to respond, but by the time I do, I have no idea what I was going to say.

I'm alone off the path with no breath in my lungs and no idea how I got here. And a cue card in my hands.

Chapter 47

Non-ADHDers often associate ADHD with constantly bouncing off the walls or the complete inability to pay any form of attention.

This is inaccurate. My ADHD spends a lot more time draining me of energy than filling me with it, and if anything, it feels like it makes my attention magnify. I don't have a deficit of attention, I have a deficit in knowing where, how, and when to allocate it. My brain doesn't wander, it latches. To a million different thoughts that I've already chased to death and a million different things that don't matter and occasionally, sometimes, to things that do.

ADHDers and Non-ADHDers alike also sometimes liken ADHD to a superpower. It can be a comfort to frame the ability to hyperfocus as purely positive or a brain that's constantly hopping to places that it isn't supposed to be in as some kind of super genius machine. My ADHD is also not that. I don't have any super-human abilities, I just have some trees, the vague awareness that people are making noise somewhere beyond them, and a cue card that makes absolutely no sense.

What ever you do, don't stop thinking about Faith. <u>Not even for a 2nd</u>!!!

Faith is a girl in our cabin. I don't know when she first started coming to Corrain. I don't know if she's here this summer, but I *do* know that she's here this summer because I count things constantly to make sure I'm not losing track of them, and I know that there are seven of us. Faith is a girl in our cabin and I don't know when she started coming to Corrain, but I do know that she's here this summer.

Faith is a girl in our cabin and I don't know why Morgan would want me to think about her and I can't remember a single conversation either of us have ever had with her except I do, don't I? I must. Because I've spent nights and days and class time thinking about her and even longer trying to plan out how *not* to think about her. Faith is a girl in our cabin and I don't know why Morgan would want me to think about her because I'm pretty sure we don't like her. Or maybe we do because I've spent nights and days and class time thinking about her and that doesn't seem like the kind of thing you do for someone you don't like. I don't remember a single word I've ever said to Faith, but I remember how to spell her name. A before I. Something that's intuitive for other people but isn't for me. Which means that if I know how to spell her name, then for some reason, at some point, I was using it enough to make sure I always got it right.

Faith is a girl in our cabin and I don't know why Morgan would want me to think about her, but that doesn't matter at all, does it? Because Morgan is also a girl in our cabin and she is constant and solid and the first time I've felt seen by someone who doesn't share my DNA and if Morgan wants me to think about her, then that must be the right thing to do. Because Morgan knows how to gently guide me through remembering to eat and sleep and take my meds and brush my teeth and comb my hair and even just remembering to *breathe* most of the time and she's never steered me wrong before, so I think about Faith.

Who is a girl in our cabin who I might not like and might something else who's been coming to camp here for an undeterminable number of years and who is probably here this summer. Who sleeps on the top bunk, I think. I'm not sure where specifically her bunk is, but I know that she always sleeps in the top one. Whose hair's black and whose eyes are... something. Whose hair's ink and whose eyes are dark and whose hands are soft. Whose hair's stories and whose eyes are eternity and whose hands are magic, somehow. And who Morgan's told me to think about.

I think of Faith whose last name I know is Harris because at some point, I decided to always attach it to her first. Whose hair's stories with words blotted out because she plucks them away when she's stressed and whose eyes are eternity yet shining, for some reason, though I can't remember why, and whose hands are magic yet solid enough that she's constantly cracking her knuckles or rubbing at the skin on her thumbs. I think of Faith who's a girl in our cabin (I think) and who's apparently an incredibly easy person to think about because I am overflowing with thoughts about her.

I don't know why or how I got here, but I think of Faith Harris who's somehow everything and nothing all at once, because Morgan told me to and thought it was important enough to write down. I might not be good at following multi-step instructions, but I can follow this one. I'm an expert at holding onto one thing long enough for it to burn a hole in my brain.

I'm thinking of Faith Harris who is a girl in my cabin who I don't like or maybe do and wondering why and how and when and where I got here, and then all at once, she's right in front of me, completely out of breath.

"You can stop," Faith gasps. "You can—"

It comes back so quickly that I double over. Faeries and changelings and capture the flag and pink, glittering dust and Faith's fingers on mine and Faith's lips on my cheek. And the red pinnie in her fist.

She holds it out. "Didn't claim it yet," she said. "Figured you deserved to get the credit for this one. Look like a hero."

I take a deep breath. My chest and mind and legs feel like fractals. And fizz and light and pink, glittering dust.

"They hid it in a fucking flower," she's still saying. "Planted it before the no magic rule went into effect. Take it. You can—"

"I'm very okay not looking good at anything at all right now."

"Okay." Faith nods. "Right, I'll..." She runs her hand through her hair. "Come with me?" She holds out her hand. "Please?"

I reach up to grab it. There's blood under my nails. I don't even remember when I started picking at my face.

Faith notices me reaching up to touch my skin and kisses my cheek. "I'll fix it," she promises. "Soon as the rest of my magic's back."

I don't know how to tell her that now that she's here everything already *is* fixed, so I squeeze her hand, try to catch my breath, and let her lead me back to the playing field.

Chapter 48

I don't know how long I spent away from the game, but by the time we return, most of our team's already sidelined themselves. Except Morgan who stayed because I asked her to so of course she did, even though I couldn't tell her why. Because of course she did.

Which means we haven't surrendered.

Faith lets go of my hand, marches right to the center of the field, and holds the flag up into the air. "We win!" she yells. "Found it! Go home now!"

I'm expecting some kind of massive outburst, but instead, the fae just simply turn around and walk away. At least they don't just pop out of existence this time. That probably would've been difficult to explain.

As the not-teenage-boys leave with their heads hanging in defeat, an outburst actually does start up from our end of the field. Boredom and exhaustion miraculously disappear the moment there's something to celebrate.

"Fay!" Sunny yells, starting the chant.

Slowly, everyone gets up to join us near the center of the field. "Fay! Fay! Fay! Fay!"

Now that it's easy to pay attention to Faith, she's the only thing I *can* focus on. She stands there (chest heaving, pinnie still clutched like a lifeline) and slowly, she begins to laugh. Loud and high and delirious, and then she's cheering too and we're all laughing and everything is perfect. Exactly as it should've been all summer.

Until all at once, the cheering stops. And everyone stares.

"What?" I giggle again, looking around. Everything looks perfectly ordinary, but suddenly, everyone's wide-eyed and slack-jawed. Even Faith. "What's—"

"Lots," Faith whispers, nodding ahead of us. "Look."

It's surprising how quickly your brain starts to process a tiny angry blue fairy as ordinary.

Faith physically stumbles back. Which also forces me to stumble back since I'm the one standing behind her. I wrap my hand around hers.

"You've revealed yourself to *more* humans, then?" His Excellentance Squirge squeaks. I look around expecting more faerie assailants to pop out of thin air, but luckily, it looks like he's the only one who's stayed behind.

Faith doesn't respond. I feel her arm shake against mine.

Squirge sighs. "We'll reset, then. With *fair* rules for the rest of the rounds. I'll need a day or two to round up new competitors."

This is my fault. We were so close, and just because I had to suggest a stupid nickname, I've ruined everything.

"I didn't..." Faith whispers so quietly that I can barely even hear it. "I wasn't—"

"She didn't," I realize all at once. I keep my hand on hers as I move to stand in front of her. I put my unoccupied hand on my hip and try to summon as much authority as I can possibly muster as I stare the little fairy down. "Now, I'm no expert on human-fae relations, but I'm pretty sure you're not just supposed to go around revealing yourself to humans all willy-nilly."

"Exactly!" Squirge squeaks. "Which is why—"

"*Which is why* I'm sure your superiors wouldn't want to hear about you dropping your disguise with this many humans around."

He frowns. "The changeling already told them!"

"Why would you think that?" I feign obliviousness.

"Lots," Faith hisses.

But I've got this. I know I've got this. "Oh my gosh." I clutch a hand to my chest. "Because we called her Fay? That's like, the most common nickname for Faith in this realm. You're supposed to be a human expert, aren't you? How could you swap someone out for a baby named Faith without realizing that?"

"I'm not..." Squirge's cheeks darken. "That wasn't—"

"Did anyone know faeries were real until a few seconds ago?" I turn to face the rest of my cabinmates. They're mostly busy staring in disbelief, but eventually, everyone shakes their head. "Alright then." I clap my hands together. "Seems that's all cleared up. Good luck with all your upcoming battles. That's..." I count everyone else out. "Five to go, I think? Six if the aid over there's paying enough attention." I nod to where she's waiting at the other end of the field. "But maybe you'll be able to convince her you were a toy or something. Hopefully none of us'll tell anyone else and add more to your plate, but like, it can be so difficult to remember to keep a secret for someone you barely know, you know? I'm sure we'll at least try, though."

His face is almost full purple now. "That's ridiculous!" Squirge tries to stomp his tiny foot against the air. "You tricked me! You—"

"We might be able to help," I stop him. "Of course. For a price."

"You do not get to negotiate with—"

I turn to Faith. She's still pale and shaking, so I take her other hand in mine to try and better hold her focus. "Does he have a... him?" I check. "Someone who's about to pop in and get mad that he just did that?"

"I'm..." she stammers. "I don't..."

"Faith." I squeeze her hands. "You're okay. You're not in trouble. Does he have a him?"

She shakes her head. "Not... only earthside fae do. Since we're the ones who..."

"Okay." I smile as gently as I can and pat her arm before turning back around. "Excellent. My colleague has decided that out of the goodness of her heart, she won't report this to anyone," I inform Squirge, "and none of us are going to say a word about it either. If you can like, somehow get Faith an extra boost of magic each morning to get her through the day. It'd only be fair since she gets a lot of hers from us and obviously you won't want us talking about her a ton after this. You've cut off one of her main energy sources."

Squirge squints at me. "I can do weekly," he eventually relents. "The deal's nullified the moment any of you reveal our secret to any outsiders."

"Faith?" I check. "Sound good?"

"I uhh... yeah." She nods. "Yes. That'll do."

I turn back to Squirge and grin. "You've got yourself a deal. Pleasure doing business with you."

After one final stomp and in a puff of air, he's gone.

The field is entirely silent. And then, the field is entirely too loud as the rest of our cabinmates erupt into pretty much every single exploitative under the sun. Faith whispers a quick "thank you" before she's pulled away from me in a fury of questions and demands and finally, I sit down to catch my breath.

"Hey," Morgan breaks off from the frenzy to find me first. She holds out a hand. "We're going back to the cabin to lie down for a bit."

I sag in relief and wrap my fingers around hers. "Thank you." She doesn't know all the other things that that 'thank you' means yet, but now that the secret's out, some day soon, I'll finally be able to tell her.

August 31

My dearest Alice,

If u told some1 u like them and they told u they like u and also u might of kinda saved there life maltipall times (metaforicly) accept only 1 of u is comeing back 2 camp nxt yr is it akward to ask for their #?

Probly yes right? Im thinking yes?

Talk at u (very) soon,
Charlotte

Chapter 49

I desperately want to talk to Faith now that there are no lives on the line, but it turns out it's extremely difficult to get a bit of alone time with someone after the rest of your friends have just found out that they have magical powers. Faith's surrounded by our cabinmates all evening and I quickly realize that I have no idea how to talk to her when there are other people around, so I just hide away in my bunk.

And she doesn't seem to notice. Or (more realistically given her heightened senses), she does and just doesn't care. After all, now that she's won her freedom, I'm a lot less useful to her. Especially considering the fact that she now has a whole cabin's worth of energy to exploit. I'm doing such a good job ignoring everything that I must not hear Morgan knocking against the underside of my bunk because she has to climb up to get my attention.

"Hey," she says.

I scoot over and hold up the covers so that she can join me.

"Today happened," Morgan says.

I nod, lying back down to stare at the ceiling. "It did."

"Faith's a fairy."

"Changeling," I correct. "Technically. Or I guess faery with an e, but she says that's less accurate."

"Good to know."

I roll over to face her fully. "Are you mad?"

Morgan frowns. "Why would I—"

"I didn't tell you," I remind her. "And I lied about why we had to win. And—"

"Lots," Morgan kisses my forehead. "I'm not mad you didn't tell me a secret that you literally weren't allowed to tell anyone."

"Okay," I sigh in relief. "That's good. Great."

Morgan throws her arm around me. I tuck my head into her shoulder and snuggle against her.

"I watched you tell off a magical creature today," she says.

I shrug. "I do that daily. Just normally the one who lives with us."

Morgan giggles. "How long have you known?"

"Since July." I wait for her to get angry at that, but secretly, I already know she won't. Morgan would never.

"That explains it," she squeezes me tighter. "We all thought you had a secret crush on her."

I blush. "I do," I admit. I'm tired of trying to keep secrets. "But we're leaving it there because she can definitely still hear us from her bunk. *And that's not even an embarrassing thing to overhear since I already told her!*" I raise my voice with that last bit.

Morgan laughs again.

Now that I can finally talk about it, I fill her in on everything that I've actually been up to all summer. (Or at least, everything that I'm okay with Faith potentially overhearing). And it's fine. Everything is so completely and totally fine that I feel kind of guilty that I was so worried it wouldn't be, but I decide that for now, I'm allowed to just blame that on general teenage insecurity instead of some kind of glaring personal flaw in need of immediate tackling. I let myself enjoy this moment where everything is fine and good and honest.

Even if our plans for next summer are constantly looming over the conversation. And even if after we say good night, I insist I'd rather sleep alone just because I'm half convinced that Faith'll pull me aside for one final secret nighttime meeting.

But she doesn't. She doesn't even try to. I wait until I can't possibly stay awake any longer, then climb down the ladder, curl up beside Morgan, and force myself to fall asleep.

August 31st

My dearest Alice,

How do u talk 2 some1 after u both know u like each other?

My curent plan is 2 just ignore her forever. Which feels very smart & practicall.

If she also dosnt talk to me right away it probly meens shes decided she hates me and nvr wants to talk to me evr again, right? Even if we almost kissed multipall times a few hrs ago?

Also HOW DO U ASK SOME1 FOR THERE PHONE #!!!

Talk at u in less then 24 hrs :):):):):):):),
Charlotte

Chapter 50

The final day of camp is essentially a half day of never-ending celebrations.

And unspecified pick-up times. Which means that Faith could be leaving for the last time ever any second now, and I still haven't gotten to talk to her at all since the battle ended.

Which I know I could solve by simply walking up to her and talking, but every time I try that, the rest of my body decides that it'd be a fate worse than death. I guess I'll just have to start coming to terms with the fact that I'll clearly never talk to her ever again.

Instead of getting closer to the music and party favours after the festivities kick up immediately after breakfast's over, all of us congregate around our tree. Even Sunny. It appears that yesterday's excitement didn't leave any Caribou eager for more. I'm doing a very good job pretending to be very busy on my phone while everyone else talks until I abruptly realize that they're *not* talking. I slowly look up to find everyone looking at me.

"Lots?" Faith's standing. Faith's the *only* one standing. "Can I umm... talk to you? For a second?"

(Gator responds to this with "oooooooh." Which I less than appreciate.)

"Sure." I fumble to put my phone away and somehow manage to miss the power button three separate times. "Of course."

We walk off towards the cabins together. (Van also "oooohs" as we do. Which I also do not appreciate.)

It feels weird that Faith doesn't take my hand as we leave, but I guess she doesn't have to anymore. None of this is a secret.

My heart should not be hammering this much over something that isn't even a secret.

"So," Faith says.

"So," I echo.

Abruptly, she turns to face me. She raises a hand towards my cheek. "I'm probably about to touch your face."

I can't tell why specifically she wants to, but I let her anyway because I want her to at least do *something* to ease the tension. But when my face prickles cold a few seconds later, I realize that she's just fulfilling her promise to close the scabs I picked open while I was trying to remember her. She instantly lets go.

"Thanks," I say.

"Sure," Faith nods. "Of course."

We keep walking. It's tense. And awkward. And terrible. And quiet.

Luckily, I'm exceptionally bad at staying quiet.

"You didn't talk to me," I accuse. "Yesterday. After."

"You didn't talk to me either."

"Yes, well..." I scrunch up my nose. "I liked this a lot more when it was just a you problem."

Faith laughs. A month ago, that would've sounded odd to me, but now, it makes everything feel a lot more okay. "I don't know how I'm supposed to thank you," she admits. "For... it feels like something too big to thank someone for."

"The fae aren't supposed to thank people at all," I remind her.

"Yeah, well, I think we're both incredibly aware that I don't do a lot of the things the fae are 'supposed' to." Faith rolls her eyes. It's such a default motion from her that normally I'd think nothing of it, but all at once, I realize that it makes absolutely no sense.

I stop walking and put an arm out to force her to do the same. "You just rolled your eyes."

She does it again. "Yes, Lots. Good job—"

"*How* did you roll your eyes?" I ask. "You can't— they're a solid colour!"

"Oh." Faith blushes. "Right. I forgot you could... it's an illusion. Only takes a bit of magic so... yeah."

"I'm sorry, you're apparently starving for magic, yet you use it for an *eye-rolling* illusion?"

Faith shrugs. "It's a great way to annoy people."

I burst out laughing. "That's ridiculous!" I exclaim. "That's—you're absolutely ridiculous."

Faith runs her tongue along her gums. "Is that... too ridiculous?"

"The perfect amount," I decide. "I don't think I could tolerate a person who wasn't at least a little bit silly." I hesitate. "You have more magic now, you know," I remind her. "You don't have to put as much effort into maintaining your attention sources."

Faith nods. "Right. Look, thank you so much for—"

"Are you still planning on acting awful again?" I blurt. "Before everyone leaves?"

Faith frowns. For a moment she looks genuinely hurt and I desperately want to take the question back. "You still think I'd do that?"

"I think you're great," I try to fix it. "I just... I think you've always been great, right? You're just good at pretending you're not. I didn't mean to... I wouldn't blame you if you still felt like it was the safest option... but I also..."

"I think I'd like to try it for a bit," Faith admits. "The nice thing." Most people who are eager to try to be nicer don't physically cringe while saying the word, but I chalk that up to years of conditioning. "And the friend thing. If you'd still want—"

"I do," I say instantly.

"And umm..." She runs her hands through her hair. "Other things too. If you'd still want to—"

I grin. "I also like other things."

I hold out my hand. Finally, Faith takes it. Finally, things feel the way that they're supposed to.

"Heard you talking to Morgan last night," she says. "Figured you might say something interesting."

"Did I?"

"Not as many glowing compliments about me as I was hoping for," Faith admits. "But you'll get there eventually." She pauses. "You still haven't told her you're not doing Leadership, Lots."

"I did a really good job with the game," I remind her. "Morgan says it seems like that was actually a lot more work than Leadership'll be. Especially now that she knows all the faery stuff. I could easily do Leadership next year."

"I can tell her for you," Faith volunteers. "If you want."

"No. She's my best friend. I just..." I sigh. "I can do Leadership. If anything, this summer proved I'll be able to."

"Doesn't mean you have to."

"But I *should*. I'm... you don't get it."

"Okay." Faith just plops herself down in the middle of the grass, as if she *knows* I'll stop walking to join her. It's infuriatingly confident. It's even more infuriating that she's absolutely right. "Make me get it, then."

I sigh and sit down across from her. So close that our knees touch. Not for magic just... because. I take off my tangle. "There are a lot of things..." I pause as if that'll help me arrange the words better, but it rarely does. "That I can't do."

"There's a lot of things a lot of people can't do," Faith fake-rolls her eyes again. I try to watch exactly how she does it, but the illusion vanishes just as quickly as she summons it. "And most of them don't have actual disabilities getting in the way."

"I might not be dyslexic," I interrupt.

Faith's eyes narrow. "Yeah, okay. I know. I literally didn't even mention it that time."

"Oh." I chew on my cheek.

Faith sighs. "Even if you aren't, even pretending it wouldn't also be valid if it was just your ADHD, you don't have to have a disability to be gentle with yourself, Lots."

"Hypocrite," I blurt before I can think it through enough to stop myself.

Faith just laughs. "Okay." She runs a hand through her hair. "Okay, fair." She leans forward. "Let's make a deal, then."

"Changelings don't deal in those."

"Maybe I do," she shrugs. "This isn't the magical kind anyway." She holds out her hands and waits for me to take them. "I am going to do my best to get better at letting myself accommodate autism stuff."

"It could just be faery stuff." I remind her.

Faith just rolls her eyes. "I'm very clearly an autistic changeling, Lots," she says. "And that's... I know objectively fine. And like, genuinely comforting to acknowledge one second and then terrifying the next, so I don't think I can say fine for me right now, but it feels better than trying to convince myself I'm not. Future fine."

I chew on my lip. "I don't know... tell me how you want me to react to this."

Faith laughs. "Just say you know, it's really obvious, and I shouldn't keep second-guessing myself every other minute."

"Right." I nod. "I know, it's really obvious, and you shouldn't keep second-guessing yourself every other minute. Seriously, though." I squeeze her hands. "I didn't mean to pressure you into... if you really think you were misdiagnosed, it wasn't my place to—"

"I know I'm autistic," she admits. "I just... also really wish someone could just scan my brain and tell me every single thing going on in there so I don't have to keep worrying about what's causing what and feeling guilty for blaming things on the wrong thing, but since you people are ridiculously slow with technology—"

"Does Faerie even have electricity?"

"Irrelevant," Faith brushes off the question. "I guess I'll just have to settle for trying to remind myself that even if one day they *can* do that and it turns out I'm wrong, accommodating myself isn't a crime. But you know like, working on that extremely gradually. Probably. Okay." She shakes out her shoulders. "Your turn. I'm gonna work on that, you're gonna work on telling your parents that you very clearly want to get an official dyslexia evaluation."

"It'd be a waste of time and energy," I instantly explain. "I'm almost done with school anyway and get all the same accommodations already through my IEP, so—"

"Yeah." Faith nods. "You said. You also keep bringing it up though, and you're obsessed with knowing things, so it obviously wouldn't be a waste of time. You're like, actively trying to be amazing at everything else all the time just because you don't have a clear answer there, Lots. If it'd make you more comfortable, knowing wouldn't be—"

"How do I even say that?" I chew a bit too hard at my lip and switch to a charm instead. " 'Hey, I know this won't give me any additional academic advantages whatsoever and we're all already kind of acting like we already know I *am* dyslexic, but also I need to waste resources figuring out which specific disabilities are causing which parts of my brain to suck'?"

"Exactly like that." Faith nods. "Without the suck part probably, though. Depending on who you're talking to."

I just keep chewing.

Faith sighs. "You don't actually have to. You were right, deals aren't like..."

"I want to," I admit. "It just feels kind of ridiculous to want to if it wouldn't change anything."

"Wanting to know more about yourself's a fair reason." Faith shrugs. "A really good one, actually. You're umm... not a bad person to try and get to know better. Just so you know. And stuff."

"What if I'm not even dyslexic?" I whisper.

"Would you want to know that?" she checks.

I nod.

"Then that's still a good enough reason to say you want to do it. Plus, ADHD and dyslexia are crazy co-morbid. Some sources say that like, up to almost half of people with ADHD also have dyslexia."

"Right." I nod. "Yeah, that's why... wait," I frown. "When'd I tell you that?"

Faith's eyes widen. "I umm.... Google did." She fixes her hair. "I think."

"Why were you googling ADHD and dyslexia statistics?"

She mumbles something too indistinct for me to hear.

"What?"

"Research is your love language," she mutters, face redder than I've ever seen it. "Or whatever."

"Love language was probably a bad word choice, actually," I correct.

"Okay." Faith focuses on cracking her knuckles.

"There's very little evidence that love languages are an actual thing. As a metaphoric expression, they're fine, but as—"

"Oh my god, are you trying to torture me?" she exclaims.

"Just a little," I admit. "I like it when you're all embarrassed. I'm also trying to share very valuable information about love languages, though."

Faith groans, flopping backward onto the grass. I giggle, scooting closer to lean over her.

"You liiiiiike me," I sing.

"Yes. Which shouldn't even be embarrassing because you already know that," she mutters. She holds out a hand and waits for me to pull her back up. "Which is why I'm gonna keep bothering you until you either go talk to Morgan or let me do it. I'm not letting you spend another summer miserable."

I fidget with my tangle. "This one wasn't... this one was good, I think. A lot, but also... I'm glad this one happened."

"Yeah," Faith rolls her eyes. "Obviously. Go talk to Morgan before I lose my mind anyway?"

I hesitate. "You won't leave before saying goodbye, right? I know you can't come back next summer, but that doesn't mean... if your parents get here, at least come and find me to... to umm..."

"I'll stay right here." Faith crosses her legs and plants herself in place. "They won't be here for a while, but if they're early, odds are you'll find me again before they do."

"Right." I nod. "Good, I umm... I'll be back!" I jog off. "Don't go anywhere!"

"Wouldn't dream of it."

Chapter 51

By the time I get back to our tree, Sunny and Brain are already gone. I didn't even get to say goodbye. I have their contact information, but that's not even the point. This is my third last summer before adulthood. And it's already started to wrap up without me even noticing.

I'm running out of time.

"Morgan." I jog straight over to her. "Can we... I want to... let's talk."

She takes my hand and leads me away.

"You're the talkative one, Lots," Morgan eventually pulls me out of my brain. I've been very busy thinking of excuses and faeries and explanations and, briefly, some TV show I haven't seen for over a decade that has absolutely no relevance to any of this.

"What?"

"You wanted to talk," she reminds me. "We're not doing that."

"Oh." I rub my hands against my pants. "Yes." I take her other hand and stand directly across from her. It feels a little too formal and a lot too much like a proposal, but that's fine because that means it also feels like the opposite of a breakup. "I umm... next year. We'd talked about next summer. And umm..." I tilt my head back and take a deep breath. "Geez, I don't know why this is freaking me out so much."

When I look back at Morgan, there's a pre-written cue card in her hands. She holds it out to me.

"You don't ever want to do Leadership," Morgan recites as I read.

I blink. "You knew?"

"For a few weeks," she admits. "I kept bringing it up because I thought you were looking for an opportunity to tell me. Then you did bring it up but said it was because you didn't think you could, so for a bit I thought it was just... I knew the whole time, though."

"How'd you know?"

She frowns in confusion, because the answer should have already been obvious. She knew because she knows me. Maybe she even knew before I did.

"I kept thinking I'd change my mind," I try to explain. "I kept... I thought we'd do the battle and we'd win and I'd realize I really, really like planning activities and running games and fostering community and it's... I didn't feel terrible, I'm glad it happened and worked and I liked feeling accomplished, but I also really, really like doing nothing."

Morgan laughs. "That's okay."

"Is it, though?" I check. "Are you sure you're not... why didn't you bring it up?" Morgan very rarely keeps her opinions to herself. Especially when they're about me because she knows how much I need to hear them.

She's Morgan and she knows me, though, so she's somehow even anticipated my follow up question. She pulls another cue card from her pocket and hands it to me.

"I thought you didn't want to, but you hadn't said that yet. And then you did and made it sound like it was because you thought you couldn't. I'd never want you to think I don't think you'd be able to do something." It's a longer message, but she still gets every word right.

"I can, though," I sniffle. "I'd be able to... isn't that the goal here? To figure out all the things I can do and then prove to the world that I can do them?"

Morgan smiles. She laughs a little. "It's summer camp. The goal's just to have fun."

I pull her closer and kiss her forehead. "I'll still see you," I say. "All the time next year, even if you're not staying in the cabin. Like, every second of downtime."

"Okay."

"And we'll obviously still text all the time even when you're busy with Leadership and hang out all the time during the school year and..." I take a shaking breath. I bite my lip. "I'm sorry. I just really didn't want anything to change. We were supposed to..."

"We were supposed to grow up," Morgan finishes for me. "It's okay if that means growing in slightly different directions sometimes."

"I love you." I throw myself at her and kiss her cheek. "I love you, I love you, I love you, I love you, I love you so fucking much. Forever."

Morgan giggles. "Have you told Faith that yet?"

I freeze. "I *do not* love Faith!" I pull away, completely aghast. "I umm... I think I might like her, though. A lot. And I— oh shit!" I remember. "I left her alone in a field waiting for me! I'd better umm..." I start to run off then jog back over to grab Morgan's hands. "You're amazing." I kiss her cheek. "I'm so proud of you. You're gonna be such a good full-time counsellor in training."

"And you're going to be great at doing nothing."

I laugh, hug her one last time for good measure, and rush off.

Chapter 52

"Faith!"

I find her exactly where she said she'd be: waiting alone for me in the middle of an empty field. She slowly turns to face me but I'm faster. A bit too fast. I slide along the grass when I try to slow down too quickly and go toppling to the ground.

"Oh my god?" Faith jumps up. "Are you okay?"

"Perfect." I spit out grass as I roll over. "Great. I'm..." I let her pull me to my feet then awkwardly shift from foot to foot. "I was worried you'd be gone already," I admit.

"I'm not."

"Yeah," I can't help but grin. "Yeah, you're not." I slip my tangle around my fingers. "So. I was thinking. About after this. I know you can't come back next summer because you promised you wouldn't so what if in the meantime... where do you live?" I realize. "I don't even know where you live."

"Milton," Faith supplies.

"Oh. That is... not very close to me." I chew on my lip. "But I was thinking. Since you can't come back next summer if you wanted to like, maybe run into each other again we could pick a place? In Toronto or something. Everyone goes to Toronto at some point, right? And then every time you're in town you can go there and every time I'm in town I can also go there and maybe I'll see you there. Sometime."

"In Toronto?" Faith checks.

"Yes."

"Do *you* live near Toronto?"

"Extremely no." I nod proudly.

"Okay," Faith says slowly. "We can do that. Might be more convenient to just swap numbers, though."

"Oh, thank god," I finally let myself relax. "I wanted to ask but then I was like, 'what if I'm not supposed to ask?' but then

I was like— I mean, yes. Very good with swapping numbers. Especially if you're the one who initiated it."

Faith laughs and holds out her hand. "Phone?"

I unlock mine and give it to her. She does the same. "You put yours in right?" She double checks when I try to hand hers back to her.

I nod.

"Cool." Faith nods back. "I'll text you, then."

"Cool." I pant. I don't know why I'm so breathless. I've been standing still for a while now (minus all the pacing and fidgeting, of course).

"I'll also see you next summer, though," Faith mumbles.

My stomach drops. She hasn't realized yet. "You can't... you promised you wouldn't," I try to break it to her gently. "Before I knew I wanted you to, obviously, but you still... we made a deal and I told you to promise."

"Yeah." Faith shrugs. "A deal I never actually agreed to."

My eyes widen. "That's not— you can't—"

I've been freaking out for weeks. Over nothing. I kind of want to attack her for that, but when I try to, I somehow end up hugging her instead.

And tackling her to the ground in the process, but in my defense, it's still mostly a hug.

"You're insufferable!" I shriek.

"You were my biggest energy source," Faith explains like it's somehow obvious. "Obviously I wasn't going to—"

"You're actually the worst!"

"Figured once you found out I'd tricked you you'd just be more pissed and I'd get even more energy out of you."

"You— ugg!" I roll off her to stare at the sky. Somehow, my fingers find hers. "I'm really glad you tricked me," I admit, "just never do it again."

Faith laughs. I hear her turn over to face me, so I do the same. "Thank you," she whispers, "for this summer."

She has to whisper, because I've misjudged the roll. She's so, so close to me. Her eyes are so, so big. I swallow. "You too. I umm... it was fun."

"Lots?" Faith says.

"Yeah."

"I have an extra tube of toothpaste in my bag. Found it this morning. And I'm pretty sure the cabin's empty."

"Oh," I say. "I do that all the time too. I always pack way too many of the things I never end up using and way too little of—"

"Lots!"

"What!"

"I'm pretty sure the cabin's empty right now, and I have an *extra tube of toothpaste in my bag.*"

"Oh," I say. "*Oh!*" I jump to my feet. "We'd better go check out the cabin one last time then," I hold out a hand to her. "Just to make sure no one forgot anything. You can never be too careful."

Faith takes my hand and laughs. "Let's go, then."

September 1

CHARLOTTE ELIZABETH KENNEDY IF YOU HAVEN'T KISSED THAT POOR GIRL YET I SWEAR TO GOD.

P.S. Stop acting like I can read social cues for people I've never even met. Especially when you very obviously already know exactly what they mean.

You better have gotten over this and told her how you felt before we pick you up,
Alice

September 1

I dont kiss & tell :P

-    *Charlotte*

Chapter 53

"Just so we're on the same page, we're actually talking about making out, right? Because I'm pretty sure we already triple-checked the—"

"We're absolutely talking about making out."

"Oh, okay. Good. Excellent."

September 1

Just kiding I absolutly kiss & tell.

Talk at u (a lot) very very soon,
Charlotte

Thanks to & About the Author

Thanks to Sasha, Ream, Maddy B., Phoebe M., and Ken Thomas for early reading this one and providing feedback :)

Alex (any pronouns, feel free to talk about me behind my back at will, I'm impossible to mispronoun) published their first book a month after turning 20, promptly decided to publish a book a month those next ten months because that was reasonable, and is now trying to hit 22 before turning 22 because he has no concept of time. She failed extremely miserably at that. This is their 19th release and their already 22.

Message alexnonymouswrites@gmail.com to get added to my email list and get updates on future releases, early reading opportunities, and to vote on upcoming genres!

Content Warnings: ableism, internalized ableism, blood, autistic meltdown, negative self-talk, mentions of fainting, swearing, mentions of death, vomit, mentions of imprisonment, mentions of seizures, physical weakness, hitting, reference to natural disasters, hair pulling, skin picking, reference to kidnapping